Also by this author

The Great Game:
Berlin-Warsaw Express and other Stories

Nothing Lasts Forever Anymore

Mundo Overloadus

Michael Lederer - **Cadaqués**

Michael Lederer

Cadaqués

PalmArtPress
Berlin

Bibliografische Information der Deutschen Nationalbibliothek
Die Deutsche Nationalbibliothek verzeichnet diese Publikation in
der Deutschen Nationalbibliografie; detaillierte bibliografische Daten
sind im Internet über http://www.d-nb.de abrufbar.

The characters in this book are fictitious.
Any resemblance to real persons, living or dead, is purely coincidental.

ISBN: 978-3-941524-40-8

All rights reserved. First Edition 2014
© Michael Lederer, 2014
© PalmArtPress, 2014

German Edition, 2014, ISBN: 978-3-941524-34-7
German Edition eBook, 2014, ISBN: 978-3-941524-41-5
Editor: Catharine J. Nicely
Front cover: Genia Chef, *Emerald Grotto*, oil on panel, 1994
Back cover: Photo by Katarina Knitter-Lederer
Printed in Germany

Palm**Art**Press
Pfalzburger Str. 69, 10719 Berlin
www.palmartpress.com

For my wife Katarina
and my friend Genia Chef,
and the memory of David Marti

"...and gave them wine saying, 'This is my blood.'"

- Matthew 26: 27-28

Breakfast in a bottle
Mama said three meals a day
And I'm such a good boy
I like to do as Mamas say

- From the song, *Breakfast in a Bottle*

"No Lost Generation here, darling. This is Cadaqués. We are *finding* ourselves!"

- Robert, a character in the book

NO LOST GENERATION HERE

Prologue

The electric buzz, the multi-tasking, the breathless pace that could keep one an arm's distance from one's own thoughts. The high-octane rush of every this and that coming at you at once, 24/7. Cadaqués was not the place for such things. A slower pace here. One step at a time. Where a mother finding a condom in a teenager's nightstand could still constitute high drama. No car chases or shady corporate mergers, or bombs exploding or bullets flying. No billion-dollar heists or shiny shoes in the corridors of power. Here, bare feet on the beach already a thrill. And having time to think. It's what *they* had come for, Picasso and the others. Not that bigger things didn't happen also. Death, for instance, visited this village too. The winding road couldn't keep that horseman from his rounds. But for the most part the dramas here were on the slower order of a chess game, versus the clackety-clack of checkers. A little sex, a little wine, a little fighting, the company of friends. In Cadaqués it was enough.

Chapter I

"Sex and drugs and rock and ROLLLL, darling. And vio-lence. That's what they want. The world they know. Can't give them beauty anymore. It's passé. Beauty is yester-year, darling. GET...OVER...IT!"

"He's drunk."

"DRUNK, Madam? I...I...," he took a deep breath. The head hung forward, the eyes closed, but only for a moment. The batteries recharged almost instantly. The eyes pried themselves back open. The head lifted itself.

"We are all drunk, on the elixir of L-I-F-E."

He stretched out the word life as if doing so could lengthen the thing itself. As he said it, his hand shot up in the air in the most gallant gesture, thrust high to a point like an Olympic flame. Then the fingers wound their way back down with slow intent to his breast. All his soul was in the moment. A few centuries earlier and he'd have been tipping his feathered hat to the lady.

Baudelaire, Byron, Robert. Of a kind. Falstaff, Cyrano, Churchill. The whole lot of them together at last in this clay lump of a man. Robert Breyer. Brighton born and bred. At twenty he had followed the grapes south. Thirty years later he was still reaping the rewards of having found them.

"Have a sip of LIFE, darling. It's D-E-LLL-I-C-I-O-U-S."

The "L" sound, played more than spoken, hung in the air forever. Long lingering English vowels rose like a slow river from the depths of his soul, rolling over consonants that stood out like sharp pebbles in the stream. This was language as God, drunk on wine, might speak it. Every "T" a tambour, every "V" a violin.

"Oh for God's sake, can we please…"

"Can we please what? Have some L-O-V-E, darling. That's what we really want, isn't it? Can we please have some love, hmm?"

In front of him, through the haze of so much Spanish wine, like visions seen through simmering desert heat, the elegant older couple stood at the wooden bar. Lady Ratkins was pulling at her husband's elbow. She wanted to go immediately and not order, but Lord Ratkins wasn't budging. There was something about this drunk man he found intriguing.

"Just one drink, darling."

"JUST ONE DRINK, DARLING," echoed Robert. "Words of a poet! And a fine one at that! 'Just one drink, darling.' Well said! Touché!"

Lord Ratkins signaled to the barman. Miguel stepped over.

"Sí?"

"Two glasses of white wine please. And for my friend here, what's your wish?"

"My wish…my wish is for love, darling," growled Robert.

The head drooped again. Again a deep breath. Then the eyes flared wide in their sockets. Red, knowing.

"Spain, darling, is the temple of love. And you are in the temple now. Welcome to it." Again, that final 't' tapping home the point.

Robert looked at Lady Ratkins. She wasn't sure what to do except hold to her husband's arm. The drinks came. Two white wines as ordered, and a red wine for Robert. The barman knew.

"Well then," said Lord Ratkins, holding his glass up to propose a toast. "To the temple of love."

"To LOVE!" agreed Robert, as pleased and pickled as he had ever been. Lady Ratkins said nothing, just took a sip.

"Where are you from? The south, is it?"

"Exactly. Brighton. And you?"

"London."

An excited gasp. "What a MAGNNNIFICENT city, hmm?" He called out. "Miguel!"

"Sí, Robert?"

"Estos son mis compatriotas. These are my countrymen. It's a British invasion, darling. Gibraltar all over again. Man the ramparts!"

"Sí, Robert?"

"Except the thing is, we thought we'd civilize you. Miguel?"

"Sí?"

"Turns out it's the other way around. You're civilizing us. Teaching us the wayyys of loooove."

Robert eyed Lady Ratkins as he said it. The vision was blurred, not too many details, but he could make out it was a woman, and a fine one at that.

The hands, brown from the sun, unwrapped a pouch of rolling tobacco. The ritual repeated every twenty or so minutes: against the bar, pinch of tobacco into the paper, the filter added, rolled, wetted tongue pressed to the glue. Nearly ready. But first, point of style, its end squeezed into a black cigarette holder and only then the fire. The curling smoke into the lungs and out again, and the sheer, obvious, delicious contentment of it. No matter how red the eyes, how stained the shirt, how unsteady the feet, the elegance of that holder and the man holding it proclaimed: This, darling, is something!

"This is your local, is it?" asked Lord Ratkins. He had the

confident casual air of one who, since the day of birth, had viewed life from the pinnacle.

"One drinks where one is liked, hmm? Where one is welcome, and where one can get credit. How is it for you in London? They give credit for a glass of wine, do they?"

Lord Ratkins smiled. "If I need it."

"Well then, to credit! And to Adam Smith, hmm? Adam."

Tipping back the glass, not a drop spilling, Robert drank.

"To whommm, darling, have I the pleasure of speaking?"

"George Ratkins. My wife, Rebecca."

"REBECCA! How wonderful that, to be named from the Bible."

"I think so, yes," said Lady Ratkins.

"Well, don't doubt it. Be proud, darling. To be named from the Bible, that's something!" The glass again aloft. "Well then, to the Good Book. And to the good names it begets."

Another sip. And another. Once, twice, thrice.

"Borrrracho."

The word for drunk. A little Spanish lesson thrown in.

She was put off, still intrigued at the same time. Despite the hairspray and the polished nails there was a rugged curiosity, the reason she followed her husband to places like this. Africa, Rio, Mustique, Spain…prepared for the wilds she, so long as there was a hot bath and room service at day's end.

"What brought you to Cadaqués, Mister…?"

"Robert, darling. Just Robert."

"What brought you to Cadaqués, Robert?"

"Dali."

"You knew him?"

He nodded. "We all knew him. Man of the village. Man of the world and the village. One as important as the other."

"Is that right?"

"Well, take either away and he wouldn't be Dali, would he? The flower has ROOTS, darling! Without those..." He didn't finish the sentence.

"So you just went over to his house, did you? Knocked on the door?"

"Met him in Paris, my brother and I. Hotel Meurice. He invited us here. As models."

"How wonderful. And that was...?"

"Long time ago. Thirty years, mas o menos. We were all young and beautiful then."

Robert and his identical twin brother Richard had been living in London. Cecil Beaton, the young Mick Jagger, Twiggy, Donyale Luna, Patti Smith, Bowie, they'd "known them all!" The swinging sixties. A quick spin around the globe then to India, Africa, the Caribbean, Paris, before Dali brought the brothers to his house in Portlligat on the outskirts of Cadaqués. To model, to play, and as importantly perhaps to share the so-called normal times when "Salvador" as they called him, was a man at work, a man of the village, and not only the mad genius celebrity. After the great painter had died the brothers had stayed on, like the hot glow of the wick after the flame is out. Though in their case it turned out there were other fires.

Two children played on the floor nearby while their mother argued with their father. A group of old men played cards at one table. Smoke everywhere in those days. Outside the front door of the Casino, a young man with a guitar sat playing on one of the wide window ledges while two pretty girls sat close to him listening. Across the road near the beach some people were smoking marijuana, the sweet smell of it wafting toward the village.

Except for the old men in the back, this was not a gambling

casino. Back to the older meaning of the word: "A noisy environment, a building or large room used for meetings, a place of pleasure." The sign high above the front read: Societat L'Amistat. Society of friends. Inside, two big rooms with high ceilings, a long bar, tables, most people from the village, some tourists, and in one corner an old TV for the games.

Robert finished his wine. "Miguel?"

"Sí, Robert?"

"Another round for my friends here."

"No, really, a bit late for us I'm afraid. Time we're off. But it's been a great pleasure."

"The pleasure is OURS, darling."

Another deep sigh, the eyes again closed. Lord Ratkins led Lady Ratkins toward the door. Before stepping outside both looked back over their shoulders. Robert was leaning against the bar, unmoving. Around him men stood talking, taking no notice of him. The television was on in the corner. Football game. One side scored a goal. A great cheer went up in the room.

Chapter II

The bus from Barcelona to Cadaqués first stopped in Roses. Most passengers got off, a few others boarded. Sitting at a window toward the back, Cal watched them. An old woman with a straw shopping basket climbed on and sat behind the driver. There were two girls with backpacks. The tall one had a big tattoo of a butterfly on her shoulder. A young guy with dreads carrying a guitar came down the aisle and sat across from the two girls.

Outside in the hot sun there were some tired looking palm trees covered with dust. A dog lay drooped in a shadow. The buildings here looked no different than in many other towns along the coast of Spain, built of inexpensive materials with shuttered windows and light colors to reflect the sun. After the collapse of fascism and the rise of tourism, many had been built in the mad rush to catch up with the twentieth century before the twenty-first would arrive. They had just made it. Only half a year left now until the century's, even the millennium's, end. That would be it then, final score for an age, as much and as little as a thousand years would accomplish.

Cal had a bottle of red wine in his pack. He took it out and looked at it. *Rioja!* Already opened, he pulled the cork out and took a sip. Then he took another, longer sip and waited. A moment later it came, that warm sweet glow stretching from the stomach to the brain. He loved how that felt, everything inside and outside softening. One more sip to be sure he had it. He did.

The door closed and the bus started to move. Across the street, two men sat smoking and drinking at a table on the sidewalk. There was a small bar behind them with a beaded curtain in the door to keep the flies out. As the bus pulled away the men watched it.

Roses, like many other towns and cities along the coast of Spain, was still sprawling upward and outward in those heady days. Another Miami wanna-be. When you were inside it, in the little corners like this one, it could still feel slow. But when you looked at it from a distance or were at its center you felt the change happening. Building cranes everywhere, men and money moving, an ejaculation of development. A bank going up here, apartments there, shopping centers, beauty salons, travel agencies...all of it pedal-to-the-metal, like the fitful day when a teenager first gets his hands on the car keys, full of self-confidence and not a worry in the world. Spain was modernizing itself now and it seemed there would be no holding it back.

Somewhere hidden behind all that stucco and the cranes and the big plans was the heart still of the old Roses that had been there forever. The 11th century monastery of Santa Maria de Roses, and the Roman ruins and even earlier Greek ruins. From the bus, the town's more distant past could be best seen in the 16th century Castell de la Trinitat high on a hill overlooking it all. Reminder of bygone days when Barbarossa, fearsome Ottoman admiral of the fleet, and pirates and privateers, would attack and pillage. Good storybook stuff. Later came newer and bigger wars, but without the torchlight and galloping horses and the silk-turbaned cutthroats, they were less fun to think about.

The bus pulled away from the buildings and soon they were out in the open again, with fields of olive trees on either side. There were no people now except for a lone bicyclist, and at one roundabout there were two prostitutes in tight skirts who stood waiting. There were more roundabouts after that, but no more hookers. That disappointed Cal. Once you begin expecting to see prostitutes along the side of a road the whole experience of travel changes. *No hookers there...no hookers there...no hookers there...*

A few minutes more and finally they began to climb over the mountain that had stood through the ages like a natural wall defending Cadaqués. Against Visigoths, against Napoleon's armies, and now in probably its most enduring battle, against bloated hoards of tourists eating, photographing and trampling their way through anything that could fit onto a four-color brochure.

Until only a hundred years before, main access to the village had been by sea. Even after the little road had been paved, and cars and buses had taken the place of horses and carriages, still it was faster, easier and more comfortable to get to so many other towns along the coast, with their sandy beaches and big hotels, and their English and German menus. Cadaqués still had only a few small hotels, not sand but rocky beaches, and the fierce tramuntana wind that would sweep down the mountain like a wild child running toward the sea. Most tourists couldn't be bothered. Cadaqués, still and forever, was for a particular kind of visitor.

Nose glued to the window, Cal watched the great cork oaks and endless terraces of flat gray stones roll by. To be an American writer in Spain on a bus to Cadaqués, with a bag of marijuana in one's pack, a bottle of wine, some money in one's pocket...this was about as good as it gets.

Cadaqués, the village of Dali the great masturbator, and so many others who had seized time away from the crazy cities to marshal their powers: Duchamp, Magritte, Man Ray, Picasso, Cage, Buñuel, Miro, Garcia Lorca, André Breton...all of them mixing so happily and long ago among the fisherfolk, the gnarled olive trees, and rocks that looked like they could spring alive at any moment or else had once lived. Here on the easternmost point of Iberia, where the great Pyrenees begin their descent toward and into the Mediterranean sea, the little village of Cadaqués had helped tip the twentieth century off its comfortable ass and set it on course for uncharted territories. Slitting an eyeball with a razor? Art! A urinal? Art! Gravity? Optional. Cubism. Dadaism. Surrealism. Younameitism. Post-Freudian dreams painted, sculpted, written and, yes, sold here. With one great leap of faithlessness in established order, the village had gone from exporting anchovies and wine to exporting the modern world.

    Left curve, right curve, left curve…up through the maze. In the distance below, Roses, the fertile plains, and all the rest of the world were drawing further away.

Chapter III

This would be Cal's second visit to Cadaqués. He had spent one month in the village the summer before.

Peering out the window of the bus now, his mind drifted back to the night in New York City, two years earlier, when he had first heard the name Cadaqués.

Cal was celebrating his 38th birthday. He, his good friend the Russian painter Grisha Yermiloff, and a small group of fellow artists and writers were at some restaurant on the Avenue of the Americas somewhere in the 50s. It was late and they were all drunk. Everyone was dressed casually, except for this one fat American lawyer named Clark who wore a tuxedo. Nobody seemed to like him. He just appeared suddenly among them. Apparently he knew Grisha from some gallery opening and spotted him at the table. Then he just invited himself over. And once he had joined them he wouldn't shut up, as if it was *his* birthday party. He kept talking about how most artists were poor because they thought of themselves as lovers when really they were whores. He said that romance was dead, and art and literature were going to die with it unless writers and artists started to think of themselves as whores, and would let him be their pimp. Then they could all be rich. Rich whores. He wore patent leather shoes and a cummerbund that looked like it was going to explode he was so fat. And even though he looked rich, and talked a great deal about getting even richer, the only thing he ordered for dinner that night was French fries. Cal could still remember the greasy fingers hard at work, and the lawyer asking the waitress to bring another bottle of ketchup.

Later, when everyone had finished their dinner and they were all standing outside on the sidewalk deciding where to go next, Clark said that wherever it was he would be happy to go along. But nobody else wanted that. So Grisha, thinking faster than the others, got down on his hands and knees on the sidewalk and started barking and growling like a dog. He kept trying to bite Clark on his legs. The lawyer kept backing away, confused and frightened.

"Grisha, stop it! What are you doing? *Stop it*! Please, don't bite me!"

"Arf! Woof! Grrrgh!"

"Grisha, *stop this*! What's gotten into you?"

"Woof, woof! Grrgh! Arggh!"

"All right, that's it. I'm afraid I have to leave you now."

The lawyer turned and hurried down the Avenue of the Americas, looking over his shoulder to make sure he wasn't being chased or followed.

"Clark, come back!" Grisha shouted, still on his hands and knees. "Woof! Woof! Come back! Grrgh!"

It was the funniest thing, and quite unexpected because normally Grisha was so polite and so gentle. As soon as the lawyer was about a block away, and there was no real chance of him coming back, Grisha calmly stood up, dusted the dirt off his hands, and looked around. There was a horse-drawn carriage making its way slowly up Sixth toward the Park. Grisha waved to it.

"Taxi! Oh, taxi! Horse taxi!"

The horse and carriage rolled to a stop.

"Cal! Raya! Come, let's go!"

Then Grisha and Cal and Raya, a beautiful Russian journalist who was a friend of theirs, climbed into the carriage.

"See you later, guys," said Grisha to the rest of their group. "Driver, through the Park...please." It was the gentle, polite Grisha again.

Their friends waved and shouted good-bye as the driver flicked his reins and the horse led them up Sixth, across 59th Street into the Park. As soon as they were in among the trees, Raya scrambled up over the front of the carriage to sit next to the coachman. She put her arm around his shoulders and asked if she could steer the horse. Because she was so beautiful the driver didn't seem to mind and handed her the reins. It was hard to say no to Raya.

In the back of the carriage, Grisha and Cal settled back for a slow comfortable ride. Grisha had a briefcase with him and now he opened it. He pulled out a package wrapped in nice paper.

"Here Cal, your birthday present. Happy birthday."

It was heavy and big. Cal unwrapped it. It was a bottle of J. Dupeyron Napoleon Armagnac, Hors d'Age.

"Grisha, how fantastic! Alcohol! You couldn't have chosen better."

"You can save it. Open it one day for some special occasion."

"Well, no occasion will ever be more special than this."

Grisha laughed. "Perfect!"

Cal peeled off the dull gold foil and pulled loose the cork. He smelled from the bottle. There was no moon that night and it was dark in the carriage.

"Grisha, does that say 'Napoleon' or 'Aladdin,' because I think I just let the genie out."

"Well then fast, you must make a wish."

Cal thought for a moment, then said, "It's already coming true."

"*Fantastic!*"

"Raya!" called Cal.

The Russian beauty turned to look over her shoulder. "Yes? What? I have a new friend here. His name is John."

"Hi John!"

The driver cocked his head toward his passengers in back and tipped his top hat. Cal reached the bottle up to them.

"Raya, you have to have the first sip, because a woman's lips will make the rest of it even sweeter for us."

Raya pressed her big lips to the bottle and drank. Then she tried handing the bottle to John.

"I can't. Sorry. I'm driving."

She insisted.

"I could lose my job."

"Or you could break my heart. Don't break my heart, John. You mean too much to me."

She was so beautiful. John took the bottle and drank. Then Raya took another sip and handed the bottle back to Grisha.

"Hors d'Age, Cal. Beyond the time!"

The bottle made the rounds a few more times. Then they all sang happy birthday to Cal. As it turned out John had the best voice, a strong graceful tenor.

Cal had a joint in his pocket. He took it out and lit it, the light from the flame flickering against his face. Leaning back in the carriage then, with the sound of horse hooves on the pavement, and the yellow light from streetlamps falling through the trees, for some moments it felt like they were a world away from the modern city with its lights sparkling in the distance. But then suddenly there was a booming voice from a loudspeaker.

"PUT THE JOINT OUT!"

Cal looked over his shoulder. A police car was crawling

along behind them at the same speed as the horse. Reluctantly, Cal began to tap the joint out on the floor of the carriage. It was the only joint he had. He figured he would put it back into his pocket, then light it again as soon as the police car was gone.

"NO! THROW THE JOINT ONTO THE STREET! NOW!"

Cal tossed the joint, still so much more than a roach, onto the pavement. He looked around trying to spot a landmark so that he could retrieve it later, but there were only trees beside the road, and in the darkness all the trees looked the same. So as the horse clippety-clopped its way along, leaving the joint further and further behind, Cal resigned himself to the loss. The police car accelerated and pulled up alongside the driver. Again, one of two officers spoke over the car's loudspeaker:

"DRIVER, YOU COULD LOSE YOUR LICENSE IF YOU LET HER TAKE THOSE REINS AGAIN."

John tipped his hat. "I understand, officer. I'm sorry. I'm very sorry."

Satisfied he had restored public order, the policeman behind the wheel pressed on the gas and the car accelerated again, disappearing into the night ahead.

"Nice guys," said Grisha sincerely as he leaned back. "In Russia they would have asked for money. *I love New York!*"

They rode through the trees and drank from the old bottle, and nobody spoke for some time. Cal could feel what smoke he had taken in and it was something. Genie or no genie, it all seemed magical.

They clip-clopped past the Tavern on the Green with its year-round Christmas lights on the trees, then past Sheep Meadow where sheep once grazed. They rolled past Strawberry Fields where the spirit of John Lennon joined them. They sang *Imagine*. And then, after the real thing, they started to invent their own lyrics: "Imagine there are no French fries...Imagine there are no lawyers...Imagine all the horses…" They kept that going for quite a while until John began to circle back toward Fifty-ninth.

"John," asked Grisha, "can you take us down Fifth Avenue to Twenty-ninth Street?"

In those days, Cal and Grisha were both living on East Twenty-ninth, between Fifth and Madison, in the neo-gothic rectory of The Little Church Around the Corner.

"I can take you as far as Thirty-fourth. The law won't let me go any further than that. That's our limit."

"Okay then, Thirty-fourth Street," said Grisha. "Like Gagarin told, "Поехали!" Let's do it!"

John pulled the horse to a stop in front of the Plaza hotel so Raya could get off. But not before kissing John three times on his cheeks.

"Good bye, John. I love you."

"I love you too, Raya."

"But you must understand, I have a husband waiting at home and I love him too."

"I understand."

Cal and Grisha hopped down from the carriage. They also wanted to give and get their three kisses on the cheeks.

"Do you love me too?" asked Cal.

"Of course. I love everyone."

Cal and Grisha climbed back into the carriage. The horse started down Fifth Avenue while Raya stood beside the fountain outside the Plaza blowing kisses after them.

"Life as it should be, Grisha!"

"Absolutely, Cal. *Fantastic!*"

Both leaned back in the carriage, Grisha with his small frame, big beard and even bigger smile, Cal with his eyes from the smoke and brandy as red as the taillights rushing past. Across the street to their left was F.A.O. Schwarz. A few moments later they would be passing Tiffany's. Toys for all ages.

With John in his top hat, and the horse poking along slowly, they said nothing for some moments. It was after midnight. Still, being Manhattan there were cars and people walking everywhere. Yellow taxis, long black or white limousines, police cars, young people jostling on the sidewalks. And above it all now, the sound of hooves against the black pavement.

"Incredible," said Grisha, "really Cal, like from the nineteenth century."

"Because it's not a horse and carriage, Grisha. This is a time machine."

"Hors d'Age!" said the Russian, lifting high the now almost-empty bottle. "To time machines, Cal!"

"Go on, pick a century. John, can you get us to any century we want?"

"Of course."

"Well then, backward or forward, what should it be?"

"We must think," said Grisha. "We must think very carefully. Because always the wishes can come true."

"Seventeenth century? London, to see Shakespeare?"

"Or maybe Antwerp, to see Rubens?"

Both thought about it, as if it was a serious choice that would have consequences.

"Or maybe...Paris in the twenties?"

"Faster to get there."

"Hemingway, Joyce, Fitzgerald..."

"Dali, Diaghilev, Stravinsky..."

"Or...or..."

"Yes?"

"Look at this," said Cal, gesturing toward Fifth Avenue stretching ahead of them. There were lights everywhere; above them towering, left, right, cars racing by.

"Maybe we just stay here, Grisha. I suggest we just stay right here, and now. This century, this place. Because it won't get any better than this."

"You know something? You are right."

"You know something else?"

"What something else? Tell me."

"This is *our* time, Grisha. *Our* place. And one day, maybe some young artist and some young writer they will think, 'How wonderful it was, New York, when Grisha Yermiloff and Cal Zander were here with their Hors d'Age.'"

Alcohol filled one with confidence.

"Everything else disappears, Cal. But there will always be the here and now. God gives to everyone their own here and now."

As they rolled past Fifty-fifth Street, Grisha glimpsed the elegant St. Regis Hotel to their left.

"Look, Cal, it's where Dali stayed every winter."

As a boy in the then-still Soviet Union, rare glimpses of Dali had shown the young Grisha a view of the West so different than the one the Communists painted. A West full of fantasy, beauty, sex, and a tradition of invention. Those last two not in conflict, but inseparable. *A tradition of invention.*

"This century has destroyed tradition, Cal. Invention without tradition is the great profanation. But Dali, he used the tradition to move us forward. It's like the difference between the real woman and its doll. He kept the woman, while the others they played with the doll."

"And he lived like he painted, yes, Grisha? Beautifully?"

"Absolutely! For him, was no difference. He said always, 'Life, it is the greatest art.' In the fall he would go to Paris, then here to New York, and in the spring back to Cadaqués."

"Cadaqués?"

"You know it?"

"No."

"Oh, Cal, you *must* know it. You will enjoy it *so* much."

And then Grisha told him…about Portlligat and the fishing boats and the nets along the beach. And about the whitewashed walls of the village, with its stone-paved alleyways and great rocks sticking through every this and that. Cal had spent nine months once living in a fishing village in the south of Spain, but he had never heard of Cadaqués up north in Catalonia near the French border.

"God and man built Cadaqués together, Cal. They did not fight each other to do it. They did not destroy the rocks to build. They built around them. And *with* them. Together, man and God *together*."

As he said it they were rolling past Saint Patrick's cathedral on their left.

"And everyone was there, Cal! You can't believe it! Dali, Buñuel, *everyone*. Even Walt Disney, he was there later. Yul Brynner. George Harrison. *Everyone* was there."

Now they were passing the carcass of the Charles Scribner and Sons bookshop. Cal pointed to it, that one-time literary lion's den that recently had become a United Colors of Benetton shop.

"Dali led you to Spain, Grisha. The first time I went to Spain was because of Hemingway. And now look!"

He explained how the publisher Charles Scribner had sold the building, and though it still looked the same on the outside it was something very different on the inside.

"Hemingway, Fitzgerald, now multi-colored underwear. Bastards."

"It is the story of this century, Cal. The selling of the soul. *This* is why we survive on the memories. More important, it's why we must make the *new* memories. A new Renaissance."

Up again with the bottle.

"What do you think, Cal? What will be after the clothing store? Because for sure it will not survive."

"Who knows? Maybe...a circumcision shop?"

"Hmm, interesting idea."

"Can you picture it? 'Christmas specials, fifty percent off!'"

"Maybe to word it differently."

They both exploded in laughter. And then they couldn't stop laughing.

"Maybe not Christmas specials, Cal. Maybe Hanukkah specials."

"No, Grisha, this is America. Here, we *all* love to get the ends of our penises cut off."

"Really?"

"Absolutely. It's very popular. We can't do it fast enough."

"Interesting."

"I can see it now, mothers lined up around the block with their babies in their arms. Jews, Muslims, other Americans, all coming together. It could be the beginning of the new age."

"The age of circumcision?"

"Why not? Less painful than some other ages."

At Thirty-fourth Street John brought the horse and carriage to a stop. Cal tried to pay for it but Grisha insisted.

"It's your birthday."

"No it's not, it's after midnight."

"It's your birthday until the sun comes up."

"I never heard that rule."

"It's famous. Everyone knows it. It's the second most important birthday rule, Cal."

"What's the first rule?"

"You have to be happy, like the song says."

Grisha paid John and gave him a fifty-dollar tip. As he was doing it the horse shit on the street.

"Oh, John," said Grisha, impressed, "she functionizes very good. What is the name of the horse?"

"Chanel Number Five."

"Nice name."

Cal and Grisha stood waving as the carriage pulled away.

"Good-bye, John!"

"Good-bye, Chanel Number Five!"

The Empire State Building was across the street. Cal and Grisha stumbled past it. They made it five blocks down Fifth Avenue, then veered left on Twenty-ninth Street. In a minute they were through the black iron gate and inside the garden of The Little Church Around the Corner.

The rector and his wife were friends of Cal's father. A few summers before Cal had housesit the rectory for them. When they returned he had arranged to stay on, renting the top floor. For some months now Grisha had been staying with him. Grisha's wife had stayed behind in Berlin where they lived, and the two guys had turned that upper floor of the rectory into a kind of neo-gothic *La Bohéme*. Surrounded by Grisha's paintings and Cal's books, they would throw not-very-church-like-parties up there. Artists and writer friends, actors, candles everywhere, Led Zeppelin or Paco de Lucia wailing through the speakers, a little wine, a little vodka...

Still standing outside the rectory door, keys in hand, they

were laughing so hard. Suddenly Grisha stopped laughing and became serious.

"Cal, one day we drink a brandy in Cadaqués, yes?"

They shook hands, promising to do it.

The following summer, Cal, Grisha, and Grisha's wife Elsa had spent a magical month in Cadaqués. And now one year later Cal was already heading back for a second visit.

Chapter IV

The bus was starting down the mountain through the Parafita pass. Looking across the aisle and out the window to his left, Cal could see the little fishing village of El Port de la Selva on the edge of the sea below. The border with France was just twenty kilometers beyond that.

They kept moving, and a few minutes and few curves later there it was, the first glimpse of Cadaqués ahead in the distance. Still about a thousand olive trees away, beside the deep blue of the sea and beneath the blue of the sky, was a line of low white buildings. Small cubes stacked next to each other. From here the village looked like something organic, not imposed on the landscape like so many other towns along the coast, but as if it had grown there, a bed of white quartz crystals with people living among them.

The biggest building was the church, Santa Maria, with its bell tower. Color of milk. Beyond it lay the little bay where white dots that were boats seemed to stretch the village out into the water. At the entrance of the bay the tiny island of Es Cucurucuc, a gray triangle-shaped rock, looked like a dolphin's fin rising out of the sea. Like all islands it was a mountaintop really, the tip of the last of the Pyrenees that could still be seen by man. The rest of the range descended under the water, a world of starfish, sea urchins, dolphins and every-colored fish that in their way were as much a part of the village as the rest of it. People also belong to the animal kingdom. Many forget or deny it. In Cadaqués they remember, some accept it, some even embrace it.

The bus kept moving. More curves in the road, and for a few moments the village disappeared again. When it reappeared they were almost in it. Something to celebrate. Cal finished what was left of his wine.

Chapter V

The bus stopped on the westward edge of the village. Close by was a copy of Bertholdi's Statue of Liberty, with two arms aloft hoisting two flames, as if promising twice as much liberty here as greets the visitor to New York.

In the hot air, his backpack slung over his shoulders, Cal walked down the thin Avenida Caritat Serinyana past a long row of shops, the village's one gas station and several bars. There were dusty trees lining the road, children running with ice cream cones and grown-ups walking behind the children. Cars and scooters motored past. Not all the scooter riders wore helmets. One of many ways Cadaqués still had a Wild West feel to it. Nothing here too careful.

At the end of the road, Cal stepped out into the main square. Straight ahead was a rocky beach with little bar-restaurants called *chiringuitos* set near the water. There was a statue of Dali, stick in hand, looking over everything with those dead eyes that statues have.

People everywhere now, tourists and locals moving past each other hardly mixing. Oil and water. There was a large raised area to the left called the passeig. A few steps led up to its surface of packed dirt. It was where children played, and where locals, especially older people, stopped to talk to each other. The summer before Cal had seen them dancing there in great circles with their arms around each other's shoulders. The dance was called the *sardana*. A traditional *cobla* band with its brass and wind instruments plus one bass and a drum had played, and everyone that day was speaking Catalan and laughing.

There was a nice breeze coming off the water. Cal stood there for a moment taking it all in. Though this was only his second time here, he felt like he had just come home. He loved this place. Not like one who knew it well of course, because he had only spent that one month here. This was a different kind of love. More like falling in love with a girl at first sight. That had its own power. You can know a person or place for a long time and never fall in love. Or you can fall in love quickly. Time didn't seem to have much to do with it.

First things first. The little wine shop was just where he had left it, at the entrance to a small alley that ran off to the left. He went to it. Behind the counter was the same dark haired girl with the sweet smile.

"I remember you!" she said in Spanish.

"Hola, guapa."

Cal spoke no Catalan, and his Spanish was not great, learned during those nine months he had once spent in the south. But still he loved to speak it. A person changes when they speak a different language, and Cal liked who he became when speaking Spanish. Looser, even faster to say yes.

The girl with the nice smile asked him what he wanted.

Cal looked over the rows of red wine on the shelves. He didn't really know the wineries or vintages. He always just selected on the basis of price and how nice the bottle looked. If he had money he'd buy a more expensive wine. When he didn't have much money he'd buy "anything wet." Now he pointed to one of the more expensive bottles with a nice label. It looked delicious.

"Tres botellas de ese."

She rang them up. Cal paid, then slipped the three bottles into his pack. Good to go.

"'a luego." See you later.

"'a luego," she smiled.

Coming back into the square he turned toward the beach. At the first *chiringuito,* the Bar Boia, he turned again and passed over a little bridge. There was a gully under the bridge that spilled onto the beach from a riverbed. The riverbed was lined with concrete and only became a river when there was runoff in the rain. At other times like now it was a parking lot.

After the bridge, a few more steps and on the right was the Casino, a large hulk of whitewashed building that together with the passieg, and of course the church, formed the heart and soul of Cadaqués. You could go into it anytime and see people you knew. Or if they weren't there yet you could buy a drink and sit and before long someone you knew would come along. The village's version of "Everyone comes to Rick's." In a bigger town or city you could miss seeing people. They were there while you were here, or vice versa. Not in Cadaqués. The village only had about two thousand residents. No one missed anyone here. Or anything.

Through one of the large plate glass windows, Cal could already see faces he recognized. The twins, Robert and Richard. And Wiggles, a down-and-out actor from London. Those three Brits were sitting together with a nice looking girl Cal did not recognize. Stepping out of the sun he went in. It was just after four and the place was almost empty. Only the most serious drinkers were at it already. As he walked toward them it was Wiggles who noticed him first.

"Well, hello. Who's this?"

Wiggles spoke the Queen's English, in slow motion. The words formed languidly, and he would sort of push them out one by one, sheer will getting them through the fog. As he spoke one could almost see the fumes spilling out of the mouth, ears, nostrils.

"Why, it's…it's…" He was trying to remember. "*Sal*, isn't it?"

"Cal," offered one of the twins. Robert or Richard, Cal couldn't tell which.

"That's it."

"Of course," said Wiggles. "*Cal*. I stand corrected. Or rather, I sit corrected." He chuckled at his own joke. "How are you, Cal? Sit down please, Cal."

Despite the awkward pace, there was a smooth pleasant quality to his voice. In a long-ago life, Wiggles had trained at London's Royal Academy of Dramatic Art. Tall, thin, forty-something, with spectacles that made him look like the reader he once was, he had had a fair career on stage, even working with some of the greats like Beckett, Gielgud and others, before he'd gone south in more ways than one.

"Well, look at you. Like a snail carrying all you've got on your back like that. You just got here, did you?"

"Yes."

"Took the bus?" asked twin number one.

"Yes."

"Well then, you must be thirsty," said Wiggles. "I mean, taking the bus, walking all the way down here into the village. Go get yourself a drink. We'll be here waiting for you. We won't go anywhere."

Cal smiled at the girl. She was smoking a cigarette and smiled back. It was one of those skinny cigarettes. The girl was almost as skinny as the cigarette. She had long dark hair and was wearing tight little shorts. Cal pulled up a chair from an empty table nearby and set it next to hers. He left his pack leaning against it and went to the bar. A moment later he was back with a glass of red wine.

"Well now there you go, that'll quench a thirst," said Wiggles. "Have a seat. Join us."

Cal sat.

"Good to see you again," said twin number two.

"Is that Robert or Richard?"

"Richard."

Both brothers smiled at the familiar question. Those who knew them well could tell them apart in an instant. Cal wasn't there yet. He took note of the shirts they were wearing so that on that day at least he would know which was which. Richard was wearing the gray shirt, Robert the white.

The twins shared boyish faces that made them look younger than they were. Like Wiggles, the brothers also spoke the Queen's English, though at a faster pace. Little machine bursts of words. Sometimes one would even finish the other's sentence, getting there first. That could happen until end of day, when alcohol eventually slowed things down. Cal knew from the summer before that there were three Roberts, three Richards. The morning versions: quiet, reflective. The afternoon versions: tongues and minds loosening. And the night versions: beyond description. Cal was jumping now into the afternoon versions. Nobody sauced. Still sauc-*ing*.

"Nice to see you again, Cal," said Wiggles. "That's an odd name, isn't it, 'Cal.' But I remember now. You told me last year. It stands for 'California' doesn't it?"

"That's right."

"That's right, California. Well, I suppose if you were from Texas, we'd call you 'Tex,' wouldn't we? And if you were from…I don't know, Alabama…I suppose we'd call you 'Al.'"

"New York?" Robert tossed that one on the table just for fun. Smiles all around as they thought about it.

"Well, let's see," said Wiggles, enjoying this. "'New…York.' I suppose we'd call him…what *would* we call him? That's a hard one, isn't it."

"What about Mississippi?" asked the girl. Even she was getting in on this.

"I guess we'd call him 'Miss.' But now that wouldn't do, would it? You wouldn't want to be called 'Miss,' would you, Cal? 'Good morning, Miss.' 'Good night, Miss.' 'You're looking good, Miss.'"

Cal looked at the girl.

"What's your name?"

"Cassandra."

"Well now look at that," said Wiggles. "He doesn't waste a moment, does he? Already knows the girl's name. Off to a fast start there, eh, Cal? Well, good for you."

"You're beautiful," Cal said to Cassandra.

Wiggles almost pissed his pants.

"My God! Do you hear that?" he asked the twins. "*That*, gentlemen, is how it's done. You can teach us a thing or two, can't you, Cal?"

Cassandra was smiling.

"Now look at *that!* She's *blushing!*"

"I'm not blushing."

"You are. You're blushing."

"You live here?" Cal asked.

"Some of the time."

"And the other?"

"Well now," Wiggles pushed his way back into it, "don't mind us. We'll just sit here, watch you seduce my girlfriend."

"I'm not your girlfriend."

"Well, I don't know. The other night up at Freddy's…"

"I was drunk. Just forget it."

"But you're *always* drunk."

"Shut up."

"Now, now," said Robert. "Enough of that."

"All friends here," offered Richard.

Cal remembered now that when Wiggles was drinking he could be a real asshole.

"To answer your question," said Cassandra, "Liechtenstein. That's the other place."

"But she and her mother come here to the village, because they find Liechtenstein a bit big, don't you darling?" said Wiggles, not giving up. He was pushing now, looking for the buttons. "Get yourselves lost in the crowd there a bit, don't you."

"Where are you staying?" Robert asked Cal, changing the tone and subject. "Same as last year? David's?"

"Yes."

The summer before, Grisha had introduced Cal to a good friend, a Catalan poet and painter named David Marin. David (pronounced Dah-veed) lived downstairs in his mother's house behind the church. The mother lived upstairs. The middle floor was rented out. Cal had stayed in that middle floor, and now he would be staying there again. This time, because he and David had become good friends, they were giving him a "special price… free."

"A good place that. Nice place."

"Close to the church. You can go pray anytime you like. Do

you pray, Cal?"

"I'm praying right now, Wiggles."

Cassandra was looking at Cal.

"You look like Brad Pitt," she said.

"He doesn't look like Brad Pitt," said Wiggles.

"Yes he does."

"Grisha? How's he?" asked Robert.

"Fine. In Berlin."

"He's coming also?"

"Not this time."

"Painting?"

"Always."

"Where do you live?" Cassandra asked Cal, crossing her legs the other way.

"New York."

"Really. Well then you should come to L'Hostal tonight. There's a DJ from New York. He'll be there. You'd like it."

"Will you excuse me?" said Wiggles, getting to his feet. "I think I'm going to get myself a nice little glass of sherry."

He was off to the bar. The others talked until he came back. Then Cal stood.

"Well, I'm off to get settled. See you all later." He was looking at Cassandra as he said it.

"Don't forget. L'Hostal. Dancing."

Chapter VI

As Cal stepped out of the Casino there were some children running by. And there was a beautiful girl walking past. Early twenties, with a big straw hat. *So* beautiful. Barefoot, carrying her sandals, the breeze blew her long blonde hair and short white dress as she walked. She was with an old man, possibly her grandfather. The old man was talking and she was listening to him. Cal watched as they headed toward the passeig. As soon as they were out of sight he turned and walked past a little tapas bar, then past the sloping hill that led up through the arch into the oldest part of the village. Two old women wearing black stood below the arch talking.

Cal kept walking, keeping close to the water. There were tourists now everywhere. Not the worst kind. No big groups. Families mostly. He walked past a string of restaurants where more tourists were sitting. After that there were some great rocks with old white buildings that rose above them. These were the white crystals he had seen from the distance. The massive gray rocks on which they were built were the ones Grisha had talked about that night in New York, part of walls that had stood since the eleventh century. A thousand years of pirates, smugglers, artists, a civil war, tourists, beautiful girls in straw hats, they had seen it all. No high sea or tramuntana wind had managed to move them. Someday they would outlast the people.

He came around the little point called the Punta des Baluard.

The road here, built for horses, was just wide enough for one car. In winter when seas were high one had to time passing around that bend as waves crashed over it so as not to get soaked, or worse. There were no waves this day though. Clear seas and sky, that soft breeze, boats anchored off to the left, children swimming by the rocks, and tourists taking photos of it all.

After the point the road bent back toward a small cove called Port Alguer. A few fishing boats with ropes coiled around their bows had been pulled onto the beach. Across the cove was a line of white buildings stretching to the left, where the little road continued toward the far edge of the village. There it would become a rough dirt trail that passed over the mountains, the old way back to Roses.

In front of one of the buildings were three arches, made famous because Dali had put them in one of his paintings. In his painting, two young women balancing jugs on their heads were about to pass through those arches. The women had soft figures and seemed to be moving. As he kept moving now, Cal felt like he was entering that painting. Except in the painting there was no man throwing rocks at the tourists trying to swim there.

"*Get out! Get out of my sea! Get out of my village! Go home, all of you. Go back to your cities. Out! Can you hear me? Out!*"

It was Dah-veed. Tall, thin, long brown hair. He was standing on the beach next to one of the fishing boats. It was a pebble beach and he was bending over, scooping up handfuls of pebbles, then throwing them one by one at the people who were swimming. Except they weren't swimming now, they were ducking. Other people stood at the edge of the beach watching. No one was trying to stop him.

"*Go on, get out! Take your pink bodies and go back to your*

England and your Germany. Out!"

Despite the mock rage, he was a delicate man. This was as much for his own amusement as anything. Though it was true, the town was changing. More visitors, prices starting to climb. Many who remembered *the old days* wanted them back.

Cal called out.

"David!"

David looked up. Seeing Cal he broke into a sweet grin. Very matter-of-factly he dropped the pebbles he was still holding in his hand. Then as if nothing out of the usual had been happening, "Oh, Cal, it's so nice to see you! Welcome! We were wondering when you would be here."

His voice was soft, ethereal. He rolled his "R's." Every word became poetry as he spoke it, the alchemy of language. The people watching weren't sure what to make of it. After some moments, a few decided he was no longer a threat and began swimming again. David and Cal walked toward each other.

"Welcome to Cadaqués, Cal. As you see, I am protecting it for us against these sea monsters!" David chuckled as he lit a cigarette. "I don't throw the big stones, Cal, only the little ones. They don't mind. And the children, I think they even are amused. It's like a game for them. And their parents, well, look at them. What do they eat to be so fat, Cal? Like Van Gogh. The potato eaters, yes, Cal? The potato eaters, right here in our Cadaqués!" He smiled. "How arrrre you?"

It was as if he tasted the words as they passed through his mouth, and they were delicious. As a boy growing up here in Cadaqués, also in Paris, he had known Dali. His parents were friends of the artist's. Many were influenced by Dali's paintings. David had been as influenced by the way he spoke.

"Come, Cal. We shall leave these monsters and bring you to

your home. *Nostos*, Cal. Home. The voyage of Odysseus ends, yes, and you now are home, back in the womb, safe. This is your home, Cal. Come."

They walked together up into the back of the village, behind the church, near the Restaurant El Barroco where Dali used to hold court. David wore a brightly colored embroidered vest from India, and on his feet rope-soled Catalan shoes called *espadrilles* with their laces wrapped around his tanned ankles. As they walked, David smoked his cigarette and spoke.

"There was a beautiful girl on the beach today, Cal. Such beauty as I never saw."

"Was she wearing a white dress, with a big straw hat?"

"No, Cal. There was no hat. No dress. She was naked. And perfect. It was Aphrodite, I am sure of it. Sprung from the sea. With brown skin. And eyes like the sun. She looked at me, and I was almost blinded, Cal. Can you imagine? Her eyes were so bright, I was almost blinded. It was like looking at the sun. I felt like Icarus. I came close to her. I wanted to touch her, but the light from those eyes…" He laughed. "Oh, Cal, what powerful magic these women have, yes? I felt my wings melting. Like Icarus."

"You will think about her until you see the next beautiful girl."

"No, Cal."

It was true, but he denied it.

"My heart is like the elephant. It's not so easy to move it."

They kept walking up the long alley that was paved with small stones.

"I will paint a thousand doves in her honor, Cal. A thousand white doves. And breathe life into them, yes? What do you think? It's a good idea? So that my love will fly to her in the night as she sleeps. She will see me in her dreams, Cal, carried by a thousand white doves with strings in their beaks. They will bring me to her, and lower me into her bed. And more important than that even, into her heart. And I will stay there forever. Do you think it's a good idea, Cal? I stay in her heart forever? What do you think? Would I be safe there?"

"Not safe, David. No. In a woman's heart you risk everything. But I think it's fantastic."

"Really?"

"Love is a risk. Maybe you win, maybe you lose. But without it, you lose for sure. And you lose everything. So you must take the risk. Go, fly with your doves into her heart."

"You are a lover, Cal. Like me."

They rounded the bend. David's studio where he worked and lived was on the ground floor of the building just in front of them now. He had painted white doves and a patch of blue sky around the door. They walked up the steep slope, around to the other side of the house. There were two doors painted blue set into the thick white walls. The blue was the same color as the sky. Cadaqués blue. David took a key from his pocket and opened the second door. Then he handed the key to Cal.

"The magic key, Cal. It is yours now."

They stepped into the little suite of rooms that looked exactly as they had when Cal had last seen them. As if he had left just moments ago. There were two small bedrooms, a bathroom, the main room, a little kitchen. This was an old house. Crooked wood beams overhead, painted tiles in the kitchen, no two the same. The walls were white and thick and cool with deep shelves built into them. The floor, red clay tiles, also cool in summer. There was a wooden statue of a saint in an alcove over the dining table. Carmen, protector of travelers. The statue was very old and some of the dull red paint and gilding had peeled off. The table and chairs were painted the same blue as the door. A large bunch of *inmortales*, a dried yellow flower picked from the hills around Cadaqués, was pinned to one wall. Its name meant "everlasting."

"It's a pity Cal, I have no wine to offer you."

Cal laid his backpack onto the flat couch.

"But *I* have wine to offer *you*."

"Yes?"

"You see? I begin to unpack," Cal said as he took the three bottles out of his bag. He set them on the table and opened one. They sat then, drinking the wine from plain water glasses.

"A l'amour! To love."

"To love. Beautiful women, beautiful friends."

David lit a cigarette.

"And Grisha? When does he come?"

"I don't know. He's working now, in Berlin."

"Like me. Always working."

"Yes."

"And you, Cal? Also working? Are you writing?"

"Always."

It was not a lie, just not true.

There was light slanting in through one window. Smoke from the cigarette curled into the light.

"In the smoke, Cal, look. Do you see it? Sometimes in the smoke, I think I see the face of God. Can you imagine? If I told the priest that, and he told the people, everyone would go chasing after the smoke. Running, grabbing at it. Can you imagine, all the people chasing after the smoke? Through the village, over the mountain. But it's what we all do, yes? We all chase after the smoke."

He exhaled. The smoke billowed up and now they both watched it.

Through his thick square glasses with dark rims, David's eyes settled on a thing and didn't move until he felt he understood what he was looking at. His brown hair curled over his collar. He had two expressions, pensive or amused.

"You don't smoke, Cal?"

"Not cigarettes. But…"

Cal stood, went over to his backpack and took out a pair of brown socks. He brought the socks back to the table and unfurled them. Inside was a bag of marijuana. He had bought it a week before in Amsterdam.

It was the amused look now on David's face.

"Marijuana?"

"Yes."

"Oh, Cal. Wine, marijuana, socks…you have brought *everything*."

Cal rolled a joint, lit it, and took a deep hit. Then he reached across the table, offering the joint to David.

"Oh, thank you Cal, but no. I don't need it. I am already, in my natural condition, intoxicated. By life, by love, by art. By that girl earlier. And by these." He indicated the cigarette he was smoking and the wine he was drinking. "These are enough for me. But it gives me joy to smell it, and to watch you smoke."

They sat talking, drinking wine, both smoking. The smoke curled around them as the room grew darker. Then David took a candle off one of the shelves, put it on the table between them and lit it. Then they watched the smoke in the candlelight.

Chapter VII

L'Hostal was a bar-restaurant-discotheque just off the passeig. At midnight it was packed tightly with young bodies browned from the day. The music spilled out onto the little street in front, and further still onto the beach beyond it. Repeated trial and error had led the owners to find the exact level where everyone could go wild enough without the music bothering the neighbors who lived above the bar or behind it. Sometimes they still didn't get it right and the police would come and tell them to turn it down. They would turn it down until the police left, and sometimes somebody would turn it back up again. If someone complained after that the police would tell them that they had already spoken to the owner.

The black logo for L'Hostal, painted boldly beside the front door, had been designed by none other than Dali himself. The story went that in exchange, the then-owner had promised Dali that for the rest of their lives he and Gala could drink and eat there for free. Of course it was good business for the owner, people knowing that Dali went there.

A DJ stood in one corner pumping out the music. Boom boom. People were dancing. Others stood crowded at the bar, drinking or ordering drinks. There were candles stuck into great mounds of wax on the bar. The mounds were from all the candles that had come before. Decades worth of candles.

Other people were sitting around the edges of the big room

talking over the music. Cal walked in, stopped inside the door and looked around. In the flashing colored lights he couldn't recognize anyone. Finally he saw Cassandra standing to one side of the bar with some people. He walked to her.

"Hey, you made it!" she said. "I'm glad."

There was a glass in her hand. She did not introduce him to her friends, just gave Cal her full attention.

"So, how are you?"

"Happy to be here."

"Me too."

"Where's your boyfriend?"

"*What?*"

She looked surprised at the question.

"Wiggles."

"Oh. Forget that. He's *not* my boyfriend."

"But he said…"

"That was bullshit. I got a little drunk the other night, that's all. I let him kiss me. Nothing more. It was a huge mistake."

"Well, I can see why he wanted to do that."

She smiled.

"How long are you in Cadaqués for?"

"A month. A year. Forever. Not sure yet."

"When were you here? Last year?"

The music was making it hard to hear each other. Cal leaned closer.

"What did you say?"

She put her mouth against his ear. "I said, when were you here? Last year?"

"Yes."

"And? You liked it?"

"Yes."

"Great."

She was not the best conversationalist. But she was very pretty, and Cal could tell already that they were going to sleep with each other. She knew it too.

"What are you drinking?"

"What? Oh, White Russian."

It took a minute to catch the attention of the guy behind the bar. When he finally came over Cal ordered a White Russian and a double brandy soda. They were standing there then drinking, using the music as an excuse to lean close, when a young man came over to them. Skinny, tall like Cassandra, he looked nervous. He said something to her in German. They talked for a minute. Then she turned to Cal.

"This is my brother, Bruno. This is Cal."

"Hi." Cal reached out to shake his hand, but her brother didn't take it. He just stared back at Cal. Then he said something else to his sister in German and left.

"He's strange, my brother. Don't mind him."

"I don't think he liked me."

"He doesn't like any man I talk to."

"Really?"

"Yeah. It's funny. He's funny."

She was looking around. Now she also seemed nervous.

When they had finished their drinks, Cal took the empty glass from her hand and put it on the bar next to his empty glass. Then he took Cassandra's hand and led her onto the dance floor. They squeezed through some people and found a spot. After a minute dancing separately he moved closer and put his hands around her waist. It was a very small waist. They looked at each other, both smiling. He held her even closer and brought his mouth to her ear again.

"You do know that dancing is just sex with clothes on."

"*What?*"

Either she hadn't heard or she wanted to hear it again. He said it louder.

"*You know that dancing is just sex with clothes on.*"

"Really? I didn't know that," she lied.

Cal couldn't help himself. She was so thin and light. He picked her up. It turned out she wasn't bashful at all. She wrapped her legs around his waist and started to laugh. They were moving around in a circle, up and down to the music, when suddenly Bruno was standing next to them again.

"Hey man, that's my sister."

"Congratulations! You have a beautiful sister!"

"Hey, fuck off. Put her down."

"*Bruno*! What are you doing?" yelled Cassandra.

Cal lowered her back down so she was on her own feet again.

"Look…"

"Just fuck off, okay?" Bruno shouted.

"Okay."

Cal didn't mean, *Okay, I'll fuck off.* He meant it as in, *Okay, you are one weird fucking brother.*

"That's my sister, man. And I don't like seeing you grabbing her like that. Not here."

"*Not here?* This is a disco, Bruno. It's all *about* grabbing."

"Bruno," Cassandra said, "stop it! Just stop it!"

"I won't stop it. Keep your fucking hands off my sister."

Cal looked at her. "One question. How old are you?"

"Never mind how fucking old she is, she…"

"Twenty-seven. I'm twenty-seven."

"She's twenty-seven years old, Bruno. You know what that

means? That means she probably has a mind of her own."

The other people dancing around them didn't seem to notice. Just boom boom and wiggle wiggle. Everyone was having fun. Almost everyone.

"Look, asshole, you listen to me..." said Bruno. But Cal cut him off.

"No, *you* listen to *me*, Bruno. I don't want to get off on the wrong foot here, little brother, but my guess is I'm about twice as strong as you, so get your fucking face out of my fucking face before you fucking piss me off. Is that fucking clear...you fucker?"

That was just a little something Cal did sometimes, zero to sixty in nothing flat. The brandy helped. Bruno stared back at him. He was trying to decide what to do. Cal waited for the decision. It was true, Cal was stronger and Bruno could see it, so after a moment he just melded back into the crowd.

"How many brothers do you have?"

"I'm sorry about that. I'm so sorry."

"You want a drink? Because I would *really* like a drink."

He took Cassandra's hand and led her back to the bar.

"Look, I'm sorry."

"Never mind. Every family has one of those."

The barman came over. Cal ordered a White Russian and a double brandy straight. He wanted to get back onto the same track they were on before.

"So, like I was saying, dancing is just sex with the clothes still on."

She tried to smile, but her mind now was somewhere else. She kept looking around. The drinks came.

"He's just...he's always been very protective of me."

"Nice. So, a lot of scenes like that over the years?"

"No. Not really. Well…some."

"Maybe he's jealous of you."

"Why do you say that? Why do you say something like that?"

"Because I've heard sometimes a brother who has a beautiful sister…"

"That's not a very nice thing to say."

"What?"

"You think that he thinks about me in *that* way?"

"I didn't say that."

"Because…never mind."

"I just meant that sometimes a brother who has a…"

Before Cal could finish the sentence, he saw something out of the corner of his eye. It was a beer bottle coming toward his head. Instinctively, he ducked. The bottle swung, just missing him. Ducking so fast made him spill his brandy.

"*That was good brandy!*" Cal screamed. Not to be funny. It just came out of him. Like the kiai one screams in karate.

Cal had taken karate once. An introductory course for five weeks. Five weeks wasn't enough time to learn much karate, except he did learn two important things: one, scream like a crazy guy at your adversary to scare the shit out of him. It will also amp you up. And second, destroy the threat.

There were no smooth moves here. Cal even slipped doing it. But he managed to reach up and grab Bruno's arm, twisting it so hard that something cracked. The beer bottle flew off somewhere, the glass shattering. Most of the people in the room stopped dancing. In just a moment, Cal was already sitting on top of Bruno with his fist raised high. But he could see there was no point hitting him. The poor guy was screaming about his arm and trying to cover his face. Without a beer bottle in his hand and the element of surprise, he was done.

"Are you going to behave yourself?" yelled Cal, his fist still hanging up in the air.

"Fuck you," said Bruno. But it was a defeated voice, just point of pride. Cal even respected him for it.

"I'll take that as a yes."

Cal climbed off him. Bruno stared up at him for a moment, then he slithered off somewhere into the crowd, one arm holding onto the other.

"Nobody ever protected me like that," said Cassandra. She was looking at Cal in a funny way.

"Well…"

"No, really. Nobody ever protected me like that. *Ever.*"

There was a big circle of people standing around watching. But with this now settled most went back to what they were doing before. Dancing, talking. The barman said something to another guy who grabbed a broom and went out to clean up the broken bottle.

Cal led Cassandra over to one corner. He made sure to sit with his back to the wall so he could see out. And then Cassandra told him the story of her life. It just spilled out of her. The Reader's Digest version. Her parents were divorced. Daddy was a banker. Mommy owned a string of six shops in Liechtenstein.

"Things for tourists mostly. T-shirts, key chains, postcards with pictures of castles and princes."

"Nice. And Bruno?"

She told him all about the cocaine and the other drugs. And about the hospital and the police, and the fire he had set once in their main store in Vaduz after the mother had threatened to cut him out of her will.

"So, he has some issues."

"I guess you could say that. Yes. I mean...yes."

About an hour later he walked her home. While they walked, Cassandra held tight to Cal's arm while he kept looking around.

"Are you okay?"

"I'm fine."

The mother owned a big house that overlooked the main square. If not the most expensive property in the village, then almost. They only used it a few weeks in the year. Came to Cadaqués for some sun, the beach, a few drinks, a party or two, and that was it. It stayed closed up the rest of the year. As they walked toward the house now there were lights on in the *piano nobile*. The doors overlooking the square were open. With their small balconies, they were the kind of doors one could imagine politicians giving speeches from to the crowd assembled below. It really was a very big house.

"You must sell a lot of postcards."

"We do."

They stopped under one balcony and he kissed her. Long, hard, deep. And again.

"Don't go home," he whispered in her ear. "Come back to my place."

"You think I should?"

He pressed himself against her leg so she could feel him, hard. He looked at her and smiled. She smiled back.

"Okay."

Chapter VIII

The next morning she left early. He went back to sleep. Later when he came to the Casino at about noon Cal found the story about the fight had already gotten around. News is like a virus in a small village, everyone gets it.

"Had a go last night, did you?" asked Robert.

He was sitting alone with a newspaper and what was left of a beer. He had his reading glasses on. There was a book on the table, a paperback biography of Wellington. The morning and afternoon Roberts read a lot.

"A little. Why? What did you hear?"

"Nothing. Nothing much. Just that Bruno, that's his name isn't it, made a mess of things over at L'Hostal. You sorted him out. Broke his arm."

"*What?*"

"Apparently. They had to take him to the clinic this morning, bandage him up a bit."

"Jesus."

"Well, I wouldn't worry about it. He'll be all right. Think about things a bit more next time."

"He attacked me with a bottle. Tried to hit my head."

Robert nodded. He looked amused. There was a fly buzzing around in the warm air.

"Nice girl, Cassandra. Like her."

Everything abbreviated when he could. Why waste words.

"Something from the bar?" asked Cal, still standing.

"Glass of wine, maybe. Tinto."

Cal went to the bar, then came back with a *carajillo*, which is an espresso with brandy in it, and a glass of red wine that he handed to Robert.

"Very kind."

Cal sat.

"Writing, are you these days?" asked Robert.

"Just notes. A journal."

"That's something. Use it later. David, he's well is he?"

"Fine. Painting, I think."

"He's been busy, yes? Heard he threw a few rocks at some tourists swimming, eh?"

"They were just pebbles."

The sweet smile again.

"Never a dull moment. He's a good man David, hmm? Like him."

"You like everyone."

"Wellll, wouldn't go that far. Not everyone."

They sat for a while not speaking. Robert read his newspaper. Cal watched the people coming and going. No one he knew yet. After a while Robert looked up.

"Off to Figueres tomorrow."

"Yes?"

"Olive press. Seeing some people there, my brother and I. Make some arrangements."

"For the oil?"

"That's it. Get a good price there. Damned good price."

Robert and Richard minded some local olive groves. It's how they survived. Took care of the trees, and in the fall saw to it the olives were taken to a press and the oil returned to the landowners.

They didn't make much money doing that, but it was enough. Wine, tobacco, food, new shoes every few years.

Robert lived alone above the village in one of the old stone shepherd's huts, long abandoned. No-man's-land. Didn't cost him a penny. There had been a house nearby destroyed during the Civil War, so there was water from an old well. He had planted some thick ivy over the hut for shade, and had made a discreet little terrace. He could step out in the mornings, see the village below and the sea, light some candles at night, keep a fire, drink a little wine. Paradise.

Robert finished his glass and stood to get another. "What's that?" he asked Cal. "A *carajillo*, is it?"

Cal nodded.

"Right."

Robert went to the bar. While he was gone Cal picked the book off the table and looked at it. There was a bookmark sticking out close to the last pages. Robert reappeared carrying drinks for them both.

"Wellington?"

"Hmm. Good man, though the French wouldn't say so. Clever. Liked his wine."

"Not Napoleon's favorite."

"No."

"Made a name for himself in France, yes?"

"Long before that, darling. India. Philippines."

"Really."

"The Peninsular War. Spain, just up here in the Pyrenees." He pointed over his shoulder. "The Bidassoa, Pamplona…."

"Pamplona?"

"Eighteen…twellllve, I think. Or thirteen. Would have to look again, hmm."

The words were starting to stretch.

"My first visit to Spain was to Pamplona," said Cal.

"Oh yes?"

"Hemingway."

A knowing nod. "Read Fiesta, did you? Or as you call it in the States, the…what is it?"

"Sun Also Rises."

"That's it. Read it when I was young. Fine book."

Cal told Robert the story of how, as a student some twenty years before, after reading that book he had taken the train from Paris to Bayonne, then hitchhiked up the mountain to Pamplona.

"It was April, so the fiesta wasn't on yet."

"Wouldn't be, would it. July, yes? Seventh day of the seventh month? Running of the bulls."

"That's right. Anyway, I hitchhiked up. There was an old man named Jesus who gave me a ride in a white car."

"Jesus gave you a lift, did he? Well, that was good of him."

"On the way up the mountain he told me how when he had been a boy he met Hemingway and shook his hand. Then when I got out of the car in Pamplona I shook that same hand."

"And you felt something, did you?" Robert smiled.

"Cadaqués reminds me of that story. And the people in it."

"Not so sure about that. Don't really think so. No lost generation here, darling. This is Cadaqués. We are *finding* ourselves!"

There were more people coming into the Casino now. A young couple sat down at the table next to theirs.

"Self-actualization. That's what it's all about here, darling. Self-actualization. And, well, getting in touch with one's self." He said all that as if in quotes. He was quoting the sixties in general. "He missed that didn't he, Hemingway? Shot himself, yes? Not an old man."

"Sixty-one in sixty-one."

"He missed the sixties then?"

"Yes."

"Pity. A lot to see there. Might have given him some new ideas."

Suddenly through the front door came an explosion. Marita. She rushed in, saw Robert and came straight toward him. She was hyperventilating.

"Oh, Robert, I am so happy to…"

She looked at Cal, recognizing him.

"Well, is it…Cal, yes? From last year? Of course."

He stood. Kisses on cheeks. They sat.

"Robert, I have to tell you something."

They waited for it but then...nothing. She froze, as if trying to decide whether to say what was on her mind.

"I'm so upset. Really, I can't tell you how upset I am. Really." She was rocking back and forth, arms embracing herself. "I can't believe it."

"Believe what?"

"Well…no, forget it. I can't say."

"Say what?" Cal pushed to know.

She thought about it.

"No. I can't say." She looked around the big room and took a deep breath. "I need a drink." She sprang up and was gone. Robert smiled.

"Crazy girl, that. But a nice one, eh? Love her."

Marita was, legitimately, a gypsy princess from Sweden. Like Robert she had come to Cadaqués in the sixties as a young model for Dali, then just stayed. Hooked on Cadaqués like it was an opiate. For some there was no getting away from it. She had beautiful translucent eyes that made her look like the fortune-teller she sometimes was. The Swedish accent was still there, in English or Spanish. And despite her years, she had kept the thin figure of a flamenco dancer, thanks to the nervous disposition of a hummingbird. Fast to smile, fast to cry, she spoke and moved and even felt in bursts. Now she was already back, wine in hand.

"Now come come, Marita," said Robert. "Have a seat. Have a drink. Settle down. Tell us."

"Well..." She sat, drank, thought, looked around, drank again, and took a deep breath. "Okay. Well, this morning, I...I was cleaning the boys' room, and what do you think I found?"

She had two teenaged sons, one thirteen, the other fifteen.

"Drugs?"

"No! Good God, no!"

"Cigarettes?"

"No."

It was a game. Cal joined in.

"A Playboy magazine?"

She looked at him. "You *almost* got it. Very good Cal, you almost got it. But it's worse than that. *Much* worse."

"Oh for God's sake, just tell us," said Robert.

She lowered her voice so no one else could hear her.

"A *condom*," she whispered. Then, forgetting to stay quiet, she blurted out, "*What is a condom doing in the night stand of such a young boy?*"

The couple sitting at the next table looked over their shoulders. Both smiled.

"Oh, Jesus. I think they heard me."

"I thought it was going to be something horrible."

"It *is* horrible. What are you saying? These are my *babies*. What are they doing with a *condom*, for God's sake."

"Who had it? Which one?"

"I don't know. I can't tell. It was in the little table between their beds. There was a spider web, and I was cleaning, and then all of a sudden I see…oh, dear God!" She burst out laughing. "These are my *babies*! I'm not ready for this. No, I'm not ready. Much too soon for this."

She drank the rest of her wine like it was water. That seemed to relax her. She grew quieter.

"Their papa must have given it to them. Okay, maybe he was trying to be a good papa, because boys…" She didn't finish the sentence. Instead, she just looked around and started to laugh again. "Oh, dear God! What am I going to do?"

"I shouldn't worry," said Robert. "They'll be fine. Just boys, that's all."

Chapter IX

Still no food in his stomach, a now hungry Cal walked alone toward the other side of the small bay. There was a restaurant on the beach beyond the village where he would eat. Keeping one eye out for Bruno or Cassandra, in that order, he walked by the passeig, past L'Hostal that looked so quiet in the day, and past the Bar Meliton where Duchamp once sat day after long day playing chess with Man Ray. Meliton was still the place where a certain *crème de la crème* from the village liked to gather. At one table toward the back of the wide terrace, Jasper Guinness of *the* Guinnesses was sitting with Lord and Lady Ratkins. At another table, an old Catalan man in a wheel chair sat with his nurse, while a rich-looking French family were laughing and smoking nearby, the blonde children sucking cold drinks through straws.

Beyond Meliton was the hulking Casa Serinyana, or *Blue House*. It was one of several grand homes built by villagers who, after the insect phylloxera had destroyed local grape vines, had sailed to Cuba hoping to find new chances in a new world. Some who made it big in Havana came back later to this village they loved and was still home. Called "Americanos" now, they built huge houses with their new fortunes. This one looked like it had been built by a lottery winner, his pockets brimming over with cash. *"Bluer! I want it bluer!...More windows!...And put another arch on that roof!"*

That happened at the start of the century, and now here Cal

was walking at the cusp of yet another new century. The centuries were ticking by pretty fast like poles on the highway. Cal stopped to look around, wondering what Cadaqués would look like in another two, three, four hundred years. Not for him to know.

He kept walking, passing the house where Picasso spent the summer of 1910. From right there the artist had stood looking out at the village, apparently thinking, *how can I change the course of art history based on all these little houses that look like cubes?*

The road then bent around a small cove. Wooden fishing boats, some painted white with Cadaqués blue trim, had been pulled onto the beach. Next to the boats were a dozen tourists splayed out on the rocky sand. There was a red umbrella stuck beside some towels, and a yellow umbrella. Some children splashed nearby. The smaller children had plastic toys in many colors. Yellow, red, purple, green. And blue.

Two young women lay without tops, their breasts pointing toward the sun.

The road began to slope upward. Looking down through bright green pines now there were more coves, and places among the gray rocks where groups of two or three or four people had found spots to call their own for the day. Boys and girls, girls and girls, boys and boys. The water past the rocks was so clear you could still see the rocks running below and out into the bay. There were green blue patches where there was sand on the bottom between the rocks. A thick stone pylon from a bygone age rose out of the water, a reminder of the heavy sailing ships that had once tied close to these shores. One could not see everything. There were still secrets down there: remains of ships, swords, Roman pottery, pirate's gold, human bones.

On the other side of the road was a row of houses with orgasms of red-purple bougainvillea splayed across their white walls.

One envied the people who lived in those houses, because they could just step out onto their terraces any time of day or night and see all this. In the sun or moonlight they could look out across those pines and that water to the white village with its church. In the night they would see the yellow lights in the windows and those lights reflected on the water. They could see it in the storms and the lightening, and when the storms cleared they could see it as it was now, sharp, clear and bright.

There was such a thing as almost *too* beautiful. Like David's Aphrodite. Or like that girl Cal had seen walking past the Casino the day before with her grandfather. He kept thinking about her. Cal was not religious, still there were moments when he would look upward and whisper thank you. He did that now.

Passing around the little point, straight ahead now was a beach with two *chiringuito* restaurant-bars. Cal went to the second of the two, chose a table in the shade of an Ombu tree and sat facing the water. He had his journal with him and put it on the table. He would write in a moment, but first...

The waiter came, a young guy with a ponytail. He looked South American. Cal ordered a half-liter of sangria. *Sangre.* Blood. So refreshing! When he made it at home, and he made it at home a lot, he would mix one bottle of decent red wine, the same amount of lemonade, a great big splash of brandy, a great big splash of rum, and a great big splash of Grand Marnier. He knew he wasn't going to get all that here, so he just told the waiter "*Fuerte.*" Strong. That was also a good recipe.

As the waiter left to get it, Cal looked at the menu. He wanted everything. Not possible. So when the sangria came he ordered: local anchovies on fresh bread smeared with olive oil and tomato paste; *escalivada*, which is a roasted vegetable salad; *navajas,* those are razor clams in garlic and parsley; and *gambas a la plancha,* which are grilled prawns with the heads still on. He would have to come back another time for the codfish *esqueixada* with orange, and the grilled asparagus, and the *rosada.*

The *carajillos* from the Casino had worn off, so he took a few fast sips of the sangria. When he finished the glass he poured another and left it sitting. It was nice to look at the pieces of lemon and orange floating in the red wine juice.

As he waited for the food to come, Cal opened his journal. If you didn't write things down it was a crapshoot. Would they still be there later or not? Some things you didn't mind losing. You even wanted to lose them, so you didn't write about them and then you waited and with luck they were gone. But there were other things, places, people, you didn't want to lose for the life of you. Sometimes just a word, like a photograph, could bring those back. For instance, say the word "Mother" to someone. You've just unlocked so many photographs and memories. Sometimes one word can even be too much.

Cal wrote more than one word now. He wrote about his friends, and the fight with Bruno, and the sex after that. It had started just inside the door, moved to the bed, then somehow wound up in the kitchen. When he was through writing he closed his journal and drank what was left of the sangria. When the waiter brought his food he ordered another half-liter. He had known he would do that when he ordered the first, but somehow ordering two half-liters seemed more moderate than just ordering a full liter out of the gate. As if trying to be moderate was a step toward the thing itself.

When he had finished everything, Cal paid his bill and walked slowly back to the village. The sangria really had been strong and the sun now was hot. He was heading toward the Casino to see if anyone was there. Before getting to it, across the square on his right was a smaller bar called the Imperial. Sometimes his friends also gathered there. He looked. No one he knew. But there was a beautiful girl with her back toward him. It looked like the same one he had seen the day before. He couldn't be sure so he walked closer. She was sitting with...*yes*, it was the same old man she had been walking with past the Casino, so it had to be her. On this day she had on a short green dress. The long blonde curls, thin neck, legs that would not stop, white sandals on those little feet...if anything, she looked even more beautiful than she had the day before. Cal had kept hoping he would see her again. He had even written something about her in his journal: *Can beauty be radioactive? What is the half-life of a vision?* As he got closer now he could see that she was holding the hand of the old man. That was sweet. She must love her grandfather a lot, thought Cal.

Chapter X

He sat at a table close to theirs. The waitress came to him. He ordered, why not, a *carajillo*.

The old man was talking, as he had been the day before. He was speaking English, saying something about "those fucking idiots." The girl was listening to him and nodding. Apparently there were a lot of fucking idiots, and he was describing them all to her.

Never, *never*, had Cal seen skin so smooth, or cheeks so softly rounded. They were like two little baby bottoms. And her eyes, like a doe's, almost almond shaped. And yes, Cadaqués blue. *Incredible.* The blonde hair curling over those tanned shoulders onto breasts so firm and big they looked ready to pop out of their little cage there. How was it possible, beauty like that? He couldn't stop staring at her. She felt it. Finally she looked over at him. He did not avert his eyes. Instead, he smiled at her. She just stared back at him. Then after a moment she turned and looked elsewhere. *Look again.* No luck.

There is beauty, and then there is something more than beauty. Behind the eyes, under the skin. Not something one sees but feels. Feels without touching even.

He watched as this girl's eyes kept looking around. She seemed so curious about everything. She was listening to the old man as he kept going on, but at the same time it was obvious she was busy with her own thoughts. As he kept looking at her,

Cal realized he had gone from watching her breasts and her legs to watching her think. That was as sexy as the rest of it.

Suddenly there was a voice above and to his left. He looked up. Cassandra. Her mother's house was next door to the Imperial, and she was standing on one of the little balconies smoking a cigarette.

"Hey, good morning," she called down.

It was after three.

"Good morning!"

"Wait a minute," she shouted. "I'll be right down.

"Great."

He waited. She came.

"I was hoping to see you here," he said, as if that had really been the reason he had come over to the Imperial. She sat...right between him and the other girl. As they talked, Cal tried to not keep looking over her shoulder.

"So, everything's okay? I mean with your brother?"

"Yeah."

"I heard about his arm. I'm sorry about that.

"Oh, it's nothing. Really, he'll be fine. He just gets that way sometimes."

"Nice. Where is he now?"

"I don't know. I don't really care."

Cal cared. He had stopped thinking about him. Now he was trying to look at Cassandra, and at the other girl, and keep an eye out for Bruno at the same time.

Cassandra was holding a pack of her skinny cigarettes, a plastic lighter, and a fat paperback. She put them all on the table. Cal looked at the book. There was a picture of a handsome man holding a beautiful young woman in his arms with a castle in the background. The title was *Never Again*.

"Is that about the Holocaust?"

"What?"

"The book. I see the title."

"No, it's not about the Holocaust."

"What's it about?"

"Nothing. I mean…well, it's about this man who inherits a castle, and there's a young girl who works in the village near the castle, and…oh, forget it. It's not so interesting."

"It sounds very interesting."

"It's not. Believe me."

The old man at the next table was still talking, and there was the noise of a scooter going past. Cal waited for the scooter to go.

"What are your plans for today? Still working?"

"A little."

"Making calls?"

"Yeah."

"For the shops?"

She nodded.

"What else do you sell in the shops?"

"What do you mean?"

"I mean, aside from what you were telling me about last night. Key chains, postcards. You sell other stuff?"

"Of course."

"Like…?"

"Oh, you know. Things."

"What kind of things?"

"I don't know." She shrugged as if it was a silly question. "Just, things. Sunglasses, hats, cups…"

"Magnets?"

"Magnets, yes. Some guide books. Maps."

"Shirts?"

"Shirts, yes."

"Shirts with pictures?"

"Some of them. Sure."

"Shirts that say things?

"Of course."

"Like…?"

"I don't know."

"What's an example?"

She thought about it. "'I Love Liechtenstein.'"

"In English?"

"Sure. But there are others that say things in French, German. Even Italian.'

"How do you say 'I Love Liechtenstein' in German?"

"Ich liebe Liechtenstein." But none of the shirts say that."

"That's a pity. I'd buy one if it said that."

"Don't be silly. You wouldn't have to buy it."

"No?"

"Of course not," she giggled. "I'd give it to you."

Over her shoulder now, the beauty finally looked again in Cal's direction. There was a little smile, as if she had been listening to all this.

"Have you been to Liechtenstein?" asked Cassandra. "I forgot to ask you last night."

"No. Never."

"Well, you should come. Visit us sometime."

"I'd love to. It's nice, yes?"

"Yes. Really, you should come. You'd love it."

The beauty had let go of the old man's hand and was playing with one curl in her hair.

"What are you doing tonight?" Cal asked Cassandra.

"I don't know. Why?"

"There's a party at a friend of mine's house up the mountain.

You probably know him. Austrian painter. Freddy."
"Of course I know him. Sure, I'd love to go."
"Great."

Chapter XI

A few hours later, Cal found Robert at the Bar Boia. Now they were sitting together behind it on the terrace at the edge of the beach. Robert had been at it, cigarette in one hand, glass of wine in the other. Eyes opening, closing, opening again. Cal had been at it too.

"*Layla?*"

"That's it."

"Like Clapton's song?"

"'Get down on your knees,' eh? Or something like that."

"And her last name?"

"Von Leda."

"No!"

"Yesss, darling. VONNN LEDAAA."

"Layla von Leda? You're joking."

"Wouldn't joke about a thing as serious as a woman's name."

"That's not a name. It's poetry. How's that possible? A name as beautiful as she is."

"Noble family. Teutonic knights. Sounds good, hmm? A certain RINGGG to it. Layla vonnn Leda?"

The sun was beginning to sink lower in the sky.

"And he? The old man?"

"Paul?"

"Is that his name?"

"Boyfriend."

"Her *boyfriend*? No!"

"Hmm."

"*Not* her grandfather?"

Robert smiled. "Not her grandfather, no."

"But...he's a thousand years old."

"Not a thousand, darling. But, mas o menos, eh? Seventy-eight, nine, something like that."

"Who is he?"

"De Beers."

"Paul *De Beers*? That's not his name."

"Wouldn't lie."

"Not Paul Revere. Paul *De Beers*?"

"That's it."

"As in, South Africa?"

Robert nodded.

"Well then, I guess I do understand."

"Of the family, but not *that* part of it. Not diamonds, no. A cousin or something. Father had a restaurant. So does he."

"A *restaurant*?"

"Two. In Manchester. Another here. Nice one here. Tapas, fish, meat. Other side of the village, near the museum. Get a nice piece of flesh there, darling. A nice piece of FLESSHH indeed!"

Robert took a once-white handkerchief from his pocket, wiped his mouth, leaned into it and closed his eyes. He slept for a moment. Cal watched him. Then,

"Robert?"

"Hmm?"

The eyes shot open.

"She's the most beautiful woman in the world."

"They all are, darling. They all are."

"And she has the most beautiful name in the world."

"Von Leda. Good one, yes? Last name's a river, somewhere north of Germany. Also our mother, darling. Leda."

"Whose mother?"

"Leda and the SWANNN. Mother of Castor and Pollux. The twins, darling. The Dioscuri. It's what Dali called my brother and me, 'Castor and Pollux.' One twin mortal, the other a god, immortal."

"And, who is who?"

"We'll find out, won't we? Time will tell, hmm? In the end."

"And Paul?"

"Her SWANNN, darling. Sweet swan of Manchester."

"And tell me something, do you think they...?"

"Sexual congress?"

Cal tried not to picture it. Too late.

"I suspect so, darling. Boyfriend. Live together. Always holding hands."

"If he's not rich, is he very smart?"

"Welll..."

"Talented?"

"Not sure about that."

"Is he a kind man? Robert? Is he a kind man? Because he didn't sound so kind, the way he was going on about everyone being a 'fucking idiot.'"

"Just his way."

"A young beauty like that could have any man on earth. Why do you think she's with him?"

"Can't say, can we? A mystery, that. After all, who amongst us knows the ways of LOOOVVE, hmm? How Cupid takes his aim? He just SHOOTS!"

Robert flashed his handkerchief in the air as if to chart the path of the arrow.

"*Jorge!*" Robert shouted out, as if to no one in particular.

The waiter came over.

"Roberto. Tell me."

Robert waved his handkerchief over the empty glasses like it was a magic wand. Message understood, the waiter went to bring two more glasses of wine.

There were small waves lapping against the rocky beach, the sun was setting, orange light shone on the boats and on little Es Cucurucuc in the distance. With a grand flourish Robert waved his handkerchief gesturing toward it all.

"Cadaqués, darling. As beautiful as any woman. And we love her. We love her."

His eyes closed again. Cal sat watching him sleep as the waiter brought two new glasses of wine. After the waiter left, Cal let his own eyes also close for a few moments.

Chapter XII

It was dark up the mountain. No moon that night, though stars everywhere. The Milky Way stretched across the sky. Wild pigs in the olive trees and scrub beyond the house, foraging. There were lights in the village below. Like more stars.

The tramuntana, that hot wind coming off the Pyrenees, swept across the terrace of the stone house. Despite the wind Freddy had managed to build a fire in an old rusted out barbeque at one end of the wide terrace. To do it, he had circled a ring of old cane-backed chairs, bleached from the sun and rain, around the fire, then spread an old blanket across them on the windward side. The wind licked around the blanket, but finally the flames took. The olive wood burned down, more was added, and when that burned down into a good bed of coals an oversized paella pan was placed over it. Stock from boiled fish heads and other things was poured in, the rice added, then saffron, clams, mussels, great prawns, pieces of chicken, peas, slices of lemon and red pepper, some olive oil and garlic. Enough there to feed the world.

A small electric lamp glowed over the pan. The cord ran inside through sliding glass doors kept open only just because of the wind. The only electricity in the house came from a gas generator in a stone shed on the edge of the property. Inside, one small electric light shone in the kitchen. Otherwise, lit candles everywhere.

It was a good-sized house made of slate stone, with heavy

wood beams and dull red tile floors, and a big white fireplace to keep it warm in winter. There was a long thick wooden table running through the main room. It used to be the bar at an old restaurant in the village. On the table were a dozen bottles of red wine, half of them already opened. There was a big basket of bread, and bowls of olives, and a wood board with white cheese and sausage on it. There was a sharp knife stuck into the cheese. And there were many small votive candles set onto plates. The flames from the candles lit the faces of the people who came close, leaning in for the food or wine.

David sat in an old chair by one window, smoking. Outside on the terrace, Wiggles stood watching Freddy stir the paella.

"You stir it clockwise, do you, Freddy? Not counter clockwise? If you stirred it counter clockwise, would that effect the taste of it very much?"

Wiggles was already drunk. Freddie just ignored him and kept stirring.

"Look, I want to help," said Wiggles. "I want to be useful. So what I'll do is I'll go inside and open another bottle of wine. Will that be useful?"

"Yeah," said Freddie. He was through stirring and was looking at the paella. Wiggles went inside, leaving Freddy alone on the terrace.

Darius Friedrich Wolff, "Freddy" to his friends, was a tall thin Austrian painter, sixty-something, with a handsome craggy face, and silver hair swept back. He had steel gray eyes, and a smile that came and went at will. He had left Austria long ago and far away. Had made his money doing this and that, here and there. A few, very few, other facts were known. He had been a street performer in Amsterdam. He had run a bar on Ibiza for some years. Later he had kept another bar in the Canary Islands. And then he had come here to Cadaqués sometime in the seventies as a special friend of Gala, Dali's wife. A short visit turned into a long visit, which was turning into forever. He had bought this land on the mountain, and over the years had built this house to his own design. Then to fill it he and Marita had made the two boys, Marko and Lorenzo.

That part of Freddy that was still and forever Austrian loved order. The part that had grown to become Spanish loved the wild. Every day, and especially every night, there was a competition between those two. You could see it in his eyes. The eighteenth century War of the Austrian Succession being played out all over again inside one man. Fewer muskets, but very possibly more wine. On this night it was still early, so for the moment the Austrian side had the advantage.

Inside the house, laughter, shouting, music. David got out of his chair and wandered onto the terrace. He stood next to Freddy, looking down at the big pan. His voice as always soft, ethereal.

"Freddy, you make for us the feast of Vitellius. Do you know about Vitellius, Freddy?"

"No."

"Oh, Freddy, he was emperor of Rome. And for him they made a feast. It was called the Shield of Minerva. Such things in it, Freddy, like you have for us here. But instead of mussels, they had the brains of peacocks. Instead of clams, the tongues from pink flamingos. Livers from fish, every strange thing they could find they put inside it. Freddy?"

"What?"

"I think your paella will taste better than the Shield of Minerva."

David took a long thoughtful puff from his cigarette. The strong wind was blowing his hair.

Inside the house people were moving around, the laughter growing louder. There was a quiet looking man, short, bald. Antonio. He took a guitar from a case and started to play. Not quiet anymore. His flamenco strumming, the rasqueado, hard, perfect.

"*Olé,*" shouted Jose Manuel, stamping his feet. He started to dance, then called out, "Marita!"

Marita shouted back down from the kitchen, "What?"

"Dance!"

"I can't. I'm in the kitchen."

"You can! Come!"

"No. Later."

"*No?* Okay then, *I* come to *you!*" His face mock serious, hands above his head clapping, stamping the floor he came toward her. Up the stairs into the little kitchen like a bull.

"Now you just let me finish here what I'm doing," said Marita, the Swedish accent insisting. "And *then* I'll dance. But later."

She was washing dishes.

"There is no later! Only *now!*"

"Esa gitana guapa!" someone shouted.

Jose Manuel grabbed her. Her hands were dripping wet, soap suds on her fingers. He carried her down the stairs and lowered her onto the middle of the table. She looked down at him. Gypsy eyes. Jose Manuel was twisting his black mustache, looking back up at her.

"Dance to the beat of my heart! Can you hear it!"

Others were shouting.

"Olé!"

"Dale!"

The bald guy was strumming harder than ever and tapping the wood of the guitar.

"Refuse and you break my heart!"
"Baila!"
"Ahora!"
She arched her back.
"Baila! Guapa!"
"Vamos!" someone else yelled.

She started to move. Fingers snapped. The heels hit the table. Antonio was playing like a devil. Jose Manuel was clapping, singing to Marita in Spanish, "You cut my heart open with your eyes! Nothing is more dangerous than Marita's eyes." He was making the words up as he sang.

"Olé!"

Freddy had come in and stood watching all this, grinning. A couple of people moved the bottles of wine from the table so Marita would not kick them over. Her elbows high at her sides now, heels stamping the table hard, fingers snapping, she turned slowly like the torero's faena passing with the cape close to the bull.

"Guapa!"

"Beautiful Marita!"

"Tercio de muerte!" cried Jose Manuel. "Now it's time. Kill me with those eyes! Look at me! Look at me, I beg you!"

She would not look at him.

"*Torture!*"

She looked at him.

"Ahhh!" He clutched his chest, pretending to die. "Stabbed by the eyes of Marita!"

Jose Manuel was an actor from Barcelona. One could tell.

Cal had brought Cassandra to the house an hour or so earlier. They had quickly disappeared into one of the bedrooms. They came out now into the big room. Marita was on the table, still dancing. The others were clapping. The guitar, candles, wine flowing. This was the best of it still.

"Okay now," said Marita laughing, "Enough of this nonsense." She got herself down from the table. "Let's get *serious* now. We are all grown-ups here. First we eat dinner, *later* we kill with our eyes."

Jose Manuel pretended to sob. He looked around, the long black curls falling over one eye.

"Quick, a knife for my wrist. The vision evaporates. The washing of dishes has waged battle with the music, and the dishes have won. Oh, cruel life!"

He took the knife that was stuck in the cheese and pretended to slash his wrist.

"*Don't bleed on the cheese!*" someone shouted.

"Fuck the cheese!"

"Don't tell him to fuck the cheese. He'll try!"

"Who said that? It's impossible. I *never* fuck cheese. It's my first rule in life, 'Do not fuck the cheese!' And besides, this is virgin cheese. Have some respect."

The guitar was softer now, gentle in the background. Everyone was getting ready for what was to come.

Wiggles, looking around the big room, spotted Cassandra and Cal standing together in a dark corner. They were holding hands.

"Well, hello there," he cried out. "How's our favorite slut this evening? Enjoying the party, are we?"

"Wiggles, shut up," said Cassandra. She was so sorry she had ever let him kiss her.

"Why look, did you hear that? She even *talks* like a slut. Straight from the docks. 'Shut up, you fucking fucker!' Go on, say it. Say the word 'Fuck.' I'm sure we'd all like to hear that. Cal? Cal would like to hear you say that, wouldn't you, Cal?

Go on, slut, say the word 'fuck.'"

"Wiggles..."

"I'm sure you can *do* it well enough, so you can certainly say it. It's even easier than doing it. Go on, say the word 'fuck.'"

Cal let go of Cassandra's hand and stepped forward.

"Wiggles, if that mouth doesn't stop moving I'm going to stop it for you."

"Ooooh! The big man is going to stop me from telling the fucking slut to say the word 'fuck.'"

"One more time..."

"Okay then, come on. Let's have a go."

Wiggles took his glasses off and set them on the table. Then he made ready for what in the old days Brits called *fisticuffs*. He started prancing about, as if whatever followed would be bound by Marquess of Queensbury Rules.

"Come on, old boy. I'm here. I'm waiting for you. Come on then."

"Not here," said Freddy very matter-of-factly. "You could break the window. Outside, away from the fire."

"All right then. Whatever you say, Freddy. Freddy's the host. He knows where he likes his guests to fight. Come on, Cal. Outside with it. You can defend the honor of the fucking slut outside."

They moved onto the terrace. Everyone followed. Antonio kept playing his guitar. Faster now. The official soundtrack.

David stood watching like a boy at the circus.

"Oh Cal, Wiggles, are you really going to combat *mano a mano*? How primitive, yes? How exciting! How wonderful!"

At the far side of the terrace, Wiggles turned, then up again with the fists.

"Right, then. I say she's a slut. A little slut. And you say that..."

Cal slapped him. Open hand.

"Now...now what was that?"

"I slapped you."

"Yes, Cal, I'm aware that you slapped me. But we're fighting here. Come on. I'm not her brother. I heard about that. I'm not Bruno. You want to defend this fucking slut, well then you'd better..."

Cal reached out fast and slapped him again, hard across the face. Then he rushed forward, pushing Wiggles to the ground. Then he sat on him. A certain leitmotif here.

"What the..."

Cal slapped him again.

"You're going to stop saying those things about her now?"

"Well, I don't know about that." He was pinned, staring up at Cal. "She wouldn't fuck me, but now apparently she goes and fucks you. Up in the bedroom there. The little bitch deserves every..."

Cal slapped him again. Just like Bruno the night before, Wiggles's hands flew up to protect his face. Everyone was crowded around. Jose Manuel was clapping his hands, shouting,

"*Olé! Hombres! Lucha!*"

Cassandra tried to sound like she was not enjoying seeing these two men fighting over her.

"Guys, please, stop it. Just stop it now."

David was fascinated.

"It's like watching the scorpion and the rat, eh Freddy? In *L'Age d'Or*, by Buñuel and Dali. You see how they do it? Like in nature."

Freddy said nothing.

Marita had been up in the kitchen again. Now she came running.

"Oh, for God's sake! What is *this*? *Stop* it, you two. Freddy, *stop* them!"

"Ah," Freddy sighed. He almost sounded bored. He had seen worse. Much worse. "What's to stop? They're just playing. No one's going to hurt anyone. Nobody even has a knife." He said it as if with disgust. "That's not a fight."

Wiggles still was not ready to call it quits.

"Well come on, don't just slap me, Cal. How embarrassing. At least punch me once, give me a black eye. Get me some sympathy at least from that little cunt."

He was begging for it. But Cal couldn't punch him. A real punch had to be in the heat of it. Because he knew how it could tear the skin off a cheek, or squeeze an eyeball from its socket, or crush a temple, or jar the brain bruising it. A real blow had to come without having time to think about those things. So he just slapped him again.

"Oh, for God's sake Cal, how humiliating."

"I like slapping you, Wiggles. Go on, say something else. Anything. Say something about the weather."

Wiggles didn't say anything.

There comes a point in some stories, as in some lives, where one might think, enough already with all the wine and madness. But that doesn't mean that a story, or a life, will back off when that point is met. Sometimes at that very moment wine and madness flow even freer and faster.

There was a loud crash suddenly on the other side of the house. Someone had knocked over the orange propane tanks that were stacked on the stone terrace next to the front door. One of the empty tanks had fallen and clanged its way down onto a stone terrace below, beside the swimming pool.

"What the *hell*?" shouted Marita. "*Now* what is it? *What is going on here? The whole world is falling apart!"*

Freddy hurried to see what it was. Marita followed. The others were torn: follow, or stay here to see how things would work out between Cal and Wiggles.

Inside the house, the wooden front door flew open and Robert came crashing in onto his knees. There was blood on his face, running down his neck onto his white shirt. Behind him were two people no one had seen before. There was a young man. He had dark hair, was handsome in a delicate way, and was wearing a woman's dress. White with flowers on it. Loose, comfortable, it almost looked like an Arabic kaftan, but it was definitely a woman's dress. The young woman with him also wore a dress. Hers was short and black. She had black hair, and black make-up under dark eyes that kept looking around.

When Marita saw the blood on Robert's face she screamed.

"Robert! My God! What has happened to you?"

"He fell," said the young woman with the dark eyes. "On one of the rocks coming up the path."

"DARLING!" said Robert, as if nothing was amiss. He was still on his knees, looking up at her. "It's nothing. Just a scratch, hmm."

Blood was dripping from the end of his nose onto the red tiles. They tried to help him to his feet, but he wasn't having it.

"I'm fine," he mumbled. "Fine here as I am." He was looking at the floor, still kneeling. It looked like he was going to vomit. Marita was beside herself. All that blood. And the truth is, she loved him.

"Oh please, someone *help* me! For God's sake, help me get him to a chair."

Jose Manuel and Freddy pulled Robert up by his arms and dragged him onto a chair beside the table.

"I'll get a wet towel to wipe that face. *Oh, dear God!*"

Marita rushed to the kitchen. David went back out to the terrace to report. Cal was still sitting on top of Wiggles.

"Cal? Wiggles?"

They both answered. "Yes, David?"

"It's Robert. He has fallen on a rock and cut himself. There is blood everywhere. But not to worry, I think he will be okay. There is a man in a dress helping to take care of him."

Robert was a good friend. Cal wanted to make sure he was okay.

"I'm going to have to stop slapping you now, Wiggles."

"I understand. Well, you do what you have to, Cal."

Cal stood, then offered a hand to Wiggles. He took it and staggered to his feet. Both men hurried in to check on their friend. The young girl in black was kneeling close to Robert, just staring at him.

"Robert?...Robert?...Robert?..." That's all she kept saying. "Robert?..Robert?...Robert?..."

The young man in the dress was grinning. Marita came back with the wet towel.

"Come on now, let me through. *Let me through!*"

Those crowded around moved aside. Marita began to wipe the blood off Robert's face.

"Robert, my God, what have you done to yourself?"

He looked up at her, smiling.

"It's nothing, darling. Just a...just a NOTHING, hmm."

She leaned in close to look.

"Well, it's not so bad. Just a little cut in the eyebrow. But my God, *how much blood!*"

The rock had just missed his eye.

"How are you feeling?" asked Cal.

"FANTASTIC, darling. Never better, hmm. Cal?"

"Yes?"

"We're well bred, you and I, hmm? Not like...not like THOSE people."

"Which people?"

"In the CITIES! With their...their..." He didn't finish the sentence. The voice trailed off. He was asleep. Marita kept the wet towel pressed to his face.

"It's like a movie, eh, Freddy?" said David.

"Well now don't just stand there, everyone," said Marita, pleading. "Someone help me get him onto the couch."

They lifted Robert up. As they were lowering him onto the cushions, someone outside shouted.

"*Fire!*"

Freddy moved so fast he pushed over two chairs. It was the Spanish side of him springing to life. The Austrian would have moved the chairs. The others followed him out like Keystone cops. With all of the distractions, no one had been keeping their eyes on the paella. The wind had blown a corner of the dry blanket onto the coals and it had caught. The cane chairs under it were also burning, like two torches.

The mountainside around the house was so dry. Trees, scrub. Just one spark and...

There was a little metal table on the terrace. Freddy grabbed it. Turning it upside down and using its legs, he poked at the burning blanket catching it. Then, hoisting it in front of him, he carried it to the side of the terrace and with a heave sent the blanket and table flying into the little swimming pool below. The blanket made a hissing sound as it hit the water, before the metal table pulled it under.

Cal grabbed one of the burning chairs by a leg and hurled it also into the pool. Jose Manuel did the same with the other chair. Then he stood there solemnly.

"A prayer for the dead chairs. *In nomine Patris, et Filii, et Spiritus Sancti,* we commit these chairs, Lord, into your care."

Back inside the house, David had wandered over to a far corner of the big room. It was where Freddy painted. His easel and brushes, tubes of paint, jars of liquid, rags, canvases, were everywhere. Leaning nearby were canvases, some finished, others in progress. Scenes of islands, strange rocks, sea life, mermaids, the village... On a wood easel was a painting Freddy had completed that day, a blue-green soft focus scene of Cadaqués with the church Santa Maria and the village spreading around it. David sat down in Freddy's chair and looked at it. After a moment he took out a heavy black marker from his pocket and thoughtfully drew a bird onto Freddy's sky. Then he lit a cigarette, leaned back and studied the canvas. A moment later he decided to draw a second bird. And a naked woman. And a sea horse with wings rising over the church. And two dolphins in the water. And... No one saw him doing it.

Finally the paella was ready. Everyone took their seats at the long table, except David who was still busy in the dark corner "improving" Freddy's painting, and Robert who was still asleep on the couch. Marita sat putting a bandage on his wound. As she finished doing it, Robert's eyes opened and he looked up at her.

"Darling?"

"What?"

"Thank you."

Everyone else was eating now. Fingers glistening wet in the candlelight, they peeled shells from the big shrimp, and sucked on the mussels and clams while more wine was poured. Jose Manuel had a bottle of tequila he was sharing with anyone who wanted some.

Wiggles kept going on about the burning chairs.

"You know what that was like? I'll tell you what that was like. That was like the story of Moses. Imagine if instead of a burning *bush* it had been a burning *chair*."

No one was listening to him, but that didn't stop him.

"My father was a deacon in the church, you see. I grew up hearing all about the burning bush. I think maybe that's why I started drinking. I was *terrified* of all those stories. Satan, falling angels, burning bushes... But now if it had been a burning *chair*, I think I might have liked that. Might have gone into the church myself if it had been a burning *chair*."

While he was going on about the chair, on the other side of the table Jose Manuel was telling a story about how the famous Mexican bandito Chucho el Roto "was afraid of mice. They kept arresting him and putting him in jail. But the jails were full of mice, and every time he saw one he would escape. You know how they finally caught him?"

"How?"

"He was hiding behind some rocks. One of the policemen, he shouted 'Mouse!' The poor guy came running out, and they shot him."

"No."

"Fucking mice. I don't like them either."

Someone told the guy in the dress that it was a beautiful dress. He hadn't said a word all night. Finally he spoke:

"It was my mother's."

Suddenly someone shrieked, "*Jose Manuel!*"

"*What?*"

"*MOUSE!*"

Jose Manuel screamed and jumped up onto his chair.

It was like that. Everyone was having such a good time.

When he was finally done, on the back of Freddy's canvas David wrote, "To my friend Freddy, on a summer night in 1999 here in our white Cadaqués. It's only a poem!" Then he signed it, as if what he had just done would please Freddy.

More wine and tequila flowed, together with the mad talk they inspire. Sitting at the head of the table, Freddy was watching all this. His work over, it was time now to play. When they were through eating, Cal rolled some joints and those were passed around. Candles flickering, the music began again. Freddy took the guitar and stood. Austria was defeated. It was Spain's turn now. The old street performer looked at his audience.

"In the hills, the goatherd can be lonely," he said, the Austrian accent holding court. "And the goats, they know it. One of these goats sees the boy coming toward him, and so the goat sings..."

Freddy began to sing the old classic *Besame Mucho*. But when he sang the word besame, which means "kiss me," he brayed like a goat, stretching it out.

"Behhhhh-same, behhhh-same mucho..."

Howls of laughter.

"...como si fuera ésta noche la ultima vez..."

Kiss me goatherd, like it will be our last time.

Whenever he got back around to "Behhhh-same," everyone else now sang it with him. A big chorus of "Behhhh-same."

And then it really began. The guitar handed back to Antonio and again the flamenco. As promised, Marita got back up onto the table to dance. Robert was asleep again on the couch, not moving.

A few people left early, at around two. One of them, Sonia, had to be at work at the bakery only a few hours later. She left a glass of wine half full on the table. Cal saw it and finished it.

"Waste not, want not," he grinned.

Cassandra laughed. "Absolutely."

Cal and Wiggles, good friends again, were in the thick of a conversation. They got back to it.

"I'll tell you what it is," said Cal. "It is what it might have been if it hadn't been for the phylloxera."

"A pox on the phylloxera," said Wiggles. "A fucking pox on it."

"And the Doors? Morrison?"

"What about them?"

"I don't know. You tell me. What about them?"

"Well how the fuck should I know?"

They talked and everyone danced and drank until the sun was up. Antonio, going for some cheese, slipped and accidentally cut off the tip of one of his fingers. It meant he would have to relearn the *rasqueado*. They put the fingertip in the freezer because some people thought that at the little clinic in the village they could probably sew it back on.

Later, the sun climbing higher in the sky already, some fell asleep in the nooks and crannies the big house had to offer. Others, including Antonio, made their way down to the village. And still others, starting down the path, in the end decided to just lie down in the warm air and fall asleep on the stones.

Chapter XIII

Later that morning, there seemed little life around the house, other than the frogs sunning themselves next to the pool, and the gecko on the wall in the bathroom, and the line of big black ants marching across the terrace from the paella pan over to a hole in the ground some twenty meters away. There were some lizards on the warm rocks with their heads bobbing up and down, and flies buzzing around trying to avoid the lizards. A tortoise starting out from one place was taking forever to get to another, while high above it all a Bonelli's eagle was circling, its sharp hungry eyes taking it all in.

Cork oaks, olive trees, Goat's Thorn, Saxifrage, Tree Spurge, European Shag, Dusky Perch, Mastic trees, heather, junipers, rock roses, and low scattered bunches of the dry yellow flowers called *inmortales* gave shelter to birds and insects, spiders, snakes, scorpions, mice, all sharing a common aim... survival.

Normally a mouse will sleep in the day. But when his mate is pregnant, the male mouse will take some unusual risks. In the scrub below the house, some bits and pieces of food had been tossed the night before. Mussel and prawn shells, bits of rice and chicken that had burnt at the bottom of the pan. A gray mouse smelled and eyed those nervously, judged its odds, then made its move. Out from a stack of wood, fast...but not fast enough. An asp viper, coiled under a rock close by, felt the air move and lashed out. In an instant the snake had its mouse. But it, too, had taken its own chance. Other eyes had seen that mouse, and it was easy enough for the eagle, already swooping down, to grab the snake instead. As it flew off, the snake writhing in the hot air, trying desperately to bend its head back to bite its attacker, the dead mouse fell onto the rocks below. Soon it would bring still others into the open, taking their own risks to get at it.

Nature is only beautiful to those who make it to the next day.

It was well after noon by the time Cal and Cassandra finally made their way to the kitchen. As they passed by one bedroom with its door open they could hear heavy snoring. Cal could see someone's feet sticking out of the bottom of a bed. An hour later he would see that those same feet had not moved.

No one else around yet as they made coffee. Then Cal suggested they go for a swim in the pool.

"The cool water would feel good."

"Sure."

Naked in the strong sun, Cal fished the two burnt chairs out of the water where they were floating. The blanket was at the bottom with the metal table. He dove in, swam down and brought them to the surface. The blanket was heavy with the water and he lugged it onto one side of the pool.

After they swam, both lay on the stone terrace, their wet bodies shining in the sun. When one side was dry they rolled over to give the other its turn. Cassandra's skin was tanned dark already because she had spent all of her days since getting to Cadaqués lying on the beach. After making her calls, she'd stretch out by the water with a book like the one she had with her earlier that day. Books about castles and banking, and handsome bankers and young girls.

Once both were dry they dressed and went back into the house. Freddy was up now, a rag and some solvent in his hand, trying to wipe as much of David's black marker off his painting as he could.

"I found it like this this morning. I don't know what he was thinking. Look at this bullshit!"

Freddy asked Cal if he would help him carry some things down to the garden. Cassandra said she would walk down to the village. She and Cal agreed to meet later at the Imperial. About an hour later, Cal also headed down the path to the village.

Chapter XIV

One could follow the dirt road down, or one could take one of the old footpaths. They were steeper, straighter, faster. They had been there over a thousand years, the original way of getting from Cadaqués across the mountain to Roses. There were painted signal markings on some of the rocks beside those paths. Small white, green, yellow or red stripes. Instructions for the traveler. *Keep going, you are heading the right way, don't give up, it's never too late.* Or something like that. Sometimes not knowing a thing for sure was nice because you could just read into it whatever you wanted. More than one philosophy had been built on those grounds.

At one point the path dipped down, and then you walked along the dirt road a bit before you took the next path through the scrub, again making a beeline for the village. On the right side of the road was a big rock. Rust gray slate, like everywhere in these parts. There was a cave inside that rock. Wind, rain and time had worn the rock down so that half the roof had broken away. But there was enough cave there still that one night the summer before, when Cal and some French girl had been walking up to Freddy's and it started to rain, they had taken refuge in that cave. And as long as they were in there waiting for the rain to stop, they had made love on the warm slanted rock floor. Cal stood looking at it now trying to remember her name. It was…it was...no use, he couldn't remember. He kept walking.

Where the footpath left the road again he scrambled down. There was another rock on the side of the path, again with those painted markings. Both the path and the old markings reminded Cal of a little book he had written some fifteen years earlier, when he was living in Andalusia in another fishing village called La Herradura near Granada. His book, that he called And Firelight, was the story of a family that lived on a small farm overlooking the sea. They had been there forever. No electricity, goats and chickens, olives and almonds, everything simple. One day a rich real estate developer offers to buy their land and their life becomes more complicated. These markings on the footpath now, whatever else they meant, pointed toward a life like theirs. To a time when goatherds would take their flocks into the hills above Cadaqués and sleep in one of the stone huts that still spotted the mountain. When horses and mules would make the trek over the hill to Roses hauling olive oil, salted fish and wine. These markings meant all of that and something more.

The bottom of the path came out near two hotels, the Rocamar and below it the Llane Petit. They were not big hotels. Human scale. Nothing like the towering eyesores one found elsewhere along the Spanish coast, in destroyed places like Torremolinos, Benidorm and Alicante. On the left was a long stonewall with a painted blue door open to a little alternative restaurant called Tao. They served Indian vegetable curries and herbal teas, and Cal could smell incense and hear drumming coming from inside. Some tourists staying in the hotels walked by. The kids carried snorkels and masks. The grownups carried straw baskets stuffed with towels and lotions. Everyone wore flip-flops and t-shirts.

The road leveled out, and there was a small rocky beach to the right. There were little fishing boats pulled up onto the stones, and some people swimming in the sea. And there once again was

David, bent over, picking up one of the larger rocks. Cal was afraid he was going to throw it at the people swimming. It really was a very big rock.

"David!"

David looked up and smiled.

"Cal! Good morning! How arrrre you?"

"You're not going to throw *that* at them, are you?"

"*This*? Oh, no Cal, this one I am going to paint."

David walked toward him, pulling open the straw bag that was slung over his shoulder so Cal could see another dozen or so rocks like the one in his hand.

"Do you know what these are, Cal? These are not rocks. They are canvases, because I will paint them. And each rock tells me *what* to paint. Like Michelangelo, yes? The marble from Carrara, he did not make them into figures, he said, because the figures they were already there inside them. He only released them. Can you imagine, Cal? The David was already inside, trapped. And Michelangelo, he released him."

David lit a cigarette.

"Cal, how exciting last night, yes? You and Wiggles."

"I don't know. You heard about the night before with Cassandra's brother?"

"Yes, of course I heard."

"That's two fights in two nights. That's not normal, is it?"

"And tell me, who will you fight tonight?"

"I think it's enough fighting for now."

"Make love not war, yes?"

"Maybe it's better."

They walked together toward the village. As he spoke, David waved his cigarette in the air like a conductor's baton.

"I had the strangest dream this morning, Cal. When I was

coming down from Freddy's. Do you know the cave in the rock by the road?"

"I know it, yes."

"I thought, I will lie here a moment to rest. But then I fell asleep. And in my sleep, there came to me a *mantis religiosa*. You call it I think 'praying mantis,' like in Dali's painting 'Cannibalism of the Praying Mantis of Lautreamont.'"

"A wonderful painting."

"So this mantis, she and I we were praying together. On our knees together, with our hands folded. And there were bats on the roof of the cave. And one of them, he was very close to me. And he had the face of death. With his red eyes he was staring at me. I could feel his hot breath on my neck, and I could smell him. Oh Cal, such a smell!"

"And the mantis?"

"With her big eyes she was staring back at death. And then there was a scream. I think it was my scream. And because the mantis could fly, I was riding her. Like Pegasus! We were flying up the mountain, and all the bats they were chasing us."

David stopped.

"But then suddenly she turned, and because I was on top of her maybe she thought I was her lover. It can be very dangerous to be the lover of the *mantis religiosa*. Do you know why?"

"Because they bite their heads off?"

"*Yes*! This is the reason! Because then the man, he makes very fast with the penis even though he has no head. Like all men, yes? When the penis is working the head is not."

"That's an old joke."

"No Cal, it is no joke, because it is true. Without his head, still he makes the woman pregnant. And so I said to her, 'Please, I am sorry, it is a mistake. I am only riding you, I am not fucking you.' But I was lucky. Because to save me then there came an army of the phylloxera, a million of them, marching in a line from Freddy's house down to the village. Oh Cal, you should have seen it. I jumped from the mantis onto an olive tree, then I rolled onto the dirt and the phylloxera, they found me. They lifted me up, and do you know what happened? I woke, and I was on their shoulders...*because it was no dream*! It is true, Cal! I swear to you, *that* is how I came down the mountain. The phylloxera carried me down. And I asked them please to leave me where you found me so I could collect the rocks. Incredible, yes?"

"Incredible. Yes."

Cal looked at his friend. David was serious. He was telling a true story.

The road kept following the beach. To their left was the white house that had once belonged to Dali's parents. The artist had spent his boyhood summers here. Wide-eyed, scrambling over the rocks, in this spot the little Dali grew. His likes, his fears, taking shape here. All children fantasize. A stick isn't just a stick, it's a sword. A table isn't just a table, it's a fort. Dali's fantasies didn't end there, they were only beginning. Later, while others saw a rock or an egg, an ant or a clock, he saw in those the seeds of wilder things. And like David he shared some of his visions while most remained behind, lurking in hidden places the world could never see.

They walked by a big rock outcropping that stuck into the road, then past some hand-painted tiles set into a wall showing locals dancing the sardana. Ancestors of those who did the dance these days. Then past the Bar Café de la Habana. Its faded whitewash made it look like Havana. An old guitarist who once played for Dali sang there every night. In the evenings when walking by it one could stand outside in the warm air and listen to him. Or one could go in and sit and have a mojito or two or three or four. Or five. Cal thought about that as the road came out again above the water.

There were more people now, tourists again. As they walked through them, Cal and David were talking artist talk, about women and love and beauty and truth, and about how words like 'dotcom' and 'email' were entering the language just as words like 'chivalry' and 'honor' seemed to be leaving it. Suddenly David stopped, took one of the rocks from his bag and plopped it into the sea.

"Do you know what just happened, Cal?"

"What happened?"

"All the seven seas just rose. Not by much, it is true, but by a little. It's like our lives, yes Cal? Maybe we do not make such a big difference, but for sure we make some difference. And that rock that I will never paint?"

"Yes?"

"My sacrifice to the gods. Because always there must be some sacrifice."

Chapter XV

Ahead of them loomed the church of Santa Maria, and those three arches made famous from Dali's painting. On the left was a little bookshop with its door open.

"Do you know this shop, Cal?"

"I don't. It's the first time I see it open."

"The owner, Joan Tharrats, he is in Barcelona usually. I will introduce you. He does not only sell books. He also publishes them. Maybe he will publish your book, Cal."

David had read Cal's manuscript the summer before and knew that still it had never been published.

Inside, the shop was like a rocky cave, painted white and lined with books. Cool, with the only light coming through the open door. There were no customers. Joan Tharrats stood alone at the back. A tall, gentle looking man with thick dark-rimmed glasses, shoulders slouched, he stood with a lit cigarette in one hand holding a book he was reading in the other.

"Hola, Joan."

Tharrats looked up. A big warm smile when he saw David.

"Hola, David!"

Those two spoke in Catalan. While they talked, Cal looked at the shelves. In Catalan or Spanish, Thoreau, Joseph Conrad, Peggy Guggenheim, Cocteau, Nijinsky, Benvenuto Cellini, Ana Maria Dali, Lewis Carroll and many others. All published by Tharrats. After a few moments David switched to Spanish so that

Cal could join in.

"Joan, te presento a mi buen amigo Americano, Cal Zander."

"Hola, Cal."

"Hola, Joan."

They shook hands.

"Tell him about your book, Cal. I said only a few words about it."

Cal began by apologizing for speaking no Catalan. Tharrats apologized for speaking no English. Then in his poor Spanish Cal told the story about the little family on the farm and the rich man that wanted to buy their world and change it.

"And David says you would like to publish it?"

"Very much. Especially here. It would be an honor to see it published in the company of books like these."

"I cannot read in English. But my daughter, she knows English. If you give me your manuscript I will ask her to read it. If she thinks it fits with these other books we publish, then we can talk about it."

The manuscript was in Cal's pack back at the house.

"I can bring it to you in about...six minutes."

Tharrats smiled.

As they left the bookshop, Cal wanted to shout and jump and hug David. Heading back to the house to grab the manuscript, he tried to get David to walk faster.

Chapter XVI

It was closer to twenty minutes before Tharrats was already holding Cal's manuscript in his hands.

"I will give this to my daughter tonight. How long are you staying in Cadaqués, Cal?"

"A few more weeks."

"You like it here?"

"I love it."

Tharrats looked pleased. They shook hands. Leaving the bookshop, Cal was so ready to celebrate. As he walked toward the Imperial there was no sign yet of Cassandra. But sitting alone at a table was the beauty. Cal glanced up toward the balconies of Cassandra's house. No one there.

He sat at a table next to hers. She was drinking a *Cacaolat,* which is chocolate milk. And she was reading a book. Cal tried to see what the book was, but it was bent back with the cover out of sight. The waitress came to him and he ordered. As he waited for his gin and tonic, he looked over at the girl whose name he already knew.

You can begin a conversation any way.

"Your parents called you Layla, or you chose it?"

She looked up from her book, surprised.

"How do you know my name?"

"I asked someone."

"And why would you do that?"

"So I would know your name."

"Well, I guess that's a good reason."

"Can I ask what you're reading?"

She bent back the cover to show him.

"*Middlemarch*. By George Eliot." A pause. Then, "My parents."

"What?"

"My parents named me Layla."

"After Clapton's song?"

"That's what everyone thinks, but no. It's from an old Persian love story, *Layla and Majnun*. My mum's favorite. But it's the same source from which Clapton got the name."

"And just guessing, Layla is the beautiful girl in the story?"

She did not blush. Just nodded.

The waitress brought Cal's drink.

"And your name is...?"

"Cal. Short for California."

"Because, let me guess, you're from California?"

He nodded.

"Do you get into a lot of fights in California?"

"Now why would you ask that?"

"Because I was there the other night, at L'Hostal. I saw everything."

"I didn't see you there."

"Well, you were pretty busy from the looks of it. With your friend, then with that guy. I saw what happened. It was definitely his fault."

"And were you there with your friend?"

"Paul? No, he wasn't there. He doesn't go out that late."

Two local men sat down at a table near them with a chessboard and began to arrange their pieces. At another table there was a heavy middle-aged woman sitting with a heavy middle-aged man. The man was looking at a map. The woman was watching him look at the map. There was a camera on their table. Now the woman looked over at Cal.

"Excuse me. I think I heard you say you're from California?"

"That's right."

"So then maybe you can you help us. We're trying to find something."

"I'll try. What is it you're looking for?"

"Honey, ask him."

The man looked up from his map.

"Well, I'm trying to see where Salvador Dali lived. But it's not marked here. Do you know where he lived?"

Cal pointed over his shoulder. "Over the hill behind those buildings. In a little place called Port Lligat."

"So then, we would have to walk over a hill?"

"We're not going to have time for that," the woman said. "What time is it now?"

The man looked at his watch.

"It's five o'clock."

"And the bus leaves at six-thirty. So honey, we're just not going to have time for that."

"I guess you're right."

"We're from Ohio," the woman told Cal. "From Toledo."

"How wonderful."

"Do you know it?"

"I'm afraid I don't."

"Well anyway, we're on a cruise ship. The ship stopped in Barcelona so we would have two days there, but we didn't like it, did we?"

Her husband shook his head. "No, we didn't like it."

"It's a very dirty city, isn't it?" she asked Cal.

Cal liked Barcelona. Loved it even.

"Well, I..."

"It is, trust me. It's a *very* dirty city. We saw the Gaudi things of course, that park and the rest of it. But then my husband suggested we come here."

"Because we heard that Salvador Dali lived here. But we couldn't find his house on this map."

"Honey, what time is it?"

The man looked at his watch.

"Almost five after."

"We're going to have to go soon."

Her husband was looking at the map again.

"It's just not marked on this damn thing. What was the name you said? Port..?"

"Lligat."

"Oh yes! Here it is. Just over that hill."

"That's right."

Cal smiled at Layla. She smiled back.

"Where does your ship go next?" Cal asked them.

"Majorca. And the other little one, what's that called?"

"Ibiza," said her husband.

"That's right, Ibiza. That's supposed to be just beautiful."

"Yes, I think you'll like that. It's very clean."

"We take a cruise every year. Last year we went to Dubrovnik."

"Did you like that?"

"Oh, yes. My word, what a beautiful place! Especially that, what was it called, Blue Mosque. That was so beautiful."

"That was Istanbul," her husband corrected her.

"Was it? Oh yes, you're right, that was Istanbul. Well anyway, that Blue Mosque was beautiful. We went to Venice and to Dubrovnik, and then we went to Istanbul. And all of those places were just so beautiful. What time is it, honey?"

The man looked at his watch.

"It's five after."

"I think you'd better ask for the bill."

The man looked toward the bar inside and waved. The waitress came to him. He paid the bill, and they stood to go.

"Well, we're off to Barcelona now I guess. It was so nice talking to you."

"You'll have a wonderful time in Ibiza," said Cal. "And I read this morning in the Spanish papers that the doctors say it's all under control now."

"What's under control?"

"That virus."

"What virus?"

"That nasty stomach virus that's been going around the islands there. I guess a couple of people died from it, and so many others got sick. But that was a few days ago. Apparently it's clearing up now, so you should be fine."

"We didn't hear about that."

"No?"

"No."

"I guess it's not really the kind of thing cruise companies like to talk about."

"Well thank you so much for telling us about that."

"Sure. My pleasure. Enjoy your visit to Ibiza."

As they walked away the wife was saying something to the husband. The moment they were out of earshot, Layla exploded in laughter.

"You're so cruel!"

"You think so?"

"Why did you tell them that?"

"I don't know."

"Is there really a stomach virus there?"

"Not that I know of."

Cal finished his drink. The waitress was passing by so he ordered another.

"Can I get you something?" he asked Layla.

"I'm fine, thanks." She nodded toward the bottle on the table in front of her. It was still half-full.

"What is that, a chocolate milk?"

She nodded.

"Isn't that for babies?"

"I guess I'm a baby, then."

You don't look like a baby, thought Cal.

She was wearing shorts, pearl earrings in the little ears, and a pearl pendant that hung above the valley of the gods. The breasts, tight as drums, were held back by a thin white cotton blouse. The buttons were just holding on.

"Good book?" he asked.

"It is, yes. But it's *so* sad."

"Really?"

"I read it once before. I just wish I could jump into it and change the ending, because I know what happens. She basically wastes her life. Did you ever read a story or watch a film and you knew the ending, and you wished that you could change it?"

"Sure. It's called *The Story of my Life*. Because I know the ending. Not the one I'd choose."

"Why, because you'd like to just go on?"

"Sitting here now, easy to see why."

The waitress brought Cal his drink.

"I never read her, Eliot."

He said that just so she would know that he knew George Eliot was a woman.

"Oh, she's wonderful."

"Do you read a lot?"

Immediately, he wished he hadn't asked that. Sounded like an interview.

"Loads. I did my A levels in English lit. As it happens I love nineteenth century. Adore it."

The interview continued nevertheless.

"Do you do any writing yourself?"

"Not really. Well, a little poetry sometimes. And you?"

"I'm a writer."

"Really!"

He told her about his book, and how there was "a very good chance" it was about to be published here in Cadaqués and in Barcelona.

"I also write poetry," he added.

"Well then come on, let's hear something."

He hesitated.

"Well?"

"Okay. I just wrote one a few days ago."

He had started it on the train between Amsterdam and Paris, and finished it on the way to Barcelona. He cleared his throat.

"In the widdle wat of time bedone
Redemptive bays and days and morrow woes
A sally mocks a minute of such one
As skyward fortals aim and toddles grow
And not to back again, but forward stretch
We one who think and touch and touch and all
What take the little piddles told to fetch

And setting over fire with no small
Desire done and done again to see
Mad things awaited long and fought to try
Withal not purpose made but all to be
Of circle to the low dunthortals high
    That when bemade all is and was and more
    Hail joyfire beckons sweet through open door"

It took her a moment.

"It reminds me of Lewis Carroll's Jabberwocky. Full of neologisms. Still, you've got your classic sonnet there. I love sonnets. At first glance that one doesn't seem to mean much, does it. But then somehow, yes, the Widdle Wat of time. I've been there, I think."

"Now let's hear one of yours."

"Oh, well, the thing is you see I'm not really a writer."

"Come on. Something. I showed you mine, now you show me yours." He smiled. She looked at him.

"Not sure I can remember."

He waited.

"Okay then, here's one. It's just a silly little thing for my sister's children:

A wish upon the sea full sail
A child on the sand
A wind to blow a dream or three
Into a waiting hand
For if like stars dreams do appear
Upon that blue black sea
One little wish I'd ask of you
Please blow one dream to me

I know it's silly. I just scratched that out for them one night last summer when I was tucking them into bed."

"In Manchester?"

"You *have* been asking questions, haven't you."

"Cadaqués is a tiny village. Everyone knows everything."

"Apparently."

"They must have loved that."

"Well the thing was, you see, for them to blow a dream toward me they had to go to sleep to have the dreams. That was our deal."

"And? It worked? I don't mean did they go to sleep. I mean, did you get your dream?"

"Well, I suppose that..."

She saw something in the distance over his shoulder.

"Here's your friend coming now."

Cal turned and looked. Cassandra was walking toward them from the direction of the beach. There was a towel sticking out of the straw basket hanging from her shoulder. When she spotted Cal she broke into a wide grin. As she came closer and saw Layla the smile didn't change at all.

"Hi there."

"Hi."

He introduced them. She sat.

"Listen, I have a great idea."

"What's that?"

"Tomorrow's Friday..."

Layla went back to reading her book.

"On Saturday morning there's a really nice little market in Ceret, just across the border in France. The farmers bring their cheese, fruit, things like that. I thought of going tomorrow, spending the night, then going to that market early. I think you'd really like it. Want to go?"

"Sure."

"Great."

Cassandra lit one of her skinny cigarettes.

"I think you're really going to like it."

Chapter XVII

Cal wanted to drive the way of the small coastal roads, through Cap de Creus natural park to the little fishing village of La Port de la Selva. They could stop there to see the old Benedictine monastery Sant Pere de Rodes, and the ruins of the castle Sant de Verderra that stood on the high cliff above the monastery. Then they could drive past scenic coves and wind-bent trees to Portbou, the last village in Spain. It was where the writer / philosopher / mystic Walter Benjamin, facing imminent arrest by the Nazis, had committed suicide in 1940. They could visit his memorial there. They could cross then into France at Corbere, with its ruined fort the Tour Carroig, and drive through vineyards up to Banyuls. A few miles beyond that and they would reach the village of Collioure. Like Cadaqués, so many artists had spent time there. Matisse and Derain, those "wild beasts." Picasso again. Braque. Collioure was also a perfect place to have lunch. Cold oysters and white wine in some nice little spot next to the water. And finally then they could swing back over to Ceret, only forty miles inland. But Cassandra wanted to take the main highway. She said it would be faster, and she was right. It was her car, so they took the highway. Up, then left. They were in Ceret in about an hour.

They checked into the little Hotel Vidal on the Place Soutine. The date "1736" was carved in stone above the entrance. The balcony of their room overlooked a narrow street lined with towering plane trees. There were people walking, others sitting at tables on the wide sidewalk. There was a big pink house with blue shutters directly across from them. Next to it was the Bar le Pablo, named for Picasso. He had lived here too. Cassandra suggested they go to it for a drink. That sounded good to Cal. There was just one thing he wanted to do first.

    She had set her make-up bag, hairbrush and toothbrush in the bathroom, had put her big book on the little desk, then taken a fresh blouse from her bag that was lying on the floor. She put the blouse on the bed and pulled the one she was already wearing up over her head. Cal didn't know why she felt she needed to change clothes after just a one-hour ride, but she did. He came to her from behind. She was not wearing a bra. He wrapped his arms around her, cupping her tiny breasts. He turned her around and picked her up. She weighed nothing. The long legs wrapped around him. They kissed. Then down onto the bed, and wild sex with the door open to the balcony and the sound of the people on the street below. As he made love to her Cal kept his eyes closed, and at the moment when it counted most he imagined it was Layla in his arms.

    He couldn't stop thinking about her. The whole drive up he had kept picturing her; that smile, the eyes, the rest of it. And now to top it off there was Middlemarch. Cal had never read it, but had heard it was a great book. So she read great books…with those Cadaqués blue eyes!

    Later, after they showered together and dressed, he and Cassandra went down. They crossed the street in the shade of the big trees and sat at one of the tables in front of the Bar le Pablo. There were warm spots of sunlight coming through the trees and people walking by. Cal drank a Campari and soda. There was a slice of orange in the glass. The sun shone on it and it looked beautiful. Cassandra had a glass of white wine. It didn't look too bad, either.

At the next bar over there was a guy playing a clarinet and another man with a tenor sax. Gershwin. *Summertime, Embraceable You, Rhapsody in blue...* And there was a big poster next to one of the trees announcing a sardana festival that would begin that night.

"That should be fun."

She grinned. She never stopped grinning, really.

They finished their drinks and were hungry now. Cassandra knew of a restaurant she liked, so Cal followed her through little alleyways behind their hotel to a square called the Place des Neufs Jets. There was an old stone fountain in the corner with children playing around it. There were a few restaurants around the square that was filled with people sitting at tables. Many tourists were in the town for the sardana festival, or the market the next day, or just because it was summer. Holding Cal's hand, Cassandra led him over to a restaurant on the far edge of the square. There was one empty table and they grabbed it. Cal looked around. Inside the open door to the restaurant he could see a stuffed bull's head on a stone wall, and dark wooden rafters on the old ceiling. The waiter came to them with the menus. Cassandra spoke to him in perfect French. He made his recommendations and left.

In the end they did not take his recommendations. Cal was not crazy about rabbit, and neither of them was in the mood for fish. Instead they ate raw oysters, shared a beefsteak tartar, then Cal had lamb while Cassandra had the duck. With a bottle of red wine from Banyuls it was very good. Cassandra looked like she was having a great time. Cal was also enjoying it, only he couldn't stop wishing she was Layla.

"Life as it should be!"

"Definitely!"

She kept giggling, blushing, looking at him, grinning. He wondered if her mouth ever got tired from all that grinning. It was obvious she was still thinking about what had happened back in the hotel.

After the meal neither wanted a desert, just two double espressos. Cal also had a brandy. Cassandra had something called a *Kir d'ici* and smoked one of her skinny cigarettes. She didn't say much. He kept trying to start a conversation.

"What a beautiful place, yes?"

"Yes."

"I keep thinking about all the artists and writers who have been here drinking, talking, thinking in this same light under these same trees, same seasons. Incredible!"

"Yes."

A moment later he tried again.

"Let's imagine how different writers and artists would describe this scene."

"Why?"

"Just because."

"Alright."

"Me first, or you first?"

"You first."

He looked around.

"Okay. Hemingway: 'There was light through the trees, and the sound of water from the fountain. People were drinking and laughing, except the waiter who was balancing drinks on his tray as he moved between the tight tables. There were as many tables as they could fit in the place, so the owners of the restaurants would make their money. In one restaurant, Le pied dans le plat, there was a bull's head mounted on the stone wall. Electric lights shone on the glass eyes that had no fight in them. It was not a bull anymore, but only what was left of a bull. Like what is left of love after two people have separated."

She giggled.

"Okay."

"Now your turn."

"No. I don't want to. You try again."

"Who?"

"What do you mean?"

"Pick a writer. Any writer. If I know them, I'll describe the place like they would."

"I don't know. You choose."

"Okay." He thought for a moment. "Dali: 'My tears, fossilized into spheres that another might call eyes, see now, as the mirror sees, all that is reflected in them. Lean forward, Cassandra. Peer close, and see how the high intelligent brow of your head is reflected, how your lips are reflected, how your grin is reflected in the eyes of Dali. See how those lips purse as you wrap them now around the skinny phallus of your cigarette, its smoke rising like the divine dream above the plane trees of Ceret, above the hairless mountains, to the translucent sea and all the womblike villages beyond. Cassandra, second most beautiful woman in the world, the temple snakes are licking your ears clean still. In all your Liechtensteinian glory, dare to peer beyond the future into the fossilized tears of Dali!'"

"You're crazy."

"Go on, now you try."

"Try what?"

"To describe this place or this moment like some famous writer would describe it. Go on."

"No."

"Come on."

"*No.*"

She was blushing again. She looked nervous. The waiter was going past them. Cal flagged him and ordered another brandy. Cassandra was still sipping her drink.

"Who's your favorite writer?"

"I don't know."

"Just name a few."

"I don't know."

"Jane Austin?"

"Yes. I like her. We had to read *Pride and Prejudice* in school. I liked it."

"So then, go on. How would she describe this place?"

"I don't know."

"Okay, well then I'll try."

"Go ahead."

Cal affected a posh English accent.

"Jane Austen: 'I do rather think that taken all together, it would appear without much question that these trees, as mighty as God could muster in a day, had he a week could not have made them any grander. And therefore, stand they as nothing less than monuments to blah blah blah...'"

She laughed.

"...Nor could nature have esteemed a place more, bestowing upon this sweet Ceret and its seasons such everlasting blah blah blah..."

She was hysterical with laughter.

The waiter brought Cal's brandy.

"Okay now, come on, fair is fair. Your turn."

"I can't."

"Sure you can. Who wrote that book you're reading now?"

"What book?"

"The one you're reading."
"I don't know."
"A man? Woman?"
"A man."
"German? French...?"
"No, he's American."
"What's his name?
"I don't know. I don't remember. I can look when we're back at the hotel."

Cal caught the waiter's eye and in the air made a signing gesture with his right hand. The international symbol for *Check please*.

"Shakespeare," blurted out Cassandra.
"What?"
"Go on. How would Shakespeare describe this place?"
Cal thought.
"When, in the mottled light love shone brighter still, and summer air arose to..." He burst out laughing, "I don't know. Something something."
"No, go on."
"I can't."
"Why not?"
"It's a love poem. I can't think of one now."
"Really?"

The waiter brought the check. Cal paid, finished his drink, and then they went for a walk. As they were leaving the square he sang.

"And you read your Emily Dickinson

And I my Robert Frost..."

Dangling Conversation. Cruel. Luckily she didn't get it.

Twisting through the little streets, then out from under the trees into the strong sun, they made their way to the edge of the town.

He wanted to see an old stone bridge he had spotted on a brochure at the hotel, the fourteenth century Pont du Diable. Bridge of the Devil. They walked out onto the center of it. Cal leaned over the side and looked down. There was not much water. In the winter and after a rain it would look very different. He pulled a joint out of his pocket and lit it. He took a hit, then offered it to her. She took a tiny puff and handed it back. He sucked it like a baby going for its mother's milk.

"You smoke a lot of those, don't you?" she asked.

"Do I?"

He had burned one on the drive up from Cadaqués, then another back at the hotel. Cal had estimated once that he had smoked about thirty thousand joints in his life. About three a day, starting at age twelve...as if life was a movie and these things were popcorn. Now he sang to her again, with a big smile.

"I smoke two joints in the morning,
Then I smoke two joints at night
I smoke two joints with my left hand
And then I smoke two joints with my right
I smoke two joints before I smoke two joints
And then I smoke two more..."

He tried to get her to dance. She didn't want to dance on the bridge. So he stopped dancing and stood there.

"Ever feel like you're not really tethered to one place? Like you've just hoisted anchor and there's no one moment or one thought that can hold you?"

"I don't know. Maybe. Why?"

"You know how sometimes the mind just floats like a balloon, and goes wherever the wind blows it?"

"What are you talking about?"

He finished the joint. He even ate the tiny bit that was left pinched between his stained fingers. The black resiny tar had a bitter, familiar taste. He liked it.

"I mean, imagine all the people who have passed across this bridge. All the horses and carts, cattle and other animals. The chickens. It's tempting to lump...dump...bump...jump..."

"What are you doing?"

"Sorry, I started thinking about writing a poem. Sorry. Anyway, it's tempting just to lump them all together into this big thing we call the past. But they were all so different, the centuries. Imagine the fifteenth century. I would not want to be heading into town to see the dentist.'

"No. Definitely not."

"Sixteenth century. Some printed books in those carts or saddlebags now, witches to be burned, knights, market day."

"You're really funny, you know that?"

"Seventeenth century. Torchlight at night, soldiers on foot or horseback, feathers in their helmets."

"Maybe we should start heading back. The music's going to start soon."

"Eighteenth century. Ruffles, hoop skirts, wigs...or were those just in the cities?"

"How should I know? I mean, I don't know."

"Nineteenth century. Napoleon's troops marching toward Spain. And last but not least, of course, the hard-to-believe-it's-so-soon-to-be-over twentieth century. Picasso would have walked across this bridge with Braque. Can you picture both of them right here?"

Cal stretched out his arms to make sure that he was occupying the same physical space as Picasso and Braque had occupied.

"Side by side, Picasso and Braque, plotting their aesthetic revolutions while crossing *this exact spot*. And now it's about to be a new millennium. Incredible, isn't it? Every second they all move further and further into the past. And they were *so modern* once! So contemporary! Even the guys on horseback."

"Come on, let's go back."

"And so what do we do now after they chopped everything up? Picasso and Braque, I mean. I guess we put things back together again, so then the old becomes the new...again. What do you think?"

She thought they should head back.

Walking toward their hotel they stopped twice. At a little *patisserie* so Cassandra could eat a strawberry tart she had spotted through the window. Cal had a glass of champagne while she ate it. Then they stopped again at a small bar for Cal to have a brandy.

"Are you sure?"

"I've never been more sure of anything in my life."

When they left the bar it was almost eight and they could hear music coming from the street ahead. The sardana festival had started. There were people everywhere, walking, laughing. They joined the crowd moving toward the Place Picasso where the music was playing. As they got close to it there was another little bar on the left. Cal wanted to have a brandy there, too.

"But you just had one."

"You said the operative word, 'One.'"

"Do you really need it?"

"I don't *need* it. I just *want* it."

She was a nice girl, but she could be so frustrating.

They went in. He drank his brandy. At his insistence Cassandra had a glass of wine. There were men standing at the bar and others sitting around on stools at high tables. The music from the street poured in. Cal loved the spirit of the place. Everyone was smoking Gitanes Brunes, that black tobacco the French love. The air was fat with the smoke of it. He ordered another brandy and drank it while Cassandra finished her wine. As they left the bar, Cal's body now was moving to the music.

Outside on the street people were laughing and dancing in great circles, with their arms around each other's shoulders. Like in Cadaqués the summer before. This was the French side of Catalonia, while Cadaqués was on the Spanish side. European history was a practical joker. Borders were the jokes.

There must have been at least a dozen groups dancing in circles. On the Place Picasso there were two cobla bands on raised stands under the plane trees. One band played while everyone danced. Then the other band played and everyone danced again. All the circles of people were moving. And children were running around. Some of the children were playing a game near the side of one building. There were two little girls and two boys. One boy stood at the wall with his back to the others. They ran toward him. Suddenly he would look over his shoulder and the others would have to freeze like little statues. Cal guessed that the object was to see who could get to the wall first during the moments when the boy wasn't looking. If you moved while he was looking you were probably out. It looked like a fun game.

There were some people getting up from a table on the sidewalk. Cal grabbed it. A waiter came and Cal ordered a brandy and soda. Cassandra wanted a mineral water. They sat there for a long time. Cal had a couple more drinks, and then they went back to their hotel.

The stone steps curved to the left. He held onto the railing as he climbed them. He was pulling himself as much as walking up the stairs. When they got to the top they had to cross the landing and go to another flight of stairs that led up to the floor where their room was. Heading from the first stairs to the next Cal could not manage a straight line. More like an "S" curve. Weaving his way across the red tile floor, he then made it up the second flight of stairs.

Inside their room, the doors to the little balcony were still open as they had left them. The music from the street was pouring in. Suddenly Cal felt a sharp cramp in his stomach. Something started to move. He made it to the bathroom just in time. He kicked the door closed behind him and dropped to his knees. His head hung low over the toilet, elbows resting on the rim, he vomited.

"Are you all right?" Cassandra asked through the door.

"Fine. I just need a minute."

Everything was moving in circles. She kept checking back, and each time he said through the door that he just needed another minute. He vomited until there was nothing left.

On the street below the bands were still playing, and the people were still dancing.

Chapter XVIII

Cal had only had two hangovers he could ever remember, a feeling that the stomach was rotten as if after death, and the rest of the body too, though not quite dead, was putrefying. A gangrene of the spirit. The head so heavy he could hardly lift it, and an overbearing weakness. Barely enough strength to retch, and even that futile because there was nothing to bring up anyway. Just dry heaves, a thick sweat, shaking, and wanting to die. He had felt all of that exactly twice, and typically today was not one of those times. Still, it was closer to it than he would have liked.

By some luck, good or bad, after a night like the one before he would usually wake up feeling only slow and heavy and uncertain. That lasted an hour or two at most. It would begin with a sound, something somewhere, then a slow movement. And finally, when it couldn't be avoided any longer, light. One eye cracking open as if scouting around to make sure it was safe for the second eye to open also. Then a slow testing of fingers, toes, mouth. A whole body inventory. With luck everything there still. Then trying to think, which is different than thinking. And testing the limits of that. To remember, to explain. Explaining was usually the hardest part. And understanding how such a good time could lead to such a bad time. Finally then legs over the bed, the rest hoisted upward, and for better or worse a new day ahead.

"How are you feeling?"

"Fine. Listen, I'm sorry about last night."

"Oh don't worry about it. I'm sorry for you."

"I don't know what happened."

"Well, you drank a lot."

"I didn't drink that much."

She counted on her fingers. It was the last list in the world Cal wanted to hear.

"A Campari soda, we had a bottle of wine at the restaurant and you drank most of it, then two brandies, a glass of champagne, two more brandies, three brandy sodas..." She was holding up ten fingers. One finger represented the bottle of wine.

He made a joke of it. "Well, at least I stopped before you had to start counting on your toes."

"Plus you smoked those three joints. In the car, here, and then that joint on the bridge."

"You have an excellent memory."

She smiled.

"What time is it?" he asked.

She looked at her watch.

"One thirty."

"We've missed breakfast?"

"Definitely."

"You've been awake long?"

"A few hours. I've been reading."

Never Again.

There was the sound of a crowd below in the street. Cal noticed it now for the first time. He walked to the balcony. Left and right as far as he could see there were many people moving slowly among dozens of stands. Each stand had a little canopy over it to protect what was being sold from the sun. Some of the canopies had the bright yellow and red stripes of the Catalan flag. And there were yellow and red banners stretched across the street.

Cal could make out fresh fruits and vegetables in baskets, and loaves of bread, and below their balcony great burlap sacks full of spices. There was some clothing on hangers under another canopy, and books and music CDs and other things.

"A lot of people."

"It's the market."

"Well, that explains it."

Sarcasm up and running, even if he wasn't.

"Should we go down? Have a coffee somewhere? And something to eat?"

"The coffee part sounds good."

He took a fast shower, hot, then cold. Then he dressed. They went down. They found a place. Cal drank coffee and a mineral water while Cassandra had a sandwich.

"Aren't you going to eat something?"

"I'm not really hungry yet."

"You should eat something."

"I will."

Later they walked through the crowds, moving past the place where the night before the bands had played and the people had been dancing. During the night while they had slept crews had taken away the stands. The sidewalks had been swept clean. And in the early hours, as the first light was appearing in the sky through the trees, others had come to set up their stalls for the market.

Now there was goat cheese and sheep cheese and cow cheese, and sausages made from wild boar and venison and duck meat. There was paella being dished out of a great pan about a thousand times the size of the one back at Freddy's. There were plastic buckets full of oysters and razor clams and escargots de mer, and Cal could hardly look at any of it. Home made jams and honeys, the fresh baked pies, soaps made of olive oil and lavender and rose, the roasted chickens, the music pumping out of the stand where the CDs were being sold, none of it appealed to him. Whatever there was, there was too much of it. Too much color, too much noise, too much smell. Still, other people seemed happy. Too happy.

There was a wild-haired man doing tricks at a stand with a sign that read *Magique*. He had huge eyebrows that looked like animals. There were old women sitting at little tables in the shade making fine lace so that people could see how it had been done for centuries. Cal did look at the lace, or at the magic tricks, or at anything else really. Even children holding their mothers' hands or riding on their fathers' shoulders just looked like more things.

They stopped for Cal to have another coffee. When the waiter came he decided to make it a *carajillo*. The waiter didn't know what that was.

"Café avec cognac."

"Oui, monsieur."

"Are you sure?" asked Cassandra.

He was sure.

Later as they drove back to Cadaqués the sun was shining and there were fields of sunflowers next to the road. And there was a big field of corn. A single sunflower seed, blown by the wind, had taken root among the corn and now there was a lone sunflower poking its head up among the cornstalks as if it was looking for the others, so close-by in the next field. Cal did not see it though, because he was sleeping.

Chapter XIX

The next day Cal did very little. Stayed home, tried to write, didn't drink much. A couple of beers, that was it. And one *carajillo* after walking alone in the afternoon just to get some air. He stayed away from the main part of the village. Too easy to see people and do things there. He didn't even want to see Layla. Not yet. Not until he was feeling himself again.

He read a bit. Problems concentrating though. A few pages each of J. M. Cohen's translation of *Don Quixote*, Kerouac's *On the Road*, and Richard Brautigan's *Trout Fishing in America*. Cal always traveled with a few books so he could transport to one world or another as needed. Never stuck in one place or time.

After sitting at the blue table he decided to keep reading on his bed. That didn't last long. He closed his eyes, and with the Brautigan spread out on his chest, which was not very good for the binding, he wound up sleeping for a couple more hours. When he woke up it was dark outside and the book had fallen onto the floor. He looked at his watch. Eleven-thirty. And now he wasn't tired. It was like a fake morning. He decided to go for another walk. A morning stroll at midnight.

As he was coming close to the Casino he could see Cassandra sitting inside. It looked like she was waiting for him. A stakeout. He stood looking at her through the window. Twice that day he had heard her knocking on his door and calling out his name.

Both times he had pretended not to be there. That was because of one thing she had said to him on their little getaway that really bothered him. And then he had said one thing back that bothered him even more. It was when they were having sex at the Hotel Vidal. She suddenly blurted out, "I love you." And then he said, "I love you too."

He turned and, keeping close to the water, walked back to Port Alguer. He sat on the beach next to one of the fishing boats. After a while he stood, stripped naked in the warm still air, and went for a swim. Probably no one saw him in the darkness. He swam out twenty or thirty meters, then stopped and while treading water looked back at the village. There were people walking and lights in the windows and he could hear laughter. He floated on his back for a while looking up at the stars. That was nice. Then he swam back to the beach, dressed, and walked home. And finally he went to sleep. Again.

Chapter XX

T he next morning everything was back to normal. Cal woke feeling fresh, strong, eager. He made coffee, wrote in his journal, then straight to the Casino.

If one was not working, and at the moment Cal was not… he was just spending down the money he had inherited when his father had died…there were few real decisions that needed to be made in Cadaqués. What to eat, drink, wear, who to sleep with, and that was about it. You did not even have to decide *where* to drink. Fate dictated. If people you wanted to see were at the Casino you stopped there. If they were not at the Casino, you kept on to the Imperial. There were other bars of course, like the Boia or Meliton, but for the most part Cal and his friends were creatures of habit. So if there was no one at either Casino or Imperial one faced the first real question of the day; where to wait for them?

On this morning, no such dilemma. Already sitting outside the Casino on the big window ledges in front were Marita, David, Jose Manuel, Wiggles, and of course Cassandra. Antonio was there too, with a big bandage over the right middle finger where he had cut it off. Everyone was smoking and drinking in the sunshine. Sometimes morning in Cadaqués looked a lot like night, only with brighter light.

Robin, a cheerful Englishman who had lived in Cadaqués for many years, had his guitar out. He was singing a bawdy old folk song. The others, glasses glued to their lips, were listening.

With his long sandy hair and shaggy beard, Robin looked and played like the English minstrels of yesteryear. Friends called him Robin Hood because he came from a village near Nottingham. He knew dozens, maybe hundreds of ballads. He sang:

"I met a young girl with her face as a rose
And her skin was as fair as the lily that grows
I says my fair maid, why ramble you so
Can you tell me where the bonny black hare do go?..."

"Tell us, Robin! Tell us where it is!" shouted Wiggles, waving his glass in the air.

"...The answer she gave me, O, the answer was no
But under my apron they say it do go
And if you'll not deceive me, I vow and declare
We'll both go together to hunt the bonny black hare..."

"He'll find it!" cried Wiggles. "Not to worry, he'll find it!" Robin smiled and kept singing:

"...I laid this girl down with her face to the sky
I took out me ramrod, me bullets likewise
Saying wrap your legs 'round me, dig in with your heels
For the closer we get, O, the better it feels!"

"Oh, that feels *so* good!" Wiggles, the one-man commentariat.
"Sigue, hombre! Sigue!" shouted Jose Manuel. "La persecucion del conejo! Fantastic!"
"Come on," shouted Wiggles, "give us another nice little

fuck tune from the old days."

There were others across the street or sitting on the other window ledges. Many of them were also listening to the music. One tourist was taking photos. As Robin began to sing the next song, Cassandra saw Cal approaching and broke into a big smile.

"Hey, there you are!" she said as he drew close. "I was wondering what had happened to you."

"Good morning."

"I looked for you yesterday. I knocked on your door a couple of times but there was no answer."

"I went for a long walk up in the hills," he lied.

"I missed you."

"I missed you, too."

If you lie often enough it gets easier. After a while, it can be telling the truth that gets hard.

She looked at him inquisitively, as if he was supposed to say something more.

"Do you want something?" he asked, pointing to the empty glass in her hand.

"No, I'm alright. Thanks."

Cal disappeared inside to get a drink. When he came out Robin was finishing his song to happy hoots and hollers. The crowd listening was growing bigger. There were more tourists. The little ferry from Roses had just arrived discorging them on the beach in front of the Casino. There were many taking photos or looking at maps.

"Come on, Robin" shouted Wiggles. "Let's have another one. Keep our toes tapping, and our blood moving."

"Alright then, this one's for you Wiggles."

Strumming his guitar, Robin sang:

"Where is me shirt, me noggin' noggin' shirt?
It's all gone for beer and tobacco
For the collar is all worn, and the sleeves they are all torn
And the tail is looking out for better weather
I'm sick in me head and I haven't been to bed
Since I first came ashore from me slumber
For I spent all me dough on the lassies don't you know
Far across the western ocean I must wander."

"Not much sex in that one," complained Wiggles. "No sex at all in that one."

Marita was laughing hard. Too hard. Everyone looked so happy.

There are two kinds of visitors to Cadaqués. Those who come and go, and those who come and stay. Among that second group there is an invisible line, and once you pass it you are neither fish nor fowl. Neither visitor nor local. A *vocal*, some call it. Most of the friends clustered around Robin now were *vocals*. Because spend even twenty years in a thousand year old village, and it's like being a pebble on the beach. Part of the thing, but not a big part. Not connected to it like the big rocks are, like the old families are. And even if you spoke Catalan, if your parents, their parents, and their parents in turn had not helped build the village, defending it against every this and that through the ages, there would always be a strict limit to your function in *the family*. Still, just wanting to be local was already something, and that something was respected. It set you apart from those who left almost as fast as they came, whose planned trajectory from the get-go was a U-turn.

Jose Manuel went inside and came back moments later with a bottle of tequila. He drank some, then began to pass it around.

Robin sipped a beer and smoked a cigarette while taking a break from his music to talk with friends. The same young man who Cal had seen on the bus the week before, with the dreads and the guitar, was drinking a beer close by. He took his guitar out of his case and started to play. Only short bursts, but you could tell from those that he was good.

Cassandra was looking at Cal, but he was not looking at her. Instead, he was looking up the road where beside the beach coming toward them now was Layla. She was alone, wearing a little yellow dress. Barefoot, carrying her white sandals in one hand just as she had when Cal had first seen her. Cal turned to Robin.

"Can I play one?" he asked.

"Of course you can."

Robin handed Cal the guitar.

"I didn't know you could play," said Cassandra, impressed.

Loudly enough so that Layla would hear, Cal announced, "This is one I wrote. It's about how important it is to have a good breakfast!"

Layla stopped walking and stood behind the others. Cal smiled at her over the crowd as he began to play and sing a basic blues tune.

"Breakfast in a bottle
Mama said three meals a day
And I'm such a good boy
I like to do as Mamas say
Oh but breakfast is over
And lunch is just one song away..."

"Yeah, baby!" shouted Wiggles. "Breakfast in a bottle!

That's the way to do it!"

"Hombre!" yelled Jose Manuel, waving his bottle of tequila in the air. "*Breakfast in a bottle!*"

Marita was laughing. It looked like she was still going from the night before. Robert and Richard had come along and were standing with the others. Robert had a bruise over his right eye where the rock had hit him, so even from a distance now it was easy to tell the twins apart. The young guy with the dreads started to play lead along with Cal's song. He really was good.

Cal's eyes stayed fixed on Layla as he kept singing.

"*...Now don't cross the street*
Before you look both ways
That's another little gem
That Mama used to say
Baby, that's way I'm leaving
'Cause I've been looking around
And there's a whole world out there
Besides just this little town..."

The guy playing lead stopped, bent down to grab a slide from his guitar case, then started in again. Most of the people were watching him now, his fingers flashing over the neck. Suddenly they were in Mississippi, on the porch next to the bayou, and instead of young and white this guy was old and black. He made Cal's little song sound much better.

"*...Oh but I'll be back*
'Cause like my Daddy used to say
It pays to go, but sometimes it pays even more to stay
I've just got to go do

*My little prodigal son thing
Yes and I'll bring you a t-shirt
So let's have no more talk about a ring..."*

Howls of laughter, bursts of applause. Robin was clapping along. Antonio wasn't clapping, but his head was moving to the music. Cal continued.

*"...Now my granddaddy
He was a wise old man
He used to take me to the woodshed
With a big stick in his hand
And he'd say "Now son,
This'll hurt me more than it will you"
And I ain't sayin' he was lyin'
But the next day, only one of us was black and blue..."*

"Black and blue! Ouch! We know about that one, don't we Cal?" shouted Wiggles.

*"...So the next time someone says to me
There's a wise old saying
I'll tell them yeah, and you just let it be
'Cause like my grandma used to say
I ain't fuckin' around
Only grandpa wasn't listening
Or I wouldn't be standin' here right now..."*

"Grandpa was a fucker, was he? A fucking grandpa! Come on, baby, give us that breakfast in a bottle!"
The chorus again as Cal wrapped it up.

"...Breakfast in a bottle
Mama said three meals a day
And I'm such a good boy
I like to do as Mamas say
Oh but breakfast is over
And lunch is just one verse away
Yes it's thirsty work
Getting out of bed each day
And like the Good Book tells us
Men and women ought to pray
So I'm praying right now
Praying to God for one last rhyme
And the good Lord must be listening
'Cause dear God, it looks like it's lunchtime!"

Cal handed the guitar back to Robin and flashed a thumb's up to the guy with dreads. He flashed a thumb's up back. Behind all of the others Layla stood smiling. Cassandra was also smiling.

"That was great!" she said.

The guy with dreads started to play something else, Spanish flames now licking out of his guitar. The crowd was his.

"Hey, listen..." said Cassandra.

Cal looked at her.

"What?"

"You haven't met my mother yet."

"You're right, I haven't."

"She'd really like to meet you. She wants to give a party and invite you. Do you have any plans for Friday night?"

He couldn't think of an excuse fast enough.

"Friday night? I don't think so."

"Great! Okay then, Friday night, nine o'clock at our house.

145

Do you like lobster?"

"Sure."

"Then we'll get some lobster. My mother and I have to drive to Barcelona tomorrow. We have some business there, and we'll do a big shopping. We'll be back Friday morning and get everything ready."

Layla was walking away toward the Passeig. Cal was watching her.

"What did you say?"

"I said we'll come back Friday morning."

"Great."

Chapter XXI

Cal and Cassandra had lunch at Casa Anita in the little alley past the wine shop. In an earlier age they used to feed the fishermen and other workers. Now the restaurant was attracting tourists. But the gambas were as good as ever, and the "wine was wet," as Cal liked to say. He really was feeling himself again.

It was an old restaurant that made you feel like you were in a cave. Day as night. No windows, low rounded roof with the stones painted white. Bottles of wine and olive oil everywhere. On the walls were old photos of Dali and Gala, some taken at the restaurant. Also, faded posters of two films that had been shot in Cadaqués. *Los Pianos Mecanicos*, 1965, with James Mason and Melina Mercouri, and *The Light at the Edge of the World*, 1971, with Kirk Douglas, Yul Brynner and Fernando Rey. There were photos of the stars, and fishermen's traps hanging on the walls. Two brothers ran the place with their wives and sisters and mother. One of the brothers had six fingers on one hand. Cal thought that maybe he should give the extra one to Antonio. Then they'd both come out at five apiece.

"These are the best gambas a la plancha anywhere," Cassandra said as she licked her fingers. She was right.

Cal didn't say much.

"Are you okay?"

"Yeah, I'm fine."

After lunch they wandered over to Imperial. The twins were

there, just the two of them at a back table on the outdoor terrace. Both smoking from their identical black cigarette holders, both with a glass of identical red wine on the table before them. Robert, marked by the bruise, but also there was something else Cal noticed for the first time. Though both brothers' eyes were the same hazel green, they did not look *at* the world the same. Richard seemed to be looking at the world, while Robert seemed to be looking over it.

"Hello, boys."

"Cal. Cassandra."

"All right with the world, gentlemen?"

"Never better. A great day of mystery, though."

"Oh?"

"Show him," said Richard.

Robert pulled a letter from his shirt pocket and handed it to Cal.

"Came today. No idea who it's from. Not signed. A great, great mystery that."

"Postmarked Madrid," offered Robert. "Have a look. Wonderful letter, hmm? Words of a poet."

The envelope was addressed to *Robert Breyer, Bar Imperial, Cadaqués, Girona*. It looked like a man's writing. No return address. Mailed two days before.

"Go on, read it if you like."

Cal pulled out the letter and unfolded it. It was on expensive stationary. He read it out loud. It was the most beautiful letter he had ever read.

"'Thou, Robert Breyer, belongest to that hopeless, sallow tribe which no wine of this world will ever warm; and for whom even Pale Sherry would be too rosy-strong; but with whom one sometimes loves to sit, and feel poor-devilish, too; and grow convivial upon tears; and say to them bluntly, with full eyes and empty glasses, and in not altogether unpleasant sadness: Give it up, Robert Breyer! For by how much more pains ye take to please the world, by so much the more shall ye forever go thankless! Would that I could clear out Hampton Court and the Tuileries for ye! But gulp down your tears and hie aloft to the royal-mast with your hearts; for your friends who have gone before are clearing out the seven-storied heavens, and making refugees of long pampered Gabriel, Michael, and Raphael, against your coming. Here ye strike but splintered hearts together. There, ye shall strike unsplinterable glasses!'"

"Incredible, Robert. And no idea who it's from?"

"None, darling. A mystery that, hmm?"

"That's not a normal writer. Robert? That's world-class literature."

"Good one, eh?"

The eyes, red, smiled. The heat of the day was inside him already.

"What a funny letter," said Cassandra.

"Do you have a friend in Madrid who's a poet?" asked Cal.

"Don't think so, no."

"That's serious literature. Well, all I can say is..."

"Here she is!" Robert blurted out.

"Who?"

"Behind you."

Cal looked over his shoulder. Layla was walking toward them. The yellow dress still. She had some books with her. Cal watched as she put them on an empty table. No one in all of human history had ever laid books on a table more beautifully than she just had. Her hands so graceful, so feminine.

"You're just in time," said Cal.

"Time for what?"

"To help Robert solve a great mystery."

"I'll try."

Layla smiled at Cassandra. Cassandra smiled back at Layla.

"So, what's the mystery?"

"THIS, darling!" Robert handed Layla the letter. She took it and began to read.

"No idea who sent it. Cal thinks perhaps it's..."

"Melville."

"What?"

"Herman Melville. It's the prologue from Moby Dick."

"How did you know that?" Cal asked.

"I told you, I did my A levels in English lit. Nineteenth century. Though in the book this is addressed to some...librarian, I think. So whoever wrote this just put in Robert's name instead."

"Well, that's it then," said Robert. "Mystery solved. Melville, is it?"

Layla handed the letter back.

"You get a reward for solving that. Anything you'd wish to drink, it's yours."

"Not necessary. I'd read Melville for free any day."

"DARLING," Robert insisted, "have a drink, on us. We're very grateful."

"Well then, maybe a...*Cacaolat*."

The chocolate milk again.

Layla looked at Cal. "I like that song you sang earlier, Breakfast in a Bottle. Autobiographical?"

Busted.

Cassandra asked Cal if he wanted to go to the beach. He did not. Then she asked him if he wanted to go to look at some of the shop windows in the village. He said he didn't really want to do

that either.
"Why don't we just sit here awhile."
"Okay."

Chapter XXII

That night, a conflict of interest. Cassandra wanted to make love. Cal just wanted to fuck. Like a tramuntana, he blew her off the bed, onto the floor, against the wall. The brandy again, or maybe he was just trying to keep anyone from saying something silly.

Somewhere inside Cal was a sweet, sensitive guy. Somewhere.

After they finished, i.e., after he finished, she said she wanted to go back to her own place to sleep. He half-tried to get her to change her mind, but she insisted. As she was leaving, she told him that the next day she and her mother would be leaving for Barcelona at about two in the afternoon.

"See you Friday, our place at nine?"

"Sure. I'm really looking forward to it."

He offered to walk her home.

"No, that's okay."

He waited until she was around the corner before closing the door.

Chapter XXIII

The next day, Cal waited until five o'clock when he was sure Cassandra would have left already for Barcelona. Then he headed to Imperial hoping to find Layla. He had his journal with him and the Kerouac. If she wasn't there he would sit and wait.

The operative word here was *and*. Sit *and* have a drink. Read a book *and* have a drink. Do anything *and* have a drink. Cal's ex-wife used to shout at him that he was an alcoholic. Bullshit. He just liked to drink a lot. He would always yell back at her, "Everyone needs a hobby!" She did not have a very good sense of humor though, which was one of the reasons that marriage failed.

After their divorce, he left California for New York hoping to find others who would understand his humor. He did. New York was just the place for it. Unfortunately, it was also the place for a lot of other things. He had wrestled his way free of those finally, and now thank god it was back to just the smoke and the drink. March of Progress.

Cal had once imagined designing his own clock. Just for fun, instead of numbers there would be drinks. *Carajillo*, Sangria, beer, wine, gin and tonic, and so on. It would take you through the whole day. What time was it now? He looked at his watch. Brandy soda time.

He ordered, then opened the Kerouac and began to read. Sucked out of the village, deposited on the road. And it was like looking in a mirror. Just as the characters in those pages,

Cal had also bummed across America. And now suddenly he was on his own memory road trip. Crossing I-80 by bus, the driver in Omaha coming back to warn him, "I smell that Mexican alfalfa." He had also driven it by car a few times. And he had thumbed across the States three and a half times. Moments long gone were back. It was Cadaqués that was far away. He was with the two guys in the beat-up station wagon in Utah who swore the cigarette lighter in the dash was a lie detector, and wanted to know if Cal had seen any "military installations" on his travels. And then again with the guy who looked like Cat Stevens who called himself Melikilikimaka, and his girlfriend with the missing teeth, who drove their truck into the desert while tripping on something and wouldn't let Cal out until they were in the middle of fucking nowhere and he thought they were going to shoot him. In that purple summer night he ran back to the highway in a zigzag pattern with his pack, while instead of shots he could hear them laughing like hyenas over his shoulder. That was fun. On the other side of the coin, there were those two pretty girls who took him to their trailer and had sex with him in the shallow river, the three of them all over each other in the hot sun, then again by the campfire later.

Funny how memory reversed some things, like a Man Ray negative. Remembering bad stuff could be fun because it was over now, while remembering good stuff could be sad for the same reason.

He didn't have to remember much else, because Layla was coming toward him finally. The third brandy soda must have been the charm. Just as on the day before she had some books in her arms, also a sketchpad and some colored pencils.

"Good morning." It was a running joke of his now. He'd say it to anyone, no matter what time it was.

"Good morning," she smiled back.

"Join me?"

Layla sat at his table. The waitress came. Chocolate milk again.

"That shit'll kill you," warned Cal. "Too much calcium."

"I'll risk it."

He nodded toward the sketchpad and pencils.

"You're an artist?"

"I wish. I'm a replicationist."

"Repli-what?"

"Replicationist. It's a word I invented."

"You invent your own words?"

"Sure. It's what we do here in the Widdle Wat."

"What do you replicate?"

"Fashions."

"Wow."

"It's only a hobby."

"Funny, I was just thinking about hobbies."

"When I started doing it a few years ago I was inspired by films. I'd see something I liked, and so I'd just make it. I love the classic look. Ingrid Bergman's outfits from Casablanca, for instance. Brigitte Bardot in God Created Woman. Catherine Deneuve in Belle de Jour. Things like that."

"What a sweet idea."

"Then about a year ago I switched to paintings. I started to make outfits that some of the figures wear in paintings I love."

"Like...?"

"Like the girl's dress from Klimt's Kiss. Also his Adele Bloch-Bauer I dress. I had to paint those, of course. It wasn't like the fabrics were available."

"Sure."

He looked at her books on the table. The one on top was *Erotic Art of the Masters*.

"And now you're doing something from this?"

"Want to see?"

"Desperately."

She opened the book to a painting by Ingres. There were five naked women in a Turkish harem. One of the women was wearing a hat."

She said, "I really like this hat."

"I think the whole outfit works pretty well. The hat together with the bare breasts."

She smiled. He leaned in closer as if to look at the hat. So close he could smell her.

"Chanel Number Five?"

"I'm impressed."

"I know a horse named Chanel Number Five."

"You're joking."

The waitress brought her chocolate milk. Cal leaned back again in his chair.

"Look, I don't want to interrupt your work, so you go on. I've got my own book here. I'll just keep reading."

"You sure?"

"Please."

She chose her colors, and then started to draw her hat. Cal opened the Kerouac and began to read. In his head it went something like this:

They stand uncertainly underneath immense skies and... her legs are as long as a summer day, or a workman's Friday... Outside Tucson we saw another hitchhiker in the...has she read ALL of Melville? How could she have recognized that passage so fast?...the whole place, a bewildering view of the...how can anyone be so beautiful?...

You couldn't really call it reading.

He kept trying to focus on the words, but no luck. And she had to know what she was doing, driving him absofuckinglutely nuts by not doing anything at all. A beautiful woman doing nothing was like anyone else doing everything. Cal gave up the not-reading and opened his journal to not-write, because that didn't work out any better. Luckily after about five minutes she broke the silence.

"Do you really know a horse named Chanel Number Five?"

"How could I lie about a thing like that? It sounds too much like a lie."

"What sounds like a lie?"

It was a man's voice. The restaurant De Beers. Out of nowhere. Every word to follow in that Afrikaner accent that would make such sense to Cal later.

"Hello darling," he said, bending down to kiss the top of her head. "What is it you're on about?"

"Oh, hello love," she answered cheerfully. "Cal, this is Paul. Paul, this is Cal."

The two men shook hands.

"Darling, Cal knows a horse named Chanel Number Five."

"Bullshit. He doesn't know a horse named Chanel Number Five."

"I don't?"

"Of course not."

The old man sat and looked at Cal. He was squinting his eyes. They looked like rat eyes. He looked like a big rat. He was smiling.

"'*Cal.*' What kind of ridiculous name is that?"

"It's short for California," explained Layla.

"Ah, I see. Well then I'm going to guess you're from California?"

"That's right."

"I never really liked California. I think it's over-hyped. A bunch of gays and surfers, everyone's always stoned. Am I right?"

"We're always stoned, yes."

Paul looked at Layla.

"Listen, put that nonsense down. Just stop what you're doing. I need you to go to the restaurant right now, get some checks from my desk...you know where they are, the top drawer... and bring them to me. I've got to pay the fucking electric bill, or they're going to fucking turn it off. And then we have to go see Consuela about, well, you know."

"Do we have to do that today?"

"Yes, we have to fucking do it today. Now go on, bring me those checks."

"Alright."

She smiled at Cal, shrugged, closed her sketchpad and stood.

"That's a good girl."

Cal watched Layla walking away. Paul watched him watching her.

"So Cal, what the fuck do you do? For a living, I mean."

"I'm a writer."

"Everyone's a writer. Do you make any money doing it?"

Who asks a stranger how they make their money? And who tells somebody they just met that their name is ridiculous? And who the fuck says "fuck" in every sentence? How could she...

"What's your last name, Cal?"

"Zander."

"Never heard of you."

"I..."

"Look, Cal, let me tell you something. I..."

And then it began. It was like listening to a river run. There was no end to it. One word led to another, one thought to the next. When Cal tried to say something finally he was told not to interrupt.

"...Now I see how you're looking at me, Cal. Don't think I don't see it. You know why I see it? It's because I see *everything*. And because I see everything, I'm going to say one thing to you now. And that is that there are three reasons why to say you are a writer is a preposterous thing to say. Unless I know your name from the bookstores, from cinema, and so on and so forth, you're not *really* a writer. You *want* to be a writer. Ah, but that's a different thing. There's a big difference, an important difference. And let me explain to you what that difference is. The difference is blah blah blah..."

A fucking avalanche of words! After a few more moments Cal stopped listening and just watched the mouth moving, the little rat eyes shifting around, and the snarky smile that seemed so fixed. Cal could have pushed his way in if he really wanted, but this was a performance, and in a strange way he was enjoying it. There was a brief intermission when Layla came back with the checkbook.

"Ah! Here's my little chungamungabunga now!"

Little chungamungabunga?

She sat and plopped the checkbook on the table in front of him.

"Now there's a good girl. You see that, Cal? She's a good girl, because she does what she's told."

"*What*? I don't do as I'm told. What are you saying?"

"I'm saying you're a good girl, that's all I'm saying."

"Well that's not very respectful."

"*Respect*! You want *respect*, now?" He rolled his eyes. Rat eyes rolling. It had to be seen. "You have to *earn* respect, darling. Respect is not like that chocolate milk there. They don't just bring it to you. And as long as I'm the one who has to run things around here..."

"What are you talking about? No one asks you to run things."

"Well you don't *have* to ask, do you, because I just run them. I do a thousand things before you even get that little ass of yours out of bed in the morning." He looked at Cal as he said it, like that was a joke between the guys. Layla started to respond.

"I..."

"Don't interrupt me! Now look, if you want to impress this man with your 'I'm a creative, independent-minded person' attitude,' well then fine, you can do it. But don't give me a lot of crap, a lot of bullshit, that I don't have to run things, because I do."

Cal spoke up finally. "I've waited a long time to say something, Paul, and here it is. 'I' and 'me' seem to be your favorite words."

"*Thank you!*" said Layla, laughing. "It's so funny you say that, because that's *exactly* what he says to me *all the time.* Don't you? You always tell me I talk about myself, and now someone you've just met has the balls to tell you the same thing."

"What rubbish! What absolute krak! I do not talk about myself any more than I need to to get my point across. And my point is that this fellow was bragging that he's a writer, and I say that..."

"I wasn't bragging."

"Excuse me, what do you call it then? You were *bragging*. To say one is a writer is an act of bragging. Because that's suggesting you have something to say that the rest of the world wants to hear, or possibly even *needs* to hear. And if that's not bragging, well then I don't know what is."

"I was just saying that..."

"You were just saying that you are a writer. That's *bragging*. If you said, I don't know...'I am a dishwasher' or 'I am a garbage man,' or 'I fix cars,' or 'I am a mathematician,' well then that would *not* be bragging. But when you say 'I am a writer,' what you're really saying is that you think you're better than other people."

"He didn't say that!"

"I didn't say that!"

"Well now wait! Just *wait*! Listen to me. Listen very carefully. Think about what it means." He spoke slowly now, enunciating each word as if English was not their native language. "It means he thinks he has something to *teach* us. That we should buy his books, and keep his books in our house, on our shelves, and talk about them whenever we can. And yes, I'm sorry, but *that is bragging*."

It was as if he was paid by the word.

A few minutes of this had been fun. Now it was becoming more like watching paint dry or grass grow. A fucking science experiment: how dull can a thing be?

"You're a very special person, Paul. I can see that already."

"Well now don't give me that bullshit, Cal. Your voice was full of irony just now when you said that."

"Oh no, I am sincere. You are a *very* special person."

"All he said, Paul, was that..."

"I *know* what he said. I do have ears, you know. You see these?" He pointed to his ears. "These are ears. And you, my dear, you are too young and too naïve to understand what he meant by what he said. Do you know how old she is?" he asked Cal.

"I don't, no."

"She's twenty-one. She drinks chocolate milk. She doesn't understand a bloody thing. But I understand. I understand perfectly well that what a person *says*, and what a person *means*, are usually two different things. Aren't they, Cal?"

"You know what?"

"What? Go on. The writer is now going to give us his opinion. Go on, Cal. We're waiting for it. What is it you want to say?"

"That I've seen you both around the village a few times now, and every time you, Paul, have been talking, while she, Layla, has been doing the listening."

"And? So? What's your point? Get to your point, Cal."

"My point is that maybe *you* should listen to *her* sometimes. Because from what I've heard, she's as smart as she is beautiful."

"I like him," said Layla. She looked at Cal. "I like you."

"Well, I *don't* like him. And I don't give kak what he thinks. He's just trying to get into your pants, can't you see that? And Cal, look at me, that's *not* going to happen. Do...you...hear...me? That's not going to happen."

"Okay."

"Of *course* she listens to me, because I'm giving her...and for that matter I'm also giving you now...the benefit of my experience, and my wisdom. Which happen to be substantial. But the thing is..."

"What's the thing, Paul?"

"The thing is, I could serve you all the wisdom of the world on a plate, and I don't believe that you would understand it. Do you know why? I'll tell you why."

"Please tell me why."

"Because you, Cal, are still on the first level, that's clear. While I am on the twenty-sixth level. And one day if you're *very* lucky maybe you *will* understand that."

"I want a dog," said Layla.

"*What?*"

"You heard me. I want a dog."

"Well you can't have one."

"Why not?"

"Because I said you can't, that's why."

"That's not a reason."

Exasperated sigh. "Alright then, if you need more reason than that, it's because I don't want fucking dog hair all over my house..."

"*Our* house."

"Okay, *our* house. Whosever house it is, I don't want fucking dog hair all over it. And I don't want to be picking up dog shit. And I don't want.... Wait a minute, what am I doing? I don't need to explain. I just don't want a dog, that's all. Alright?"

Another, overwrought sigh. Again, the rat eyes rolling. Cal opened his journal and scribbled a quick note to himself: *Write song called Rat Eyes Rolling.*

"Well," said Layla, taking all this in good humor. She was obviously used to it. "I know what I'll do then. I'll wait until you die, and then I'll get a dog. And I'll name him Paul. And then I'll say, 'Sit, Paul!' and 'Do this Paul,' and 'Don't do that Paul,' and 'Be quiet Paul.' I'll treat him just like you treat me. Like a *dog*."

"Oh for God's sake, this is...."

"Actually no, I won't. I could never be so cruel. I'll treat Paul the dog *better* than you treat me."

Cal stood. He went inside and paid the bill. Then he came back out. He took his Kerouac and journal from the table.

"Well kids, this has been a lot of fun. Really. You know what I'm going to go do now?"

"What?" asked Layla, smiling.

"I'm going home to write. I'm going to write until my fingers drop off. Because you, both of you, have given me so much to write about."

Chapter XXIV

"It's not about his age, David. If he thought like Einstein, or had the talent of Picasso, or the soul of Gandhi, or looked like Sean Connery, well then I could understand the age difference. But he's *not* like them. He's a...he's a...I can't even think of the word. I have to invent one. He's a...bolby. No, a...tadigogue. No, a...*bolbigogue*! That's it. He's a bolbigogue!"

That tasted right.

"Bolbigogue?"

"Exactly. Definition: someone who knows he's only six percent of the man he wishes he was, and claims to be."

"Oh, Cal, you begin the new mythology. Bolbigogues. How do they look?"

"Their mouths are bigger than their heads. Like the Mick Jagger mouth on a neck."

"I can imagine them, yes, in the desert maybe? Or rising out of the Sea?"

"Armies of Bolbigogues. And if you get a thousand of them together, they still can't tell a rock from an egg. So they all go hungry, because their mouths are so big, there's no room for a brain."

"Cal, you are so cruel."

"Only to Bolbigogues. Because the way he treated her...she deserves better."

They were sitting downstairs in David's studio, surrounded

by leaping porpoises, white doves in flight, naked women, vaginas, penises, long-necked swans, winged chariots and horses of every color. And boats. Everywhere boats. Behind David was a large painting he had just finished, an oil on canvas. On it, happy creatures of the sea and sky, a radiating sun, all in bright blue, green, red and gold. A young man stood beside a river coursing across the canvas from mountains to the waiting sea. He was about to board a ship being rowed not by a single ferryman, but by a dozen beautiful young women. They would bring him to the other side of the river.

Sea urchins, shells, those rocks from the beach now painted, not an empty space anywhere. Calder-like mobiles with more of David's creations hung overhead, together with a great bunch of those dried yellow *immortales* tied to a black thread. Like Damocles' sword.

Upstairs in his own space Cal had been writing, then hit a block. So he had grabbed his journal and pen, a bottle of wine and a joint, and hurried down to David's.

"David, please, I have a big favor to ask of you."

"Of course, Cal. Anything. How can I help?"

"Explain women to me."

"Ah, well then maybe you should sit down, because this could take some time."

So here they sat, drinking, smoking, trying to decipher women.

"Have you seen the wind, David?"

"Of course. Here in Cadaqués the tramuntana is very strong."

"I don't mean have you seen what the wind does. Have you seen the wind itself?"

"No Cal, one cannot see the wind."

"*Exactly*! *This* is the problem with women. It's easy to see *what* they do. But *how* they do it, and *why* they do it..."

"These are mysteries, Cal. You search for the Holy Grail of love."

"And I have another problem."

"So many problems. Tell me, what is this new problem?"

"Nothing rhymes with 'Layla.'"

"Cal, you are already writing poems for her?"

"Only one."

"You have been bitten by the snake."

"A little."

"A little bite of the snake can be enough."

"Anyway, it's impossible. 'Layla.' It's worse than 'orange.'"

"I don't understand."

"In English, nothing rhymes with 'orange.' Or 'Layla.' Listen..."

Cal flipped open his journal and read from it:

"*Layla*
C'est la
Vie
Fait accompli
Can't you see
You were born for me
Layla...we'll have a gay...la, ma,
sha...geisha...nightingale...a...

You see the problem?"

"No. What is the problem?"

"Nothing rhymes with 'Layla.'"

"Well then, why not write another kind of poem? Without rhyme."

"Okay. Good idea. But then there's *another* problem. I'm not really in love. *Yet*. But I can be. I *will* be. I think."

"So then, this is something you are *planning*? To fall in love?"

"Yes! I am planning on falling in love with Layla."

"You see, Cal, I am not the teacher, I am the student. I did not know love could be planned like this. It is very interesting. And when will you do this? When will you fall in love with her? Tomorrow? What time? In the morning? Maybe the night. Night is very good for falling in love, Cal."

"Okay, well maybe I do feel something already. A little love."

"A *little* love? Is there such a thing? And Cassandra, what about her? The other night up at Freddy's, you two..."

"A temporary solution to a long term problem."

"That does not sound so romantic. Does she know she is only a 'temporary solution'?"

"Not yet. But look, David, the only one I want to talk about is Layla."

Cal poured more wine into their glasses.

"It's like...like when you *start* to fall, but you haven't fallen yet."

"Well then, why not write a poem about falling? Not about love, but about falling."

"You know where you are, David?"

"In Cadaqués?"

"No. You are on the twenty-sixth level."

"Oh, Cal, I am a little afraid of the heights."

The smoke circled around David's head as he held his cigarette. He was fingering it like it was a rosary bead.

"Love is like the smoke, yes, Cal? It fills the space it is in. If it is in a big heart it will grow. C'est formidable. You have a big heart, Cal. Do not be surprised if your little love becomes something bigger, and stronger. A tiger in a cage is still a tiger. Give it your heart and it will not remember that it is not in the jungle."

Cal opened his journal and quickly began copying David's

words so they would not be lost. Seeing this, David continued to dictate as if his words now were being chiseled in stone.

"Cal, you are Endymion, and you have seen your Selene." He thought for a moment. "No. It is more dangerous than that. You are not Endymion. You are Majnun, the crazy one, with your poetry. And now even with your own Layla. Do you know the story?"

"She mentioned it, but I've never read it."

"Oh, Cal, you *must* read it. It is so beautiful. An old Persian love story by Nizami. I read it when I was very young. Can you believe it, Cal? I was young."

"You will always be young, David."

"'Majnun,' it means the crazy one. Because the boy, he is crazy with love for his Layla. She is the most beautiful woman in the world. But he cannot have her. And so he writes her name in the sand while he wanders in the desert because her father, he will not allow it. He has heard the young man is crazy. He does not understand that it is only the madness of love."

"I am not so crazy yet."

"No, but you *plan* to be."

"I do."

"I have the book here if you would like to read it."

"Oh yes, please!"

David stood, crossed to a shelf and brought back the book. It was in Spanish. Cal would manage it.

"And poor Cassandra? What about her? I think she is already a little crazy for you. Be careful, Cal. She is so skinny. It has to be a little heart that will break easily."

"I know."

"She is always waiting for you at the Casino."

"Not now. She's in Barcelona with her mother. They're shopping for a dinner they want to give for me Friday night. Do you know the mother?"

"Oh, Cal, I know the cow. She bought a painting from me. And *still* she has not paid me for it. It is more than one year. Half a million pesetas, about three thousand dollars. Can you imagine? And they have so much money! A castle in Liechtenstein, that big house here, and so many of those little fucking shops."

"I heard about those."

"Do you know what they sell in those shops, Cal?"

"Magnets, shirts, postcards..."

"Their *souls*. They sell their souls. Can you imagine, not to pay the artist? Three thousand dollars, for them it is like a grain of sand on a mountain. But have you met the mother?"

"Not yet."

"Well, you will see. Probably she *ate* those half-million pesetas. She is as fat as the other one is skinny. Like two different species. Like the brother they are all crazy, the whole family. Because of drugs, because of money, because of love..."

On David's table between his pens, paints and brushes, Cal noticed three pills. One blue, one yellow, one white.

"What are those, David?"

David looked down at them. He said nothing for a moment. Then, "My medicine, Cal. These are my medicines."

"For what?"

"For everything, Cal. For everything."

Chapter XXV

Middle of the night. Two candles burning. Open bottle of wine. Cal sat at the blue table. He had begun reading *Layla and Majnun*. Mad with love, the young man had fled to the desert to be alone with his passions. "He fell to his knees in the dust." When Cal read that he remembered David's words about the poem, and suddenly it came to him. His first haiku:

I tried not to fall
But there was nothing to hold
Onto but the falling

This was crazy. He hardly knew her. A few words, that was all. And yes, okay, she was smart, she was beautiful, she was... He actually made a list now in his journal:

Smart, beautiful, laughs easily, no bullshit (yet), writes poetry for children, creative, loves serious literature, playful... It was like a shopping list. Tomatoes, potatoes... She had it all.

And now on top of it, he wanted to save her from the bolbigogue. From those rat claws that were at her this very moment for all he knew. Probably he wasn't a bad man or she wouldn't be with him. Would she? Cal didn't know her well enough yet to answer that. But the old fart was certainly that, treating her and others with derision and taking such delight in doing it. That little smirk of his, judging all the "fucking idiots" from up there on the twenty-sixth level.

Another bottle of wine, another joint, and still there was no way Cal could sleep. So out into the night for a long walk, then down to Port Alguer for a swim. Stepping into the black water set off little phosphorous sparks in the sea.

The Holy Grail of love. It had to be somewhere. He swam as if heading toward it. The little sparks in the water. Lights from the boats and the village. Later, floating on his back he saw a shooting star. And suddenly it wasn't enough. None of this.

Chapter XXVI

Friday evening, nine o'clock. Wearing shoes, not sandals, and a clean shirt, Cal walked to Cassandra's, passing by the Casino where Marita and Robert were sitting at one of the tables. They waved to him. He waved back and kept walking. Wiggles was at the Imperial. He was leaning over the bar saying something to the barman. He did not see Cal walk past to the nearby door of Cassandra's mother's house and push the bell. A moment later Cassandra appeared on the little balcony above.

"Hi," she shouted down.

"Good morning!"

"I'll ring the buzzer. Then just push the door open. We're on the first floor."

"Great."

The buzzer rang. Cal followed instructions and went up the stairs. The big door to the apartment was already open. Cassandra was standing there, grinning.

"Hi."

"Hi."

Kisses on cheeks.

"Come in."

"Thanks."

Cal stepped in to the big, spacious apartment. High ceilings, white walls. Hanging on the walls was some of the worst art he had ever seen. But the colors were nice, big splashes of orange and red on canvas. And there was a big woven tapestry at the end of the hall, a copy of the photo of Audrey Hepburn smoking a cigarette with a long holder...in yarn.

Breakfast at Tiffany's. Dinner at Cassandra's.

Suddenly behind Cassandra appeared her mother. David had been right, they looked like two different species. The mother was huge, round, with a pretty moon face and massive grin. Her teeth, earrings, necklace, rings, all sparkled. Money so new you could still smell the ink.

"Hello, Cal. It's so nice to finally meet you. I've heard so much about you."

She stuck out her hand, brown from the sun. Cal shook it. Her hand was as big as his, made heavier still by all the gold rings and bracelets. The moment she had ahold of him she pulled him closer. Big kisses on both cheeks.

"This is my mother," said Cassandra.

The mother's breasts were enormous. Cal couldn't help bumping into them as she kissed him.

"Won't you come in!" It was not a question.

Cal stepped further into the apartment as the door closed behind him. The mother still had hold of his hand.

"My name is Aya."

"What a beautiful name."

"It is, yes."

"Aya. That's not a typical Liechtenstein name, is it?"

"No, you're right. It's not. It's from Morocco."

"You're from Morocco?"

"No," Cassandra giggled. "Of course not. But she visited it when she was young."

"That's right. I went with a boyfriend, Dobie. We hitchhiked everywhere. The Riff mountains in the north, Ketama, then all the way down to the south. Ait-Benhaddou, Zagora. It was magical. We met a girl with the name Aya, and Dobie started to call me that too. I'm not sure why. I think he just liked the name. Anyway, for some reason it stuck."

"'Aya' means 'miracle,'" said Cassandra. "Also 'sword' in old German."

"And, which one are you?"

The mother laughed. "Oh, probably both. It depends on my mood. Isn't that right?"

"That's right," agreed Cassandra.

Aya was still holding onto Cal's hand.

"Now please come in and meet everyone."

Pulling him after her, the mother led Cal through wide double doors into a big room with half a dozen people standing around. All had drinks in their hands. Cassandra followed.

"Everyone," Aya announced in a booming voice that silenced the others, "I want to introduce Cassandra's friend, Cal Zander. Come Cal, I want you to meet everyone, and of course for them to meet you."

She led Cal over to three men who were standing next to the open door to the balcony. The oldest of them was around 60, heavyset, tall. He wore a white linen shirt nicely pressed, expensive looking trousers, and a massive gold Rolex on his wrist.

"This is my ex-husband, Bruno. Cassandra's father."

Aya released Cal's hand so he was free now to shake hands with the father.

"Cal, very nice to meet you. We have been hearing so much about you."

"That's not true," said Cassandra, blushing. "I mentioned you once or twice, that was all."

"And this," said Aya, her eyes directing Cal to the second

man, "this is Herr Warning."

A short man in a gray suit, no tie, reached out his hand. He spoke with a thick German accent.

"Very gut to meet you."

"Herr Warning is my banker. He is visiting Cadaqués for his first time."

"Do you like it here?" asked Cal.

"Vell, you know, vat can I say? It's Spain."

Herr Warning handed Cal his card.

"Here, please."

"Thank you," said Cal. "I'm afraid I didn't bring my cards with me."

"Don't vorry, I'm sure zat vee vil meet again. You can give it to me za next time."

The third man now reached out his hand. Tall, thin, with little wire glasses. Like Cassandra he could not stop smiling.

"And this," said Aya, "is my business partner Albrecht von Hoffman."

Another card handed to Cal.

Two more men who had been standing across the room next to the unlit fireplace now came over. Aya introduced them.

"My lawyer and friend, Jonathan Freyburg."

More shaking of the hands.

"And this gentleman here, this is Rico Fuentes. If you ever have any questions about real estate in Spain, Rico is the man to ask."

"Oh Aya, you flatter me."

"It's true!"

Everyone laughed.

Aside from Cal, it seemed that Rico was the only other non-Teutonic guest. He had a black moustache and black eyes and wore a white jacket.

"Are you from Cadaqués?" Cal asked him.

"No, originally Madrid. But now I am living in Barcelona."

He pronounced it 'BarTHelona.'

"And what about you, Cal? Do you like Cadaqués?"

"I love it."

Again everyone laughed.

"Let's get Cal something to drink. What would you like? We have everything."

"Everything sounds good."

"No, really, what would you like?"

"Maybe a...vodka tonic?"

"Cassandra, go tell Sonia to make Cal a nice big vodka tonic. No, on second thought, I'll do it. You stay."

Aya left the room. Cassandra's father looked at Cal.

"Cassandra tells us you're a writer. What kind of things do you write, Cal? Fiction? Corporate?"

"Fiction."

"Interesting."

"Thank you."

"She also told us your father was a professor at Harvard?"

"Yale, actually. And Stanford."

Cassandra looked confused.

"I thought you said Harvard."

"No, Yale and Stanford."

"Well, those are good schools too, aren't they?"

"Yes."

Herr Warning wanted to know what subject Cal's father had taught.

"History."

"*History*."

"That's right, history."

"Interesting."

"Very interesting," agreed Herr Freyburg.

Aya returned with a glass.

"Here you are, Cal. A nice big cold vodka tonic."

Cal thanked her, took a sip, and looked at Cassandra.

"Is your brother here?"

"He's in his room. He'll come out and join us when it's time to eat."

"Nice."

"We heard what happened," said Aya. "I want to apologize for my son. It was definitely his fault."

"Oh, well..."

"No, really, it was his fault. And hopefully that taught him a good lesson."

"That boy's been fucking up all his life," said Cassandra's father. "So many times I wanted to break his arm myself. So good for you! Life is going to teach him a few hard lessons like that. Then maybe finally he'll learn."

"I just hope he won't hold it against me."

"Of course not," Aya assured him. "He's not like that."

Cal noticed a big painting by David above the white sofa.

"What a wonderful painting."

"Really? You like it?"

"We hate it," said Cassandra.

"Well, we don't hate it," her mother corrected her. "We just don't like it very much. We have some problems with it. You see that tree in the painting?"

"Yes. What about it?"

"That was supposed to be a lemon tree. I told David I wanted a lemon tree. Nice splashes of yellow...here, there..." She was pointing to the places where she wanted lemons. "But that's not a lemon tree. Those are pomegranates."

"Or apples," said Cassandra.

"Or apples. One can't really tell, can one?"

"Well..."

"And those horses?"

"What about them?"

"They were supposed to be white."

"Like Lippizaners."

"But he made them brown."

"And red."

"Whoever heard of a red horse?"

Herr Freyburg laughed. "I've seen a lot of horses in my life, but never a red one."

The talk then turned to investing. Herr Warning wanted to know about real estate in California vs. real estate in New York.

"I don't really know much about it," Cal admitted. "It depends where in California, of course."

"I mean in za better parts."

"North? South?"

"Vat vould you say is za difference?"

Cal took a long sip from his drink.

"Well, in the north, near San Francisco, you have Silicon Valley where the computer industry is developing."

"Yes? And, zo?"

"And zo, I would guess that as that industry grows, the demand for real estate there will also grow."

Everyone was looking at Cal.

"And in za South?"

"Well, in za south you have Hollywood. But of course the movies are already a well-established industry."

"Zo you sink zat in Silicon Valley zer is greater growth potential?"

"Of course, that's only a guess."

"What about stocks?" Herr Freyburg asked. "The Americans are all so crazy about their stocks. Especially these so-called I.T. stocks."

Cal told them what he knew, which was very little. Herr Freyburg looked disappointed. Cassandra's father jumped into it.

"Now that Germany is reunited, I personally believe it represents a market with enormous potential for a new renaissance. Maybe even bigger than the last renaissance!"

More laughter, heads nodding, Cassandra grinning, ice tinkling...

Rico said that as people in the north had more money, surely soon they would be buying more second homes in the south.

"Aya is a perfect example. And I am sure many more will follow her."

Rico and Bruno then got into a friendly debate about whether people would be wiser to invest their money in the north or south. As he listened to them, Cal finished his drink.

"Cassandra darling, go bring Cal another drink. And while you're in the kitchen, tell Sonia we're ready for some food now."

Cassandra nodded and disappeared. A moment later she was back with another vodka tonic. A little woman in a white apron appeared behind her carrying a big silver tray. She brought it straight to Cal.

"This is chocolate covered fois gras," Aya said, pointing to the tray. "You must try one of these."

"You'll love it!" Cassandra assured him.

Both women watched closely as Cal reached for some strange looking things on a stick.

"What do you think?"

"They're French."

"But we bought them in Barcelona."

"At a little shop off Las Ramblas."

"Aren't those delicious?"

Cal wanted to spit it out, but couldn't because they were both still watching him. He liked fois gras, and he liked chocolate, but together...

Sonia circulated around the room with the tray. Moments later she was back already with figs stuffed with hot goat cheese, then again with frog legs, coriander encrusted shrimp, and some other things. Finally Aya announced it was time "To *really* eat!"

Cal and the others followed her down a long corridor past some closed doors, out onto a wide terrace at the back of the apartment. There were lit Tiki torches stuck into big clay pots overflowing with white and purple bougainvillea. A water fountain built into the side of one wall trickled perfectly. A lemon tree rose beside its orange cousin, the splash of colors reminding everyone that they were as far from the colder north as one could get in a ten hour drive.

There was a long table in the middle of the terrace. It was laid with starched white linen, candles, silver glistening, and in the dead center there was a huge gold-plated urn with birds of paradise and other exotic flowers sticking out of it. Aya sat at one end of the table, Bruno Sr. at the other end. Cal and Cassandra were instructed to sit on either side of Aya. Everyone else took their seats.

"Sonia, tell my son it's time to eat."

"Si, Señora."

Sonia disappeared inside. Moments later Bruno Jr. came out. His right arm was in a sling. Without looking at the others he

181

took his place next to his father. Then, lifting his head slowly, he looked up and across the table at Cal. He picked up his knife with his good hand and began to play with it. Light from the candles glistened off the sharp blade.

The food started to come: mussels in a creamy saffron sauce, cold asparagus in mayonnaise, little truffle soufflés, and something else, green in red aspic. Wine was flowing. And the conversation never stopped. Herr Freyburg and Herr Warning had both driven from Liechtenstein, so there was the classic Mercedes vs. BMW debate. Then talk of immigration, import quotas, private equity, leveraged buyouts. Subjects shifted like gears on a fine car. The European Union and the great "power-grab" by Brussels, Herr Freyburg actually approved of it while Herr Warning had his second thoughts. And everyone had an opinion about the coming euro, even Cassandra.

"I like it. It will make everything much easier at the stores. Though of course we will still get Swiss francs."

"Well, I will miss my little peseta," said Rico sadly.

Cal agreed. Herr von Hoffman looked at him.

"Now why, Herr Zander, would you say that?"

"Yes," Cassandra asked, "why would you say that?"

"Well, because of the...the romance of difference."

"What is that, the 'romance of difference'?"

Herr von Hoffman pulled an ironed handkerchief from his pocket and blew his nose as Cal answered.

"Well, it's just that some differences are interesting. Like for instance, the difference between a man and a woman. You don't want *everything* to be the same."

Silence.

"I mean, it used to be that Spain was Spain, yes? And France was France. And that's why we traveled, to see different things.

But now it's all starting to become the same. 'McWorld,' someone called it."

Bruno Sr. now spoke up from his end of the table.

"But that's always been true. You get a cup of Indian tea in London, a French crepe in Manhattan. What's the difference?"

"The scale is the difference. Because it's all happening so fast now."

"And so, what's wrong with that?"

"It's disappointing, that's all. At least it is for me. Last year for instance when I drove across the Pyrennes..."

"Yes?"

"I crossed into France near Andorra, from Puigcerda into Bourg-Madam. I was heading to Llivia, and at the frontier there was no one there to check my passport."

"Thank God!" said Herr von Hoffman, tucking away his handkerchief.

"There was just an old border crossing gate. It was rusted and stuck up permanently in the air. Who knows, maybe there's a McDonalds there now. That would also be convenient."

"Oh-oh, watch out Aya!" cried Rico. "He's a Romantic!"

"A rose has thorns. Don't forget it!"

It was time for the main course. Aya looked at Cal.

"I hope you like surf 'n turf."

"Oh, I *love* surf 'n turf."

It was true. The only problem was that he was already full. He could vomit he was so full. Sonia served. While Cal ate his slowly, he watched Bruno Jr. across the table trying to cut his lobster and steak with one hand. Not easy. Everyone ate in silence. Then, wiping something from the corner of her mouth, Aya turned to Cal.

"So Cal, what do you think of our apartment? Do you like it?"

"It's beautiful."

"It is, yes. But I have to tell you, I've been coming here for so many years already. As beautiful as it is, I think it might just be time for a change. Which is why I'm thinking about getting someplace in the Caribbean. Costa Rica, maybe. Or Jamaica. Someplace like that. We'll see."

"But wouldn't you miss Cadaqués?"

"Oh, I could still come here. Because you see, if I do decide to get something in the Caribbean, well then I'm going to give this apartment to Cassandra. You know, to help her get her own start in life."

Bruno Jr. stopped poking at his food, and was staring across the table at his mother.

"When did you decide to do *that*?"

"I didn't decide. It's just something I'm thinking about, that's all."

Bruno said something to her in German. Then his father said something to him in German. Suddenly there was a lot of German flying back and forth. Cassandra interrupted them.

"I don't think this is right. I mean Cal doesn't speak German. And besides, we shouldn't really be talking about this. Not here, not now."

"You're right," said Aya. "I'm sorry I mentioned it. We'll discuss this later."

After everyone had finished the main course, there were two cakes, one chocolate, the other raspberry fudge. And there was a mango sorbet. Bottles of Calvados, Cognac and various eaux de vie appeared on the table together with oversized snifters. Sonia brought coffee. A few people smoked cigarettes or cigars.

Cal poured himself a good portion of the Calvados. He had been drinking wine all dinner long, on top of the vodka tonics earlier, and as he drank now he could feel it starting to add up.

Puffing a cigarette, Herr Warning looked across the table.

"I meant to ask you earlier, Herr Zander, vat is your own approach to investing?"

"Well, let's see, my approach is that I like to take all my money..."

"Yes?"

"...put it into one big pile as it were..."

"Yes? And? Zen?"

"And zen I like to spend it."

There was some nervous laughter around the table.

"Zat's very funny."

"Oh, but I'm serious," said Cal, swilling the apple brandy in his hand.

"But surely you must invest *some* of your money?"

"*All* of it! I invest all of it. Because my philosophy is that spending *is* an investment...in *life*."

"He's joking."

"Of course he's joking."

Cassandra looked at Cal. "You're joking, aren't you?"

"I'm not joking. I'm serious."

"But..."

"I invest in experience. Carpe diem. Because you can't take it with you, can you?"

"That's not the point."

"No?"

Aya and Bruno Sr. were looking at each other across the table. The mother turned to Cassandra.

"Cassandra darling, why don't you take Cal back inside. I've just remembered something I need to ask your father, and it will be easier if we speak about it in German."

"Sure."

Cal followed Cassandra back into the apartment.

In the big living room, Cassandra sat on the white couch under David's painting. Cal wandered over to the big doors still open to the balcony. He stepped out to look at the view. The moon was coming up behind Es Cucurucuc. The light from it sparkled on the water beyond the beach, and on the white boats that moved up and down as the water moved. There was laughter from below. Cal heard a familiar voice. He looked and could see Wiggles, Jose Manuel and David sitting together at Imperial. He shouted down to them.

"Gentlemen, you look like the three musketeers!"

Seeing Cal standing on the balcony, Wiggles shouted up.

"Well, what's this? The lord of the manor now, eh, Cal? Well, that's a nice position. A very nice position indeed!"

"Hombre!" yelled Jose Manuel. "Pareces el rey del mundo allá arriba!

"Si," agreed David, "the king of the world, Cal. That's what you look like up there."

All hoisted their drinks toward him.

"Go on, your Majesty, give us a speech. Give your poor little subjects down here a nice speech."

"Good people," said Cal, waving his snifter of Calvados in a sweeping gesture through the warm air, "you look well satisfied down there. Is there peace among my people? And contentment?"

"Oh yes, Cal, we are very happy," David shouted up. 'And you? Are you happy up there? With the cow?"

"Abundant happiness, David. Abundant!"

"Cal, please, can you do me a favor?"

"What's that, David? Anything for you."

"Please, can you throw down my painting? The one they never paid me for."

"I don't know about that, David. Anything but that. I'm their guest, you see. They might consider that a little rude, taking things off their walls and throwing them down there to my friends."

Cassandra suddenly appeared on the balcony beside him.

"Oh-oh," cried David. "It is the little cow. The calf."

"David, just shut up! Why don't you just shut up? We'll talk about that painting some other time, okay?"

"What other time, Cassandra? It has been more than a year. Give me my money, or else give me back my painting."

Cal stood caught in the middle.

"Well now to be fair, David, they did ask for white horses. I heard all about it earlier. They wanted *white* horses, David. So why the fuck did you paint *red* horses?"

"Who told you about the horses? The cow?"

"Yes, the big one. She asked me, and I must say she's right. I mean, who the fuck ever saw a red horse?"

"*I* saw them, Cal. In my dreams. There were many."

"David knows his own dreams, Cal," shouted Wiggles.

"That's not the point."

"No? What *is* the point? For God's sake Cal, get to the fucking point."

"The point is that aside from David's dream, who the fuck ever saw a red horse? A red horse doesn't even match the couch, David. I mean, not really. Not like a white horse would. Because you see, it's a *white* couch. And wouldn't that look nice? You have to *think* about these things, David."

"He's right, David, you have to *think* about those things. He just wasn't thinking, Cal."

Cassandra now was laughing.

"And *lemons*!" Cal shouted down. "That's another thing. Where are the fucking lemons, David? I heard about the tree." Cal looked over his shoulder through the open doors at the painting inside. "I'm looking at it right now, and to be honest with you David I don't see one fucking lemon."

"Tell him they're pomegranates," said Cassandra.

"She says those are pomegranates."

"How can you tell?" Wiggles wanted to know.

"Because, Wiggles, lemons are yellow. Often *very* yellow. And these things are *not* yellow. Her mother was ready to pay you David...*by the lemon*!"

Cassandra was almost doubled over with laughter.

"One thousand dollars for every lemon. I mean really, all you had to do was paint three fucking lemons. How hard is that?"

"Tio," shouted Jose Manuel, "que pasa ahi arriba? Hombre, lo que está pasando? ¿Hay una fiesta allá arriba? Abre la puerta, que venimos!"

Translation: Open the door and let us in so we can join the party.

That wasn't going to happen.

Instead, Cal shouted down, "This is *life*, David, not some dream. This is economics! These people are from Liechtenstein! You can't fool them. All you had to do was paint three fucking lemons, and then..."

Cal never finished his sentence. Because suddenly standing off in the shadows behind Imperial, he noticed Layla. She had been walking by from the direction of Bar Boia, and had stopped to watch and listen to this back and forth.

"Oh no, quick, someone call a doctor!"

"What's wrong, Cal?" yelled David.

"What's wrong?" asked Cassandra.

"My heart just skipped a beat."

"What are you talking about?"

"I've seen something not from the natural world. A spirit. A demon. An angel!"

"What are you talking about?"

"In the shadows just there, the most beautiful angel ever."

Layla could see that he was talking about her. She smiled up to him.

"The angel smiles! So cruel to that poor old moon up there that's trying to get our attention. But now, no chance moon! Give it up! There's only one light, and its name is...Layla."

"I don't think this is funny," said Cassandra.

She stood there as Cal continued.

"Look gentlemen, you see how an angel can turn a shadow into light, like magic. Only there's something wrong with this picture."

"What's wrong, Cal?"

"She's supposed to be up here on the balcony, isn't she? Isn't that how the play was written?"

Wiggles strained to see into the shadows beyond the bar.

"What the fuck are you talking about, Cal? I don't see any angels."

"Don't look, Wiggles! Don't do it! You'll blind yourself! It's like looking into the sun. Fast, shield your eyes or go blind!"

"I'm going inside," said Cassandra. She turned and disappeared.

"Cal," said David, "ask the angel to talk."

Cal called out to Layla, "Angel, please, we beg you, talk to us. Tell us what has brought you here to our little village."

Layla just stood there, her eyes and white dress standing out in the darkness.

"She says nothing. What of that? You know why she says nothing, David?"

"Why, Cal?"

"Because angels don't talk. You know why they don't talk?"

"Why, Cal?"

"Because they know that we already know what they're thinking."

Layla's voice now came floating out of the shadows. "And so go on, tell us, what do angels think?"

"You think that where men have faith there is hope."

"Hope in...?"

"Redemption."

"*Redemption*?"

"Yes, Angel, redemption. Because you know that only you can save me. Save me, Angel. Save me from...Liechtenstein!"

Cal turned to look inside. Cassandra was not on the couch. She was nowhere. He was about to turn back to Layla and his friends when Bruno exploded into the living room. He was screaming.

"*What the fuck are you doing? My sister is crying, man!*"

"Hey look, Bruno, don't..."

"*She's fucking crying! Because you're talking to some girl from up here?*"

"I was just..."

"Yeah, fuck you, I heard what you were doing. We all heard."

There was a bronze statue on a side table. A man holding a pocket watch. Bruno picked it up with his good hand.

"*You're hurting her, man! So now I'm going to fucking hurt you!*"

He ran at Cal.

"Bruno, stop! I don't want to..."

Too late. Bruno tried to hit Cal with the statue. Cal jumped to one side and the statue just missed him. Then Bruno came at him again. Backing away, Cal tripped over the coffee table and fell. Something else also fell.

"*Bruno, stop it!*"

"*Fuck you!*"

Cal grabbed the legs of a nice ivory-colored ottoman and used it as a shield against repeated blows of the statue. Cassandra, Bruno Sr., Aya, Rico, Herr Warning and the other Herrs all came rushing together into the room. From below the balcony there was shouting.

"*They are all freaks, Cal! Be careful!*" yelled David.

"*Tio, tira aqui abajo al hijo de puta!*"

"*Stop this!*" Aya shouted. "*Bruno, stelle die Statue wieder hin!*"

"Fucking Liechtenstein!" screamed Wiggles.

"*Stop this right now!*" yelled Aya. "Both of you, just stop this right now!"

Cal wondered what it was he was supposed to stop...ducking?

"Bruno, you heard your mother! Stop it!"

It was the father's turn now. "Bruno, ich rate dir dringend, stelle die Statue an ihren Platz."

But Bruno Jr. just kept at it, swinging, missing, swinging again. He was defending his sister's honor. There was actually something sweet about it, thought Cal as he kept crawling behind things. Bruno kept swinging and screaming, "*You fucker!*"

The word 'fuck' is a great word. It allows one to vent one's anger and frustration and not keep those things bottled inside. But still, sometimes that word, as strong as it is, isn't enough. Sometimes to really make your point you also have to try to hit someone in the head with a bronze statue.

Cal kept scrambling away while Bruno kept swinging. A little table was knocked over. People were yelling. A lamp crashed to the floor. From below, other people were laughing and shouting.

Cassandra was sitting on the white couch again, crying. Bruno Jr. was breathing hard, doubled over. He had hurt something. Cal's friends were still shouting from outside. Cal looked at his hosts.

"Well, it's been a wonderful party, really. The chocolate covered fois gras...*unforgettable*. Thank you so much for everything! But it's getting late now, and I think maybe I should be going."

Cassandra's crying grew louder. She was sobbing uncontrollably. Bruno Sr. and Aya were standing shoulder-to-shoulder by the door, which meant Cal would have to squeeze past them to go out the way he had come in. He really didn't want to do that, so instead he turned and went back out onto the balcony. He looked down. It was only a one-story drop. He swung one leg over the iron railing.

"What are you doing?" asked David, matter-of-factly.

"It looks pretty obvious to me," said Wiggles. "He's going to jump."

"Hombre, salta! Salta! Jump! Jump!"

"Be careful!" shouted a girl's voice from below. It was Layla.

Cal lowered himself down, then let go. It really was a very short fall. When he landed he fell backwards, rolled, and picked himself up. Wiggles and Jose Manuel rushed over to congratulate him. Hearty pats on the back. David and Layla came over to see if he was okay.

"I'm fine."

"Are you sure?"

"I'm sure, yes. I've fallen much further than that."

Wiggles and Jose Manuel were laughing like crazy. Cal said after that he was ready for a drink. All agreed that Imperial was not the best spot, too close to Cassandra's house. As they began to move toward the Casino, behind them there was a loud crash. Bruno Jr. had thrown the statue after Cal. Because he had to throw with his left arm it didn't even come close. It hit the paving stones a few meters short. There were voices coming from inside the apartment above. The voices were very loud, still Cal could not understand them because everything being shouted was in German.

THIS IS MY BLOOD

Chapter XXVII

Inside the Casino, smoke, noise, people everywhere. Sitting together off to one side of the big room at the front, the usual suspects: Robert, Richard, Marita. With them was an older woman named Senalda del Ponte. Also the young guitarist with dreads who had played with Cal the day before. As Cal and Layla, Wiggles, David and Jose Manuel came swooping in to celebrate "Cal's escape from Liechtenstein," the others waved them over to join them, both parties doubling in size at once.

"DARLINGS," growled Robert, "have a seat. Join us."

Another table pulled close, and chairs gathered.

Something dripping out of Richard's mouth. With abandon, he wiped it away with a sweeping gesture. Whatever it was went flying, hitting a woman carrying two beers from the bar. A tourist, she had no idea where it came from, or what it was.

"Well, isn't this wonderful!" cried Senalda as the others sat.

In her late sixties, she looked like a mother hen surrounded by her chicks. Casual chic, radiating delight toward any and all, Senalda was another *vocal* who had lived in the village for years. Born in Germany, brought to England as a child after *the* war, later she married an Italian, lost him somewhere, and now lived in Spain. Grinning ear-to-ear with white teeth that matched the white hair and long flowing white cotton dress, she stared at the others with *those eyes,* one blue, the other green. *Heterochromia iridium* the doctors call it. And she made sure one couldn't miss them behind bright red-framed Italian glasses. *Look at me* they screamed even as they looked at you. For that and a few other reasons, some of the older women in the village actually suspected her of being a witch, which was nonsense.

"I am so pleased you're here to join us! *Now this really is a party!*"

For added oomph, almost everything Senalda said had an exclamation mark after it.

The guitarist's name was Filip. Richard introduced him. For both twins, despite the little fraying around the edges, grace and fine manners never far off. Introductions mattered.

"From BOHEMIA!"

Filip smiled. "But now we just call it the Czech Republic."

His guitar lay on the floor next to him. Cal told him how much he liked his playing.

"Thanks, man. And I liked your song. Cool lyrics."

"And Cal, you know Senalda of course?" asked Richard.

"My word, yes!" exclaimed Senalda. "We met last year. You were at my home for a dinner with your friend Grisha and his lovely wife. What a wonderful night *that* was. I shall never forget it!"

Marita jumped in. "Now *I* want to say something..." But she forgot what she was going to say.

Layla sat there, as quiet as the others were loud. While Wiggles, David and Jose Manuel took turns telling the story of what had just happened, Cal also said nothing. He was feeling a little bad about Cassandra, and about her party that was more or less ruined toward the end there. As they were telling the part about him jumping from the balcony, he turned to Layla and asked what she wanted to drink.

"And please, don't say chocolate milk."

"All right then. Maybe, an orange juice."

"Are you sure? How about a white wine?"

"I don't drink. Never really liked it. Gives me headaches."

"Alright."

Cal went to the bar. Jose Manuel followed him. They were back in a moment, Cal with two bottles of red wine and an orange juice, and Jose Manuel with his tequila. Everyone was laughing at something Wiggles had just said. He continued.

"...and so of course the show went on, as they must. But now I'll tell you something else. Do you know what Samuel Beckett once said to me?"

"What did Samuel Beckett once say to you?"

"He said, 'Wiggles, would you please bring me a cup of coffee?'"

"No. Did he *really* say that?"

"I swear to you. On my mother's grave."

"And so then you went off, and he was just sitting there waiting for his cup of coffee?"

"Now just a minute, I can see where you're going with this, Cal. But no, I'm sorry, good try, but I do *not* believe that Godot represents a cup of coffee. I mean, can you imagine if Sam had called his play *Waiting for a Cup of Coffee*? What a fucking disaster that would have been!"

"Well I don't know about the rest of you," said Senalda, "but in the morning waiting for my first coffee there is *definitely* an existential crisis at that moment!"

Wiggles stood suddenly and climbed onto his chair. In a booming voice that harked back to his training at RADA, with half the room turning to look at him, he kind-of-sort-of quoted Beckett.

"In the qua qua qua of the Apathia, waiting for my fucking

coffee..."

"Oh-oh! This is how it begins," shouted Jose Manuel. "The revolution! A man gets up on a chair or a horse, starts shouting something, and suddenly everyone is shooting."

"*Don't shoot!*" cried Wiggles, tottering on his chair. "For God's sake, *don't shoot!*"

Marita was choking with laughter.

"Le theatre de la vie dans notre ville!" grinned David.

"Hombre en una silla! Así es como empieza cada revolución!" Jose Manuel yelled to the rest of the room so they would understand what was happening. "The revolution, she is beginning!"

Most just ignored it.

"Well I never!" cried Senalda. "I shall see peace on earth before I see anything so wonderful again as Wiggles reciting Beckett on a chair in the Casino."

Wiggles was about to say more when, shifting too much of his weight onto one side of his chair, he fell backwards crashing onto Filip's guitar.

"Are you alright?"

"Wiggles?"

Wiggles picked himself up.

"Oh God, Filip I'm sorry. I am so sorry. Now look what I've done."

"It's okay, don't worry about it. Really. It was an old guitar."

Filip was too kind to add that he had been given that guitar by his father. He picked the thing up. Beyond repair. The wood in front crushed, the strings slack.

"I'll buy you another guitar."

"It's okay."

"Well then at least let me buy you a drink."

Marita blurted out, "Come on Cal, you're the damned writer.

Make us happy again. Tell us a beautiful story now."

"About?"

"A horse. Tell us a beautiful story about a horse."

Cal thought. One came quickly to mind.

"Alright. Well, I was at my friend Dan's ranch in California..."

Wiggles had pulled his chair upright and was sitting again.

"Go on Cal, tell us. So you were at this fucking ranch and..."

"Old broken down house. We were in the kitchen. We were drinking beer and Dan was rolling a joint from this huge trash bag full of marijuana he had grown himself."

"Well done. This sounds like a very nice story."

"And then suddenly, clippity-clop, clippety-clop, his horse Butternut comes through the living room."

"No!"

"Yes."

"Then what?"

"Well so then Butternut sticks her head through the little window into the kitchen and starts to eat the marijuana. Dan stands there in his cowboy hat and watches her for a minute, and then he says, 'Dang it, Butternut, I told you not to eat my marijuana. If you want to get high, have a drink.'"

Wiggles again. "I just hate that when a horse eats your grass."

"Darling," said Robert, "let him finish."

Layla was watching, listening.

"So Dan takes out a bottle of Jack Daniels. He pours some into his hand and offers it to Butternut. Butternut doesn't know what to do of course. She stands there looking at the pot, then at the whiskey."

"Well that's a very difficult decision. And making a horse decide like that, that's cruelty to animals if you ask me."

"Butternut decides to have the drink. She swings her head

over and starts slurping up the Jack."

"Good girl, Butternut! There's a horse after my own heart."

"So then of course Dan and I, well, we had a couple of shots too."

"As you would."

"And then I said to Dan, 'Dan, I think I'd like to ride Butternut.'"

Senalda's hands shot up in a praying gesture. "Oh no! Dear God! You didn't!"

"So we go outside. Dan put a fistful of the pot in his hand so the horse would follow him out of the house."

"That's the way to do it. I'd follow him too."

"He leads her over to the barn and saddles her up. And then I get on her, and we take off at a gallop through this pumpkin field. And so we're flying along then at a full run, and I'm whooping and hollering, and Dan's watching us, laughing his ass off, and suddenly Butternut trips in a gopher hole."

"Oh no!"

"What happened?"

"Well...this is not the funniest part of the story."

"What happened?"

"She broke her leg. Dan had to shoot her."

Senalda put her hand over her mouth.

"That poor horse."

Everyone fell quiet. Cal looked around.

"I told you it wasn't the funniest part of the story. I mean, it wasn't supposed to end that way."

"Don't you know any funnier stories than that?" asked Wiggles. "Because really, Cal, that isn't very funny."

Layla stood up and said that she had to go.

"It's late. I'm sorry. I'm tired, and in the morning I have to go to Figueres to buy some fabrics."

"Are you sure?" asked Cal. He offered to walk her home.

"That's okay, really. Good night, everyone."

Cal and the others watched her go.

"Looks like your angel is flying off, Cal."

"Come on," said Marita. "Don't you know any funnier stories than that?"

Chapter XXVIII

The next day, a late start as usual. The list of people Cal needed to avoid had grown. Bruno Jr. of course, the parents, Cassandra herself, Herr What's-his-name and the other Herrs. In a small village no place to hide really, so better to just charge ahead and get it over with, whatever *it* was. Layla had gone to Figureres for the day, so no hope of seeing her. Cal didn't really know where he was heading. He was just heading there anyway.

Passing by the Casino he saw Marita standing inside at the bar. She was leaning over. Some man Cal didn't recognize had his arm around her. It looked like she was crying. Cal went in. There was a strange mood at the bar. People seemed just to be shuffling about. One older man stood staring at the floor, shaking his head. Marita was hunched over. Cal went to her.

"Marita, what's wrong?"

She looked up at him. Her eyes were swollen red from crying.

"What is it?"

It took her a moment.

"Jose Manuel."

"What about him?"

She couldn't bring herself to say it. Someone else said it.

"Dead."

"*What?*"

"Last night."

"You're joking."

Such a stupid thing to say. Why do people say that?

"How?"

An old woman said something in Catalan. Someone else said, "Auto. Auto."

Cal looked around. One of the twins was sitting alone at a table in a corner. Richard. He walked over to him.

"Richard, what happened?"

"Jose Manuel. He died, yes."

"That's impossible."

Richard nodded. "But it happened, hmm."

"How?"

"Accident. On the mountain. Damn pity, eh? They found him this morning. Jorge, from the Boia, saw the skid marks and the rail gone. Looked over the edge, saw the car. Jose Manuel still inside it. Damned pity, eh?"

"But when? Last night?"

"Hmm. About three in the morning must have been. Mas o menos. He told Wiggles he was heading over to one of the bordellos in Roses. Asked him if he wanted to go. Wiggles said he didn't have any money, so looks like Jose Manuel, well, just decided to go on his own. Never made it though, eh? Shame. Good man, that. Damned good man. Good friend. We'll miss him."

There were people moving around the Casino. Those who didn't know about it sounded as they would any day, holiday makers laughing, talking. Those who did know just sat or stood quietly.

Cal looked over at the tables where they been sitting together the night before. Only a few hours earlier Jose Manuel was *right there*, twirling his black mustache, with those wide smart eyes of his so full of mischief. Joking about revolution. All of them laughing, until Cal had told that stupid story about the poor horse.

He had to remember to stop telling that, or else invent a different ending. It was funny up until the ending. And now Jose Manuel was gone, dead forever. That was the problem with death. It lasted so long. *Fuck!*

Marita was sobbing still. There were more people around her now. They had been friends so long, those two. Cal wanted to go to her but decided not to. He'd stay with Richard. Maybe have a drink, a glass of wine. Or better yet a tequila in Jose Manuel's honor. No. Better to have nothing, considering what had happened, and why. So he sat there drinking nothing for some moments. Richard rolled and lit a cigarette, then stood to go to the bar.

"Tinto?" he asked Cal.

"No thank you." He changed his mind. "Well, actually..."

"Right."

Richard ordered from Miguel, then turned to Marita and patted her on the back. He said something to her. She nodded.

Nothing to do about it.

Cal looked around the room, remembering now a conversation he had had with David and Grisha the summer before. They had been sitting in David's studio drinking a bottle of old port. It was evening and there was a candle on a table, and for some reason the conversation turned to death.

"It's a stupid system. You know what I'd suggest?"

"What would you suggest, Cal?"

"I'd suggest that death last, let's say, a thousand years. You go off, you rest a bit, recharge the batteries, and then you come back. Because forever is definitely too long."

"And where do you go to make this suggestion?" asked Grisha. It was a pointed question. Grisha "had" religion. Cal did not.

"I don't know where I'd go."

"And what about your loved ones? They come back, too?"

Cal was thinking on his feet, as if it was a real proposal that someone somewhere would take seriously.

"Well, actually, that would be like the difference between heaven and hell. If you'd been good, you'd get to say who else comes back. All the people you love, care about, like even. But if you'd been bad, the ones you *don't* care about come back. And you're stuck with them forever, or at least every thousand years or so. 'Oh no, *you* again!'"

Cal knew that his friend believed in Paradise, and so for him the idea would be no improvement over the existing system. And David believed in reincarnation. So it was only Cal, with his death-is-a-bummer, we-go-as-the-vegetables-go, no-gods-but-the-ones-we-make modernism who really wanted to change the rules.

Richard was back with two glasses of wine. He sat. Neither said much. Others came in who had heard the news or were hearing it now. When Cal finished his wine he stood to go.

"See you later, Richard."

"God willing, hmm? Should be here. Not going anywhere. My brother'll be along soon."

As Cal was heading toward the door, he saw Tharrats sitting in a far corner with another man. He went to him. Had he heard? Yes. In Spanish, an exchange of kind words about Jose Manuel. Then Tharrats mentioned Cal's book.

"My daughter read it. And she loved it."

"Really?"

"And so Cal, if you still want, I would like to publish it."

As he left the Casino, Cal didn't know what to feel. Happy about the book, so sad about Jose Manuel. All he could do was walk, and to keep walking for a long time.

Chapter XXIX

Only sadness in the usual places. The same words being said that wouldn't change a damn thing. And to make it worse, still no sight of Layla. Cal wanted to apologize to her for that stupid story about the horse, and explain to her...whatever.

No good waiting for her at Imperial, because the balcony doors were open at Cassandra's and he would be more likely to see one of *them*. Finally he went to Paul's restaurant. He was told Paul was in Figueres until the next day and that she was with him.

Enough with people. A quick trip to the store, then home to pack. He would take the rest of the day alone to think. A block of goat cheese, some nice *jamon iberico de bellota*, olives, bread, a few of the hot red chili peppers he always travelled with, and a bota bag full of water. Cal decided that for the rest of this day he would keep a clear mind and not drink alcohol or smoke pot. Still, he packed a bottle of wine, a corkscrew, two joints and some matches just in case he might change his mind. His journal, two pens, the Brautigan, knife...set to go. His little daypack slung over his shoulder, he made his way past the two hotels Llane Petit and Rocamar, down toward the beach Sa Conca, then up the little road that morphed into the trail that led out to the lighthouse.

The old lighthouse Cala Nans sat on the rocky point at the entrance to the bay. Cal had always wanted to go to it. It would be a fine place to look back at the village or out to sea and think. Or feel. He hadn't figured out yet if those two things were different, thinking and feeling. Two sides of the same coin probably. He'd go out to the lighthouse now and toss that coin, and just see which side came up most.

Poor Jose Manuel...His book was going to be published... Layla. Thoughts, feelings, twisting like the road, he kept climbing.

There was a cactus with broad leaves on the side of the path. Some people had carved their initials or names on it. *C.B...Argo... Teo loves Dolores.* Their bid for immortality. Good luck. There were pine trees laden with small cones in their own bid for immortality. In the end everyone wanted the same thing: no end. Some sought that by trying to delay the inevitable, popping vitamins, eating their bio yoghurts, trying to bench press and crunch a few more years into their story. Others painted paintings or wrote books they hoped would last, or cloned children. The lucky ones like Grisha were even convinced death was just a bridge to some sweet forever on the other side. But if that was so, why all the glum when someone died? Nobody seemed too happy now about Jose Manuel. They were acting like it was a *bad* thing. If you believed those stories, he hadn't passed away, he had passed *over*. Yipee!

The road narrowing, Cal kept climbing, his body busy while the mind did the real work.

Maybe that was the bond between a writer and his readers. That we are all stuck together here on the Titanic, we know that iceberg is ahead and we are hurtling toward it, and that knowing it makes no fucking difference because there is not a chance in the world to divert. The writer describes or the artist paints the deckchairs, or the waves on the sea, or the faces of the passengers, and others buy that book or painting and stare at it like one stares at an accident beside the road. That could be me, we think, because of course one day it will be.

We do stuff then die. The whole story in just five words! A pronoun, verb, noun, adverb, then one more little verb. Comedy is shorter still, only the first three words needed. No comedy this day, though. Now suddenly Jose Manuel was as dead as any of them. You can't get much deader than that. Dead like a professional. The expert dead.

Cal had started once to write an essay he called *The Theatre of Help*. Like so many other projects he hadn't finished it, but he figured it was a good idea and one day probably he would get back to it. He had been to see some play in Berlin when he was visiting Grisha and Elsa. The play was dank, depressing, gray people on a gray stage saying depressing things. He left the theatre feeling completely deflated. Then he had this idea. He wanted theatre, books, paintings, any art to *help* him. Life isn't just about death of course, it's about all the stuff before it. Still, a lot *did* connect to death, and he wanted help. To understand it, to confront it, to ignore it (*that* was always helpful!) and also just to know that he was not alone in fearing it. What fear Jose Manuel had to have felt as that car was going over the abyss. No way he could be happy about it.

After a few last scattered houses set into the hillside, the road roughened into a narrow path. Trees, scrub, dry grass and rocks marked the furthest edge of the village. The natural world trumped the manmade now. Still, just beyond another bend were two stone outposts extending both the good and evil of man into the wild. A goatherd's hut, disused and long collapsed, conjured images of slow moving bucolic days when the line between people and nature was less clearly marked. And not far from it, on the edge of the hill overlooking the village and the little bay below, were the stubborn remnants of a gun battery left over from the civil war. A trench had been dug into the earth, a concrete wall poured with sight holes for the riflemen and two rounded enclosures for the big guns. Looking at it from the side of the sea, by those being shot at, it would have looked like nothing more than just the hill. The earth itself armed. Men had been firing from there at other men just sixty years earlier. Because the wild is within man as well as without.

Cal stood close to that gun emplacement looking down at the church and white houses and the blue water that on this day looked so peaceful. He could hear bells from Santa Maria. He counted. ...five, six, seven o'clock. On Sunday mornings those same bells would ring more urgently. It would be God phoning, calling the faithful to prayer.

A seagull landed on some rocks nearby and started to laugh. That's what it sounded like anyway. A second gull flew down to join him and together now it sounded like cackling laughter in a madhouse. Seagulls can sound like hyenas, or cats in heat, or braying mules, or madmen laughing, but only a madman would describe it as "birdsong."

The trail leveled out now, and there was a man running toward him. He was a big man with a long beard and long hair and he had no shirt on. He wore old shorts and had a big stomach and he was jogging, and as this bear of a man ran toward and past Cal he didn't even look at him, just kept running. Cal watched him until he disappeared.

The lighthouse was maybe half an hour away. It was hot. Cal was sweating and there were flies buzzing around him and he kept walking through the flies. One fly got sucked into his mouth. His tongue probed to find it and he spit it out. *Bad news for us both,* thought Cal. He tried imagining it from the fly's perspective. One minute you're flying around with your fellow flies happy enough, then suddenly you're in some guy's mouth getting spit out. The Jose Manuel story with wings.

There was a pine tree just above the path. He climbed up to it now and sat in its shade. He kept thinking about stuff and wanted to write about it in his journal. But first, maybe he'd open that bottle of wine.

No. Not this day. Keep a clear mind. Okay. Good boy.

He opened his journal and began to write. He wrote about wanting to open that bottle.

Then he tried to think about Layla, and about his book being published, but his mind kept coming back to Jose Manuel. It was like that old children's game of rock, scissors, paper. Death trumped. And then he remembered that shooting star he had seen while swimming. That meteoroid was long gone, and yet here he was still remembering it. Just like he was remembering Jose Manuel. He decided to write a poem now for his fallen friend. Another sonnet. Some trial and error, scratching this out, adding that, and finally he had the first quatrain:

As a shooting star are we today
Within eye's sight but for briefest time
And though we would we cannot stay
Yet we can always linger in your mind...

Four lines down, ten to go. He was thirsty now.

Come on, open that bottle. No, don't do it. Okay I won't. Good boy. Maybe just smoke one of those joints then. Don't do that either. You don't need it. Okay. Good boy, I'm proud of you. This is stupid. You brought it all the way up here. Some say wine is even good for you. The French, for instance, and they live forever. It's good for the heart and has all those anti-oxidants. Fuck it.

There it was, the winning argument. *Fuck it!*

Cork out, wine in. And as long as he was drinking, he torched one of the two joints he had brought. Death floated away, taking its ugly-ass dark hooded skull face with it. Instead, the face and body and smell of Layla, the breeze in the pine tree above him, the warm air, the orange sun setting over the Mediterranean, all that was good in the world now wrapped its sweet arms around him.

He did not finish his poem that day. And he did not make it out to the lighthouse. He decided that it would be better to do that some other day when he could get an earlier start. Maybe with Layla. He leaned back and finished the bottle, imagining what he would do with fame and fortune in case his book became popular. He ate the food he had brought, and also smoked that second joint. And then, as one by one the stars were appearing overhead, and with the lights from the village twinkling below, like Sysyphus Cal made his way back down the hill.

Chapter XXX

The following day, across from the Meliton in the bright sun, some children were kicking a red plastic ball on the beach.
"But did it really happen like that?" asked Layla.
"It did, yes. But that was a long time ago. And it taught me a huge lesson. I'm sorry for the horse."
"Butternut."
"Yes. I'm sorry for Butternut. All I can say is I'd never do anything like that now. I mean, get a horse..."
"Drunk."
"Yes."
"And stoned."
"And stoned, yes. I wasn't thinking."
"That poor horse."
"Yes."
A waiter came to them. She ordered her usual.
"You know, I think I'll try one of those too. I used to love chocolate milk when I was a kid."
"Really?"
"Really. They couldn't get me to drink regular milk, but the chocolate milk, I loved it."
As the waiter left, he told her the news about his book.
"Hey, congratulations! How wonderful. You must be so thrilled."
"I am."

"I'd love to read it."

There were two kinds of people in Cal's world. She had just joined the much smaller group.

"I'll get the manuscript back from Tharrats."

She was watching the children. The waiter brought the two chocolate milks. He tried his.

"Wow, that's delicious."

"That's so sad about Jose Manuel. I wish I had known him better. Were you two very close?"

"Not really. I only met him last week at a party at a friend's house."

"So full of fun, yes?"

"Yes."

"And his funeral?"

"Thursday."

"It's so sad."

One of the children on the beach had hurt herself, stubbed a toe or something, and was crying.

"Like flowers really, aren't they?"

"How do you mean?"

"Well, despite all that energy, so delicate still. They need enough of anything, but not too much. Get it right and they're the most beautiful things in the world."

"Absolulely."

"I suppose the only thing you can't give them too much of is love."

Chapter XXXI

The clock on the church tower read two o'clock. No bells at this late hour though, only the sound of the water as Cal sat alone smoking next to the old wooden wine press overlooking Port Alguer. Across the little cove was the bookshop beside the three arches.

He was too excited to sleep. Tharrats had given him back the manuscript and he had brought it to Layla. It was a small book and she said that she would read it that same night. They would have lunch together the next day, and he would hear then what she thought of it.

There were no people anywhere now, only the peace of this moment as his mind moved with the water. Wave after small wave onto the beach then back again, like a metronome. Lay-la...

She wasn't just one of those party girls, spending her beauty and youth like there would be no end to those, on the beach, or at nights flitting from one good time to the next. A yellow smiley-face instead of the Mona Lisa. With so little to show for it all years later, maybe a photograph or two. Not this one.

Everyone's feelings ran deep. You could hurt a person easily, or bring them to anger, or make them smile. But in her case there were more than feelings, there were ideas there. The three L's. She looked, listened, learned. And then when she spoke you didn't want to miss a word. What she had said about children needing love. Cal tried now to think of something smarter than that, but couldn't. So simple, like a plumb line. He even liked the fact that she drank chocolate milk and orange juice. He could take care of all the other stuff for the both of them.

He listened to the water a while longer but still wasn't tired. Finally he decided he could not sleep here, or he could go back to the house and not sleep in his bed. He decided to go not sleep in his bed.

Chapter XXXII

He had not fallen asleep until it was light out, and then he had overslept. Now it was already past one, and he was late.

Layla had suggested they meet for lunch not in the center of the village, but "somewhere a little quieter" where they would be able to talk about his book. He mentioned the little *chiringuito* out beyond the point, and she had said it sounded perfect. Now he was walking as fast as he could, almost running. Hurrying by Imperial he glanced up and quickly saw that the doors to Cassandra's balconies were shuttered closed. Maybe it meant they had left Cadaqués. Great. He was about to keep on when he heard shouting. It was a familiar voice, one of the twins.

"Why don't you just shut up!"

Then someone else yelled, "Don't you fucking tell me to shut up!"

An angry dog was barking. Cal stopped and looked. On the terrace in front of Imperial either Robert or Richard, he couldn't tell at this distance, was standing next to a man in a blue and red shirt sitting at one of the tables. Cal had seen the man before but did not know who he was. He turned and walked toward them.

"Well then just stop it, do you hear? Just *stop* it! He was our friend."

It was Robert.

The man sitting had long red hair and a thin red beard. His dog, still barking, was tied to his chair with a short leash. Wiggles was sitting at the next table over. The man was leaning past Robert, trying to explain to Wiggles the difference between the Catholic and the Protestant churches.

"It's all bullshit, man. All of it. Like some fucking theatre, man. You know why they're going to bury your friend? So they can make some fucking money from it. That's what they do. Squeeze every fucking peseta they can out of you, even when you're dead. And you know the difference between the Protestant church and the Catholic?"

Wiggles didn't want to hear about it. "Look, I..."

"I'll tell you the difference. At least in the Catholic church you get forgiven for your sins. But they charge you for it, man. They fucking charge you for it. It's fucking medieval, man. You still have to pay to get forgiven for your sins, and it's not cheap. And your friend there, what was his name? Jose Manuel? He was driving to a whorehouse, right? I heard about it." He laughed. "So probably he's got a lot of sins to pay for. But now his family's going to have to pay for them, so he can get forgiven. And man, they're going to charge for that."

It wasn't a German accent, but something like it. Later Cal would learn the guy came from Basel in Switzerland. Called himself Tor. Another "vocal." Cal would also learn that he sold drugs for a living. Anything to anyone. Cal hated drugs, except for the ones he loved. Nobody ever behaved like that on mushrooms, or after smoking. Drink, maybe, but still...this guy had something else in his blood. You could tell by the way he was twitching.

"Look," said Wiggles, "can you just be quiet please? Have a little respect."

"*Respect!*" The guy was spitting out his mouth. Cal stood at the edge of the terrace watching this. "I don't have any fucking respect, man. For that fucking church? Are you kidding? When my time comes, just throw me to the fish, man."

The dog was going nuts. Jose, the owner of the bar, told the guy to leave but he wasn't moving.

"Go on," said Robert, tottering over him. "Just *go*! Can't you see you're not wanted here?"

"Look, that was our friend," added Wiggles. He sounded so reasonable. "So please, if you'd just..."

"Fuck your friend, man! And fuck that church!"

Wiggles stood up. The guy stood up. The dog was showing its teeth. It was an ugly brown dog.

"Yeah, you want something? Come on, man! I'll fucking give it to you."

Poor Wiggles. Poor Robert. Both wanted to defend the good name of their dead friend, but how to do it against this coked-up asshole and his rabid looking wonder dog?

Super Cal. All he needed was a phone booth and a cape. He shouted, "Yo!" as he charged toward the guy. The guy looked over, as if at cavalry reinforcements appearing suddenly on his right flank.

It was a great system really. How many fights had Cal avoided over the years by just looking like he would love it?

Only this time it didn't work. Tor pushed the table out of his way. His bottle of beer and glass fell to the ground, the glass breaking. But then suddenly he froze. Cal figured he had frightened him, which felt great. But then he noticed the guy was looking off in the distance over Cal's shoulder. He turned and looked. There was a police car driving past slowly, the regular patrol through the village. Tor didn't need any attention there.

"Okay, man. No trouble. Just a misunderstanding, all right. No trouble."

He took his dog and left, down into and up along the riverbed.

He kept looking behind him, like that lawyer Clark in New York.

And he hadn't paid for his beer.

The guys were still standing there.

"Well, that was very kind of you, Cal. Really. But Robert and I, we could have handled that."

"No, Wiggles. I'm the only one who gets to fight you."

"Well alright, if you say so."

The owner of the bar smiled at Cal. Someone else started to laugh. Then they were all laughing. For such a peaceful little village...

Suddenly Cal remembered Layla.

"Oh *shit*! What time is it?"

"Ten minutes before two."

Without another word, Cal rushed off, running as fast as he could across the passeig. He flew past the Blue House, and was about to head up the hill toward the point when there she was, Layla, walking toward him. She had his manuscript in her hand. He stopped. He was sweating and breathing hard.

"Sorry. I'm so sorry I'm late."

"No worries."

"I have this alter-ego, Super Cal, and..."

He told her what happened.

"Well, it sounds like you did the right thing."

"I tried. I really tried."

Lemonade out of lemons.

His breathing settled down. Then he told her about his brother.

"When we were kids, I had him convinced I was Super Boy. We'd be standing there talking and suddenly I'd say, 'Did you hear that?' He'd say, 'Hear what?' Then I'd say, 'Oh, of course you couldn't hear it. You don't have super hearing. Wait a minute,

I'll be right back.' Then I'd wait just a second and say, 'Okay, I'm back.' I'd tell him how I'd just flown around the world and saved some girl from some bad guy. My brother was about five or six, and he really believed me. Later, when he learned I wasn't really Super Boy, I think it traumatized him. And I've been disappointing him ever since."

"Everyone needs heroes. With or without super hearing."

They were standing in front of the house where Picasso had lived.

"Do you know what Picasso's real name was?"

"No," said Cal. "What?"

"Pablo Diego José Francisco de Paula Juan Nepomuceno Maria de los Remedios Cipriano de la Santisima Trinidad Ruiz y Picasso."

"Okay. No wonder he wanted to break things up. Imagine his mother calling him in to lunch by that."

"By the time she got it out, it would be time for dinner."

It was just silly talk. Good, fun silly talk.

Did she still want to have lunch? No, she had eaten something finally while waiting for him. The Meliton was close to where they were standing.

"Then how about just a drink at Meliton?"

"Sure."

She was wearing a white transparent blouse with a black bikini under it. As they walked, his peripheral vision kept taking it in. They sat on the same terrace as they had the day before, facing the sea.

"It's kind of turning into our place, isn't it?"

She smiled *that* smile.

His manuscript was on the table.

"I loved it."

"Really?"

"The way you described how it was. How it is. It's always hard, isn't it, going from 'then' to 'now.'"

"Can be."

"And what they're being asked to give up. Of course someday it could all go horribly wrong and we could be right back where they are, growing our own food, scratching a living off the land."

"The old man doesn't think it's scratching. He loves it."

"Well, that's the other thing. It's all in how one looks at the world. One person's refuse, another's treasure."

"Exactly."

"Anyway, I really feel for them all. The young mother dreaming about electricity and having a washing machine. The poor husband having to decide. I like the way you show each side of it. Rashomon."

"Thanks."

The waiter came. The *Cacaolat* for her.

"Well, it's either the chocolate milk again," said Cal, "or a beer." He pretended to think about it, then in Spanish he said, "I think today I'll go with the beer."

The waiter left. They sat for a moment saying nothing.

Then, "Why nineteenth century?" he asked.

"You mean, literature?"

"Yes."

She thought a moment.

"Well, our house was Victorian. I suppose that had something to do with it. Great, big, scary looking thing, though I loved it. Lots of fine places to hide. And then *Alice in Wonderland* and *Looking Glass*, those were my favorite stories as a child. *Tales from Shakespeare,* by the Lambs. *Christmas Carol* of course, doing the right thing in the end. Then oddly enough, *Count of Monte Cristo*."

"Did your father read you that one?"

"No. No he didn't. But the book did belong to him. I found it on a shelf and just read it by myself."

The waiter brought their drinks.

"And Melville?"

"Well, that came later of course. But there were others in the meantime. *Doll's House* by Ibsen, I suppose that *really* got me going. I was thirteen when I read that. A very impressionable age. Nora, the role of women in society, sorting out I suppose who you really are, who you want to be. Going off to find that out. That sort of thing."

"You were a precocious thirteen year old."

"Well, in some ways I suppose. In others, perhaps not."

She looked off in the distance a moment, then back at him.

"And then I came here to Cadaqués one summer with my mother. I was fifteen then. There were all those stories about Gala, another strong woman. And I heard some people talking about the Modernists. I asked somebody what made them so modern, and the man I asked, a friend of my mother's, he told me it was a lot of nonsense really, because people had always considered themselves modern, and had always been trying new things."

"Yes, but it was a new brand of modern."

"As it always is. Now you have 'Post-modern.' What's next, 'Post-Post'? And then, 'Post-Post-Post'? How long can they keep that up?"

"Well but after the war, big industry, loss of faith, the absurdity of it all..."

"But the world's *always* been absurd, hasn't it? So much of it, anyway. That didn't start just one lifetime ago. Love failing, families failing, minds failing. I mean read Büchner's *Woyzeck*, for God's sake. And as for lack of faith, again nineteenth century, too many freethinkers to count. And you already had your industrial revolution. I mean, *gunpowder*, let's go back to that if we want to point to a time when a man or woman couldn't hide behind a wall even and feel themselves safe."

"You're right. And so then..."

"So then back to school after that summer, to Queen Margaret's in York. And I began to see my mother's friend was right. I mean, William Blake goes back to the eighteenth century even. Have you seen his paintings?"

"A few. Not many."

"Well, they're as modern as anything if you ask me. And his poems?"

"Incredible."

"Mary Wollstonecraft, also very early. Her daughter, Mary Shelley. That was another one of my father's books I read, *Frankenstein*. It frightened me of course, but I loved it. And then my favorite of all, Acton Bell."

"Is that a title or the author?"

"Author."

"Never heard of him."

"'He's' a she, actually. Anne Bronte. Her book, *The Tenant of Wildfell Hall*, well I have to say that one touched me deeply."

The waiter was walking past. Cal asked him to bring another beer.

"And there were so many other fine women writers of that period. Dickenson, George Eliot. No, for me the nineteenth century felt something like a neglected child, or puppy. And I fell in love with it as one would with those." She was getting excited now. "I mean, jump ahead just a bit and, same century, already

225

you have Rimbaud, Jarry with his pataphysics, Freud no less." Cal sat there just watching her. "What is it Robert always says, 'The flower has roots'? So I guess after all the mad talk here and everywhere about the twentieth century, I wanted to dig a bit deeper, that's all."

The waiter brought Cal's beer.

"And, so who are some of *your* favorite writers?" she asked.

Cal thought. Of all the writers she had mentioned, he had read just a few. He had basically drunk, smoked, screwed, snorted his way through high school, later playing what catch-up he could. To say there were holes in his education was like saying there was some water in the sea. He might be the writer, but it was clear that she had read as much, and probably much more, than he had. So he did what he always did at moments like this, steered it back to the few writers he did know.

"Well, Hemingway probably had the biggest impact on me. Brautigan, Kerouac, Cervantes. Eliot, Joyce, Kesey..." He had read *Lolita*. "...Nabokov, Beckett, David Foster Wallace, Steinbeck..."

He was trying desperately to think of a woman writer he had read.

"...Harper Lee..."

"Did you read *East of Eden*?"

"No. That one I didn't."

"Did you see the film, with James Dean?"

"I don't think so, no."

"So you don't know the name of the main character?"

"No."

"Cal."

"You're kidding."

"Cal."

"I thought I was the only one."

He was about to say something about Gertrude Stein and Virginia Wolf, when trundling toward them across the passeig, Paul. Coming closer with arched eyebrows, those rat eyes making a fast and unhappy appraisal.

"Ah, so *there* you are! Hiding out in the open. Clever strategy. And I see the fox is with you."

"What are you on about, darling?"

"The way he's looking at you. Like a fox looks at a chicken. Stop staring at her breasts."

"*Paul!*"

"I'm not staring at her breasts. I was before you came, but I'm not now."

"Darling, don't be so rude. Forgive him. He's incorrigible."

"Do *not*, repeat, do *not* apologize for me. I have nothing in the world to apologize for."

He plunked himself down. The waiter came over. In English, Paul said, "Nothing." The waiter turned to go. "On second thought..." He called him back. "Give me a diet cola, no ice." The waiter left.

"Now, what are you two plotting?"

"We're not plotting anything. Don't be so paranoid."

"I am not paranoid. I'm a realist."

"We're just talking about Cal's book."

"What book?"

She pointed to it on the table.

"This one. It's about to be published."

"Is it really. And, what's it about? A fox and a chicken?"

She laughed. "No, it's about..." She told him the story.

"How fucking ridiculous. What does he know about living on a farm in Spain?"

"Well, you can ask him. He's sitting right here."

"All right." Paul looked at Cal. "So tell me, what the fuck do you know about living on a farm in Spain? Are you Spanish?"

"No."

"Are you a farmer?"

"No."

Paul turned to Layla. "And you've read this?"

"Yes."

"I don't like the sound of this at all."

"You're just jealous."

"*Jealous*! Of *what*? Why should *I* be jealous of *him*?"

"Because you've always said you wanted to write a book, and you haven't. Yet."

"Look, if I wanted to write a book, I'd do it. And it would be about a foolish young girl who doesn't know what the fuck she's talking about."

Layla smiled and shrugged and looked at Cal. Water off a duck's back. The waiter brought Paul's diet cola.

"If anyone's jealous, it's him. Because I have more money than this...whatever he is...will put together in his whole pathetic lifetime."

"What does *that* have to do with anything?"

"Oh for God's sake, be practical."

"Stop being so rude."

"Why should I? Give me one good reason."

"Because I like him."

"*Will you please stop saying that!*"

"Why?"

"Because I *don't* like him."

"*Why* don't you like him?"

"Because I don't. Does one need a reason not to like a

person?"

"Yes!"

"Well then, I don't like him because…"

"Because I do, is that it?"

"Now *stop* this!"

"No. I want to understand."

"How *can* you understand. You don't understand a damned thing."

Cal jumped into the game now. "Paul, talk to her with some respect."

"*You* stay out of this."

"But this was *about* me."

"This was *not* about you. Why must you think everything is about you?"

"Paul, he's just trying to..."

"Let me finish. This is not about him. This is about you liking people before you have any good reason to like them."

"But you just said…"

"I just said what?"

"You just said you don't even need a reason *not* to like a person."

"That's right."

"So why should I need a reason *to* like a person?"

"Oh for god's sake, this is stupid. Neither of you has a clue."

"Clue to what?"

"To anything at all!"

"Bolbibogue," said Cal.

"What? What did you say?"

"Nothing."

Paul's face was red now, and for the first time the little smile was gone. He pointed a finger across the table at Cal.

"Look, I am *richer* than you, I am *smarter* than you, I am *wiser* than you..."

"You mentioned that last time."

"But obviously you didn't absorb the lesson."

"Paul, please, you're getting yourself all excited over nothing."

"It's *not* nothing. Just because you're too stupid to see what's going on here..."

"Don't talk to her like that."

"He's right. Don't talk to me like that."

"'Stupid' is a strong word, Paul. Only fools use it lightly."

"I've had enough of this. I'm going."

Paul stood up, paused, then sat down again.

"No. What am I doing? I'm not going. That's exactly what you two want, isn't it? Well fuck you! I'm staying right here."

Layla reached for his hand. He pulled it out of reach.

"Look, I'll be dead in three months. Just wait for it, and then you can charm her all you want with your little stories once I'm gone."

"You're dying?"

"Yes, of course I'm dying. We're all dying. I'm just going to do it a bit faster than you, that's all."

Layla rolled her eyes.

"Look," said Paul, the smile back, "do you know why you like to write? I'll tell you why you like to write. Because as a writer you can manipulate situations."

It was the first smart thing Cal had heard him say.

"Well, this here is one situation you're *not* going to manipulate. Because this is not some story, this is *life*."

"What on earth are you talking about?" asked Layla.

"Look, don't you see what this is all about? It's not about some damned book. He's trying to charm you. It's disgusting.

He doesn't know his place. And at my age I have seen this far too often. Everything is fine. Then someone gets it into their head that it's not fine. And then guess what...it's *not* fine. Well I have news for you. Right here, right now in Cadaqués, everything is just fine. You are not going to upset the perfect order of our world, and that's all there is to it."

"For God's sake," said Layla, "we were only talking about his *book*. No one is trying to..."

"Of *course* he is!"

"Look, Paul..."

The little pink rat eyes were glaring at Cal.

"Go on, get out of here! Do you hear me? Take your fucking little book and clear away from us!"

"Paul, if he goes now then I'm going also." Layla turned to Cal. "He doesn't mean any of it. He hasn't had his nap, that's all. He gets a bit crotchety if he..."

"*Fuck* you! Fuck *both* of you!"

Paul stood up. He looked at Layla who stayed sitting.

"Are you coming with me, or aren't you?"

"No, I'm not coming with you. Be reasonable."

He waited a second. She didn't move. He stormed off. But only for a few feet. Then he turned, came back, and slammed some coins from his pocket onto the table.

"There! I won't have this idiot paying for my drink!"

Then off he went. They watched him. He seemed lost. Started to walk one way, turned, then walked another, huffing and puffing his way across the passeig until he was out of sight.

"I don't know what's wrong with him. I really don't. He's been getting so excited lately. It's not good for him. He's already had two heart attacks."

Chapter XXXIII

"I should go check on him, really. See how he's doing."

Cal paid the bill, and left Paul's coins on the table for the waiter.

He would walk her as far as the Casino. From there she would head alone up into the old part of the village toward Paul's restaurant, which was called *Paradisio*.

As they walked slowly, neither saying anything, they passed by the statue of Dali that stood at the edge of the beach. Cal looked up at it.

The village was his now. The artist's body had left it, but his spirit hung over the place like a night sky. Every bit of madness or beauty, every act of invention or whimsy, every confusion or certainty, reverence or denial, for a thousand years would bear his imprimatur and unfold under his watchful gaze. The great painter had remained childless, yet the village now was peopled by his adopted sucklings, his in all but name. They had adopted each other. And soon even the oldest ones would be ever younger than he.

Outside the Casino, Layla turned toward Cal. Kisses on both cheeks.

"Congratulations again about your book."

"Thanks."

"What's a 'bolbigogue'?"

He told her.

She smiled. "I thought so."

As soon as she was gone, Cal headed inside the Casino.

Sitting to one side, as much a part of the place as the tables and chairs, the twins of course, Wiggles again, and Filip with a new old guitar in his lap, a cheap looking red thing. Also there were two young ladies, twenty-somethings, sitting with them. Very pretty. And another young man. Waves, welcoming smiles.

On the other side of the big room, sharing their own table, Senalda was sitting with two other women. Those three also waved at Cal. For a moment he stood like a donkey equidistant between two bales of hay. Then he walked toward the women.

"Ladies. Double double toil and trouble?"

"Non," said one of the women, "don't tell me we look like witches?"

That from Vivienne, who looked like anything but. A great beauty then, now, and forever. With her French accent and French curves and French sparkle in the eyes, a big kitten. Anything she ever did or said suggested sex, no matter that a few years had slipped by. She could still pick fish bones from her mouth in a way that would give any half-healthy man an erection. Over the years in Cadaqués, going back to its "glory days" in the mad seventies, she had left a string of broken hearts like stones on the paths. She stepped over them every day with a barely-muffled laugh.

Next to her sat Chasey, American. Her piled mass of dark hair was so thick a stork could nest in it without her knowing. She looked at Cal with eyes so blue. He had only seen that color once before, in one of Grisha's paintings. They had met, he and Chasey, not here in Cadaqués but in New York years earlier at a party on the roof of the Chelsea Hotel. Grisha had been there also. And then one day last summer, when Cal and Grisha were walking together near the passeig, a voice by the Boia had called out to them in a New York accent, "Hey, you two!" And then they just picked up where they had left off, as if that party at the Chelsea had never ended.

Rounding out the circle here, Senalda. The blue eye, the green eye, those white teeth grinning. Today she wore a loose linen smock, olive green, with a light yellow scarf. The three women were sharing a bottle of Veuve Clicquot.

"Ladies."

"Hello Cal."

"Won't you join us?"

Cal sat. A few niceties. Then, women's intuition.

"What's the matter?"

"Yes, what's wrong?"

"I'll make a deal with you," said Cal, looking at all three. "I'll pay for that champagne you're drinking, if you can please explain to me why the fuck Layla von Leda is with..."

He didn't even get to finish the sentence.

"...that old fart?" asked Senalda.

"Yes."

"Ah! Well..."

The three women looked at each other. Cal would have to pay for the champagne.

"First off," said Vivienne, sounding French in more ways than one, "I completely understand it. Some people have the sexual appetites different than the others. For instance, they are fascinated by the, how do you say, 'prosthetics?' The false body parts. Or else they enjoy maybe the fat people? Or someone from their own sex?"

"Or S and M," added Chasey.

"Or S and M, of course, I forgot it. Paul, he has the artificial teeth, yes? Who knows, maybe when she sees those in the glass at night, maybe that excites her."

Chasey shook her head. "No, that's not it. At least I don't believe that's it. Do you know what I think?"

"What?"

"You have to know her story to understand it. Her father left her and her mother when she was still a baby."

"How do you know that?"

"Everyone knows it. This is Cadaqués. Everyone knows everything."

"Go on."

"Well, so the father left. And as far as I know they never heard from him again."

"No no, that's not true," said Vivienne. "They received a postcard from Morocco. Or India. One of those, I forget. He said he was sorry, but he had to leave and that was all. He told his daughter he would write again, but then he never did."

"The bastard!" That from Senalda.

"Anyway," continued Chasey, "listen to me, I've been a gestalt therapist in Manhattan for twenty years...okay, thirty years... and so this is what I think. I think that if she was with the kind of man that everyone *thinks* she should be with, you know, younger, handsome, real husband material, well then probably she's terrified that a man like that might leave her one day."

"Interesting," said Vivienne, nodding. "Yes, I think maybe you are right. I remember when she first came to Cadaqués with her mother. Layla was fifteen, sixteen, something like that. She had a boyfriend that summer, and ooh-la-la there was a big scene when she found him with another girl."

"I remember that!" said Senalda, excited. "She was sitting at the Boia, weeping like a willow. Her mother, and you Vivienne, and some other people were all talking to her."

"So you see," Chasey summed it up, "I think she's with him because she knows that he won't leave her."

"But at his age," said Cal, "he's going to *have* to leave her one day."

"But she's so young, she doesn't get that yet. At her age, one still believes that people live forever."

"Wouldn't that be nice," Senalda mumbled.

"But Cal is right," added Vivienne, putting the words in his mouth, "She should not be with such an old man now. I saw his passport once. He's seventy-nine..."

"He tells everyone he's seventy-two."

"It doesn't matter. These are the years when she is her most beautiful, with her whole future ahead. She should be with the kind of man who one day could be the father of her child."

"No, no, no. You don't get it," said Chasey. "She already *has* a child. And his name is Paul. Everyone thinks because he's older, and because he's so loud and full of himself, always ordering her around the way he does, because of that everyone thinks that he's the one in control. *He* certainly thinks it. But I've watched them. And I'm telling you, he needs her a lot more than she needs him. And *that's* the attraction right there. Every man *wants* her. My god, she's so beautiful. But what *she* wants is to be *needed*. And as long as she feels Paul *needs* her, she feels safe and secure. And in a way, she's right. Because he's not going to leave her, is he? For *what*?"

"Such a pity," said Vivienne. "What a waste."

"I mean, he probably sucks on her tits all night, curled up in some kind of fetal position."

"I really wish you hadn't said that," said Cal.

Vivienne laughed. "Mon dieu. What a disaster."

"Well I never!" Senalda chimed in. "And the reason you're asking us about her, Cal?"

"Well it's obvious." Vivienne glanced at Cal like a co-conspirator, "it's because he desires her. Isn't it so?"

"Maybe."

"Humph! 'Maybe.'"

"Well now it all makes perfect sense," said Senalda. "I mean as you say, she is certainly one of the most beautiful women in the world, and she's just taking that for granted. I mean youth doesn't last forever, does it?"

All three women sighed.

"Unfortunately."

"It's a damned waste. And he's always telling people he will die soon," said Chasey. "I've heard him say it a dozen times to anyone who will listen. But a man like that, with his ego, he can live another twenty years. And then what will she be, forty-something? Never having had children?"

"It's so sad," said Vivienne.

Senalda was suddenly furious. "He should have the kindness, the maturity, the *decency* for God's sake, to push her out of his bed. To tell her to go and find a man who can one day become the father of her children."

"He's too selfish for that."

"*Much* too selfish."

"And of course she is not going to leave Paul because it would break his heart, maybe even kill the old bastard. And she doesn't want *that* on her conscience, now does she?"

"She has really, how do you say it, cubed herself in?"

"*Boxed* herself in."

"That's it."

"Oh dear."

The three women drank, while thinking hard. Watching them, Cal realized that he had forgotten to get himself something to drink. He excused himself and went to the bar.

"Well, what can we do about it?" Chasey asked the others.

"I have an idea," said Senalda. She explained, and all agreed.

Cal came back, a brandy soda in one hand, a fresh bottle of Veuve Clicquot in the other.

"Another bottle for you, ladies."

"Mais non!"

"Mais oui! And I have to tell you, this is the best investment I ever made. The veil of ignorance has been lifted, you have given me sight, the blind can see!"

"Well," exclaimed Senalda, rubbing her hands together. She was like a bubble now floating through this world. "Just sit down. While you were gone, everything solved."

She would throw a party.

"A small dinner, very intimate, to celebrate your book being published. And with any luck, we shall get this whole business off the ground in proper fashion."

"That's so kind of you."

"Not at all! And I tell you, we need it! We really do. All of us. Everyone's mood is so sad because of poor Jose Manuel. But life must go on, mustn't it? It absolutely must."

All nodded.

"And so we shall have a party, and I shall cook the most delicious everything you can imagine. And we shall drink to Jose Manuel, and we shall drink to your book, and we shall drink to drink, and we shall be happy."

"How did you know about the book?"

"I told you," said Chasey, "this is Cadaqués. Everyone knows everything."

Senalda was grinning. "And I, I am just heeding the call of fate. I shall delve into my books of magic, and conjure recipes guaranteed to awaken deepest feelings. We will drink love potions, and I shall make aphrodisiacs for dessert, and you will do your part, I'm certain of it. You shall be the magician and I, I shall be the sorcerer's apprentice."

Glasses hoisted high. They drank "To love!"

Some American tourists at the next table asked Vivienne if she would snap a photo of them. She said of course. They handed her a camera. She stood, stepped toward them then leaned forward, presumably to get the best view. In her tight dress with her little *derriére* sticking high into the air, all were watching her, no one looking at the tourists posing for the photo.

"Do you want another?" asked Vivienne, still posing herself.

"Sure," said one of the Americans. "Why not?"

Chapter XXXIV

Chasey had it wrong of course. Not everyone knew everything in Cadaqués. Even in a little village, as with any bigger town or city, wherever there are windows there are secrets. Even as one story unfolded there were others here of equal weight.

At that very moment, in a darkened bedroom behind lace curtains, an old woman was reminding her husband, *again,* of the time years earlier when he had lost all their land gambling it away in a rousing game of *botifarra.* While on a wide terrace, Guinnesses sat in white cotton listening to the sound advice of lawyers and accountants as dinner was being made ready in the kitchen. The son of a fisherman had gathered his courage and was explaining to sad parents his dream of life in a big city. A painter was deciding on a stroke of the brush here, a shadow there. And over at Imperial, a queen was being sacrificed in the hope that some moves later a pawn might triumph.

Cal didn't know or care about any of those things now. He was focused like a moth on the flame. After leaving the Casino he only wanted to find Layla to ask if she would like to join them for Senalda's dinner. She would probably be with Paul still, soothing those frayed nerves. And for the first time, Cal understood why. He would go now to sit alone at the Meliton, have a drink and wait hoping to see her. It was their place now. Also none of his other friends went there, so nobody to have to talk to. He could be alone with his thoughts.

Brandy soda time.

Cal sat watching nothing or no one in particular. He finished his drink and ordered another. When that was done he realized it was silly just sitting there. The sun was still high in the sky. In the warm air he decided to go for a swim. Moving some parts of his body would take his mind off other parts.

He headed up toward the point, then climbed down onto the rocks. No one watching, so off with his clothes and into the water. Usually to swim naked one went all the way around to the other side, to Sa Conca. He couldn't be bothered. The moment he was in the water a deep breath, then down into the blue green of it. Pulling hard and like a frog kicking, his eyes open, the cool water swept against his face and body like a woman's hair running over him. Ahead of him now rocks, then no rocks where the sand started. A few more strokes and finally the stillness, just hanging in it, arms and legs suspended. Bubbles out through mouth and nose, keeping only what he needed. Then the slow silent float back toward the surface. He repeated that a few times, though the coolness now was gone.

Then a hard swim, first stomach down gulping at the air. Later on his back, watching the village grow more distant. Motor of a small boat getting closer, he stopped to look. No danger, so again plowing through it. Forty years old and feeling his youth still. He was his own audience, all his strength on display, being tested. *More...further... come on...just one more burst!* Then that was it. Spent. On his back floating, chest heaving, then heaving less, finally everything still again. The sky so blue over him, a bird, another bird, a small cloud. No knowing who or what had watched him. Unseen eyes below, they knew he was there. And those birds, so disappointed he wasn't something else.

Now back like a frog again, looking at it all slowly. Pulling the water from in front of his breast, again and again into those voids. Mountains in the distance, the village, people in or near the water, children splashing, small boats, the light bouncing off it all. And somewhere in the middle of all that, Layla.

Reaching land underfoot he stood for a moment waist high, half his body in one world, half in the other. A quick look around. No one watching, so a quick scramble onto the dry rocks so hot from the sun. He grabbed his shirt that was lying by his sandals and trousers, then lay on the flattest surface he could find and draped the shirt over his penis. He could care less. Loved to show it, even. But there were holiday families strolling past on the road above. Germans, French, Americans. Americans were the prudest of all. Call their fucking lawyer if they saw him. *Irreparable damage to the children.*

The water beaded on his skin as slowly the sun took it back until there was none left. Then he dressed, back up to the road licking the salt from his lips, and down again toward the Meliton. She was there now. He wanted to think she was waiting for him.

In her hands, *Middlemarch.* She was close to the end of it now.

"How is he?"

"Paul?"

"Yes."

"He's fine. It was nothing. He just acts like a spoiled child sometimes."

"I understand."

Cal sat in the chair closest to her.

"Listen, you know Senalda...green eye, blue eye?"

"Of course. The witch."

"*What?*"

"It's just a joke around the village."

"Anyway, she's having a party, a small dinner Tuesday to celebrate my book being published. You want to come?"

Cal had worried that it would be hard to get her there without Paul. It was easier than he thought.

"And of course you can bring Paul. Only..."

"Only what?"

"It's going to run very late. You said he doesn't stay up?"

"That's true."

"Also, there are a lot of stairs. And they're very narrow."

"That could be a problem for him. His knees."

"Of course, I'd love to have him there."

"No, it sounds like probably I should come alone."

"Okay."

Chapter XXXV

In the oldest part of the village, the little Plaza de la Estrella was tucked between white houses. The plaza was paved with small stones, arranged in the middle to form an eight-pointed star symbolizing the eight winds: Gregale, Levante, Sirocco, Ostro, Libeccio, Ponente, Mistral, Tramuntana.

On this night it was the tramuntana blowing again. In summer it was usually a gentle wind from the north that cleared the sky. In the winter, the same wind blew with a strength said to carry souls away.

One house on the square, built high into the archway leading to it, belonged to Senalda del Ponte. To sit, drink and eat at one of Senalda's dinner parties was to know one's purpose on earth. The kitchen as altar. It didn't matter the when or why, the coming together for a meal of her making was enough to set all doubt aside and know there was such as thing as the divine.

Inside the little house this evening: Senalda, Vivienne, Chasey, Tharrats and his daughter Rosa, Cal, David, Robin the minstrel, and the German writer Daniel Zapf, another *vocal*. This was the first time Cal and Daniel had met. Senalda's idea to bring the two writers together. Finally a thud from the brass knocker on the door below. Layla. She was the last of the guests to arrive. Cal offered to go down and open the door.

Layla stood in the open doorway wearing an outfit that looked familiar. Tight green bodice hung low off bare shoulders, a short ruffled yellow skirt, ballet slippers.

"I've seen that outfit before."

"Degas. His Little Dancer."

"Of course. How beautiful."

"Thank you."

Cal had not lied, there were stairs. Following behind her, he watched Layla as she climbed them. As they reached the first floor, on their right side was the little kitchen. This was the heart and soul of the place. Cracked blue and white tiles in the sloping walls, the old bread oven now used for keeping pots and pans, and on the gas stove things bubbling. Maddening smells from the oven, and Senalda bent over it all. The sorcerer's lair.

"Now I won't be but a moment," Senalda called out over her shoulder. She was busy sprinkling something into something. "You two go on upstairs and join the others, and I shall be along in a tinker's moment."

The scene was so beautiful, Layla and Cal stood together a moment longer watching it. Shelves of an alchemist's workshop were set into the thick walls. Bottles and jars filled with every colored potion and oil. Valerian, basil, sage, rosemary and rue and other dried herbs hanging from the rafters, a pot of mint growing in the window, and three candles burning. One glimpse or whiff of it all a few centuries earlier and, all joking aside, they'd have been screaming "*Witch!*" from the little square below. Thank god we live in saner times.

Cal leaned closer into the doorway where Layla stood for a better view of the scene. As he did, his shoulder pressed against hers. He could feel her breathing. After a moment she shifted, not away, but leaning into him harder still as they both watched this woman cooking. As Senalda mixed, stirred, beat and folded things into the magic of the meal to come, they could see very clearly on the stone counter beside her woven baskets full of onions, potatoes, lemons, oranges and avocados. Spices everywhere, brought from the furthest corners of the globe: Maldon sea salt from England, black peppercorns from Indonesia, cinnamon, clove, green, yellow, purple things not even Senalda could pronounce. And hanging from the gnarled wood beam above the hearth, a hand-painted sign with the old joke *Life's a Beach.*

"Are you still there?" asked Senalda without looking.

"We're just watching you."

"I had no idea I was so interesting. I tell you what, as long as you're here perhaps you wouldn't mind taking a few things up with you."

On a small table nearby were two wooden trays. On each tray there were five plates, and on each plate were three things. Small portions.

"What are these?" asked Layla, looking them over.

Senalda pointed to each item, "Oysters in a pomegranate marinade...."

"Incredible."

"...avocado cubes in honey and basil with white truffle shavings..."

"You're joking."

"...and last but not least, chilled asparagus spears, al dente, that have been sautéed with a secret ingredient."

"What's the secret ingredient?" Cal prodded.

Senalda stared at him disbelievingly.

"Well if I told you it wouldn't be a secret, would it? No no, you go on, just take these upstairs if you would and I'll be along in half a heartbeat."

Both stood staring at her with big smiles.

"Well go on you two. Bob's your uncle!"

As Cal and Layla climbed the curving stairs they could hear laughter, voices and a guitar coming from the room above.

It was not a big room, the walls white except the stone wall with the white hearth set against it. A stack of wood stood to one side already waiting for winter. For now, cream-colored candles aflame inside the fireplace and on the small glass table, also on the white shelves with their rock crystals, moonstones, and purple amethysts. Candles everywhere, like Christmas lights.

A spirit of the sixties hung over this twelfth century house: more crystals hanging in the windows, brass incense burner on one shelf, and behind it a photo of a young Senalda next to a man with long hair. The heavy wooden rafters above had been painted white. Large potted plants in each corner included a purple flowering mandragora. And through the open glass doors, the little terrace with its white cotton hammock, and beyond it a sliver view of the sea past the square and through the houses.

Robin sat at the edge of the hearth playing his guitar softly. Tharrats and his daughter Rosa were on the white couch. David sat alone in a far corner smoking. Vivienne and Chasey, one dressed more beautifully than the other, sat on either side of the writer Daniel, both leaning in close toward him. Thin, blonde pony tail, fast eyes, fast mind, fast to smile, the young German had lived in Cadaqués for years.

Ooohs and aaahs from Chasey and Vivienne over Layla's outfit. She returned compliments. And everyone was excited to see the food.

"Cal," asked Chasey, "do you remember the first poem you ever wrote? Daniel just told us his."

"I do remember it, yes."

"Well come on then, let's hear it."

"I was fourteen."

"How sweet."

Cal recited his first poem.

"Roses are blue
Violets are red
LSD taught me
It's all in my head"

"And you were *fourteen* when you wrote that?"

"Yup."

"Your childhood sounds very different than mine."

"Oh, childhood was over a long time before that."

There were bottles and glasses on the table. Cal poured a juice for Layla and a red wine for himself.

"That was in California. Palo Alto. At nights my friends and I used to go over to the cemetery next to our school. We'd take acid, then wait for Bluebeard to step out of one of the graves. It was fun."

"Well at least you wrote poems about it."

"At least."

Cal sat down on the cool stone next to the fireplace. Layla sat close next to him. Senalda appeared at the head of the stairs urging everyone to get started on the hors d'oeuvres. She described again what each thing was. Daniel smiled.

"Senalda, everything here is an aphrodisiac."

"Is it? I hadn't realized. But my word, you're right, aren't you. Now how did that happen?"

Layla took one of the asparagus spears and ate it slowly. Cal watched her. Oysters followed.

"What is that you are cooking downstairs?" asked Rosa. "The smells are driving us all very mad."

"Ah! Well, here's the surprise. I have recreated the very same meal that the young woman serves to the family in Cal's book."

Cal looked at her. "No."

"Yes, I have. Except she starts out with a garlic soup, and presses cloves of garlic into the lamb. I thought we'd just do without the garlic tonight." She looked at Vivienne and Chasey, who smiled back at her. "This room's too small, and the air here is too warm."

Rosa was translating for her father.

"Senalda," said Tharrats, "es fantastico!"

"Yes, yes it is. And do you know what I realized not a moment ago?" asked Senalda, the green eye and the blue eye flaring wide.

Robin stopped playing his guitar.

"What did you realize, Senalda?"

"I realized that we are making literary history here tonight. Joan Tharrats is going to publish Cal's book. And coming, as I'm told it will, in December of this the year of our Lord nineteen ninety-nine, that means that Cal's is going to be one of, perhaps even *the*, last book published in the twentieth century! Which means, I can hardly believe it, that *all of twentieth century literature has been leading all along to my very doorstep!*"

She had a way of placing herself at the center of all things. Senalda del Ponte. The sign. The bridge.

"I mean, *can you believe it?*"

Wine poured, glasses raised, toasts made. Then Senalda excused herself. Back down to the kitchen to ready the main event.

As always at Senalda's parties, as much food for thought as for the stomach.

"Back in the twenties," said Chasey, "you can imagine it, yes? All of them here from Paris or wherever. Duchamp, Man Ray, Dali, Garcia Lorca, Buñuel... There are some great photos of it. No cars, all the fishing boats. Cadaqués was a real fishing village. No tourists then. The real changes hadn't started yet."

"Each century gets its own twenties," offered Cal. "We'll get ours soon enough."

"That's true, isn't it?" Daniel nodded, grinning. "I'd never thought of it like that."

"And they'll share something, our twenties, their twenties, and all the future twenties. Because in the twenties, you've left the last century behind and so you're feeling more advanced. Somehow superior."

"Like the living feel themselves superior to the dead."

"Exactly!"

"That's a very temporary superiority," said Layla.

From his corner, David laughed. "Vive la vie. Tous les jours. La mort c'est un autre monde."

"You're right, David. Absolutely right."

David smiled, then disappeared back into his thoughts. Here but not here.

"At the same time," Cal continued, "in the twenties one feels oneself young as a century, because of course most of it still lies ahead. Even if one is already old, in the twenties you feel again the possibility of youth. The twenties are to a century what the twenties are to a life, the start of it all."

Tharrats, listening as Rosa translated, nodded.

"Sí, hombre. Es verdad."

"But still you have to envy them in a way," said Layla, "those last twenties. That mad rush of invention, turning everything upside down or just letting it float. What did Gertrude Stein say, that in Paris in the twenties they 'invented the twentieth century'?"

"And now?" Cal asked her, "Who's inventing the twenty-first century?"

"Steve Jobs, Bill Gates..."

"You're saying science is the new art?"

"Well, they're like Robert and Richard, aren't they, science and art. Mirror images of each other. One takes a step and the other follows. In the seventeenth century, Cyrano de Bergerac dreams up a rocket to the moon, then fast forward and some engineer makes one. Or someone builds a massive factory, and then you get Chaplin's Modern Times. It's like a dog chasing its own tail isn't it, art and science."

Cal was staring at her.

"Too beautiful, too smart. What else are you too much of?"

She smiled the answer back, then added, "Now when a *man* says something half-intelligent, do people act surprised?"

Half the room blurted out, "*Yes!*"

Laughter. Tharrats proposed another toast, then the talk turned back to Cal's book.

"I love how you have the young woman make that feast on the Friday when they're supposed to be fasting," said Layla. "And the dead wood between the old man's legs when he goes to split the almonds. Great image."

Falling...

"Daniel's writing a wonderful book himself," said Vivienne.

"How is it going, Daniel?"

"Oh, well, getting there. Almost finished. But then I've been saying that for about three years now."

"What's it about?" Cal asked.

Daniel shrugged.

"Okay. Well, it's about this young guy who was hitchhiking around Spain. He comes to Cadaqués in the sixties, and he hears this legend about this island near Cap de Creus. Called *Massa d'Or. The Mass of Gold.* It's also called *The Rat,* because it looks like a rat. Has the shape. Anyway, the legend is that if you walk

251

across it at the widest part you'll become immortal. Only you have to do it on one special day of the year, and no one knows what day that is. So this guy, he's done a little too much LSD." Daniel grinned, with a knowing nod to Cal. "And so he really believes it. So then he spends one whole year walking across it every day."

"Incredible."

"Yes. *But*, you see the thing is at the end of the year he realizes it's 1965, which was *not a leap year*. And now he's afraid maybe February 29th can be the magic day."

"And now he has to wait around three more years to walk across it," said Cal.

"Exactly! And there are these killer rats defending the island, and these sea monsters like giant squid, and he keeps taking LSD, so he's not sure if they're real or just that he's seeing them. And the reader's not sure either."

"I'll buy it!"

"Me too. Another copy just sold."

"Fantastic!"

"And then...?"

"And so then, while he's waiting these three years, he hears about *another* legend, that the Holy Grail is buried up at the old monastery San Pere de Rodes. It's about thirty kilometers from Cadaqués. Beautiful place. Magical already just by itself."

"So this guy, he..."

"...he goes up there with a shovel, and of course he starts digging. Every day. He gets obsessed with it. He really wants to live forever. And then one day he's digging and he finds this old box. But it's late, the sun's going down, and he can't get to it. So he goes back the next day. He's so excited. He digs, unburies it, but it's nothing, just some old bullets left over from the civil war.

And then suddenly he realizes that day was February 29, and he forgot to go back to the island to walk across it."

"So now he has to wait another four years," said Layla.

"Exactly! It's like that. And every time the leap year comes around something else happens that keeps him from walking across the island on that day. And so it turns out he never leaves Cadaqués. But of course he doesn't really mind that because it's the most beautiful place on earth. And besides, now he's looking for the Holy Grail, and if he finds that and drinks from it, well then he'll also have immortality."

"But maybe he's immortal already," offered Layla. "Maybe one of the days he already walked across the island was the right day."

"Well, *exactly*! Very good! But he won't know that until, well, until he doesn't die. So he decides that if he reaches his 120th birthday, then he'll know it really worked and he's immortal."

"And how old is he now in your story?"

"Oh, well that I can't tell you. You'll have to read the book."

"Sounds great."

"Cal?"

"Sí, Joan?"

Tharrats said that he thought a first printing of one thousand copies of Cal's book would be enough. He wanted to know if Cal agreed.

"Sí, hombre. Perfecto."

Tharrats asked about the cover. Cal suggested they use a painting by Grisha. In Spanish he said, "Not because he's my friend, but because he's the finest living artist I knew of."

From his corner of the room, David said nothing.

Layla went downstairs with Vivienne to see if Senalda might

need help. As soon as she left, Cal quickly drank his wine and poured another. By the time she came back he had finished that too and poured one more. Probably it looked to Layla like it was the same glass as when she had left.

The food was served.

Moments later, plates balanced on laps, Tharrats stood to offer another toast. Generous words about Cal's book, the writer, and their hostess. David then stood to say some sweet words. Now Cal's turn. The wine was in him and working. He got emotional. Layla saw it, and smiled.

He thanked everyone. Then, "To the here and now!"

"To the here and now, Cal!"

Layla and Cal sat close to each other still, arms touching, even legs touching. When he said something about how talented she was making her outfits...the Klimt, Degas, and others...she leaned her head on his shoulder for a moment as she thanked him.

Vivienne said Layla's outfits reminded her of Cadaqués in the old days.

"It was so different then. Art not just in galleries like today, but in the life. And at nights...ooh-la-la!"

She described L'Hostal.

"It was...surreal. Dali and Gala would come in their big black Chevrolet. To El Barroco, or to L'Hostal, that was the center of our world. Young girls, young boys. So many boys! The waiters wore white gloves. There were gold candelabras on the tables. The Captain would bring his ocelots Babou and Bouba. Girls dressed like butterflies, men like matadors in their tight pants. Everyone dressed not like today," she grimaced. "Blue jeans, dirty sandals. No! We were beautiful, and we wanted to be more beautiful."

"And we were!" said Chasey. "We really were."

Both women sat digesting the memories with their food. David wandered alone onto the terrace to smoke. Then Senalda announced the dessert.

"Frozen bananas dipped in bitter chocolate, and fresh figs stewed in sauterne with vanilla bean."

"In other words," said Vivienne, "penises and..."

"Exactly! Everyone here represented."

"Did you know," said Chasey, "vanilla beans are seeds from the ovaries of an orchid?"

To wash those down, a bottle of *Garnatxa*. Robin reached for his guitar as if it was a woman. A quiet version of Clapton's *Layla*. When he finished, Cal asked if he could play a song.

"This is something I wrote a couple of days ago, after a certain someone said a certain something about a certain fox."

He looked at Layla as he said that.

Another blues melody.

Found me a woman
Found me a woman for this man
Now I'm crowin' like a rooster
Like a rooster what found his hen
'Cause I'm startin' to love this little chicken
Love her 'till the break of dawn
But she's runnin' so fast!

Layla was looking back at him. No expression.

Is it something I said, Lord?
Something I did or didn't do?
Now won't you go talk to her please
'Cause she can't run away from you

Tell her I love my little chicken
And I'm feelin' so blue

From Vivienne, "Oooh-la-la."

Whatever it was Lord
Tell her I won't do it again
'Cause the thing is this rooster
This rooster ain't no good without his hen
We're talkin' Cock-a-doodle-doo Lord
We're talkin' that sweet Cock-a-doodle-doo
See, I'm not the fox babe
I'm the rooster!

"I don't think this song is about a chicken," said Robin, laughing.
"Go on," said Vivienne, "finish the story."

And I'm startin' to love this little chicken
Love her to the break of dawn
And unlike that chicken and egg stuff
We know where this gets goin'
I'm talkin' Cock-a-doodle-doo, babe
Talkin' 'bout that sweet Cock-a-doodle-doo

"Nice," said Layla.
"You liked that?"
She nodded.
Robin played again. *Perfidia* the way Nat King Cole sang it, slow and sweet.
Later, warm thank you's to Senalda, then Layla let Cal walk

her home. Not the fastest way. Through the Plaza Estrella, down the cobbled path to the Port Alguer, then back toward the village along the water. There was no moon, just stars in the clear sky and yellow lights in the windows. They walked slowly, neither speaking. Below them to their right the water was moving. They could smell it and they could hear it. There was a white sailboat moored close by. There was a white light on the tip of its mast, and when the water moved the light moved against the darkness.

As they came closer to the village there were a few other people strolling now. Couples mostly. A boy and girl sat on one bench embracing. They kept walking. Finally Cal said something.

"Did you ever swim in Cadaqués at night?"

"No. Why, should I?"

"At night, sometimes when you move the water you see little lights, like stars. It's phosphorous from the plants in the sea." He added, "You should have Paul take you swimming at night once so you can see that. The water is warm."

"Don't be cruel."

Passing the Casino, familiar faces. They didn't stop.

"So, where do you live?"

"On the other side behind Es Poal. And you?"

"Back by the church."

The passeig was crowded, with music and people spilling out of L'Hostal. Young women in small dresses, young men clustered around them. Behind the little cove Es Poal Cal followed Layla up one of the small dark passageways. She stopped.

"Well, this is where I live."

It was a white house, with bougainvillea climbing up its side.

"Nice."

They stood there a moment.

"Well, good night."

"Good night."
Slow kisses on cheeks. Right cheek, left cheek.
"Good night."
"Good night."
He turned and walked back the way they had come.

Chapter XXXVI

No way, no fucking way, he could sleep after that. Straight to Imperial. No one. Then to Casino. Everyone.

Cal didn't hear a word his friends were saying. Didn't even pretend to pay attention. All of it was just background din while over one calvados after another he kept playing certain scenes over again in his mind.

Finally one last drink, then back into the night.

Only one thing to do now. Since he couldn't kiss her good night, he would kiss her house good night. He made his way back to it. There were shadows against the wall as he pressed his lips to it, his hands slowly rubbing against the white paint.

"Good night," he whispered to the wall. "Good night."

Chapter XXXVII

"Were you kissing my house?"

"What?"

"I said, were you kissing my house? Paul said that last night he couldn't sleep, and so he went outside on our terrace for some air and he heard something so he looked down, and he says he saw you kissing the front of our house. Why would you do that?"

"Umm..."

They were standing on the packed dirt of the passeig.

"Why would you do that?"

"Because."

"Now you sound like Paul. 'Because' is not an answer. Why would you kiss the front of my house?"

"Because...those were magic kisses."

"What's a magic kiss?"

"A magic kiss is a kiss that passes through walls, and then it floats inside a house, and then it waits just inside the front door for a special person to come home. And every time she comes home, if she stops inside her door and closes her eyes she can feel the magic kiss."

"Oh. Well, okay then. At least now I understand what a magic kiss is."

Chapter XXXVIII

Paul's restaurant *Paradisio* was on a hill toward the back of the village near the museum. Like all the buildings surrounding it, it was old. The ground floor where the restaurant was located dated back to the fifteenth century. One would not know it.

The laminate flooring that had been laid over the original stone floor looked like it came from IKEA, because it had. The nine tables, each a different color plastic, were surrounded with matching chairs. There were cushions on the chairs to make them more comfortable. Blue neon lights ran the length of one wall behind a clear plastic screen, and there was a waterfall at the end of the screen. There were orange and yellow lights suspended from the ceiling, and flowers on the tables. Paul had designed everything himself.

If you wanted to get away from Cadaqués but didn't have time to do it, this was the place to come. You felt like you were in Las Vegas or Los Angeles. That was the concept. Still, in deference to the village there was a lifesized figure of Dali near the front door holding a small tray with business cards and toothpicks on it.

"I do not want you to see him again."

"What are you talking about?"

"You heard me. I do not want you to see him again."

"Why on earth not?"

"Because he was kissing the fucking wall of my house, that's why."

"*Our* house."

"Our house. Even worse."

"So what?"

"So, next he'll want to kiss something else. And not just kiss it."

"Oh for god's sake, he's just a friend."

"Friends do not kiss other friends' houses."

"You're getting yourself all worked up over nothing. He was just trying to be charming, that's all."

"It was three o'clock in the fucking morning. There was no one there to charm."

"Do you know how cute you are when you get angry?"

"*Stop it!* Do not change the subject. I want you to agree right now, and to promise me, you will not see him again."

"This is Cadaqués. One can't take two steps without bumping into people. How do you expect me not to see him?"

Paul thought a moment.

"All right, well then that's all there is to it. We're going to Manchester."

"*What?*"

"You heard me. Go home, pack your bags, we're leaving tonight."

"I'm not going to Manchester tonight."

"Yes you are."

"No I'm not."

"You're not?"

"No."

He thought again. Then Paul smiled.

"All right then, I'll go alone. You can stay here and do whatever you damn well please."

"*No!* You can't go."

"Of course I can."

"I won't let you."

"But that should make you very happy. I shall go, and then you can do whatever you like, wherever you like, as often as you like."

"Paul, just stop it. You're not going anywhere."

"You can have that nice big house all to yourself, and the bed to yourself, and you can take meals by yourself. Or maybe your friend Cal would like to join you. And then you won't be alone."

"This is *not* funny."

"Well then, go home and pack your bags, and if you like you can come with me."

"You're *not* leaving. And I'm not leaving. What about your meeting with Adrian?"

"Ah, yes. I forgot about that."

"You see? You're just being silly."

She stood and came over to him. She brushed the little wisps of hair off his ears.

"You're so cute when you're jealous. Did you know that?"

"I am?"

"Very."

She bent over and kissed the top of his head.

"Now enough of this nonsense, alright? Nobody is going anywhere."

He looked up at her.

"All right. But promise me you're going to be a good girl."

"I promise."

Chapter XXXIX

J ose Manuel's funeral would be the next day. His family had come from Barcelona. Mother and father, the two sisters, the little brother, were all sitting at Imperial on the terrace surrounded by Jose Manuel's friends. The friends were saying things to let them know they were not alone in their grief, what a good man Jose Manuel had been, and how much he would be missed by so many.

"The finest, darling. He was the finest. La mejor!"

"Always kind," added Wiggles. "Always helpful. Great sense of humor."

"He was hilarious."

The mother didn't speak a word of English, but she understood the tone of what was being said and sat nodding.

"Siempre un buen hombre. Y un buen amigo."

The mother began to cry.

Marc, a tall thin Frenchman spoke now. Full of compassion. A viscount from an old family descended from the French corsair Surcouf, he and Jose Manuel had been close friends for years. In his t-shirt, shorts and sandals, the Viscount Surcouf leaned in close toward the mother and smiled. In poor Spanish, the words perfect nevertheless, he told the family, "Your son, your brother, had many friends here. We loved him. He was so full of joy. I feel the joy now when I think of him."

The little brother leaned against the mother. She wrapped her big arm around him.

Marita was there. She tried to say something but couldn't, she just started to cry. Now the parents were comforting her.

"He was a good man," said Marc. "And we all loved him."

Chapter XL

As the scene with Jose Manuel's family was unfolding at Imperial, up the little alley behind the wine shop Cal and Layla were sitting inside Casa Anita's. She had sent word to him via David that they should not meet at Meliton anymore. That bar was too close to her house. Paul walked by it a few times a day, and likely would see them together and worry "over nothing." Casa Anita, with its cave-like atmosphere, was tucked away from everything and everyone.

"Jealous? Of what?"

"I told him it's silly."

Layla had her straw shopping basket with her. She reached into it now and pulled out something wrapped in thin paper.

"Here. I made this for you."

"What's this?"

"Nothing really, just a little something. Go on, have a look."

It was a white shirt with short sleeves.

"It's beautiful," he said. "You made this?"

"I know it looks like just a plain white shirt, but actually it's a copy of the one James Dean wore in East of Eden. For the character Cal. Look at the pocket."

In white thread so fine you could barely see it, she had embroidered the name 'Cal.'

"I was lucky. I found a photo of Dean wearing that in one of my books about classic films. It didn't have the name on it, but I thought, why not?"

She was sitting across the table. Cal reached for her hand, pulled it gently to his lips and kissed it.

"Thank you," he said.

At that same moment, back at Imperial, Paul stood asking if anyone had seen Layla.

Chapter XLI

Night again, in the Casino again.

"What a lonely, lonely buffoon," rumbled Robert.

"Him, or me?" asked Cal.

"HEEE, darling. HEEE is the lonely buffoon."

Cal and Layla had been sitting together with friends. He was wearing the shirt she had made for him. Paul had just come bursting in to collect her. Something about needing Layla's help writing a letter to Ferran Adria, owner of the famous El Bulli restaurant in Roses.

"Can't it wait?" she had asked. "We're all here thinking about Jose Manuel. His funeral's tomorrow."

"I know his funeral is tomorrow."

"Well so can't the letter wait?"

"No, it *cannot* wait. This is important. Now come on!"

Paul looked around at all the faces. About twenty people clustered together. Gathering of the tribe. The Red-Eyes.

"And not to worry," said Paul, surveying the scene, "these pathetic drunks will be perfectly able to get even more drunk without you." He pointed at Cal. "Especially *that* one. Just look at him, those red eyes. Fucking alcoholic."

Layla shrugged, stood, smiled at everyone, then left with him. Paul was holding onto her hand like a parent taking a bad child from a shop. Cal had thought of saying something but decided against it. Now he felt bad. He was supposed to be thinking about Jose Manuel, but all he could think about was the empty chair next to him.

The party continued around him.

This was not just the usual random drinking. This was committed, world-class, professional league ritual drinking. Serious stuff. You had to know what you were doing, to have practiced, to have trained for this. An amateur here would only make a fool of himself.

They had pulled half a dozen tables together, like cowboys circling the wagons. One whole side of the big room was theirs. Bottles everywhere, cigarette smoke, people talking at the same time. Filip was there with his new old guitar, a cheap red thing. He played while people talked. His sister Bara, Ellayne, Valmont, Lia, the Hungarian Josef, the viscount, both twins, Wiggles. The beautiful Sonia. Antonio with his bandaged finger. David, Cal, Senalda, Vivienne, Chasey, Robin. Full court. Also with them were some of Jose Manuel's friends who had come from Barcelona. Off to one side, Marita had a deck of the gold-edged Tarot cards Dali had painted. One by one people were coming to her for readings. Past, present, future, obstacles, opportunities, all right there. The Tower, World, Moon, Fool, Judgment. Some took it more seriously than others.

Freddy walked in, a rare trip off his mountain to celebrate the memory of a lost friend. He came over and sat next to Cal. In Layla's chair. Altonio said something to Freddy, but was so drunk you couldn't understand him. Sounded like he said "Bullshit."

"Jah, it's all bullshit," Freddy agreed.

Josef poured the last of one bottle of tequila into his glass. It was Jose Manuel's favorite and they were all drinking it this night. Out of respect for the dead. There were other bottles, some spent, others full and waiting on the table. David was watching Josef.

"Josef?"

"Yes, David?"

"There is no worm in the bottom of that bottle. I think maybe the worm has escaped."

From across the table, Robert. "No, darling. You're thinking of MEZCALLLLL."

Wiggles shook his head sadly. "So much potential."

"In mezcal?"

"Well yes, that too of course. But I mean Jose Manuel, all his plans. He had big plans to grow rich, you know. The twins remember, don't you? He was going to grow those worms they put in tequila."

"MEZCAL," Robert shot back.

"Yes, well, mezcal, tequila, whatever. He wanted to plant these cactus plants..."

"AGAVE plants."

"Agave plants, thank you. He wanted to plant those fucking agave plants on the terraces above the village where the grapes used to grow. At the same time, he was going to start a worm farm..."

"No, no, no," said Robert. He explained that the so-called 'worms' are really moth larvae that infect the agave plants.

"Damned shame about that whorehouse being in Roses," said Josef. "Him having to drive over the mountain like that. Someone should start one here in Cadaqués."

"What, a whorehouse?"

"Why not? Save the commute."

"Who would be their biggest clients? Let's try to imagine it, shall we?"

"Hector, from the fish market."

"Definitely."

"Tourists, of course."

"I might have a go," said Wiggles. "Now and then. Special occasions."

"Like...?"

"I don't know. Christmas. Easter. My birthday."

"Jose Manuel would have given them some good business."

"He was a horny one, wasn't he? I've seen him with...well, let's just say he was a horny one."

"In Barcelona you've got everyone. And everything."

Wiggles again. "A man gets horny enough, it's like Pan with his goat, yes? You know that famous Roman statue?"

"From POMMMPEI," grinned Richard.

"Herculaneum," his brother corrected him.

"I mean sometimes you just have to fuck a goat," said Wiggles, pressing his case. "Freddy knows that, don't you Freddy? With your Behhh-same mucho."

Freddy grinned. "Jah."

He had a glass of tequila in his hand now, and was part of it. A few people who knew Freddy's version of the song started to sing, "Behhh-same, behhh-same mucho..." Filip was playing along on the guitar.

"I tried to fuck a beach once," said Cal over the singing.

"A bitch?" asked Wiggles.

"A *beach*."

"Well now, how did you do that?"

"It's about as easy as it sounds, Wiggles. You make a hole in the sand, and then you..."

"Yes, Cal, I can imagine *how* you did it. I'll rephrase the question. *Why?*"

"Because this girl who was supposed to meet me on the beach never showed up."

"And, how did that turn out? I imagine the beach must have been awfully flattered."

"I'm not sure it gave it much thought."

"Well, it probably thought it was a child digging. Oh, I'm sorry, not to offend. It probably thought it was some great construction machine burrowing into it."

"It's not the perfect situation."

"No, I don't imagine it would be."

"The hole doesn't stay small enough."

"Well, that's always the problem, isn't it. I mean, even with..."

It was like that. Just kept going. A while later Robert stood, clanging a spoon against the side of his glass.

"Darlings, let's not forget why we're here, hmm? Jose Manuel. Our friend. With us always, yes? And we love him."

"To love, and friends. Can't replace them."

"For Jose Manuel then. Live well. Live long."

"Marching forward!" someone shouted.

Later, much later, Cal and David walked home together. Cal had a bottle of brandy in his room. He went to get it and then brought it down to David's studio. They sat at David's worktable with a candle between them. David was smoking.

"I don't know, David. I don't know. I'm just so tired of it all. Of the stupid games. Girls, always leading you to think one thing. Or you *want* to think one thing, that's probably more like it. And it turns out it's something else. You understand what I mean? David? David?"

"Yes, Cal?"

"Do you understand what I mean?"

"Yes, Cal. I think so."

"I mean, maybe it's me. Maybe I just look for the right things in the wrong places. You have to be in the right place. And if you're not, you're fucked."

Cal took another sip of the brandy.

"But Layla, she's not like that. Not at all. And I knew it the minute I saw her. She was walking...walking past the Casino with Paul. There are no games here. I could tell that from the start. She just didn't look like someone who likes to play games. She says what she thinks, she thinks what she says. And of course, yes, she's beautiful. On the inside as much as on the outside. *Jesus*! This is the one, David. I really think this is the one."

"Cal?"

"What?"

"Do you think there is a God?"

"Maybe. I don't know. Why?"

"I think there is a God."

"If there is, David, he made her. And he did a damn good job of it. Like a great painter. Because she's like the Mona Lisa with blood pressure." Cal laughed. "You want another drink, David? I don't mean this. I mean, do you want another drink? She doesn't drink. I mean, she drinks of course. Everyone drinks. Only she drinks chocolate milk. I used to drink that shit when I was kid. I used to love it."

"Really, Cal?"

"Oh, yes. I used to love it."

Chapter XLII

Cal was in no mood to return to his bed alone. So, what to do? Layla by now was warm in Paul's bed. No people out, the village still, everything closed. One dog on the street searching in vain for its owner. In the silence, Cal had begun to walk. And as he walked, he decided that probably the best thing to do would be to climb up onto the roof of the church to watch the sunrise.

It was a big church, and he had to study the possibilities. Two cypress trees stood in front. He stood on the wide terrace looking up at them. Unfortunately, neither was high enough, too far still from the top of the tallest tree to the roof. So he walked around the back, past the studio of the artist Richard Hamilton. Everything was too something. Too low, too high, too smooth. Finally, in a narrow passageway behind the church, there were small pebbles arranged as an arrow on the stone ground. The arrow pointed toward the church. Cal took it as a sign. *This is the way you are meant to climb onto the roof of the church.*

So he did it. First up onto a stone wall. Easy enough. Then up to the next level. Not a problem. Then a harder bit. There were some protruding buttresses, but too far between them to shinny up. He was about to give up and climb back down when, luckily or not, he spotted a drainpipe. Being either very clever or very stupid, he took off his belt and, looping it around the pipe, up he went like a telephone repairman climbing a pole, though not as gracefully as they do it. Grunting, laughing, talking to himself making silly jokes, he was doing fine until he got to the top. Then suddenly the pipe began to give under the strain. There was a jerk, a creaking noise, the metal slowly bending. Cal looked around for something else to grab hold of. Nothing. Nada. The pipe was prying itself loose from the wall. Less by thinking than by instinct, his left hand flew up and caught the lip of the roof. As it did, whatever had been holding held no more. Twisting and groaning, the pipe pulled away from the wall as Cal's second hand flew up to grab hold of the roof, doing everything it possibly could to help the first hand. And now he was just hanging there, feet dangling, holding onto little more than an agnostic's prayer. With fingers slipping, he thought as fast as he could under the circumstance. He was less afraid of falling *onto* the first roof below than falling *through* it. *If that happens,* he thought, *put one hand over your throat, and another over your eyes, so no pieces of timber pierce either of those. What you really need now is a third hand to cover your balls at the same time. Shit!*

    A deep breath to steady body and spirit, then a 'Hail Mary pass.' Letting go with one hand, he tried to grab one of the curved red tiles on the roof. He hoped the curved shape would give him something to hold to. It didn't. He was literally holding onto nothing now. With that famous luck reserved for drunks and idiots, still for a moment something seemed to stick. He could feel moisture though. Not good. He was sweating, and his hand was slipping. With his wrist he felt something sharp. One of the tiles was cracked. There was a jagged edge. He grasped at it. Tips of his fingers clawing at something, anything, he managed somehow to swing his left leg up onto the edge of the roof. As he did, he could hear a ripping noise. The shirt Layla had made for him had caught on the broken pipe. More tearing sound then as the second leg, so eager to follow the first, scrambled its way up.

And finally he was up on it, the roof of the Church of Santa Maria.

Crouched low like a cat he paused to catch his breath. All the village was spread out below him now, with the dark sea ahead. So beautiful! Keeping low, he inched his way along the damp sloping tiles, stepping lightly on the old roof that rattled in places as his weight shifted. He took a few tentative steps. There was a cracking noise suddenly as his right foot broke through one of the tiles. A moment later there was a second noise, an echoing clatter far below. He pried his foot free from the hole. Something had cut him. His leg was bleeding. His fingers also were bleeding. Keeping on all fours now, trying to distribute his weight over as wide a surface area as possible, he inched forward until at last he made it to the front of the church.

His plan was to sit there, smoke the joint that was in his pocket, and wait for the sun to rise. He got the sitting part of it okay. But then he discovered he had no matches. Just as well. Smoking now after all he had drunk probably would have made him sick. He was already feeling dizzy. He wanted to keep looking at it all, this hard-earned bird's eye view of Cadaqués, but now suddenly everything was spinning. The church, the rooftops below, the mountains in the distance, all of it was moving. Cal pressed himself against the sloping roof so he wouldn't fall. And then after some minutes, lying there with his head resting on one arm, he closed his eyes and fell asleep.

As he slept, below and above him all the natural rhythms of the morning played themselves out. Seagulls and swallows followed their routines paying little attention to him. The few fishing boats that still worked their nets at night returned to shore with their catches, but Cal didn't see those. He didn't even wake when, at eight o'clock, the bells began tolling out the hour as they would throughout the day. He slept right through those, believing only that he could hear bells in a dream.

And so he never did see the stars disappearing above him as the purple sky turned red then orange and yellow and finally blue. And he never did see the sun rise beyond Cucurucuc at the entrance to the little bay, or below him the street sweepers with their stick brooms shuffling along the beach. Or the old woman in the bathing suit who, as she did every day in every season, walked resolutely from the village into the sea as if it was all one in the same. Or the police and the old men who came into the Casino in the early morning for their *cafés solo* or *cortados*. And he never saw the car delivering shucked garlic and herbs, leaving those outside the doors of restaurants still closed. Or the men unstacking chairs and tables on terraces outside the cafes, or the bakery with its fresh warm bread in the racks opening its doors. Or the old woman selling fresh fish out of plastic buckets in the little square by the archway. Cal missed all of that, and more.

Instead, he was rolling now, as a child rolls down a hill of grass, nothing to hold onto, screaming, rolling faster and faster. He was sweating. Somewhere there were bells tolling. The bells wouldn't stop. His eyes cracked open and there was a bright light. The bells were still ringing, and birds were circling close, and the heavy heat of the sun was on his back. In a panic, Cal sat up and saw that he was not really rolling. It was only a dream. Those bells were not a dream, though. They kept clanging in the belfry that loomed so close. My god how they clanged! They were not counting out the hour, unless it was a thousand o'clock. Just ringing wildly. Then he remembered. *Of course, Jose Manuel's funeral!*

He inched toward the edge of the roof and peered down. There they were, starting to gather. Jose Manuel's family, friends, almost everyone who had been at the Casino just hours earlier.

And there she was, Layla, standing off to one side with Paul. She was wearing a simple black dress. The old man was wearing blue jeans and a t-shirt and a hat. He looked like he was going to a fucking ball game.

The two cypress trees that grew at the front of the church were below Cal. Another fifty years maybe and the taller of the two would be high enough to climb down. He couldn't wait that long. The drain pipe was no longer an option. What to do? He looked around. Maybe he could climb not *down,* but *up* the bell tower, get into the belfry, and then get back down to the ground that way, *inside* the church. He looked up. No way. He needed to do something, before someone spotted him up there and called the police. He had to look like a burglar, crouched up on the roof like that. Also he had damaged the roof and that pipe, and did not want to have to explain to the priest and others how that had happened. How embarrassing.

At last, mercifully, the bells stopped ringing. Thank you God. He looked down once again. They were still there. He thought of that scene in Robin Hood, Errol Flynn on the balcony telling Olivia de Haviland which soldier below he could jump on to cushion his blow. The fattest and best prospect here was of course Paul. And if he did that it could kill two birds with one stone. Not going to happen.

As he watched, the crowd started shuffling in to the church. Cal waited until they were inside. Even though it was too low, the Cypress tree looked like his best bet. Lowering himself down from the roof until he was hanging from it as before, then looking down through his feet, he aimed for the tree and just let go. It did not work as well as he had hoped. The top branches were not strong enough to hold a man of his size. It was more like sliding down a fireman's pole, if that pole had sharp jagged sticks poking out of the side of it. His hands and legs were desperately trying to latch on to anything. At last he grabbed hold of something that held back. Then, scratched and bleeding, he climbed down the rest of it. Worst of all, Layla's white shirt was completely shredded, and there was blood on it. He wanted to go home and change, then come back for whatever was left of the service, but suddenly the door of the church swung open. Andreu, the old caretaker of the church, stepped out. He smiled at Cal. He spoke a little English.

"Are you right?"

"Yes. Thank you. I..."

"I know. I saw."

"I'm sorry. I didn't mean to..."

"Is okay," he reassured Cal. "Is very beautiful, you wanted to see every part of our church."

For some reason Cal did not think to switch the conversation to Spanish. They continued in English.

"How did you know I was up there?"

Andreu smiled again. He had a gentle face, and eyes that sparkled. "I find the pieces on the floor this morning. I climb up and I see you from belfry. I want to help you, but was too late. You already climbing down."

"I will pay for any damage."

"Oh, no, no, no, please, you not worry. Is old roof, and we must fix very soon. I only happy you are okay." He looked toward the door to the church. "He was friend, yes? Jose Manuel?"

"Yes."

"Then come. He like you to be here."

"I think maybe I will just run home fast, wash, put on some nicer clothes."

"The fishermen what build our church, they not have fancy

clothes. You are welcome. Please."

Andreu gestured toward the door. Cal could not say no. He stepped inside the church.

Chapter XLIII

The priest was speaking in Catalan. Cal made his quiet way down the aisle, stopping behind the last pew full of those who sat with their sad faces forward. Layla was sitting next to Paul in the back row. The old man still had his hat on. Cal sat just behind them.

The casket lay surrounded by flowers and candles. From the great gilded alter, carved wooden figures looked on. Two large painted fishermen stood below, shouldering the rest of it. And at the center of it all, Mary was holding her child, the golden figure of the sun hanging low over her loins.

As the priest kept talking, Paul leaned in toward Layla. Cal could hear him whispering.

"This is so fucking ridiculous. Bunch of hocus pocus."

"Shhh..."

"Don't 'shhh' me. If that priest can talk, I can talk."

"Darling, please, can you just..."

"What do these people think? That Jose Manuel is going to float up to some fucking cloud, they'll uncrush his skull, and then he'll sit around up there smiling for a few billion years? Playing cards or whatever it is they do with the angels? He'd probably try to *fuck* the angels. What a massive, fraudulent, putrid vat of vomit, all of this."

"Stop it, darling."

Paul's voice grew louder. Sotto voce, he continued.

"I *won't* stop it. This is all a fraud, and I'm going to call it what it is. Am I the only one around here who has the courage to..."

A few people were looking over their shoulders, fingers raised to lips.

"Oh, okay, okay. If they're not ready for the truth, then they can just go on listening to all this krak. Bunch of fucking nonsense. They're welcome to it. Idiots."

When it was over and everyone turned to go, Layla saw Cal standing behind her. She gasped.

"Oh my god, what happened to you?"

"I'll tell you outside," said Cal.

Paul was grinning. "You look better with blood on your face," he said. "It suits you."

Everyone filed out. The priest, casket, family, friends. They would head now toward the cemetery that was on the path to Port Lligat. Jose Manuel would be buried there among the olive groves, above Dali's house. Standing on the terrace near the foot of the Cypress trees, Paul glared at Cal.

"You look like a fucking wreck. What is wrong with you?"

"I heard what you were whispering inside there, Paul. What's wrong with *you*?"

"Now listen..."

"Darling, I'm afraid he's right," said Layla. "That was not your finest hour."

Jose Manuel's family was standing nearby. They could hear them arguing. Cal couldn't help himself.

"This is *their* moment, Paul, not yours. They need this. Also, didn't anyone ever tell you to take your hat off inside a church?"

"Well look who's talking," said Paul. "With your shirt torn..."

"The shirt!" Layla just noticed.

"I'm sorry," said Cal. "I'm really sorry."

Cal felt a hand on his arm. It was Wiggles.

"We're heading now to the cemetery."

"Well I'm not going," said Paul. "It's too far up that damned hill. And besides, I've had enough of this damned theatre. Come on," he said to Layla, "let's go."

"No. I'm going with them to the cemetery. You go home. I'll be along."

"But I said..."

"You go on home. I won't be long."

Paul stood there watching as the procession, with Layla in it, wound its way down the passageway and out of sight. As the last of them disappeared he mumbled to himself, "Fucking idiots!"

Chapter XLIV

On the crest of the little hill that rose between Cadaqués to its south and Port Lligat to its north, just a stone's throw from either of those, lay the village cemetery. The tiny chapel of Saint Baldiri stood at one corner of it. High walls stretched around like arms embracing the quiet patch of earth where some, whose lives had unfolded so close by, had settled in for the "ever after" part of their story. As Jose Manuel joined those who would not be walking back to the village at day's end, his family and friends gathered to say their last good-byes. The mother wept. The little brother played nervously with some pebbles he had picked off the ground. Both sisters were comforting the mother. The father stood stoically, with his head bowed.

Cal and Layla were standing next to each other. When the priest finished, and it was the gravediggers' turn now to earn their living, the group turned to go. As they were leaving, David pointed toward the bell that hung above the chapel.

"Do you know, Cal, where they got the bell?"

"Where?"

"Dali, he gave it. His father is buried here. And so it was his gift. But first, Dali he put it in a painting. So the bell, it lives twice now. Here, but also in the painting. Like the person, yes, it was reborn."

Cal and Layla and David stopped and turned to look at the bell as the rest of the group began to file back toward the village.

"It's a beautiful place," said Cal.

"To be reborn, yes, Cal? On this hill one day I will also rest. The body will stay here even as the soul flies, like an echo from the ringing of the bell. Cal? Layla? Life, it is like an echo from the ringing of a bell, yes?"

"Yes, David."

"And the echo, it does not stop. Over the sea, over the mountains, it keeps going. We are echoes, too. Jose Manuel, he is an echo now. His karma pushes the echo."

"It's incredible," said Cal. "I wrote a poem for Jose Manuel and part of it is about an echo."

He had finally finished that poem he had started on this walk toward the lighthouse. He recited it to them now.

> *"As a shooting star are we today*
> *Within eye's sight but for briefest time*
> *And though we would we cannot stay*
> *Yet we can always linger in your mind*
> *If you'll recall our passage like your own youth*
> *Gone, as beauty, in deed but not in name*
> *Remembrance of a past as sure as truth*
> *Your memory now for us the truest flame*
> *For sure as light reflects and echoes sound*
> *Both mind and heart can hold that which has passed*
> *Till nature's game must child-like come 'round*
> *And all once gone instead forever lasts*
> >   *Still, as your own star now flies fleetingly through time*
> >   *Look to the day when it will follow mine"*

"Oh Cal, I did not understand every word, but it sounded very beautiful," said David.

"Yes," agreed Layla. "Very nice."

There was no sight of the others now. David smiled.

"Look, Cal, they have all gone back to the world of the living."

David lit a cigarette.

"I will go for a walk to the sea. In moments like this, maybe best to be alone yes, to think, to pray. Because *all* of this," David gestured toward everything, "this *also* is a church."

Cal and Layla stood watching as David walked not toward the village, following the funeral party, but alone along the road that stretched past the cemetery toward the sea. Beyond the chapel, the blue water stretched toward an unseen world beyond. Rocky islands close to shore looked like stepping-stones.

"Should we follow the others?" asked Cal. "I think the herd's heading to the watering hole now."

"And you want to join them?"

"Well, I..."

"I just thought that, considering how Jose Manuel died, and after last night..."

On the walk up to the cemetery Cal had explained to her what had happened; the drinking, the climbing on the roof of the church, and how the shirt that she had made for him had ripped.

"Or what do you say, let's go the other way? For a little walk maybe?"

"Okay," said Layla.

They turned and headed down the narrow lane that led toward Port Lligat. Dali's house was below and to the right. It was separated from the cemetery by a grove of olive trees on the hillside. There were drystone walls running along both sides of the road. A small car passed them. Otherwise they were alone.

"How does your face feel?" she asked. "And your back?

And your hands?"

"Ask me how my left foot feels."

"Okay. How does your left foot feel?"

"Great! That's the way to do it, isn't it? Think about the things that don't hurt to get you over the things that do."

"Is that the formula?"

"That's my formula."

There was no wind. Only the sun on the olive trees behind the wall, and the sound of a small bird perched on a telephone wire. Some tourists were coming up the road the other way. A man and woman wearing hats. The man had a camera in his hand.

"How's it going with your book?" Layla asked.

"Fine. I spoke with my friend Grisha on the phone."

"The painter?"

"He's mailing us some images he thinks might work as a cover. Paintings he's done with Spanish themes."

"Excited to see your book published?"

"Yes."

"Fifteen years is a long time between writing a book and having it published. And you never wrote another one after that?"

"Not yet. I started a few. Didn't get very far."

"Busy with other things?"

Cal nodded.

"Do you think you'll ever write another book?"

"Absolutely."

In front of them was the quiet bay stretching out. It was even smaller than the Cadaqués bay on the other side of the hill. Two rocky islands at the mouth of Port Lligat kept the waters here calm. There were little fishing boats moored offshore, others pulled onto the pebble beach ahead, and others tied to the stone quay that ran past Dali's house on their right. The house was a museum now. There were about twenty tourists milling around outside it, tickets in hand, waiting for their turn to take the tour.

Dali's whimsy loomed about the place. There was the Cypress tree growing through the wooden fishing boat beside the entrance to the house, the first sign to visitors then, as now, that things here were not as they were elsewhere. There were the huge eggs and heads of Castor and Pollux balancing on the roof. And behind the house, the penis-shaped swimming pool. In their youth and tight-skinned beauty, Robert, Richard and Marita and others had splashed in it as the great masturbator himself had sat at the head looking on. In this quiet place, in the painter's studio that was at the heart of it all, dreams Freud had so assiduously probed were splayed out on canvases for the modern world to see. In this quiet place, the line between what was real and what was fancy became no more fixed than Europe's borders.

At the end of the quay there were no people. They walked to it. As soon as they were on the smooth stones Layla took off her sandals and carried them. They sat then, dangling their feet over the water, the tourists over their shoulders in the distance, birds circling above the island, the water like glass.

"It looks like one of Dali's paintings."

"That's bass akwards, isn't it?" asked Cal.

"You mean the paintings look like this?"

They were sitting close together, and quiet for some moments.

"You never said anything about my song that I sang at Senalda's."

"You mean, about the rooster and the chicken?"

"You never said anything about it."

She just looked at him.

A small yellow boat appeared at the mouth of the bay. It was coming toward them.

"So what's with the drinking and climbing?" she asked.

"Well, there was this rumor the sun was going to rise this morning. So I climbed onto the roof of the church to see if there was any truth to it."

"To the church, or to the rumor? You could have killed yourself."

"Everyone has a hobby, right? Mine is drinking and climbing."

"Don't joke."

"I'm not joking. It used to be drinking and driving, but I decided that was too dangerous. Jose Manuel proved it."

She looked disappointed. "Okay, forget it."

"Serious answer? It started when I was about twelve. My parents had divorced. My brother and I lived with our Mom. She never figured she'd have to work for a living, just planned on being a professor's happy wife, but that didn't really work out. So she tried different things, like selling encyclopedias door to door. Not a lot of money or fun in that, so what she'd do is she'd come home and drink a whole bottle of bourbon to make herself feel a little better. Or at least not as bad."

"I'm sorry."

He shrugged.

"What can you do? Anyway, it wasn't much fun for us, either. I didn't like hearing her complain. And twelve years old, it didn't seem like there was much I could do to help. So what I'd do is, when she wasn't looking I'd drink a little of that bourbon too, and then I'd climb up onto the roof of the house because she could never find me up there. Or else I'd climb up a tree. That worked too. I had this little fort. Why she never bothered to look up, I don't know. Too drunk to think about it probably. Or maybe it was just too hard to lift her head. Anyway, I had discovered the joys of drinking and climbing. This is *not* my favorite subject, by the way."

There was a group of tourists that had broken off from the larger group, and now they were watching the yellow boat getting closer. There were more tourists in the boat, and it looked like the boat was going to drop off the one group and pick up the other.

"And so what, you're still hiding from your Mom?"

"Maybe."

"And that story about the horse..."

"Oh, I have lots of stories. Because the thing is, if you survive that shit it makes for great stories."

"Does it?"

"It better. Otherwise there's nothing to show for it."

The little yellow boat's name was Gala. Dali's wife. They could see the name now written on the bow in black letters. It stopped near the museum. The tourists on the boat got off and the tourists off the boat got on.

Cal had also taken off his shoes and rolled up his pant legs. There was a scar over his ankle.

"What happened there?"

"Umm..."

"Come on, let's hear it."

"That's my *maximum* drinking and climbing story."

"So, go on. Once upon a time..."

"Okay. Well, once upon a time there was a boy, and he was living in Andalusia writing this little book..."

"And?"

"And he lived in a little apartment on the fourth floor of this little building next to a little beach. And one night he didn't have his key..."

"His little key."

"That's right, he didn't have his little key, so he figured he'd just climb up the balconies."

"And then?"

"And then this piece of wood broke, and he fell from the fourth floor down to the little parking lot."

"Are you joking? You're so lucky."

"I was pretty lucky. I just broke my leg, that's all."

"But that still didn't stop you from drinking and climbing?"

"Umm, apparently not. When the cast came off a year later I was in New York. A friend of mine had an apartment there. 666 West End Avenue. Nice building. To celebrate we went up on the roof to have a drink and smoke a joint. It was twenty-two stories up. I remember the number, because I kept jumping over this one gap in the edge of the roof, an airshaft or something, and my friend Gordon kept yelling at me, "Are you fucking crazy? It's a twenty-two story fall.""

"And? Are you? Fucking crazy?"

"I guess. Because I didn't stop doing it. Instead, I said to Gordon, 'Now watch, I'll do it with my eyes closed. And so then....'"

"No. Okay, enough. Stop. I don't want to hear any more."

"Sorry. Hey, I've got a great idea. Let's stop talking about me and start talking about you. Your turn. I want to hear some secrets. And not just your average run-of-the-mill little secrets. I like my secrets big, dark and heavy, like my coffee. Come on."

She thought a moment.

"Okay. I stole five pounds from my Mum once. I was thirteen. My friends and I wanted to go to the cinema, and my Mum wouldn't give me the money for it, so I just took it."

"Wow, there's a dark secret. That could ruin a life if it got out. I promise I won't tell anyone. And I really appreciate your honesty."

"I can't really think of..."

"What's with the Paul thing?"

"What do you mean, 'the Paul thing'? You mean because he's a bit older than I am?"

"For instance. Let's see, you're twenty-one and he's..."

"Seventy-nine. He's fifty-eight years older than I am. What of it?" She shifted her body. "Well, okay. Here's something that not too many people know. My father left my mother just after I was born. And we haven't seen him since. But Paul is *not* a father figure for me. I know that's what some people think. I love him. He's a good man. Really he is. I know he comes across as a little gruff sometimes, but that's just because he's got his own wounds. And they're so deep. He's just trying to protect himself with that...that strong thing that he shows to people."

"That 'strong thing.'|"

"Yes. I mean, there's more to it than just that."

She started to say something else, then stopped herself.

"So, he's the one for you, is he?"

"Yes. I mean, yes. Definitely."

"What about children?"

"What about them?"

"Well, the way you were talking about those kids on the beach the other day, and that poem you wrote for your sister's kids. Are you and Paul thinking of having your own kids one day?"

Chapter XLV

"What did you say to her?"

"I'm sorry?"

"What the fuck did you say to her? Because when she came home yesterday after that damned funeral, all she could do was cry."

"That's what people do after funerals, Paul. They cry."

"Now don't get smart with me. That wasn't it. I tried to find out what was wrong, and she wouldn't tell me. So *you* tell me. What the fuck did you say to her?"

"Nothing."

"Look, you bloody fucking asshole, I know what you're up to. Well stop it. Just stop it, right now. You have no idea the kind of pain you're causing."

"To her, or to you?"

Paul glared down at him. His hands were leaning on the table. All this unfolding on the terrace of the Meliton. The two young waiters stood nearby watching them.

"Now listen to me, I may be seventy-two years old, but that doesn't mean I don't still have some tricks up my sleeve. And I will defend what is mine. So I have just one thing I'm going to say to you now. Are you listening?"

"I'm listening."

"Are you sure you're listening?"

"What is it?"

Paul leaned closer. For the first time he lowered his voice so that no one else would hear. Then, almost whispering, he said,
"I have a gun."

Chapter XLVI

That night and the next day, and the day after that also, Cal did not see Layla. Finally he had David go up to Paul's restaurant pretending that he had something to give her. But the waitress told him that she didn't know where they were. Cal waited, walked, then waited again, at Meliton, at Boia, at Imperial. No luck. She had left Cadaqués.

Chapter XLVII

It began with a word. Sometimes you had to dig for it, like for a truffle in the roots of what you already knew you wanted to say. Other times you would trip over it easily like a stone in the path that couldn't be missed. You'd look down and there it was, one word standing out from all the others. And you'd pick that word up in your hand and put it on the paper, and everything else you wrote after that would hang on it, as on a keystone. You'd find another word then, and another, and just keep stringing them together until you had your poem or your book or whatever else you were building to say what you needed to say.

It was like that now. Cal sat at the blue table, and as it had for so many before, all trying to say the same thing as he was now, there was really only one word that could get it started. He was even luckier than that. He had more than just the one word, because it came to him in a question.

How fast is love?

Chapter XLVIII

The third day now and still no sight of her. Looking left, right, everywhere, while walking by the Imperial Cal spotted Angela, Jose's wife, the owner of the bar. She was looking toward him and waving something in her hand. He went to her. It was a letter.

"Es para ti."

Layla had written the bar's true name: *Cal Zander, Café D'Es Canto, Cadaqués, Girona.* He opened it and read,

"In Roses. Back soon. Love, Layla."

All day and that night he kept taking the letter out and reading that last part of it again.

Love, Layla
Love, Layla
Love, Layla...

Chapter XLIX

The next day there she was, sitting inside the Boia alone. Cal came to her and sat.

"I didn't know what happened. I thought maybe he took you back to Manchester."

"We were in Roses. You got my note?"

"Yes."

"I didn't want to go but Paul insisted. He said he needed me there. Just an excuse, really. He's quite upset. Apparently he thinks that you..."

"That I what?"

"That you're falling in love with me."

"That's ridiculous."

"That's what I told him."

"So he took you to *Roses*?"

"Well, there was more to it, of course. He's been trying for almost a year now to get Ferran Adria interested in starting a new restaurant with him."

"Ferran Adria? Of El Bulli?"

"Yes."

"And?"

"Well, Adria's not at all interested, of course. Paul keeps writing to him and he never answers his letters. So he wanted to go and see him in person."

"And, what happened?"

"We couldn't even get in. We kept eating pizza at this little place on the beach, staying in this horrible little hotel. And then we kept going back to Bulli, and back again, and of course he wouldn't see him. There's no interest there whatsoever."

"Adria's the number one chef in the world. One can't get a reservation at his restaurant even a year ahead of time. What makes Paul think he'd be interested in going into business with him?"

"I keep telling him it's ridiculous. But he keeps writing these letters to Adria, telling him he has this wonderful idea that would make Adria's cooking 'even better.'"

"I'm so glad you're back."

She smiled. Cal flagged the waiter.

"Do you want something to drink?" he asked. "Chocolate milk? Orange juice?"

"No, I'm fine."

Cal ordered a sangria for himself.

"Listen, I told you my friend Grisha was sending those images as possible covers for my book?"

"Yes."

"Well, they came. And tonight Tharrats and his wife Dolores are making dinner at their house. We're going to pick which image to use. Would you like to come?"

"I'd love to. I really would. But I can't. Paul said if he sees me with you again he's going to do something crazy."

"Like what?"

"I don't know, but he was in tears as he said it. He's so sensitive."

"So what, we don't see each other again? We say good-bye now, before we ever really said hello?"

"No, of course not that. I just think..."

In the distance, she could see Paul walking toward them.

"I have to go. I'm sorry. Really, I'm so sorry."

Cal watched as she stood and walked to Paul. Those two spoke for a moment. From the bright sun, the old man could not see Cal sitting at the table in the shade.

Chapter L

The following day Cal had not shaven. He was wearing the same clothes he had worn the day before. The wind was coming off the sea, and the trees were moving and there were gray clouds overhead. On the edge of the passeig, a cluster of about ten young people were lying with their backpacks beside them. As he walked by them, Cal could smell marijuana and smiled. Filip was sitting with them, playing his guitar. When he saw Cal he shouted out to him.

"Hey man, you coming to our concert tonight at the Boia?"

"I'll be there."

That night, Cal had showered and changed, and as he walked toward the Boia he could hear the music already coming across the water. It was warm and the wind was blowing still. There were waves breaking on the rocks below the Punta, and many people walking. Couples, families, friends.

At the bar, Cal squeezed through the crowd onto the terrace in back. Filip, another guitarist, and a young man with drums were playing at the edge of the beach. There were people dancing. Robert and Marita and David were sitting at one table. There was an empty chair at one of the other tables. Cal asked the couple sitting there if he could take it. They said yes. He lifted it over people's heads and brought to the table where his friends were. He sat. The waiter came and he ordered.

Filip's guitar, fast and loud, sounded like an electrical storm.

As if to match it there was a flash of light in the sky beyond Es Cucurucuc. Cal kept looking around to see if Layla was there. After about an hour, still no sight of her, he said good night to his friends and went home.

Chapter LI

The next day, Cal sat again on the empty terrace of the Boia. Wherever he had seen her last was the place he wanted to be. The wind was strong still, though the expected rain had not yet come. Cal sat with a drink watching the waves, and wondering what to do and where to go next. Then her voice.

"Hi."

He turned. She was alone.

"Join me?" he asked.

She sat next to him. "Well, did you do it?"

"Do what?"

"The other night. Did you find the image you want to use as the cover of your book?"

"We did, yes."

She pulled something out of her bag.

"Here, I have something for you...again."

It was a shirt, like the one she had made for him before.

"Try not to tear this one, alright?"

"I promise. I'll be very careful."

"No more church rooftops."

"I have something for you, too."

"Really? What?"

"I can't tell you. Not here anyway."

"Well, give me a clue at least."

He thought a moment.

"It doesn't weigh anything, and it will last forever."

"Mysterious. And, when do I get this mystery gift?"

"Now, if you want."

"I want."

"But we have to go around to Port Alguer."

"Okay."

"You're not afraid he'll see us walking together?"

"He had to go to Figueres. Meeting someone at the bank there. He won't be back for a few hours."

Cal paid for his drink. Together then they walked to Port Alguer. As they reached the beach, where the edge of the road wound above it he jumped down, turned, and offered up his hands to help her. She leaned forward. He put both his hands around her waist and lifted her down.

"Follow me."

He led her to the edge of the water, then turned to face her.

"Okay, now I have to explain something first. What I'm going to do now is hopelessly, shamelessly, ridiculously romantic."

"Oh my god. What are you going to do?"

"People don't do this anymore, if they ever did. Probably they never did. But I've planned this very carefully. Even the weather."

"You planned the weather?"

"Yes. I made a call."

As she stood watching, he bent down and began to clear stones away from the water's edge. The sand here was hard-packed and already smoother than the rest of the beach.

"What are you doing?"

"You'll see."

A couple of small children who were playing close-by

stopped and stood watching him. Their parents at the other end of the beach were gathering up their towels because of the wind. As Cal kept clearing the stones, he called to Layla over his shoulder.

"I learned to do it like this from the manual."

"What manual?"

"*Layla and Majnun.*"

"You're joking."

He finished clearing a small swath of the beach, then smoothed it over with his hands and feet and began to look around. She was watching him and smiling. He found a small stick, picked it up then came to her.

"Okay, now I'm going to write something. And as I write I need you to read the words out loud, okay?"

She nodded.

He bent down, and with the stick he wrote in the sand, *How fast is love?* She just stood there.

"You have to read it out loud, remember?"

She spoke the words.

"How fast is love?"

"Excellent! Now the next line..."

He wrote, and again she read his words out loud.

"Is it like light? Like fire? Like waves upon the sea?"

He had already used up all the space in the sand that he had cleared. So he stopped writing and walked to her. Standing in front of her now, he just recited the sonnet he had written for her.

"*How fast is love?*
Is it like light? Like fire? Like waves upon the sea
When the storm sends forth its ripples against the shore?
Could such love I feel for her she feel for me?
And if so, then would I love her all the more?

> *Can her feelings now, like so many sunrays through a glass*
> *Through the prism of her heart burn such a fire*
> *That focusing on me I dare to ask*
> *If the colors of her love match my desire?*
> *For were it so, then would my very dreams alight*
> *And life itself in their place take wing*
> *Then would my footsteps instead give way to flight*
> *And I too dumb to speak must loudly sing:*
>> *Let both the thundering surf and skies above proclaim*
>> *That on this day a man was born again!"*

He was watching her, looking for her reaction.
"Too romantic? That was too romantic, wasn't it?"
"No. It was okay."
"Not very modern."
"Not very."
"I could write something more modern."
"No, it was okay. Really."

The wind was blowing her hair and the white dress that she was wearing. Her arms hung at her side.
"I never had anyone write a poem in the sand for me before."
"Are you joking? I'm the first? Really? I can't believe that."
"I remember now, Majnun, he writes in the sand for Layla. And the other night, when you kissed the wall of my house, that was also in the story, wasn't it?"

He stepped closer to her. Only inches away now.
"What are you doing?"
"Kiss me."
"What?"
"Kiss me."
"I'm not going to kiss you.

"Kiss me."

"I said, I'm not going to kiss you. I'm with Paul, remember?"

He stood there, just looking at her.

"You're afraid."

"I'm not afraid. Afraid of what?"

"A real relationship."

"I'm *in* a relationship. With Paul."

"You're using him."

"How am I using him?"

"He's protecting you from a real relationship."

"That's...that's not true."

"You're afraid of being with a man who might one day leave you, like your father left you. And you think because Paul needs you so badly, he won't leave you. But he's almost eighty years old. He's going to have to leave you one day."

"Why are saying these things?"

"Didn't you listen to my poem? There was your answer. Come on, just do it. Put your lips together and..."

"*No.* And besides, that's not kissing. That's whistling. I saw that movie."

"It also works for kissing. I promise. Here, I'll show you." He leaned toward her. "Just put your lips together and..."

"*No!* And it's *not* because I'm afraid."

"I'll never leave you."

"What did you say?"

"I said, I'll never leave you."

"Why did you say that? What gives you the right to say that?" He leaned back.

"Okay, I tell you what. If you won't kiss me, at least come for a swim with me."

"*What? Are you crazy?*"

"You see, you're afraid. Afraid of a real relationship, afraid of a little kiss, you're even afraid of going for a swim."

"There's a storm coming!"

"So?"

"So? It's a *storm*!"

"Alright, forget it. I'm sorry I asked. Because if you're afraid of a little warm rain even, well then..."

He turned and began to walk away. She called out after him.

"I'm not afraid of anything."

He kept walking.

"Okay. I'll go for a swim with you."

He turned and reached out his hand. She came to him and took it. Together they walked up the little road through the arches, past the cafés and restaurants where tourists were eating and drinking. The umbrellas next to the tables were folded and tied closed because of the wind. Just beyond the Café Habana there was a break in the wall to their left. A narrow passage led down to the sea. At the other end of it there were some rocks. There were no people there.

"I don't have my bathing suit."

"This is Cadaqués."

Before she could say anything else, Cal stripped off his clothes and dove naked into the water. When he resurfaced and turned to face her she was still standing there. A light rain was starting to fall.

"You know you're crazy, don't you?"

"It's only rain. Come on."

Treading water, he watched as she took off her clothes. Every part of her body was as beautiful as he had imagined it. Stepping carefully over the rocks she came down toward and finally into the water. He swam to her. He looked down for a moment to make sure that he was not stepping on a sea urchin. His feet probed the rocky bottom, found a firm footing, and this time he didn't ask. With one hand braced on a rock, he wrapped an arm around her and kissed her. Gently at first, and then suddenly she was kissing him back, their mouths pressed together, one hungrier than the other. Both her arms were around him, and then her legs were around him, and a moment later he was inside her. She made a noise. He was afraid that she had cut herself on a rock.

"Are you okay?" he whispered.

"Don't stop. Please, don't stop."

When it was over he helped her climb out of the water. As she was stepping over the rocks he saw it. There was blood on the inside of her thigh. And then he understood.

There was an overhanging balcony on one of the houses near the water. He grabbed their clothes and they sat together under that balcony. He kept his arm around her, and hung his own shirt over her to keep the wind off her. Her head was leaning on his shoulder.

"I didn't know."

"It's alright."

A few minutes later she looked up at him.

"Please, take me home."

"You mean to..."

"To your place."

Chapter LII

He watched her sleeping, her hair almost dry now, the shape of her body outlined by the sheet he had pulled over her in the warm little room. The shutter on the window was closed, and behind it was the sound of the wind and rain. He had understood when they came here that she did not need to make love again, but needed to hold him and be held and to feel safe. She had whispered to him that she had wanted to be close since that first day when he had read Widdle Wat to her, and that finally she had needed to be close and there was nothing he could feel sorry for. That she was grateful, and that she had waited for him. And they agreed that now they were in the Widdle Wat together, that it was their space, and they would be happy in it.

He watched her sleeping for a long time. Her slow breathing, the little hand resting on the pillow. Then he stood and went into the other room. On the blue table lay the 'magic key' David had handed him that first day. Also there his journal, laptop, some books, and the bottle of brandy he had begun to drink the night before. He opened the bottle now and took a few sips. He stood there thinking for a while, and then he went back into the room where Layla was still sleeping. He slipped into bed and lay watching her again before finally he too fell asleep. But not for long. A noise outside woke him. Something sharp and long, like a scream. She had rolled onto her other side with her back to him. The noise had not woken her. And so again Cal stood and went into the other room. He sat at the blue table and lit a candle. It was dark now, and the storm outside was blowing harder.

He had heard stories about the winters here in Cadaqués, and the famous tramuntana. Gabriel Garcia Marquez had written a story about it. He had not read the story, but he knew about it, and as he listened to the wind and the rain against the house words began to come to him. He took another long sip from the brandy, then opened his journal imagining the worst of it. It began as a poem, but quickly became a song as the noise of the wind was giving him the melody.

Tramuntana blows, tramuntana knows
That something's coming down
Wild cats howl, mad dogs growl
And there's a rumbling underground
High seas are rising
Beating boats against the shore
A faint light is shining
Through an open door
Church bells ring, children sing
There's a stranger in the town
Tree tops bend, roots upend
And the wind is blowing 'round
In the bars they are drinking
Waiting for the judgment day
Hopes quickly sinking
As some drink their lives away
Young girls dream, young men scheme
As the rain begins to fall
Someone cries, the old man spies
A shadow on the wall

Scrambling footsteps
Echo down the cobblestones
In darkened alleys
They are battening down their homes
Tramontana blows, Tramontana knows
That something just came down
And the rain is falling down
And the wind is blowing 'round
And the wind is blowing 'round

The words came out of him like water running down a hill, easily. Still, it surprised him that he had not written a poem about her.

"Cal?"

Layla's voice from the other room. He blew the candle out. Slipping in next to her, his hand cupped her face. He stroked her cheek.

"I'm here."

"Where were you?"

She could smell the brandy.

"I couldn't sleep because of the noise outside."

"What time is it?"

"I don't know."

She twisted her head to look toward the little window.

"It's dark outside."

"It's the middle of the night."

She sat up.

"How's that possible? How could I have slept so long? I have to go."

"Why?"

"I have to go. Paul will be scared to death. He has no idea

where I am. I have to tell him. He has to know that I'm okay."

She stood, looking for her clothes.

"Layla, please don't go."

"I have to."

"In the morning we can..."

"No. He'll be terrified something's happened to me. I can't let him worry like that."

He told her what Paul had said about the gun.

"*What?*"

"At the Meliton. He even whispered it, so no one else would hear."

"Oh, he was just saying that. Out of frustration, or pain, or maybe anger. But believe me, he doesn't have a gun. If he had, I would have seen it."

Chapter LIII

The rain had stopped. The stones under their feet were wet and shiny and they could hear the waves before they saw them as the noise echoed up the narrow passage. He was holding onto her hand.

"What are you going to say to him?"

"I don't know yet."

There was no one else out. Blackened windows, and the sky dark as the sound of the sea grew louder still. Soon they were out in the full of it, in the open of the little plaza above Port Alguer, with the wind warm on their faces and pulling at his shirt. The tops of the trees were moving. As they kept walking, heads bent forward, the water was breaking against the beach to their right. Where he had written in the sand for her was being pounded by the waves, his words long gone.

They rounded the bend in the road. Ahead now were the lights of the village. Street lamps threw shadows from the moving trees onto the dirt of the passeig. Cal kept thinking that this was a mistake, and that she should wait. Then again, she was right that Paul would be worried.

"Please don't tell him about us. Not yet. Not when you're alone with him. Just tell him that you fell asleep at a party, at Senalda's."

"Don't worry, I'll know what to say. Trust me."

Around the corner from Paul's house she stopped to kiss him.

"I'll find you later. Please, don't worry."

He stood watching as she walked toward the house. She knew he was watching her. When she reached the corner she stopped and looked back and smiled at him. Then she disappeared.

Nothing else he could do. He couldn't follow her. And there was no way he could just go home to be warm and safe in that bed without her now. He had no idea what Paul would do or say. If he would even believe that she had been at Senalda's. If he didn't know the truth, he would at least suspect it.

There was a doorway nearby out of the wind. Cal went to it. He would wait and listen, stay there just in case. Craning his neck, he saw a light come on in a window overhead beside their terrace.

A black cat appeared from some unseen place. It paused to look at him, then walked across the little passageway and disappeared through a gap in a wall. Cal did not believe in omens. He was not superstitious, although he did knock on wood when some things were said to avoid tempting fate. As if directing fate could be that easy.

There was a light on in another window now. An early riser, someone who worked in the markets maybe, or a fisherman. And there was the noise of a wooden shutter banging in the wind. The noise stopped. Someone must have fastened the shutter.

Cal was crouched down in the doorway on bent knees. When his legs got tired he sat on the stone step. It was not cold, still the wind was on him and he pulled his collar up against it. He closed his eyes and thought about Layla and then he fell asleep. A sharp noise woke him. His eyes shot open. He saw a woman with a key locking a blue wooden door near by. She was looking at him. The noise must have been the door closing. She turned and walked off.

The first purple light of day was spreading in the sky. Cal looked up. The light in their room was off. Probably they were asleep by now. He stood and, walking slowly, made his way back toward his own house. It was growing lighter and the storm was passing. The clouds were lifting and on the mountain ahead he could see the hermitage of San Sebastian surrounded by cork oaks. And there were people on the street now. The village was waking up.

Chapter LIV

Brandy in the morning is stronger than brandy at night. Cal had a few sips to help him sleep. Then he took off his clothes and climbed into bed. He reached for the pillow where her head had rested so recently, and he held that pillow as if it was Layla. He tried to smell her in the pillow, and rubbed his hand over the place in the bed where her body had been.

This was different. Not just another summer affair, a good time destined to become another memory on a stack of memories. He had enough of those already. What he needaed now was a best friend, a partner, a lover. And maybe, yes, maybe even a wife. Why not? There had been so many false starts, and now...

The thoughts tapered off as sleep came. That invisible line that once you cross it you don't realize you've crossed it. Like a little death. Only this was better, because it didn't last like death lasts.

Hours that seemed like minutes later there was a knock on the door. Cal jumped up and, with a towel wrapped around his waist, standing a little back from the door and to one side just in case, he called out.

"Yes?"

It was Layla. Cal opened the door. She had a bag with her. She had been crying. She came in. He closed the door after her, locking it. She put the bag down and he held her. She was crying again.

"It was so bad," she said. "I hurt him so much."

She had said what Cal told her to say, about being at Senalda's.

"At first I thought he believed me. Because I know he wanted to believe me."

She had gone to bed then, and slept. But then he woke her, yelling at her that he wanted to know the truth.

"But then I didn't have to tell him, because he told me the truth."

He had guessed, of course. So finally she told him he was right.

"I was afraid he might hit me, which he's never done. But then he just went over to this chair by the window and sat. He wasn't crying. He didn't even look angry anymore. He just sat there. I kept saying things to him, but he wouldn't answer. Finally he just whispered to me, 'Get out. Get out of my house.' I tried to say something, but he kept saying the same thing. In this voice that was so calm, so bloody calm. 'Get out of my house. Please, get out of my house...'"

"I'm sorry. Layla, I'm sorry."

"Finally I just grabbed a few things and, well, here I am."

They slept for a few hours. In the afternoon they showered and dressed and went for a walk. They needed to eat something. They went up to L'Estable. The sky had cleared and everything had been washed clean by the storm. The air was clear and bright, still they ate inside where no one would see them. And afterwards they went for a slow walk, up to the Hotel Llane Petit. They turned there and as they were starting to walk back they saw a helicopter above the village. It was taking off. They watched as it rose up and disappeared over the mountain. Back at the house then, they were in the kitchen making coffee when there was a knock on the door.

David's voice shouted out.

"Cal? Cal, are you there? Cal, if you are there please open the door."

Cal hurried to the door and opened it.

"What is it, David? Is everything okay?"

"Did you hear the helicopter?"

Layla was standing next to Cal.

"We saw it. Why?"

"Cal, Layla, it is Paul. They have taken him to the hospital."

Layla cried out. "Oh my god, no. What happened?"

"I do not know. The helicopter landed in the football field above the village. They have taken him to the hospital."

Chapter LV

Cal and Layla hurried together toward the village center. Cal kept thinking about that fucking gun. Someone shouted out to them. It was Consuela, the accountant for Paul's restaurant. From across the street by the Casino she came to them.

"Layla, I'm so sorry."

"What happened? Consuela, please tell me."

"I had to go to the house. We were to meet. We have to file for the taxes tomorrow. I knocked, but no answer. The door was open so I just went in. I found him on the floor. The gun was next to him."

"What gun? What are you talking about?"

"I was so afraid, Layla. I thought maybe he..."

"Oh no, dear god. Please, don't tell me..."

"But was no blood. Only he was lying on floor, sweating, in so much pain. And he was making these strange noises...was so horrible!"

"Consuela..."

"I called ambulance. They came fast. They think probably was heart attack. Please Layla, do not worry. I am sure he is going to be okay."

"Where did they take him?"

"I don't know. The helicopter came. But, somebody will know."

As the Casino was right there they hurried into it. Information central. Robert stood at the bar. He had heard they had taken Paul to Figueres, to the hospital there. Someone else said no, they had taken him to Girona. The two ambulance drivers walked in, coming to have a coffee. Miguel called out to them in Catalan from behind the bar. They had heard over their radio that the helicopter had diverted to Barcelona.

The German writer, Daniel, had been sitting alone at one table. He came over to them. He had a car. Cal and Layla were welcome to borrow it.

Chapter LVI

That evening in Barcelona, after a long walk around the nearby Sagrada Familia, they went back a second time to the hospital. Layla asked again to see Paul, but was told still no visitors.

"But can you tell me at least how he is?"

It was an old nurse with a kind face.

"He is resting. Come back tomorrow."

Hospital de la Santa Creu i Sant Pau is a modernist marvel. Walking down the sculpted corridors, past the great columns and vaulted ceilings and the grand staircase, craning his neck to look up at the tiled domes, Cal thought that one wanted to live, not die, in a place as beautiful as this. Maybe that was part of the therapy.

There was a little hotel, the Esperanza, near where they had left the car in a garage on the Diagonal. Three stars, but looking at it Cal thought one would have been enough. It was on the big road itself, with all the heavy traffic and the windows of the hotel dirty. Layla thought it was good enough and they should just get a room there since it was close to the hospital. Cal thought differently.

"Look, as long as we're here let's stay someplace nice. You're under a lot of stress. We should relax, charge the batteries."

"Alright. Where would you suggest?"

The summer before, just after getting the money from his father, he had spent two delicious nights at the Palace Hotel. It was also close by.

He flagged a taxi. The little black and yellow car stopped and they climbed in. First to the garage for Cal to grab their bags from the car. They had each brought a change of clothes and toiletries, expecting to stay one night, maybe more. Then to the hotel. Cal held Layla's hand in the taxi. He felt bad for her. He even felt sorry for Paul. Whatever he was planning to do with that gun, the stress from just thinking about it had proven too much.

At the hotel they found his name in the system.

"Welcome back, Señor."

Cal would take a deluxe room. He told the man standing behind the desk that they were there to visit a friend who was in the hospital. The man said he was sorry to hear it and upgraded them to a junior suite.

A bellman offered to take their two small bags. Cal let him, pausing a moment to look around. The last time he had walked through those revolving doors, past the marble columns and heavy drapes and the gold trim on the walls, there were two young prostitutes with him. Now he was with a woman he loved. This was better.

Once alone in the big room, Cal came to Layla and held her.

"It's going to be okay. Don't worry."

He suggested that maybe they should go for another walk. Las Ramblas was close by. They could have a bite and a drink somewhere. Layla didn't feel like it. She just wanted to stay in. He drew a hot bath for them in the large marble tub. As the water poured, he looked over the menu on the desk. Layla said she wasn't hungry, but Cal convinced her that she had to eat something. He phoned down asking for the food and a bottle of good *rio-ja* to be brought up in one hour. And he wanted a bucket of ice now. Layla undressed and went into the bathroom. Cal also undressed, and was standing in the hotel's white robe, looking out the window at the courtyard below when there was a knock on the door. The ice. Layla was already in the bath. Cal went to the mini-bar and poured three little baby bottles of vodka into a glass. He waited a moment for the vodka to get cold, then drank it. Then he joined Layla. Her skin was smooth in the water as he lay looking at her. Cal always traveled with a small candle in his toiletry bag. He had lit it and set it beside the bath. With the bathroom lights off, watching her through the steam in the candlelight, her eyes sparkling, the round cheeks glowing, she tried to smile. Still so hard for him to believe she was his now.

Afterwards, both in their robes, the food came. They ate from the folding table with the white linen and the rose in the little vase and the silver-plated flatware. It was midnight as they climbed into the big bed. They held each other and then Layla fell asleep almost immediately. Cal lay there thinking for a long time before he too finally fell asleep.

The next morning both woke early and feeling fresh. Layla immediately phoned the hospital. A nurse told her Paul was sleeping, and if she was planning to visit she should come later in the day. They went down for breakfast. A grand buffet with everything. Layla drank fresh squeezed orange juice while Cal had two glasses of champagne from the open bottles in the big silver bucket. When they finished they went back upstairs to use the bathroom and plan their day. Cal suggested again that they go for a long walk. It was a beautiful morning. They could wander down Las Ramblas. Later they could roam through the Gothic quarter, which was also close by, and then have lunch at a good restaurant he knew, the 7 Portes. After lunch they could take a taxi to the hospital.

"He should be awake by then. He'll be so happy to see you."

They walked the three blocks to the Plaza Catalunya, where

Las Ramblas began. Flipping the normal order, here it was pedestrians taking to the wide center, with cars relegated to the thin throughways on either side. Big plane trees, like those in Ceret, shielded the ant-like throngs wending their way down the storied avenue. The sun was already strong and patches of light broke through the leaves onto the people. Catalan flags, unmoving in the warm still air, hung from the iron balconies of brown buildings. Bullet holes and shrapnel scars from the Civil War had long since been filled in, but they were there still under the patches. Old men and old women bearing their own scars sat on benches. The old women wore dresses, and the men had their shirts tucked in and their hair combed. They would be gone soon. But for now they sat together still, as they did every morning, looking on while another generation chewed gum and videotaped each other making faces and eating ice cream. There were tourists dragging their suitcases clickety-clack over the patterned tiles, and students with backpacks and passports excited by everything. Everyone was moving past each other. Holding hands, Cal and Layla strolled down the center of it.

Some children were splashing water from a fountain that had gold colored spigots, and Barcelona's city shield on it. The Font de Canaletes. It had served this neighborhood since days when many apartments did not yet have running water. There was a legend that if a visitor drank from that fountain they would return to the city. Both Cal and Layla went over now and took a drink from it.

Newspaper stands also sold magnets, keychains, and Sagrada Familia egg cups. There were birds in cages. Layla said how cruel it was that they could not fly. The man selling them heard her but didn't give a damn. There were flower stands, and round kiosks with posters for upcoming concerts. On the right side was the famous food market La Boqueria. Layla had never seen it so Cal led her through, past crowded stall after stall brimming over with everything. Big jamons and sausages and bananas and strings of garlic and red peppers hung over every tropical fruit and cheese and candy they could squeeze into the place. Oysters and other sea food nesting on shaved ice, freshly squeezed juices, tapas, people eating the tapas, people drinking the juices, parents videotaping their children pointing at the candies. Smiles and cameras everywhere, so this abundance would be with them always. It was like first prize in the lottery of life, with this happy crowd of winners slowly oohing and aahing their way through it. Next year their neighbors and cousins would be here too.

The men and women selling it all were shoveling money into their purses as fast as the tourists could grab things. A few of the sellers looked almost bored if not for the money. Some of them even looked bored with that. Everyone was basically happy.

Cal and Layla emerged back onto Las Ramblas: Canaletes, Estudis, San Josep, Caputxins, Santa Monica. Each stretch of the boulevard had its own name, though most just lumped them together. People walked over Miro's pavement mosaic, not realizing they were stepping on a real Miro. To the sides, overpriced cafés sold frozen paella and watered down drinks to tourists who had only a few hours before having to get back to their ships. Looking at them, Cal remembered the fat man and his fat wife in Cadaqués who by now had seen Ibiza with its Blue Mosque, and "that other one."

There were two young black men selling real genuine sunglasses by Dolce & Gabbana and Dior and Armani and Versace from blankets spread out on the edge of the wide walkway. The year before, Cal had seen how fast one of those blankets could be gathered up as the police approached checking sales licenses, and how wonderfully young men could run when being chased by police. Cal had sympathy for them. Live your life somewhere with limited opportunity, or come here and try for a slice of the big pie. Everyone had to make a living.

There were street artists lining both sides of the wide footpath now, sitters poised self-consciously on stools as the charcoal copied chin, nose, eyes, hair onto large sheets of paper that would be rolled and taken home and put under the bed and forgotten.

And finally the living statues: a bronze cowboy, a white painter, a black gargoyle, a green statue of liberty. The statue of liberty was on his break, his red eyes scanning sideways watching the crowd as the cigarette hung from his copper lips. The cowboy got down from his pedestal, walked over and said something to the statue of liberty, then went back to his pedestal.

At the end of the last Rambla was the big traffic circle with all the cars again, and at its center the stone column with Christopher Columbus standing on top pointing toward a new world. Behind Columbus was the port with the cruise ships. There were black lions around the base of the column. Every lion had a kid crawling on it, and there was a proud parent taking a photo or video of the kid. There were young pickpockets standing close by watching the parents.

After all that, Cal and Layla were ready for the quiet of the back alleys of the Gothic quarter just a stone's throw away. Thousands more were looking for the same quiet. There was a group of English guys still drunk from the night before. One of them wore a t-shirt with a British flag on it. Another wore a t-shirt with the word *Trojan* and a cartoon of a smiling condom. They had their arms around each other and were singing limericks.

"There once was a woman named Jill
Who swallowed an exploding pill
They found her vagina

In North Carolina
And her tits in a tree in Brazil"

Holding Layla's hand, Cal followed behind them hoping for another. He was not disappointed.

"There once was a fellow McSweeny
Who spilled some gin on his weenie
Just to be couth
He added vermouth
Then slipped his girlfriend a martini."

"Do we have to?" asked Layla.

"Have to what?"

"Do we have to follow them? It's embarrassing."

They turned down a little side alley. The sound of the singing grew fainter.

"I mean, coming from England that's the last thing you want to hear. Some people think that's how we are. The drunk British."

"Robert and Richard. Wiggles."

"But it's not *just* the English, is it. There are drunks everywhere."

She was right of course. And besides, *that* was not *this*. At his drunkest, Robert might approach a beautiful girl he didn't know and ask her, "Please, darling, may I KISSS your hand?" *Please. Darling. May I?*

Lions vs. alley cats.

They were in the maze now.

"Which way is it?"

Cal pointed with both hands, one left, the other right.

"*That* way."

Laughing, she followed him as they plunged further into the quarter. Left, right, then left again. Migrating in the general direction of the restaurant, looking up at the balconies, the red geraniums in flowerpots, the laundry hanging to dry, the sharp shadows, the faces of old people staring back down at them. Around one bend it opened up suddenly and they were in the little Plaza George Orwell. Named for the writer who had fought here during the Civil War. There was a plaque with his name on it. Next to the plaque was a security camera. Big Brother had a sense of humor.

Cal half-remembered the square from the year before. He had been here doing something with someone. There was a bar to one side, the Oviso. It looked familiar.

"What do you think, a little something to drink?"

"Alright."

They sat on metal chairs at a metal table. A waiter came. She ordered her Cacaolet. Cal ordered a "Mojito double."

"You're not going to start singing limericks, are you? Please tell me you're not going to start singing limericks."

"No chance."

The waiter left.

"There was a young lady named Layla..."

"No, don't."

"Okay."

"No actually, go ahead. Let's hear it."

"There was a young lady named Layla,
Cal looked at her like he was a saila..."

"'Saila'?"

"...And then he said
Later in bed
I promise that I won't fail ya."

"Not bad."

"Not good."

"No, but not bad."

When they finished their drinks, Cal paid and they left.

He aimed them back toward the water. Soon they were at the restaurant. The summer before Cal had asked an old taxi driver for his recommendation. Best way to find anything in a new city. Ask young drivers where the girls or drugs are, ask the old drivers about restaurants. The driver had told him this was where he brought his own family when they were celebrating something special.

The Seven Doors, oldest restaurant in Barcelona, second oldest in Spain after Botin's in Madrid. Vaulted arcade outside, inside the black wooden beams overhead, black and white tile floors, waiters in white jackets and black ties, the maître in black jacket, starched white linens on the tables. Not snootyish, just old-worldish. Layla's beauty, plus Cal's obvious joy at being here got them one of the best tables, beside one of the big curtained windows where they could see and be seen.

They shared the house specialty, a *paella parellada,* or "rich man's paella." Layla drank a sparkling water. Cal had a half-carafe of wine, followed by another half-carafe. Later, they both had the rum and raisin flan. Layla had an espresso, and Cal had a carajillo. Then out into the heat of the day, and the first taxi straight to the hospital.

At the nursing station, they wouldn't even give her a report.

"I am sorry. Your name is von Leda, yes?"

"Yes."

"If you are not family, we are not permissioned to give information."

"But I was told I could see him this afternoon."

"I'm sorry."

There was a young doctor in the corridor nearby. He was looking at Layla. He went over and said something to the nurse. Those two talked for a moment. Then the doctor came over.

"Señora von Leda?"

"Yes."

"I am very sorry to tell you, but Señor de Beers, he does not wish to see you. He gave strong instruction to the nurses."

"But, I want to see him. I *need* to see him. You don't understand."

"I am sorry, señora. We have to respect this patient's wishes."

"Oh my god."

Tears. The doctor looked at Cal.

"Please, come with me."

Layla and Cal followed him down the corridor.

"Can you at least tell me how he is?" Layla pleaded.

The doctor stopped and looked over his shoulder at the nursing station.

"I think he will be okay. His family has arranged he will return to England, to a hospital there."

"But..."

"You must call the family if you have more questions."

In the taxi back to the hotel, Layla told Cal about Paul's son Donald.

"He's fifty-three, maybe fifty-four years old. We met once."

"Does he like you?"

"A bit too much, I think. Paul and he got into a terrific row one night after Donald said something."

"What did he say?"

"Paul wouldn't tell me."

Up in their room, Cal sat by as she made the call. After she put the phone down she looked at him.

"Well, you heard, his son said that Paul never wants to see me again."

Tears.

Cal crossed, kneeled next to her and took her hand.

"I'm sorry."

"I didn't want to hurt him. I never wanted to hurt him. He was so good to me."

Cal said everything he could think of to make her feel better.

"He needs bypass surgery, but they have to wait. They'll do it in Manchester, at the Royal Infirmary there. But I mustn't go. Paul would be angry."

Did she want to go out? No. Did she want to take a bath? No. All she wanted to do was write a letter to Paul. Cal stood and went to the window. He opened it, lit a joint, took a deep hit, then exhaled the smoke outside watching it curl in the still air.

"Must you do that?"

"It calms my nerves."

He stood there smoking as she sat at the desk writing out her letter to Paul on hotel stationery. Then a quick taxi back to the hospital to leave it at the nurse's station.

The next morning, checking out of the hotel, there was a problem with Cal's credit card. Declined.

"That's impossible. Please try it again."

The man behind the desk tried again.

"I am sorry, señor. Maybe you have another card?"

"I don't understand it. I need a phone, please."

The clerk pointed to a desk across the lobby.

"You can use that phone, señor."

Cal called the number on the back of his card. He was told that a hold had been placed because it seemed there had been insufficient funds in his account to make the last payment.

"How is that possible?"

"I don't know, sir."

He didn't understand how that was possible. He had transferred ten thousand dollars when he was in Amsterdam, and that was only a few weeks ago. There was a clock on the wall. Eleven-thirty. Only five-thirty still in New York, too early to phone his father's retirement fund to order another transfer. Besides, the signal numbers were in his pack in Cadaqués. He would have to call from the village. Even then, he knew it would take at least forty-eight hours before the funds would be in his own account. Meanwhile he would not be able to use his card. If there were insufficient funds, it meant he couldn't even use his ATM card to pull cash. He checked his pocket to count what money he had. Eleven thousand pesetas. Less than one hundred dollars. Cal could feel sweat beading on his forehead. As he walked toward the desk he wiped the sweat onto his hand, and his hand on his pants.

"I'm sorry. I don't know what to do."

"I have a credit card," said Layla.

It was linked to Paul's account.

"I'll have the money in two days," said Cal. "They just have to transfer it into my account. I'll pay you back immediately."

While signing the bill, Layla saw a charge for twelve items from the mini-bar. Later, on the drive back to Cadaqués, Cal said that he needed to grab something from the trunk. He pulled over. In the little side mirror, Layla saw him standing behind the car on the shoulder of the autopista as he took a drink of sangria from the bota bag.

Chapter LVII

Greatest pain and greatest pleasure both push everything else away. Stub a toe hard enough and a king forgets his armies in an instant. Rapture also focuses the mind like a laser. Nothing in the world but that. And so began what began as the happiest time. Whatever it was, together and a joy. In the village or beyond it, everything and everyone else only background now, faded into the kind of details that exist beyond the frame of a photo or a story. There was only Cal and Layla. If that even, as where one ended and the other began was not always so clear. With nothing to hold them back any longer, they made love anywhere and everywhere they could. In morning light, in dead of night, above the village on a picnic blanket spread out by the old Torre de les Creus. Or out by the lighthouse Cala Nans. Cal finally made it there with Layla. Beside the water, in the water, under the stars, all the hidden places were theirs now.

She had found the one she could depend on, who had promised never to leave. And finally, finally, he had found one who loved him as much as he loved her. All those years he had no idea that she would be waiting for him at last in a little fishing village on the edge of the world.

Beyond just the love making, it was the little things. Shopping together. Squeezing the fruit in the market and the silly jokes that came with that. Just the sight of a fig or a banana could send them rushing home to bed. Then the cooking together. Dressed or not, in the kitchen tasting the sauce, arranging the plates, lighting the candles, pouring the wine. She teased Cal about the wine. He told her he only drank to celebrate "the seven major holidays."

"What are those?"

"Monday, Tuesday, Wednesday..."

"Don't joke."

Later that night, when he seemed to be gettting a little drunk, she returned to the subject.

"I'm just following the rules," he told her. "Wine, women and song. Drugs, sex and rock 'n roll."

"So then, where's my music?"

He sank onto one knee as if proposing, and sang to her. Words by Nizami, tune by Clapton:

"I am yours
However distant you may be
There blows no wind but wafts your scent to me
There sings no bird but calls your name to me
Each memory that has left its trace with me
Lingers forever as a part of me."

As he finished the tune he lost his balance and fell onto the floor, laughing.

"Look, you see what you do to me? You knock me off my feet!"

The ten thousand from his father's retirement fund had finally made it over to his own account, and there was still a good deal left where that came from. His father had been a prudent and hard-working man. And so, flush again, Cal took Layla to all of the best little restaurants in Cadaqués. "Spreading the wealth," as he put it. L'Estable, Casa Anita, the little mermaid La Sirena, Casa Nun, La Galiota. Sometimes Layla would wear outfits that she had made herself, and Cal would have to guess what film or

335

painting they were from. If he got it right he would get a reward.

"Do you want your reward now, or later?"

If they had not left for the restaurant yet, the answer was usually "now *and* later."

Deep in the night they would watch each other sleeping. And when they couldn't bear to watch any longer, one would wake the other and the whole cycle would begin again.

Freddy had a small boat that he called The African Queen. For obvious reasons, because it looked like that; an old beat up wooden thing. To see it float was to see a miracle. Still, he let them use it, and to Cal and Layla it was the finest vessel on the sea. On calm days they chug-chugged their way out to Sa Sebolla or Port Lligat, stopping in hidden coves to make love, swim, and then make love again. One day they took the Queen, as they called her, to Es Cullero cove with its Great Masturbator rock that Dali had made famous in his painting. The little boat rocked, little waves slapping against the hull as they made love until at the last minute Cal stood up and, with Layla watching, his seed spilled into the sea, left to become a part of that place forever.

"That was appropriate!"

Laughing then, it was on to Agulles cove with its tiny beach, Portalo cove with its shallow water that looked like blue ice but was so warm, and then to Jonquet cove where, Cal's batteries fully recharged, they were already at it again. Hidden by the coast rocks with their twisted shapes, the curves of their bodies offered up their own inlets and promontories. Layla had waited so long to do anything, now she was ready to try everything.

One day they took the boat into Hell's Cave, that slanting hole in the tip of Cap de Creus. Sailors call it the "Devil's Cape" because the wind, rocks and water there can turn, as luck turns, in an unsuspecting instant. From there they motored out to the little island Massa d'Or, where Daniel's character had by now hopefully found his immortality. Anchored on the leeward side, they joked that they had found something even better. She was lying on top of him. Her long hair fell down around both their faces. Looking at each other, noses almost touching, it was as if they were inside a secret fort.

"Come home with me."

"You want to leave now, already? But it's so nice here."

"I don't mean here. I don't mean Cadaqués. I mean, I want to take you to see my home in California. *Our* home in California."

"Well, this sounds serious."

The boat was moving slowly in the ebb and flow of the water.

"You'll love it. It's on a place called Cobb Mountain, up in the wine country north of San Francisco."

"I thought you grew up in Palo Alto?"

"I did. But then I told you I left California for New York. And last year after my Dad died I bought some property on the side of this mountain. I wanted a place to get away from everything, all the craziness. Those ten years in Manhattan were a little nuts. I needed someplace quiet."

"And so now you're living up there on your mountain all alone?"

"With the dogs."

She broke into a big smile.

"You have dogs? Really?"

"Dada, Suetonius and Moocow. German Shepherds. Dada is the mommy, Suetonius and Moocow are her babies."

"Who takes care of them when you're not there?"

"A friend."

She rolled off him, then lay with her head resting on his chest. The sun was on them, their eyes closed against it.

"And there's a house on your property?"

"Not exactly. I told the real estate agents I wanted to see the funkiest things they had. Instead of a house, there's a little Quonset hut. You know Quonset huts?"

"Those round things?"

"Exactly. This one has a view that goes on forever, down the whole valley. And there's a little cowboy town below it in the distance called Middletown. I still have to fix the place up, but I think you'll like it. There's a fireplace near the bed, and snow in winter. Pine trees. I made a hot tub outside by the deck. In the summer the air is so clear you can see the Milky Way like crazy. But my favorite's the winter. Your body in the hot water, snowflakes coming down, the silence."

"It sounds beautiful. Does it have a name, your property?"

"Firelight."

"After your book?"

He turned and looked at her.

"The only thing missing there has been you. We could fix it up together. What do you say?"

"I've never been to California."

Chapter LVIII

When they were ready finally to let a chosen few re-enter their orbit, they found many in Cadaqués wanting, as Robert put it, "to share the LOVE."

Friends watched them holding hands, arms around each other, lips drawn together like magnets.

"Get a ROOM, darlings!" became a running commentary.

Wiggles would look away.

"Oh dear god, must you?"

The child-like David, just the opposite. He would stare at them wide-eyed.

"Oh Cal, Layla, you are like a story now, yes? A beautiful story. Vive l'amour!"

They were like children playing. Through the little stone passageways, slipping through the shadows back into the light, poking into all the art galleries, watching the sun rise or set. Anyone watching them would think the world had become a better place.

At Sa Conca one night, swimming together Layla finally saw those "stars in the sea" from the phosphourus Cal had told her about. Moonlight sparkling on the warm water, Cucurucuc poking out in the distance, a little fishing boat motoring past it.

"Paradise."

"Yes."

Still, we are curious animals, and after a while even paradise repeated yields to a hunger for the new. The proverbial apple. So eventually their sights set further, new places and new experiences sought out, as long as they were together. Cal rented a car and they made that same journey he had hoped once to make with Cassandra, to France by way of the little coast road.

Below the looming monastery of San Pere de Rodes, they discovered the tiny village of La Vall de Santa Creu. Only 26 people lived there. On the terrace of the little restaurant El Coto de Rioja, a fine gazpacho, black rice, and the gilt-head seabream in salt crust. Cal found the first bottle of wine so good he wanted to order a second.

"Are you sure? You're driving."

"You're right."

They shared a crème Catalan, then an espresso for her and a *carajillo* for him before driving up to the monastery.

Poking through the dark stone corridors, having heard Daniel's story it was not without a glimmer of hope that both actually kept an eye out for the Holy Grail.

"*There* it is!"

"Are you sure it's the Grail?"

"No, you're right, just a rock. Though from this angle..."

Laughing, they kept up the search. An hour later, when they still had not found the Grail, it was back to the car and on toward France. But first a quick stop in Portbou. At the Walter Benjamin monument, a descending passage cut through the earth into the cliff above the sea, Layla stood staring down steps the color of dried blood, shaking her head.

"Are you okay?" asked Cal.

"He killed himself because he thought the Nazis were about to take him," she said.

"Yes."

"Because he couldn't bear the thought of what would happen to him in the camps. Just because he was Jewish and an intellectual. I read something once he wrote about Baudelaire. It was so brilliant. How can people treat other people like that? How can we do that?"

"I don't know."

They drove on.

At the frontier, or what was left of it, the gate stood upright, frozen, no longer in use. On the other side of the now-invisible line, almost immediately there were heavy green vineyards stretching up the side of the mountain.

"I love watching grapes grow. Only it makes me so thirsty to see it."

"Don't joke."

"I'm not joking."

On this day, the bota bag was not in the trunk. It was on the floor under Cal's seat. He reached for it. Using his knee to steer for a moment, he untwisted the cap. Then he hissed a stream of wine into his mouth while he looked past it toward the road twisting in front of him.

"Do you really think you should drink and drive at the same time?"

"This isn't wine. It's sangria. It's mostly lemonade."

He closed the bota and slipped it back under the seat.

They drove past a cemetery with a commanding view of the coast spreading below.

"Not much point in that," Cal observed. "I mean, who's looking?"

"The families, when they visit. Also, I suppose those who know that someday they'll be here. It must make dying here a little easier."

The road bent down. Soon they passed through Cerbere, with its little green and yellow and salmon pink restaurant-bars across from the water. There were posters attached to lampposts advertising a circus coming to Banyuls the next week. The posters showed a tiger and a horse with Spiderman jumping over them. At the far end of the town the road began to climb again. There were rocks and brown scrub on the left, and more vineyards. The car windows were open and the warm air blew Layla's hair. Cal kept looking over at her. She had her white skirt pulled up high, and the sun through the window shone on her browned legs.

Cal took another drink from the bota bag. Even in the car he liked to hold the bag as far away as he could so the stream would travel.

"You're really a professional at that," she said, watching him. "I'm impressed."

At the bottom of the next hill there were some children playing. There were two little girls walking, and there was a boy on a bicycle. The boy was about ten years old. He had a plastic sword in one hand, and was pretending that his bike was a horse. He waved the sword high in the air, and rode in front of the girls and they laughed at him. Then the boy circled back to do it again. His bike was still on the dirt shoulder, but closer to the road than it should have been. Coming down the hill, Cal was fumbling to close the bota bag. He took the turn too fast. Layla saw the children and screamed. Cal looked up and cranked the wheel just in time. The car swerved. The boy on the bicycle just kept riding, while the two little girls stood watching Cal's car disappear.

"You almost hit him," said Layla. She was fighting to catch her breath.

"He was almost in the road. So dangerous to be riding there!"

As they pulled into Banyuls-sur-Mer, there were palm trees

and people sitting on benches at the edge of the wide sidewalk. There were ice cream stands with pictures of different kinds of ice cream. The beach was off to the right. There were many cars now and the traffic slowed. There was an old black Citroen in front of them with the canvas sunroof pulled back. And in the other lane rolling by was a yellow Chrysler convertible, also from the fifties. A great big thing, the Chrysler was polished beautifully and sparkled in the sun. Both those cars dated back to a time when men and women here in the south of France took greater care dressing than those shuffling by today in their t-shirts and flip-flops.

"You could have killed him."

"Come on, don't exaggerate."

"You almost hit that boy."

"It wasn't *that* close."

"It was too close."

"He never should have been riding his bike next to the road like that. Especially around those bends. His parents should be more careful. *Much* more careful."

Layla was staring ahead.

After leaving Banyuls-sur-Mer, the road wound up along the steep hill. Signs told them they were on the Route des vins. Vineyards on both sides of the road proved it. Other signs pointed to Port-Vendres and Collioure, and beyond those to Perpignan. They would spend the night in Collioure.

Some local farmers had stands along the road selling fresh fruits and vegetables. Cal asked Layla if she wanted to stop. She did not want to stop. Then passing Port-Vendres he asked her again.

"The Romans called this the Port of Venus. Very deep water here. Shall we park the car, have a look around?"

"We're almost to Collioure, yes?"

"Yes."

"Let's just keep going."

Collioure was to French Catalonia what Cadaqués was to Spanish Catalonia. To get the twentieth century kicked off in high style, artists had been drawn to the seaside town to paint their hearts out, splashing their own chosen colors onto canvases like "wild beasts," as they were called. The Fauvists. What was red became blue, what was blue became red, yellow, green, all the spectrum rearranged as if God was having second thoughts about what should look like what. Henri Matisse, Andre Derain, Braque again, Picasso again, all here in a mad rush to claim this corner of the world as their own. France, Spain, Catalonia...trinity for a new age that was not going to look, on canvas anyway, like any age that had come before it. From Paris, Ezra Pound's mantra "Make it new!" rang out like a clarion call. As in Cadaqués, it was as if an eighth day had been added for invention of the world to proceed. World 2.0.

Settling into the room at their hotel, Le Relais Des Trois Mas, Layla peered through the window. The hotel was built on the side of a cliff above the water. There were stone terraces and a swimming pool and pine trees. Beyond the trees and pool lay the bay with the Royal Castle to their left, and across the water the church Notre-Dame-des-Anges that was once a lighthouse. Its stone tower rose over the bay like a phallus with its pink domed top.

"Beautiful hotel."

"Yes."

"Very expensive?"

"Not really. I just thought that this is such a special weekend."

Layla lay down on the bed. She looked at Cal.

"What am I going to do with you?"

He came toward her.

"Well, I've got a good idea where to start."

"That's not what I meant."

He knew what she meant.

"I'm sorry about that boy. Really. You were right. I should have been more careful."

"And next time?"

"I'll be more careful. I promise."

The smile was back.

"Come here."

About an hour later they had showered and changed. At the desk, Cal reserved a table for dinner at nine o'clock. They could watch the sunset over the bay then, and the lights coming on at the church and on the castle walls and in the village.

Stepping out of the hotel, Cal stopped to look at Layla. He had watched her dressing inside, and now under the shade of the pine trees, with the strong afternoon sun throwing shadows onto them, he needed to look at her again. As always, so incredibly beautiful. She was wearing a dress she had made herself, the same as she had mentioned to him long ago, from Casablanca. The one Ingrid Bergman as Ilsa wears in the market while looking at lace and telling Bogie the truth finally about her and Laszlo. A white overdress, sleeveless, with broad shoulders and falling just below the knees, with a thin white belt pulled tight around her little waist. Under it was a short-sleeved cotton blouse with blue and white horizontal stripes.

"I had to guess the color of the stripes, of course. Because the film is black and white."

"Sure."

To top it off, white gloves, white shoes, little white hand purse, and a show-stopping white hat with wide brim that framed her face like a halo. She smiled under it now as Cal took a photo of her.

"Wait a minute."

He wound the film forward. A bellman was standing close by. Cal asked if he would please take a photo of them together.

"Mais oui, monsieur."

Cal stood with his arm around Layla, smiling. It was a photo he would look at many times in the years ahead.

They went for a walk then through the village. The winding medieval streets with flowers everywhere, purple, pink, rose red, yellow. Nature imitating art here, as if having seeing the Fauvists at work the world was shouting back, *you want color, here's color!*

Younger people didn't seem to pay much attention to them. But many older people turned to look at Layla.

"You're bringing back memories."

"Do you think so?"

"They're remembering when people used to dress as you're dressed. When beauty was still in fashion. It's a bit of a bad word now."

"You're too kind."

They sat at a little café by the water for an ice cream and coffee. And that's just what Cal had, a coffee.

"I'm proud of you."

"For drinking coffee?"

The ice cream came in flared glasses, with whipped cream and nuts and fruit on the top, and a thin sweet biscuit sticking out of it. Rather than eat their own, with long thin spoons she fed him hers while he fed her his, and they laughed a lot. When they were finished, Cal paid and they kept walking. There was a little shop selling men's clothes.

"Let's get you something," she said.

He was wearing khaki pants, sandals and a plain t-shirt.

"What's wrong with this?" he asked, looking down at himself.

It was like a mother choosing clothes for her child. When they came out of the shop, Cal was wearing loose white slacks, and a pale blue collared shirt rolled up at the sleeves. He carried his old clothes in a bag.

"We need to get you some white shoes."

"We don't need to get me some white shoes."

They got him some white shoes.

They walked past cafés with people drinking beer, and past bars where men stood drinking other things, and they did not stop.

In the late day, as the sun was starting to come down slowly, they walked the *chemins du fauvism*, or Way of the Fauvists. Paintings by Matisse and Derain were reproduced, standing in the same spots where the artists had painted them. Also, there were empty metal frames one could look through to see the same views, inviting you to imagine how you would paint those scenes yourself. It was all like a painting now. Layla, Cal, this time together.

At dinner that night Cal drank two brandy sodas before the meal, one bottle of Banyuls wine with dinner, and a Calvados after.

"I'm not driving tonight."

"No," she agreed, "you're not driving."

He laughed. He couldn't stop laughing.

"What's so funny?"

"Well, just look at me. You've Gatsbyfied me!"

"You mean the white shoes?"

"All of it. The white pants, the fucking white pants. I mean, who wears white fucking pants anymore? And white shoes?"

"You look very good."

"No, *you* look very good."

He tipped his glass to her.

"I say old chap, here's looking at you."

She smiled.

"Do you know what I'm not going to have?"

"What?" she asked.

"I'm not going to have another Calvados. Do you know why I'm not going to have another Calvados?"

"Why?"

"Because one is enough. And..."

"And what?"

"And because I want you to want me. I want that more than anything in the world, Layla. More than anything else in the whole world, I want you to want me. I need it. I need you."

There was a candle on the table, and no wind. They could hear the smooth sound of the water against the rocks below. The moon was up, with Venus rising beside it. Across the bay, someone was playing a saxophone.

The next morning, Cal stood in his new white pants, no shirt, smoking a joint out on their balcony. Layla came out to sit and to watch the light through the trees and the view beyond it. Both wished that they could stay an extra day. Not possible. This had to be it. The next morning Cal would meet at Tharrats' home with the man who was going to translate his book into Spanish. And so in the late afternoon they would have to drive back. This was just an appetizer trip to Collioure.

"Don't worry, we'll be back."

"Do you really think so?" she asked.

"Of course. Do you know why?"

"Why?"

"Because we have time to do everything always."

He started to sing to her. The Louis Armstrong song from an old James Bond film, *We have all the time in the world...*

Later, as they stepped onto the wide terrace about to take their seats for breakfast, she asked him if he would do her a favor.

"A little experiment."

"What's that?"

"Don't drink today."

"All right."

She put a hand on his cheek and looked at him.

"Thank you."

After breakfast they spent some time in the Musée d'Art Moderne looking at the paintings. Then they wandered together outside looking at the museum itself, the old monastery, the mill, the gardens, and some of the small streets, smaller the better. At one little shop Cal bought a book about Collioure.

Later they stopped for lunch at Les Templiers. It was an old classic hotel-restaurant with a wood bar and heavy beams and many paintings on the walls. The waiter came to them. Layla ordered a Perrier. Cal asked for the same. When the waiter came back with their drinks they ordered. While they waited for the food, Layla suggested they look through the book. Cal took it out of the plastic bag and opened it. He was sitting across from her.

"Incredible, the history of this place. The Knights Templer were here, the Count of Barcelona, D'Artagnan and the King's Musketeers, Wamba..."

"Who's Wamba?"

"King of the Visigoths."

"That's it!"

"That's what?"

"My name for you. Wamba."

"Really?"

"What a beautiful name, Wamba. Such fun to say it! Will you be my Wamba?" she asked.

"King of the Visigoths?"

"No. The other kind of Wamba. My Wamba."

"All right."

It was a very good lunch. Afterwards they took in the church and the castle much too quickly. Cal was eager to drive back to Cadaqués, but Layla wanted first to visit the little cemetery where the Spanish poet Antonio Machado was buried.

"We can't leave without seeing that."

"All right."

As in the photo of it in the book, draped over the tombstone was a red, yellow and purple flag of the second Spanish republic that had stood before Franco squashed it with his bloody boots. Fresh flowers, photos of the poet, drawings, poems, and other offerings rested on the grave. Attached to the headstone was a letterbox to receive messages. Letters to the poet. *Dear Antonio, I would like to...*

Cal and Layla stood close together looking down at the tomb. One of Machado's poems, from his *Campos de Castilla*, was reproduced in the book Cal held open in his hands. They took turns reading it out loud. Cal began it.

"Wanderer, your footsteps are the road and nothing more
Wanderer, there is no road, the road is made by walking..."

Then Layla read.

"...By walking, one makes the road, and glancing behind
One sees the path that never will be trod upon again..."

They read the last line together.

"...Wanderer, there is no road, only wakes upon the sea."

As they were climbing into the car later, about to begin the drive back to Cadaqués, an ambulance raced past them with its siren blaring.

"You promise we'll be back?" she asked. "So much we

didn't see."

Cal's hand was twiddling, his fingers tapping on the wheel.

"Are you okay?" she asked.

"Yes. Fine."

"You look nervous."

"It's nothing."

He stopped twiddling and smiled at her.

They passed Port-Vendres and drove through Banyuls-sur-Mer. There was music playing on the radio and Cal did not say much. In Cerbere he said he needed to use the toilet. He parked and she waited as he went into one of the restaurant bars. About five minutes later he came back.

"Sorry it took so long," he said, rubbing a hand on his stomach. "Something funny with my stomach."

"You think it was something you ate?"

"It could be."

"But we ate the same things."

"Well, I don't know, just some kind of reaction. Anyway, I'm feeling better now."

Chapter LIX

It was their place now. Her things beside his in the closet, her books stacked by the bed mixed in with his. Cal had gone out. He had told her he would be back soon. He was just going to the shops to pick up a few things.

Layla sat at the blue table, so happy she was humming to herself. She was cutting patterns and sewing a new outfit. Rita Hayworth's black dress from the film Gilda, the Put the Blame on Mame number. The black satin sheath to the ankles, slit high in the front to show the legs. With bared shoulders, cut so low across the breasts the nipples would be tucked just out of sight. And to match it, long black satin gloves stretching above the elbows. She was even making those. There would be a full-moon party at Cap de Creus lighthouse restaurant the following week. Many people from Cadaqués would be wearing costumes, and she had decided to go as Gilda. Layla knew her own beauty. And with the full moon, and Cal holding her as they would dance, she was so eager to show him that beauty could intoxicate as well as anything that came in a glass.

At Imperial, Cal was taking a break from his errands to sit with the twins, Wiggles, and David. Marita was also there. Already out of it, she sat looking at the others, silent, laughing, then silent again. One of her sons, Lorenzo, came to her to ask a question. She told him to ask her later and he left.

"Nice to have you back, Cal," offered Wiggles. "We've

missed you."

"He's been busy though, hasn't he?"

"Now now, DISCRETION, gentlemen."

"Well, it's nice to be back," said Cal.

Angela brought Cal the vodka tonic he had just ordered. He looked at it. Americans use more ice than Europeans. Even when he said "con mucho hielo," and he always said it, still they took that to mean two cubes intead of one. Three if he was lucky.

"What is it with the ice here? Is ice something precious?"

"Cal hasn't been drinking much, has he?"

"Been on his best behavior, haven't you Cal?"

"Is that right?"

"I saw him with Layla sitting the other day at Meliton. Forgive me for spying, Cal."

"It's fine."

"Do you know what he was drinking?"

"What was he drinking?"

"A chocolate milk," said Wiggles.

"Are you serious?"

"Were you really, Cal? You were drinking a chocolate milk?"

David was saying nothing. A cigarette in his hand, he was looking past the others at something in the distance.

Wiggles lifted up his glass of red wine.

"Well so then, a toast to chocolate milk."

They all drank to chocolate milk. Marita was hysterical with laughter. She was doubled over with it, trying to say something.

"No...you...it's..."

She couldn't speak through the laughter.

"So tell us, Cal, what have you been doing with yourself?"

"We KNOW what he's been doing. And *not* by himself."

Smiles all around.

"Well, last week we went to Collioure."

"And, how was that?"

"Delicious."

Cal finished his drink. Angela was walking past. He caught her attention and pointed to his empty glass.

"Y por favor, Angela, con *mucho, much* hielo."

Angela nodded. Some minutes later she brought Cal a fresh drink, and a little bowl with ice cubes and tongs.

"Perfecto! Gracias, Angela."

There were people sitting at the next table. Angela went to take their orders.

"Do you know what I was just thinking?" asked Wiggles.

"What were you thinking?"

"You know that old game, saying 'Toy boat' ten times very fast?"

"It can't be done, darling."

"Well try this. Say, 'beach party beach party...' ten times very fast."

They all tried it.

"Easy."

"Not a problem."

"Alright. Well now, try *this*. *This* is what's so interesting. Say 'party beach party beach....' ten times fast."

They all did it.

"Get to your point!"

"Well, it's just interesting, that's all. I mean, it's a totally different experience, isn't it? It's not like 'toy boat.' I mean it doesn't trip you up in the same way. Still, you can feel the difference in your mouth. There's a big difference between saying 'beach party beach party' or reversing it and saying 'party beach party beach.' In the end it's the same thing, but it *feels* different."

"What the *hell* are you talking about?" asked Marita. She was squinting at Wiggles, looking so serious. "I mean, what the *hell* are you talking about? Beach...party...party..." Couldn't even say it once.

"Cal's the writer. Can you explain it to us, Cal? Why those two feel so different?"

Layla was walking toward them. Wiggles saw her.

"Oh oh, Cal."

"What?"

"Here she comes. You'd better change that to a chocolate milk fast."

Smiling, Layla came straight over to Cal, bent down behind him and wrapped her arms around his neck.

"Here you are. I thought you were only going to be gone some minutes?"

"We hijacked him," said Richard.

"Not his fault."

"It's true. I tried to leave, but they wouldn't let me."

She saw Cal's glass on the table and the bowl of ice.

"What are you all doing with my Wamba?"

"Your *what*?"

"Wamba. She calls me Wamba."

"What's a Wamba?"

"It's him," Layla answered, still smiling.

"I beg your pardon," said Wiggles. "I'm confused. 'Cal' is now 'Wamba'? I thought Cal was Cal."

"Cal to you, Wiggles. Wamba to Layla."

"Oh, I like that. 'Wamba to Layla.' I like that a great deal. 'Wamba to Layla, Wamba to Layla, do you read me Layla? This is Wamba.' I mean, it sounds like something from a Tarzan movie, doesn't it?"

Marita was doubled over again. David was smiling. He was paying attention now. Layla sat on Cal's knee.

"So tell me, what are you all doing here? Just getting battered in the middle of the day, are you?"

"We're CELEBRATING, darling."

"Celebrating what?"

"Robert just learned he's a father."

"*Again.*"

"Really!"

Cal explained.

"He just heard from a woman in Venezuela that he hasn't seen in, what is it, seven years?"

Robert nodded. He looked embarrassed.

"It seems they had a child together. A daughter she never told him about."

"Incredible, Robert. Congratulations."

"Big surprise, that."

"And tell her about the grandchild."

"What grandchild?"

"Well, that comes just one week on the heels of having learned that he *also* has a seven year old *grandson* he didn't know about."

"Both the same age, seven years old?"

"Family's growing!"

"Incredible, yes?"

"But how could you not know you had a seven year old grandson?"

"His son never told him."

"Robert, is that true?"

"Well, you can't keep track of them ALL, can you, darling? I mean, it's a busy world. Everyone on the go."

There was a nice breeze coming off the water. David closed his eyes to feel it on his face.

Chapter LX

Cal couldn't stop laughing.
"What are you talking about?" he asked.
"It's a simple question. Where are you?"
"I'm right here."
"No, you're not," said Layla. "You're somewhere behind those eyes. Those red eyes. Just go look at yourself in a mirror."
"Listen, Layla..."
"No, *you* listen. What's happened? You're so clever, and it's so interesting to talk with you when you're here. But you're not here, are you. It's like...like talking to someone over a wall."
Cal stopped laughing.
"Look, I just asked you a simple question, that's all."
"About 'beach party' being different than 'party beach'?"
"Yes!"
"Well, I have no idea, do I? No idea what you're talking about."
"I was just saying that when you..." He tried again to explain it. "Don't you see, how different it feels to the mouth? 'Party beach' or 'beach party'? Depending on which word you put first. It's just interesting, that's all."
"No. It's not. It's not interesting."
They were sitting on a bench close to the Punta des Baluard. The Casino was off to their left. It was very late. They had been arguing. It had started when Cal had asked Layla to give him a

blowjob.

"What, *here*?"

"Why not?"

"Because it's a bench, in public."

"*So?*"

"So? People could see."

"It's the middle of the night. No one will see."

"Well they might, mightn't they? There's no knowing when someone could walk around that point."

"Well, that would just be part of the excitement."

She sat there staring at him. He was laughing again.

"In fact," said Cal, "I have another great idea."

"What?"

"We should do a fuck guide to Cadaqués."

"A *what*?"

"A fuck guide to Cadaqués. And we could call it..." He thought a moment. "...*Not Lonely Planet*. It could show all the best places to fuck."

"Are you serious?"

"Absolutely. Make us a fortune. Look at all the places you and I have already fucked. Made love, sorry." He started to list them. "Up by the old tower, on almost every beach, behind the museum right by Paul's restaurant..."

"That was a mistake."

"...out by the lighthouse, on the rocks by Llane Petit..."

"All right, stop it. Enough."

"...on those steps down to the water by L'Estable. And we could do it here. And then we could make a map, showing all the best places to do it. And people could buy the map, and then fuck in all the places that we've fucked."

"You're being so vulgar."

That's when she made the comment about his red eyes.

"What's happened to you?"

"What's happened to *you*?" he asked back. "You've gotten so serious suddenly. Can't we just have a little fun?"

They sat there quiet for a few moments.

"Beach party beach party beach party...party beach party beach party beach...well, *I* think it's *very* interesting. The way the brain organizes information like that."

Cal took a joint out of his pocket and lit it. Layla stood up and started to walk back to the house. He followed, calling after her.

"Where are you going? Layla? Layla?"

He caught up and walked alongside her.

"Look, I'm sorry. You're right. That was not the best place to make love."

She kept walking.

"You're drunk," she said. "And stoned."

"Well, yes, okay, maybe a little. But come on, it's been a long time. I've been drinking fucking water, and fucking chocolate milk..."

She wasn't stopping.

"Listen, for god's sake, what's wrong? Can't we just have a little fun?"

They were walking past the old wine press.

"Okay, I have an idea," said Cal. "A serious idea. You're going to like this. I'm being serious now."

She stopped. "What?"

"Let's make love here. Nobody would see us doing it here."

Chapter LXI

In the middle of the night, Cal woke to go pee. Layla had insisted on sleeping on the couch in the living room. In the light from the yellow streetlamp coming through the little window he saw her lying there. Squeezing in, he lay down next to her. In the end he convinced her to come back to bed with him. In the morning he made breakfast for them. Layla offered to help.

"No, please. This is my sorry-I-was-such-an-asshole breakfast. I promise, everytime I'm an asshole you'll get a very special meal afterwards."

On the blue table, fresh squeezed orange juice, espresso, scrambled eggs with goat cheese, a red pepper salad.

"Almost worth the trouble, yes?"

"Well, I don't know about that."

"I can try to be an asshole earlier in the day once, in time for dinner. What do you like, lamb, salmon..."

"I just want my Wamba. With his nice clear eyes, and clear head."

He went over and wrapped his arms around her.

"One clear-eyed Wamba coming right up."

"You promise?"

"I promise!"

Chapter LXII

The party at Cap de Creus was just days away. Layla needed black shoes for her Gilda outfit. There were shops across the mountain in Figueres. She thought they should take the bus, but Cal insisted on renting a car.

"Why spend a little money when you can spend more?" she asked.

"It's not that, just that it's nicer to drive ourselves."

Pulling out of the village, they passed the roundabout with the Statue of Liberty holding up her two flames. Cal's eyes were focused straight ahead. The road began to climb. He reached over to take Layla's hand, then a moment later pulled it back as he needed his hand to downshift on the turns. They drove past the spot where Jose Manuel had gone off the road. The guardrail there was shiny and new. Cal looked over at Layla to see if she had noticed it. She was smiling at him. She had not noticed.

In Figueres, he parked the car in the shade of a big tree. Then, walking along the Carrer Peralada, they visited three shoe shops before Layla finally found a pair she liked.

"They're not perfect. The heels could be a little higher, but these are close. They'll do."

Cal insisted on paying for them.

"Still part of my charm offensive."

"Is there a Tiffany's in Figueres?"

"I'm not *that* charming."

Cal suggested they visit the Dali Theatre and Museum near by. The artist had designed the museum. It was said to be his largest work. As they walked toward it they could see the big eggs on the roof, just as at his house in Port Lligat.

"Symbols of..."

"Breakfast. Each egg represents breakfast."

"Or a chicken."

They ran through all the things the eggs might represent.

"Rebirth..."

"Egg nog..."

"No, I'm pretty sure it's rebirth."

There was a long line of tourists stretching from the door of the museum across and around the little plaza and down one of the side streets. Twenty minutes at least waiting in the hot sun while people in funny hats tried to sell you things. They had both been to the museum before, and decided it would be better to see it again one early morning before the lines formed, or during shoulder seasons when crowds were thinner.

Both hungry, and Cal saying that he was thirsty, they kept walking away from the museum until they were past the tourist spots. Along a small side street they saw workers sitting in one restaurant, a sure sign of good authentic food at fair prices. Two men in blue workclothes were getting up from a table against the back wall and they grabbed it. The waiter came over and cleared the table and then wiped it with a damp rag. He slapped two menus on the table. He must have thought they were tourists, because he was not very friendly and said nothing to them. There was a sign on a wall with the menu of the day written on it. Tuna salad, oxtail stew, flan, wine included. They both ordered that. The waiter looked disappointed. The tourists were not even going to spend much money.

At the next table, a man and woman were speaking Catalan. There was a television on in one corner. A Spanish soap opera. A beautiful young woman was looking at an older woman and crying. Nobody in the restaurant seemed to be watching her cry. She was crying for nothing.

The waiter brought their salads, and left a bottle of red wine on the table. There was no label on the bottle. This was the old way. They were free to drink as much or as little of it as they liked. Cal poured a glass for himself. When he finished it he poured another.

"You're not going to drink that whole bottle, are you?"

"It's only wine."

"And you're driving."

When they were through eating, Cal paid and they stood to go. He paused to take a last look at the bottle on the table. It was still half full. As they walked back to the car he kept thinking of the money wasted.

They drove past dusty shops, through the narrow streets, then slowly over the railway tracks and soon they were beyond the edge of the city and out in the open again. The mountain and Cadaqués were ahead of them. There were big modern stores set back along the road with windows and things you could stop to buy.

"I have to say, that was complete bullshit."

"What was?"

"You not letting me finish that bottle of wine."

"Why? Did you need to?"

"I didn't *need* to, no. But it was included in the price."

"So?"

"So, it was a waste of money."

She said nothing. A few minutes later though he came back to it.

"The thing is, I've always had this incredible tolerance to alcohol. That's why sometimes I drink a little more than other people. I just can't feel it."

"Really?"

"Well, okay, I feel it, yes. But I have to drink *so much* before I really feel anything. It's strange."

He said it as if he was asking for sympathy. Sympathy for a condition where he had to drink a lot to get drunk.

"But you're driving now."

"I told you, it was just wine. And it was so weak. I think they water it down there."

"Really?"

They came to a roundabout. Cal slowed, swung around it, then sped up again.

"And let me tell you something else. You want to know what driving drunk is?"

She looked at him.

"It's not just having a little wine in your head. Let me tell you what driving drunk is. My mother used to get so drunk that sometimes, when she ran out of her bourbon, she got my little brother to go with her in the car to the liquor store. She was so plastered, she knew she couldn't handle the steering wheel. Double vision, things out of focus, everything spinning probably. My brother was about nine, maybe ten. And so what she'd do is, she'd have him lean across and do the steering while she worked the clutch and the brakes. *That* is drunk driving! And I have never, *never* driven like that in my life. And I never would."

The mountain was getting closer, and there were olive trees again on either side of the road.

"I don't know why, I just really don't feel alcohol that much. I just have this incredible resistance, or tolerance to it. I have to drink so much just to feel a little buzz. It's always been like that."

He laughed.

"You know how much money I could save if I could just feel alcohol the way most people feel it?"

They were on a straight stretch. He reached over to take her hand.

"Stop worrying. Really. I love you, Layla."

"I love you too."

"And I promise you, I'll be a good Wamba."

"Really?"

"Really. I promise. I'll be a very, very, very good Wamba."

Chapter LXIII

Friday, 27 August, clear skies. The full moon party was that night. All over Cadaqués hair was being done, nails polished, costumes tweaked, mirrors being stared into. The stranger the better here. Other towns could have their little dress-up nights. This being Cadaqués, more, much more, was expected. The spirit of Dali would be looking on. Layla had surprised Cal with a white dinner jacket she had made for him. If he was going to be escorting Gilda to the lighthouse, he had to look the part. He stood in the bedroom about to dress. She called out to him from the other room.

"Do you want to see it now?"

"Let me see the gloves first."

"Before the dress?"

"Why not?"

"Okay."

He stood there waiting. A moment later she was in the doorway, naked except for the black satin gloves reaching up beyond the elbows.

"And the shoes?"

A little smile. She disappeared. Then she was back in the doorway, taller now, legs stretching from the floor to her little waist. Her breasts pointing straight at him. Never ever a woman more beautiful than this! It was almost painful to look at her.

"What's happening to my body?" he asked her.

"What do you mean?"

"It's doing something strange. Come look."

She walked toward him.

"Look closer."

As she watched, he pulled the waistband of his shorts down. His erection sprang up into the air. She slowly sank onto her knees. He couldn't see her through the mass of her blonde hair, but he could feel her. The warm wet movement of her tongue, the black satin of the gloves touching, holding every part of him. Then suddenly so deep. And again. *How could she do that?* His hands wrapped in her hair, eyes closing, opening, he looked down to see the long line of her legs splayed out behind her, the thin black heels pointing away as she took him again, and again. After some moments he pulled her back up toward him. He needed more already, needed all of her now. Both mouths starved and feasting at the same time, he was breathing hard like a horse racing.

Her breasts up against his chest, he pulled her back, then head bent forward, his mouth took in one nipple, then the other, then back to the first again. He couldn't have enough of her. Dropping to his knees as if in worship, slowly he ran his hands along the smooth legs, his face pressed into her stomach kissing her. One, two, a thousand kisses, each one with such love. And with every kiss he even said it, "My love...my love...my love..." Somewhere above, she said it too. Then back onto his feet, to her mouth that was waiting for him. No stopping now. Cal turned her around. Bent forward with her gloved hands spread out on the bed she let out a sound. He was inside her now.

Again and again he pressed into her as she pressed back, gravity or something very much like it drawing them together, both straining to get him into the center of her. Then he turned her, lifted her up. With her arms around his neck, legs high around his waist, a thump as one shoe fell to the floor. He was feeling all his strength. She was feeling it too, as both looked down to watch their own bodies moving. His legs tiring finally, inside her still, he carried her back onto the bed and lowered her down. Then, neither caring that the little window was open, they came at the same moment. She screamed with it. And his voice, from the throat, louder even than hers. Like an animal. Outside the window two young men applauded, shouts of "Bravo! Bravo!"

The explosions kept coming, his body convulsing. She held him as the twitching finally lessened, was back, then faded again. Finally both lay still, Cal fighting for breath, she already quiet. In the hot little room they pulled back to arm's length for air, his body drenched in sweat and hers with it. They lay there for a thousand years. Gradually, more sounds from outside. A child walking by singing to herself, a small dog barking, a motor scooter, a woman's voice.

Later a cool shower together, then dressing. She was standing in the middle of the room in the black dress posing for him. His own Gilda.

"Men will die tonight, looking at you."

"Do you think so?"

"*And* women. There will be only one dream in all the beds of Cadaqués tonight. The same dream."

Cal went into the bedroom to put his shoes on. She called after him.

"Shall we eat a little something before we go? There's that avocado that's ripe, and those shrimp from yesterday."

"All right."

He was sitting on the edge of the bed putting on his shoes. Her voice again from the other room.

"What's this?"

"What's what?"

"This."

It was the way she said it. He knew. He stood and went to the door. Standing next to the blue cupboard by the kitchen, she was holding up a bottle of rum.

"I was taking a bowl to make our salad, and look what I found on the bottom shelf."

"Layla..."

"You promised me."

"I..."

His brain was racing, trying to figure out what would be the most believable. *Someone else must have left it there. It was mine from before I made that promise. I was only...*

No good.

"All right," she said, "I get it. A promise isn't exactly a promise."

She was standing there, just holding the bottle, looking at him.

"Okay. You know what," she said, "you win."

She unscrewed the top of the bottle, raised it to her mouth and took a sip.

"What are you doing?"

"It's a full moon party, isn't it? We have to celebrate the full moon."

She took another fast sip.

"Layla, please, don't."

She took another sip.

"Layla, stop it! What are you doing?"

Wiping her mouth with the back of her hand, she looked at him.

"You know something, that's delicious. That's really delicious.

But, am I doing it right?"

She brought the bottle back up to her mouth again.

"Stop that!"

"Why? I just want to have some fun, too."

Cal rushed toward her and grabbed her arm.

"What's the matter? Afraid I'll drink it all?" she asked.

He took the bottle from her hand.

"Layla..."

"You lied to me."

Cal took the bottle into the kitchen and, as she watched he poured what was left of it down the sink.

"What a damned waste," she said.

"Stop it. I'm sorry."

She crossed to the blue table and sat.

"Maybe you have a joint for us to smoke? I'm serious. Let's be crazy tonight. Crazy together."

"Come on. Let's get ready and go."

Silence. She looked around.

"Where's my necklace?"

There was a little rhinestone necklace lying on the coffee table next to the sofa. She pointed to it.

"There it is. Now be a good Wamba and help me put on my necklace. Go on. Help a girl put on her necklace, for god's sake. Can you do that? It's much easier than telling the truth."

"Layla..."

He went over to the table and picked up the necklace. She twisted in the chair, her back to him, and lifted up her hair.

"We're going to have the craziest night ever," she said. "You'll see. We're going to have *so* much fun."

He fastened the necklace around her neck. In the light from the window the rhinestones looked like real diamonds.

Chapter LXIV

*D*onde hay luz hay sombras, y donde hay sombras hay luz. Where there is light there are shadows, and where there are shadows there is light.

Cap de Creus is the easternmost tip of Catalonia, and of Spain. At its edge stands the old lighthouse. Many have followed its beacon to safety. Others to their end, as the rocks and swirling eddies below exact a high price to those who do not know these waters. During days, especially in winter but during other seasons too, the wind by the lighthouse can reach such a pitch that one can stand leaning into it and not fall. Arms stretched out, it can give one the sensation of flying. Flying without leaving the ground.

It was almost ten o'clock when Cal and Layla arrived. The tricky sun, already gone now as the days were growing shorter, still managed to light the scene, reflecting off the full moon that loomed above this place and the people here, and on the silver sea that spread below. So bright in the clear air that one could hardly see the stars. The wind had died down by this time, though it was strong enough still that it blew the leaves on the bent trees that stood between the rocks beyond the wide terrace. It was a warm wind, and felt good on their faces as Cal and Layla stepped together toward the music.

Sitting at the edge of the terrace, Filip with his guitar, another friend Omar singing, and a third man Pablo with bongo drums cradled between his knees. The music was smooth and fresh; a mystic Spanish love song, an Afro-Cuban beat, Moroccan rhythms... The wind carried the music around the terrace where happy people sat at tables drinking and talking. Beyond the terrace, more happy people were sitting on the rocks, smoking, laughing. Smells of hashish and women's perfume and the hot food being served; Indian curries, grilled fish, roast lamb and chicken. Bottles and glasses and eyes sparkling as the full moon sailed slowly above it all.

No candles up here because of the wind. Instead, a colored pinwheel sent purple, blue, red lights cartwheeling around the heads of the people, and up the sides of the building and on the big open space where some were already dancing. The old restaurant with its yellow walls had been a military outpost in the Civil War. The lighthouse itself, towering above the rocks beyond the restaurant, cast its own white light far as it circled around and then around again. Cal and Layla stopped to look and find their place in the scene.

Cal had stuck a small pin into the lapel of his white dinner jacket. Alfred E. Neuman from Mad. He had found it years before on the sidewalk in New York, the boy's face with the words "What, me worry?" in red letters below. No one was looking at Cal or at his pin. But many now were looking at Layla. One could not not-look at her. The moon was like a spotlight as she stood there in the black satin dress and the long black gloves, with the rhinestones sparkling around her neck.

Not everyone here was in costume. Most were not aware even that this was a full moon party, lusting to be as surreal as possible. There were many tourists looking like tourists anywhere scattered among the tables. And student types in jeans and t-shirts, all part of the regular restaurant crowd that would have been here full moon or not. It was only those from Cadaqués, clustered together at one end of the terrace, who were making of this something strange and wonderful, "divine" as Dali would call it. They sat, stood and drank apart from those untouched by the mad beauty of the village. With love of Cadaqués there comes a sort of madness. As if she the village was Layla, and those who loved her, men and women alike, the majnuns. The crazy ones. Hard wired in the DNA now, that madness. Destined to be passed from one generation to the next. In their own way all here were writing in the sand.

Vivienne, Chasey, Senalda, Valmont, Lia and others had strung white Christmas lights above that end of the terrace closest to where the music was playing. There was a mattress on the ground with a white cover, and circled around it tables with white cloths and red flowers. Thin white curtains suspended on wires blew in the wind like ghost dancers. Around the mattress and tables, the tribe. The Red Eyes, as Paul had always called them.

Robert and Richard had white sheets wrapped around them and were wearing sandals. Cal and Layla stepped toward them.

"Darling, you look DE-LICIOUS," said Robert, eyeing Layla up and down. "My god! A VISION, darling, that's what you are, hmm."

"Cal, you've got yourself a beauty there," growled Richard.

Looking back at both, Layla grinned. "And you two are...?"

Wiggles was holding a comic Greek mask on a stick. He held it over his face as he explained.

"Robert is here as Richard, Richard as Robert."

"No, no, no, that's not it," corrected Robert. "Castor and Pollux, darling. In our TO-GAS!" He had a glass of wine in his hand.

Layla laughed.

There was Daniel with a Dali moustache, diving mask and

seaweed hair. Freddy, dressed as a pirate, with silk scarf wrapped around his head, a gold earring, high leather boots, and a stuffed parrot pinned to his shoulder.

"Is it real?"

"Jah, well, it was."

"Does it talk?"

"No. It's dead."

David wore a pink bow tie and a massive tarantula ring on one finger. Senalda was dressed as herself. Chasey was a gypsy. Vivienne, standing next to her, was a kitten with little whiskers, and a long tail she kept bending over to wave at people. There were *two* Mad Hatters, and a jellyfish, and a round white thing that turned out to be Hector from the fish market.

"He's the full moon."

"I thought so."

Robin the minstrel stood wearing coconut breasts and a little coconut hat. The American painter Bob Venosa and his wife Martina were there. Martina had butterflies in her hair and another painted on her cheek. Venosa had a white square thing on his head, half buried in his heavy brown-grey curls. In his New York accent,

"It's a sugar cube with LSD in it. The idea is I'm not really here. If you can see me, you're tripping."

"I like it," said Cal.

"Me too," grinned Layla.

At this end of the terrace, of life, the exceptional was normal. Dali had set the bar about as high as it gets, and those here were jumping at it still. Marita, with gold hoop earrings and a lace shawl tucked behind her arms, sat staring out with those eyes that had once threatened to kill Jose Manuel. She looked at Layla.

"You are *so beautiful*, my dear. Cal, you take good care of this one. Do not fuck this one up."

She knew about the others. Cassandra, and the French and Russian girls he had brought up the mountain the summer before.

"My *god*, she is beautiful!"

A waiter was delivering food to one of the tables.

"What will you drink?" Cal asked Layla.

"What are you drinking?"

"Not sure yet. Why?"

"Because whatever you're drinking tonight, I'll have."

She had thought this through on the drive up.

"That's not fair."

"Isn't it?"

Something strange in her voice. As if she could still feel that little bit of rum she had earlier. Not possible, thought Cal, only those few sips over an hour before. Though in the car she had been acting funny. Laughing.

"I'm going to have wine," said Cal, afraid now to order anything stronger.

"Then I'll have the same. Or else..."

"What?"

"I know. Better yet, let's have champagne."

"Are you serious?"

"Why not? Let's be crazy. You remember how to be crazy, don't you? My crazy Wamba, with his hidden bottles."

"Layla..."

"And you still have some of your father's money left, don't you? Let's see if we can't spend that tonight. You like to spend money."

She got the young waiter's attention. He came over to them.

"*Sí?*"

"Go on, Wamba, order us a bottle of their best champagne."

"You don't want..."

"I do. I want it so badly. Come on. Or shall I order for us?" She looked at the waiter.

"Que champagne tienes?"

He answered in English.

"We have cava. Or if you want champagne, we have Veuve Clicquot."

"That's it, that's the one. Veuve Clicquot. Bring us a nice cold wet and shiny bottle of the widow Clicquot. Perfect. That will make my Wamba happy. And bring it to us in a silver bucket won't you, just like in the movies."

Cal stood staring at her. She looked like she was in a movie, her face, eyes, glowing. He couldn't decide if he was happy she was doing this or not. The waiter turned and left.

"This is going to be so much fun!" said Layla. "I haven't drunk champagne in such a time. Almost forever."

Wiggles had been watching, listening to this. Holding the mask over his face, "Well, I underestimated you, Layla. What have you gotten yourself into here, Cal?"

"I don't know."

"Darling, welcome," said Robert, grinning. He raised his glass toward Layla and drank to her.

Omar, leaning into his microphone, called out,

"This next song is called Monsters in the Sky. Is for all the monsters here."

Filip's guitar then, the bongos rolling, and Omar's voice. As he sang, more people stepped onto the terrace to dance, arms around each other. This was a slow one. Sonia, wearing a tight pink sari, with a crystal bindi sparkling on her forehead, stood and was dancing with herself. Grinning. Omar sang in his thick-accented English.

Hurts so good, knew it would
Don't know if to laugh or cry
Like a child, running wild
The truth is that I lied
Alibi
Had a dream, didn't seem
She was very far away
Nuns and girls, prayers and pearls
Showing me the way
Yesterday
Angels on the ground
Monsters in the sky
Lost until you found me
Darling darling don't ask why
Please don't cry
No good-byes

The song finished. Scattered applause. The waiter brought the champagne in a tin bucket.

"That's not silver," said Layla, pouting.

There was a hissing sound as the waiter turned the bottle, unloosening the cork. No popping noise. The waiter put the bottle back into the tin bucket and left. Cal filled their glasses.

"To the most beautiful woman in the world," offered Cal.

"And to the trickiest Wamba in the world," said Layla, smiling back at him.

She drank her glass in one go, as if it was water.

"Not so fast."

"No?"

"What's gotten into you?"

"What do you mean?"

"You drank that so fast."

"What's wrong, can't a girl have some fun? Besides, it's so light."

She waited for Cal to finish his. When he had, she reached out her empty glass.

"Next."

He just stared at her.

"Why are you looking at me like that?"

"What is this?"

"What is what?"

"You don't drink."

"Don't I? Come on, be a good Wamba."

Reluctantly, he filled her glass again. This time she sipped it.

"Like a lady. Isn't this how a lady does it?"

Filip and the others were playing a new song. *Mi querida Cadaqués.* My Dear Cadaqués. Filip's guitar so slow to start it, then Pablo shimmering a tambourine, a dull roll of the drums again, and Omar's voice floating into and above it. Soft, smooth, the rhythm picking up, bodies around the terrace moving with it. Layla set her empty glass on the table and reached for Cal's hand.

"Come. Dance with me."

Onto the floor then, hungry eyes on her from all sides. There was another girl also beautiful close by. But showing so much tits and ass those lost their power. Layla made you wait for it. Made you imagine. Arms hanging limp at her side, her head tilted, the soft curls falling over one shoulder. She moved her head to the right, curls shifting to the other shoulder. Her gloved hands began sliding upward. Slowly, so slowly, she was touching what everyone watching wanted to touch; hips, waist, then higher still as bare arms stretched toward the moon. And finally her body moving, all of it, the music deep inside her now. *Mi guerida Cadaqués.*

My Dear Cadaqués. *My dear Layla. My dream come true. The one. Thank you, god.*

Omar singing words about mountains, wind, sea, dreams, heat. Layla writhing, moving like water. You knew it was coming. Faster, faster still, and suddenly Filip's guitar on fire. Spanish flamenco at the heart of this love song to a Catalan village, those two like man and woman, interwoven here, inseparable.

Cal didn't listen to the music as much as watch it, the music coming through Layla, her eyes back on him always with that smile. And something else there he had never seen before.

Another song then, and another. Cal was ready again to dance the next, but Layla wanted to return to their table. They moved through the crowd. She sat not at the table but *on* it, the long slit in her dress pulling apart as her bare leg hung in the air. She took her empty glass from the table and held it toward Cal.

"Bubbles, please."

"What's gotten into you?"

"Bubbles. Bubbles have gotten into me."

She watched as he poured.

"Now, I've been meaning to ask you a question," she said.

"What's that?"

"What's your real name? I mean, Cal's not your real name. What's your real name?"

"Max."

"Don't joke."

"I'm not joking."

"Max?"

"Maximilian."

"And a middle name? Every boy has a middle name."

"Alexander."

"Maximilian Alexander Zander?"

"Yup."

"Well, that sounds rather pompous."

"I'm pretty sure it was my father who pressed for it. Dreams of empire."

"So then, you grew up as Max?"

He nodded.

"Well, Maximilian Cal Alexander Zander Wamba, you know what I suggest?"

"What do you suggest, Layla von Leda?"

"I suggest we finish this bottle of champagne before any more bubbles escape. Did you know that's how they charge for champagne, by the bubble?"

"Layla..."

"The widow Clicquot had to be very clever, don't you think? While others were selling their wine, she was selling bubbles. Made a bloody fortune doing it."

She didn't wait for him. With her gloved hand, she lifted the bottle from the tin bucket and refilled both their glasses.

"I've never seen you like this," he said.

"Like what? Never seen me like what?"

She was twisting her ankle slowly, the black heel winding up the men and women watching her. And there were many watching her. She knew what she was doing. A beautiful woman feels her power like a soldier feels his. Other side of that coin. Push vs. pull. Instead of *don't* fuck with me...

"Do you know what we're going to do later?" she asked Cal.

"What?"

"We're going to make love right here on that mattress. Will you do that for me, Wamba? Will you make love to me on that mattress?"

The three musicians finished their set, and carrying their instruments left the stage to applause. A moment later a DJ took over, music now pounding over speakers. He stood at a sound system set up under a tree, an old stone bread oven behind him. The colored lights were flashing as more people crowded onto the dance floor. The song playing was Ricky Martin's La Vida Loca. It was everywhere that summer.

The bottle of Veuve empty, Cal tipped it upside down into the tin bucket.

"Should we get another?" asked Layla. "Let's get another."

"No."

"But you..."

"Come on," said Cal, reaching for her hand. "Let's dance."

She slid down from the table. Back onto the floor with all the others, then into the middle of it. Everyone was moving.

She'll make you take your clothes off and go dancing in the rain
She'll make you live her crazy life but she'll take away your pain
Like a bullet to your brain. Come on!

You have to be able to take your liquor. That was the key. Cal was lucky. Some couldn't do it.

No slow moves now. Layla was tossing her hair, arms stretched high in the air, winding down with her little knees bending. Turning, rubbing up against Cal's body, then pulling back. And laughing. Hands cupping her own breasts, then lifting her hair, turning again, slowly she began stripping off one of her gloves. Like in the movie. Gilda. Her eyes fixed on Cal, Layla's left hand rolled the black satin glove down off her right elbow, then lower still, turning it inside out as she peeled it off her fingers. *Dancing is just sex with your clothes on*...until the clothes come off.

Upside, inside out, she's livin' la vida loca
She'll push and pull you down, livin' la vida loca

Layla came toward Cal and, wrapping the glove around the back of his neck, pulled him close. Reaching up to kiss him, as their mouths met he felt her tongue. A quick lick, then just as fast she was away again, twirling the glove in a great circle. All watching her were waiting to see if anything else would come off. Again moving close she knelt down in front of Cal, reaching for him now.

"Stop that!"

He pulled her back up. She just laughed, looking at him.

They danced the next song, and the next. Cal's shirt was sopping wet with sweat. Layla did not stop moving, as if she could not stop. She didn't even notice until the next day that the little gold ring she always wore, with her family's crest of a swan in blue stone, had flown off her finger. Cal took her hand finally and together they wound through the people back toward their friends. There was no one on the mattress. Layla sank onto it, pulling Cal down with her. She had barefeet.

"My shoes!"

"Where are they?"

"I don't know. I must have lost them out there dancing."

Cal went back onto the floor to look for them. Minutes later he was back.

"I couldn't find them."

"Oh well, doesn't really matter. Heels were too short."

Layla lay coiled on the mattress smoking. Someone had passed her a joint.

"What's that?" asked Cal.

"You don't know?"

She took a deep hit and started to cough. Cal took it out of her hand and passed it to someone, anyone, without taking a hit himself.

"Layla, stop this. You don't smoke. You don't drink. What are you doing?"

She couldn't answer. Too busy coughing.

Close by, Marita was arguing with Chasey.

"I mean no *real* gypsy would be caught *dead* wearing such a thing! Pink flowers like those. No! Never!"

"It's just a costume."

"Listen, my grandmother traveled in a horse wagon from Hungary to Sweden in the middle of the night, and if she..."

That kept going, the real gypsy telling the pretend gypsy how real gypsy women dress.

Layla had stopped coughing. With her gloved hand she reached again for Cal.

"Come here. Lie down with me."

Cal knelt next to her.

"Do you know what I want, Wamba? What I want more than anything else in the world?"

"What?"

"I want you to order us another bottle of champagne."

"No, Layla..."

"What's the matter?"

"You don't need anymore."

"I don't *need* it. I just want it. That's what you always say, isn't it? You know what else I want?"

"What?"

"I want you to fuck me. Will you do that, Wamba? Will you fuck me right here, right now."

She kept reaching for him and he kept pulling her hand away.

"Stop this!"

"*Why*? We're going to make a fuck guide to Cadaqués, remember? Show everyone. I'll let you fuck me here, and then we can put it on the map, and they can even put a plaque or a stone here with a little sign saying, 'This is the place to start fucking.'"

She was laughing so hard now.

"'Start fucking here, and go to the next spot on your map to continue fucking.'"

She reached again for his zipper. Again, he pulled her hand away.

"Stop it! You're drunk."

"Don't be silly. I'm not drunk. But I know one thing."

"What?"

She looked at him very seriously.

"Try saying 'Fuck suck fuck suck,' and then reverse it. Go on, do it. Then try saying, 'Suck fuck suck fuck.' Just try. It's a completely different experience."

"Layla..."

She was pouting again.

"What? I'm just having some fun. Don't be so serious. Why are you always so serious?"

"You know what?"

"What?"

"You're the most beautiful woman in the world."

She fell back onto the mattress, face framed by her hair, looking up at him.

"Do you know what I wish?"

He lay down close next to her.

"What do you wish?"

"I wish people would say to me, 'You're the most decent person in the world.' Or, 'You're the kindest person in the world.' They never do, though. All my life, men always told me how beautiful I am. But they never called me decent."

"Well, you are. You're the most decent person I've ever known."

"They never say how smart a girl is, or how talented. Or how decent she tries to be. It's always the same thing. And I do like to hear that, of course. I mean, who wouldn't? But sometimes, just sometimes..."

"You're all those things. Smart, talented, decent, *and* beautiful."

"Really?"

"Really."

"Wamba?"

"Yes?"

"Do you think the moon is a bubble?"

"Maybe."

"Look at it up there. That's what it looks like, doesn't it? Like a big, decent bubble."

She sat up. She was holding onto her stomach.

"Oh god."

"What's wrong?"

"I think I'm going to..."

Layla got onto her knees and tried to stand. Her dress caught. She pulled it free and climbed onto her feet. Cal was helping her. She made it to the rocks at the edge of the terrace and bent over. Cal stayed with her as the music continued in the background.

Chapter LXV

"I'm sorry," said Cal.

It was the next morning. Layla was packing, putting her things in a bag. Books, clothes...

"Layla? Please, I'm sorry. Stop it. Just stop it."

She did not stop. Just kept packing.

"I'm so sorry you got sick."

"That's not it," said Layla. "That's not it at all."

More books, more clothes into the bag. Cal felt sick now, watching her. He was leaning in the door to the little bedroom.

"Then *what*? Explain."

"It's what happened before that."

"*What* happened? We were having fun, that's all! We were dancing. And, okay, yes, I drank a little. It was a fucking party. And you drank a little. And you didn't like it. Okay, but..."

She stopped now and looked at him.

"It's *not* that I didn't like it. Don't you understand? The problem is I *did* like it. I liked it very much. Until..."

She looked down a moment, took a breath, then began putting things into her bag again.

"So if you liked it, what's the problem? Look, to be a little wild just one night..."

"*It's not about one night!*"

"Then *what*? Stop packing, explain this to me."

"Listen, I can't change the way you are, Cal. It's okay. You are who you are. But this is not for me. It's too...dangerous."

"*What's* too dangerous?"

He moved toward her and tried to put his arm around her.

"Please don't."

"Layla..."

"I said, *don't*. I'm sorry, Cal. It's over."

More clothes into the bag, make-up and lotions from the bathroom... Cal felt weak in the knees.

"Layla, please, I beg you. If you'll just tell me how..."

"Listen, I told you my father left us when I was a baby."

"I know."

"But I didn't tell you how it was before. The stories I've heard from my mother. He was drunk, *always* drunk. The day I was born he was out somewhere with his friends. My mother thinks he just forgot he was having a child that day."

"I'm sorry."

"We had a dog, Daisy. I don't remember her because I was just a baby. My father left her in the car one day, and she died because of the heat. To this day my mother still cries to tell it. All these stupid, stupid stories! So many of them!"

She looked frightened.

"And after he left us, as I was growing, she used to always say to me, I hope you won't turn out like your father did. And also his father before him."

"Layla please..."

"And then, when I was eleven, I was at a wedding. A friend of my mother's. There were these glasses of champagne on the table. I sat under the table. Nobody saw me, and I kept reaching up and taking those glasses and drinking what was in them. And I loved it. I mean, *I really loved it.* Because for the first time in my life I felt..."

"What?"

Tears now.

"...like I was closer to my father. Because somehow that's what that meant to me. And then it happened again, a few times. And I became so afraid...afraid that I was turning into..."

She was crying hard. Again Cal went to put an arm around her. This time she let him. The shutters were closed and there was just a dull light in the little room. They stood together with her head on his shoulder. After some moments she spoke again, through it.

"When we came here to Cadaqués, I was just a girl still. And all these parties on the beach. Every night. And the boys, always..."

"It's okay. Shhh. It's okay."

"...and then, Paul. I was only sixteen when we met. He rescued me one night. I mean, he literally saved me. There were these boys, and they had this car, and they were taking me to it. And I was drunk. Paul saw them and he stopped it. Told them to leave me alone. He took me to some place, some café or restaurant, and sat with me. And I told him I didn't want to see my mother when I was like that, so he took me home with him and left me alone to sleep. Do you understand? He left me alone. And then he became..."

"What?"

"He became like my best friend, because he protected me. He did not drink, and he did not want me to drink, and he protected me. Later I had a boyfriend. And when I wouldn't...we got drunk on the beach one night, and he wanted to have sex. I said no. And then he called me all these horrible, horrible names, and he left me. Told me he didn't want want to be with a girl who..."

"Look at me. Layla, look at me."

She wiped her face and looked up.

"I swore, Cal. I swore on everything I believe in that I would not turn into my father. And that I also would never be with a man that was like him. I don't want that. I don't want it for myself, and someday, when it's right, I don't want that for my..."

She didn't finish the sentence.

"Be my Paul," said Cal. "Please, Lay, help me. I know...I know that I've been overdoing it a little. It's not so easy for me. Those stories about my mother...just like your father. And I don't want this either. Please, help me. Let's be healthy together."

She took his face in her hands.

"I do love you so much, Cal. So very much."

Chapter LXVI

That day, and the next day, and the day after that even Cal drank nothing. And there was no more talk about Layla leaving. She put her things back as they were, they had meals, took long walks, telling each other stories about the dreams, but also now about the nightmares. They learned more about each other in those few days than in all the time that had led up to them. On the fourth day, Layla had to go see a hat maker from Barcelona who had a weekend flat in Cadaqués, somewhere up behind the Blue House. Layla had decided she wanted to make a copy of the hat Marcel Duchamp wore as Rrose Sélavy.

"Who?"

"You know, when he dressed as a woman. The name means Eros c'est la vie...desire is life. There's a Man Ray photograph of Duchamp wearing this wonderful hat. I thought it would be fun, but I haven't the faintest idea how to make it. Paul has this friend Nuria. She makes hats. She's going to show me how to do it."

"So then meet you later, at Meliton?"

"Perfect. Where Duchamp sat playing his chess games. That seems appropriate."

A sweet kiss, and off she went. Cal sat at the blue table for a while writing in his journal. Things he had learned about Layla, and also about himself. And he had so many ideas suddenly. He even had an idea for a new book. About a boy and a girl both lost in a forest, and they come to the same spring from different directions.

Cal began to sketch it out, not sure if it was meant to be a children's story or something more complicated. Then he went for a short walk on his own. He put on the white shirt Layla had made for him *again*, then out and up toward the Llane Petit. He was avoiding the Casino and Imperial. Too many temptations there.

As he walked past the Café Habana there was music coming from inside. The guitarist normally was there nights only, and though it was still light for some reason he was already playing. Cal decided to go in and listen to the music for a moment. There were people sitting at the bar and at tables, many of them drinking the famous mojitos. Cal looked at the drinks, with the ice and pieces of green lime and the sprigs of fresh mint, and he decided that he had been so good for three days, it would not hurt to have *just* one. When that was finished he decided he would have *just* one more. That was it then. He left. And as he walked, he was feeling so proud of himself for not having had a third drink, though he could have so easily. As long as he kept everything as moderate as he had now, there would be no more problems. He knew that he could do that, and that knowledge gave him joy.

He stopped at L'Estable to have a quick sandwich with ham and cheese and lots of onion. No point in Layla smelling those two mojitos and worrying for no reason. And really he was so happy. If he was going to drink at all, from this day forward it would be as most people do. One or two, maybe three on a Saturday, that would be it, and he and Layla would live happily ever after. He even laughed to think of it now. She had *already* helped him!

Heading back toward the center of the village, he was walking past the Casino as Senalda was coming out of it. She looked upset. Cal waved hello and she smiled at him but did not stop. Then Richard came out of the Casino, a glass of red wine in one hand.

He shouted up the road after Senalda.
"Next time, darling, YOU can buy ME a drink!"
"Richard."
"Cal."
"Everything okay?"
"Wellllll, just that...it's always the same, isn't it?"
"What is?"
"She, Senalda. Sits at the table, drinks her wine...the best they have, mind you...and then she expects you to pay for it."
"Does she?"
"Well, not having it! BASTA, darling! Enough! Not very elegant, that."
"No."
"What a witch, eh? The only magic there, avoiding the bill."
The sweet smile then.
"My brother's inside. Join us?"
"I can't. Sorry. I'm meeting Layla."
"Darling, she'll find you here."
"I can't. Sorry."
"Cal?"
"Yes?"
Richard held up his glass of wine.
"This is my blood," he said, smiling. Just a joke. "Sure you won't join us?"
"Next time, Richard."

As Cal kept walking past the Boia, he thought back to the way he used to be and to the new Cal that he now was. He had said no to a drink with the twins, had said no to a third drink at the Café Habana.

How different even friends at the Casino seemed to him suddenly. Incredible, he thought, how fast things can change if you want it badly enough.

At Meliton he sat waiting for Layla while drinking a Bitter Kas. That's like a Campari without alcohol. He asked for a lot of ice and the waiter brought it. He sipped the red bitter drink with the slice of lemon in it while watching the people, and it was not long before Layla came.

"Well, how did it go?"

Layla was bubbling over as she sat.

"Fantastic! She told me everything I need to know. I'm going to make Duchamp's hat, and later Nuria said she'd even help me make others. Like that flying saucer thing Audrey Hepburn wears in Breakfast for Tiffany. You know the one."

"But don't you already know how to make hats? That one you wore in Collioure?"

"I cheated with that one. I actually found it in a shop in Paris last year. I was there visiting some close friends of my mother's. It's what gave me the idea. I just made the outfit to go with it."

Excited, she stood again, came over to him and knelt close.

"I'm so happy, Wamba. Thank you."

"Thank me for what?"

She looked at the bottle of Bitter Kas on the table.

"Thank you," she whispered.

He smiled at her.

"Kiss me," she said, leaning closer still. "You remember when you said that to me on the beach?"

"Yes."

"Well go on then, kiss me."

Their lips pressed together, she said, "You taste like onions."

"I had a fast bite at L'Estable. Just a sandwich. There's nothing in the house. We need to do a shopping."

She looked at him.

"What do you think," he asked, "maybe we go do it now?"

"All right."

Cal paid for his drink and together holding hands they walked toward the market. They had to go past Imperial. Tor was sitting alone at one table with a beer. Cal had seen him a few times since that day they had almost gotten into it. They had avoided each other. But now, as Cal and Layla walked by passing close to his table, Tor looked at them and grinned. In his Swiss-German accent, he shouted out.

"Wow, man, congratulations."

Cal didn't say anything back, didn't even look at him. Just kept walking. Tor started to laugh.

"Man, you've got yourself a nice piece of pussy there, don't you? A nice sweet little piece of..."

Cal let go of Layla's hand and flew at him. Layla screamed for him to stop. Too late. Fists flying, Cal tore into him like the world depended on it. The guy had hardly gotten out of his chair when, his nose already broken, he fell back on the ground. There was blood on his face and on Cal's hands and on the shirt that Layla had made for him. Layla kept screaming.

"Cal, stop it! Stop it! Don't!"

He didn't hear her. Or he didn't want to hear her. On his knees now, hitting Tor again and again, in the face, in the chest. He just kept hitting him. When he stopped finally and stood he looked down at Tor.

"Don't you *ever...ever*...say that about my woman again. You fucking slime bag. Do you hear me?"

Tor didn't answer because he couldn't. He just lay there trying to cover his head in case there was more coming. Jose, the owner of the bar was standing close by looking at Cal.

"Hombre, no mas, eh? Bastante."

Someone else said, "Come on, Cal. Enough, eh? You showed him."

"I'll fucking show him again if he says something like that again." Cal stood there breathing hard, staring down at Tor. "Have some fucking respect. You fucking slime bag."

Tor was wiping his red face with his sleeve. Cal turned toward Layla. She was not there. He looked around. She had gone.

Back at the house he found her. Packing.

"What are you doing?"

"It's over. It's really over."

"What do you mean, it's over? You heard what he said. Layla..."

"No! Cal, it's over."

The books, the clothes, all of it. She was stuffing things into her bag as fast as she could.

"Layla, *stop* it! That was not my fault!"

"You were like an animal. A bloody animal!"

"Okay, maybe I shouldn't have hit him so hard."

"*So hard?* He was on the ground, and you just kept hitting him."

"I'm sorry. He said that about you, and..."

"I don't care! Who gives a damn what anyone says? Let them say what they want. You don't go smashing a person's face because they've said something."

Her voice lowering, "And you drank."

"What are you talking about?"

"You drank. And then you went and ate some silly onions. It's not something one smells in you, Cal. One *sees* it. I could *see* it in your eyes."

"Layla..."

"No. It's over. Forget it. You're not going to change. You're never going to change."

In the silence now, he watched her.

Not with anger, instead with such sadness she zipped the bag closed, then turned to look at him.

"I can't watch you hurt yourself anymore. Or hurt others. I'm sorry, but I just can't do it. And I don't want to be hurt. Not like this."

"Layla, listen to me. He sells drugs, hard drugs..."

"It's not *about* him! It has nothing to do with him. It's about you. And until you see that, nothing else is going to change. It'll just keep on like this, and I don't want it. I haven't the strength. I'm sorry. I wish I did."

She started toward the door. He stood there blocking her.

"Please Cal, let me pass."

He did not move.

"Let me go by."

"I'm *not* going to let you go."

"Well then, what are you going to do? Keep me here by force? Maybe hit me, like you hit him?" A moment. "I'm sorry. I shouldn't have said that."

Cal still wasn't budging.

"Please, Cal. Let me go."

Slowly Cal pulled aside. He sank to his knees, his back leaning against the frame of the door.

Cry. Sob. Weep. There was not really a word to describe what Cal did next. It was like taking what was inside you and putting it on the outside. Like peeling back the skin and just leaving everything under it exposed, the wet pink soft bits unprotected now. His whole body was shaking. Layla stopped next to the door and stood there.

"*Oh, god. Please, god. No. No. No...*"

After some moments she put her bag down. She couldn't leave him like that. She turned and looked as he moved to the bed and lay there. He was rocking, curled in a fetal position, gripping his stomach and making these strange noises.

"Oh god, I beg you. Please, Layla...I love you *so* much!"

She came back, sat next to him, and put a hand on his shoulder.

"It's going to be okay," she said.

"Please...*please* don't leave me."

"You're going to be fine, Cal. What I said earlier, it wasn't right. Things will change, I know they will. But please, get some help. Because I don't think you can do this on your own."

"I want *you* to help me. I *need* you to help. Please. Please..."

"No, I see it now. You're not ready for this yet. Not until you get things sorted a bit. And it will happen. I'm sure it will. Because I know you can do it."

There was something so calm, so damned calm in her voice. And so determined. She was slipping away. Was already gone.

"*No! No! Oh, god, please...*"

Again, such strange noises out of him, the bed already wet with his tears and his sweat. She sat there. It kept going until his stomach hurt so badly he had to stop to catch his breath. Then it started again.

He begged her, again. "I'll stop! I swear to you, Layla! I'll stop...I *will* change..."

Finally Layla stood. She went into the other room. She picked up her bag and went to the front door, opening it. Cal heard it open. And then he heard it closing. He wanted to die. Would die.

"*No!*" he screamed to the empty space. "*No! Oh god, no. Please god, no. No...*"

The light outside was gone, and still in the dark room Cal lay rocking, wailing from the pain of it, holding himself. Begging, promising, negotiating even as if she was still there.

"I promise you. I love you. Oh Layla, I love you..."

But there was no one there to hear. He was alone.

Chapter LXVII

Through long days and even longer nights Cal waited. He would sit at the blue table staring at the door, or lie in bed hoping, praying even, that she would come back. She had to feel his pain. Know how badly he loved her, missed her, needed her. Silly, but he actually tried sending his vibrations out into the universe hoping that somehow, like a homing beacon, they would lead her home. It did not work. As often as he imagined it, still that door did not swing open, she there with her little bag telling him that she had tried but just couldn't stand facing a life without him. That somehow together they would pull through this. There was only the fucking silence.

He tried not drinking, and after three days that still did not bring her back. Couldn't she sense he was doing that? He would smoke a joint, sitting down by the water, and instead of fingers unclasping from his throat as usually happened, there was just a thick sad fog. The sadness would hang over him and get under his skin and he couldn't shake it. Nothing to do, and nowhere to go to get away from it.

Finally he tried drinking again, to see if that would dull the pain. And it did seem to work for a moment. But then the feeling was back, that he was going to vomit up his heart.

On the fourth morning, while looking for his sandals under the bed he found a book she had left behind. Virginia Woolf's To the Lighthouse. Cal dressed as fast as he could and hurried to the Casino to sit reading it there. As he turned each page, doing it made him feel closer to her. And just as importantly, if she did show up and saw him there reading her book she would be reminded of all that was good between them. Their common interests, his sensitivity, his feelings toward her...

He had a *café cortado*, nothing more than that, and got as far as the bits about rapture and love and the glove's twisted finger. He was making sure to read so that the cover of the book faced the door. If she did walk in she couldn't miss seeing it. But then instead of Layla it was Robert who wandered in and came to him, a newspaper tucked under his arm.

"Cal."

"Robert."

Robert left his newspaper on the table, went to the bar and came back with a cold beer. He sat, and for a while they read across the table from each other. Then Cal went to the bar to get himself a beer. It was nice not being alone, sitting here reading, feeling her in the pages of the book. This was the best he had felt in days. Later other friends came and sat with them. Everyone said nice things to try to make Cal feel better. *She'll be back... Don't worry...You'll find her...If it was meant to be...*

He didn't just sit and wait, of course. Later that day he searched for her. Again. He revisited all the places they had been together, dreaming that he would find her at one just sitting, waiting for him. Each time he returned home he imagined that he would find a note from her on the door. But it did not happen.

Senalda and Vivienne both knew the mother. He went to them to ask where she lived.

"Manchester, wasn't it?"

No, they had sold that house years before. Nobody knew where the mother lived now. And so that was it, she had gone.

And finally Cal understood that he had to go also. It was too hard being here without her. He packed and said thank you and good-bye to David's mother. Then he went downstairs to David's studio to say good-bye to him.

"Don't worry, Cal. She gave herself to you, yes? This can never be taken. She is Psyche for you. And in your heart, she can never be taken."

"I don't want her just in my heart, David. I want her in my life."

David took a long puff from his cigarette and stared down at the painting on the table in front of him. It was another boat, in another river, with another mountain behind it. The colors were shades of brown.

"Cal, I must work. You excuse me, yes?"

"Yes, David."

David lifted up his brush, and as Cal stood watching he was already back at it.

"Good bye, David."

His friend didn't answer.

From there it was up to the bookshop to say good-bye to Tharrats. The translator was finishing his work on Cal's book. Tharrats wanted to know where he should send the galley proofs.

"You already have the address, on the back of that envelope Grisha sent you with those illustrations."

"You are going now to Berlin?"

"Yes."

Tharrats smiled.

"I would like to go to Berlin one day."

They talked about when the book would be printed. Tharrats wanted to have a little event in the spring, a publication party. Cal promised he would return for that to read.

"Hasta entonces, Joan."

"Hasta entonces, Cal."

They shook hands, then Cal headed back to the house to grab his backpack. For the last time he locked the blue door behind him, and left the magic key in the postbox as David's mother had asked. He walked down the long passage to Port Alguer as they had walked, turned as they had turned, drifted past the little beach where he had written out his poem to Layla. At the old wooden wine press he stopped to take one last look back.

So beautiful this place out here on the edge of everything; hermitage of San Sebastian on the mountain in the distance, little Cucurucuc rising out of the water as it always had and always would, the lighthouse Cala Nans standing at the entrance to the bay. The little buildings the color of clouds. Cal stood looking at it as if he had already left this place; all of it just a memory now.

There were people passing. He couldn't help hoping still to catch a glimpse of Layla among them, just as they had looked for the Grail that day up at San Pere de Rhodes.

This was a ghost town now. Funny how just one person missing can suck the life out of a place.

He was so fucking sentimental! He had friends in New York who could take anything, hard as rock. Why couldn't he be more like them? He began to drag himself away like a child having to go home before he's ready. *You can't stay darling. It's time to go. Say good-bye now. Good-bye, Cadaqués.*

Through the big plate glass windows of the Casino he could see the twins and Marita and Wiggles sitting together, glasses of wine in hand or on the table, smoking, laughing. He watched them for some moments, and then he walked across the little bridge past the Boia, and past the passeig. He stopped at the little wine shop to buy three bottles of rioja for the trip. *Rio-ja.* Up the Avenida Caritat Serinyana then. The bus for Figueres was already waiting. He climbed on and sat at the back. That night he would board a train in Figueres and head toward Berlin. He had phoned Grisha and his wife and they were expecting him.

PERSISTENCE OF MEMORY

Chapter LXVIII

The train pulled into Berlin Zoo station in the mid-afternoon. A gray September sky matched the gray dust-covered walls and windows of the station, and the gray clothes of the people shuffling along the raised platform. Here and there a man and woman embraced as one stepped off the train into the other's arms. Through the crowd, Cal spotted a young woman with her back to him. Long blonde curls like...was it...he slung his backpack over his shoulder and, pushing past people, headed toward her. Maybe Layla had followed him, taken the same train even, or known somehow that he would be arriving now and... The girl turned her head. It was not Layla. Cal stopped. He turned and headed down the stairs to find a taxi below. The line was to his left. Three people ahead of him. He waited. The driver helped him put the backpack into the trunk of the pale yellow Mercedes and Cal got in. He read from the slip of paper that he pulled from his pocket.

"Mommsenstrasse 57, bitte."

As the taxi began to roll, out the window three immediate signs this was Berlin. Atop one building, the emblem of the crossed words for Bayer chemical and pharmaceutical company. Atop another building, the Europa Center, a giant revolving emblem for Mercedes. And below those two, the stubbed spire of the ruined church the Gedächtniskirche, or Kaiser Wilhelm Memorial Church. Destroyed in heavy fighting during the last days of World War II, Berliners had kept the ruins in the heart of this shopping district as a daily reminder of the consequences of war. A cynic might say that in a cost-benefit analysis, that glimpse of the ledger a stiff lesson that there were wiser investments.

The taxi turned onto Kurfürstendamm, the wide tree lined boulevard locals call simply Ku'damm. At a bus stop, Cal saw two men sitting, one old, one young. Dirty clothes, red faces, a dozen empty bottles of beer scattered on the ground by their feet. The old guy was holding a bottle of vodka and saying something to the young guy. Walking past them were throngs of people heading from one place to another. The year before, on his first visit to Berlin when Cal had come to spend some weeks with Grisha and his wife, he had been so excited to be here. Now he was sick to be here without Layla; the empty seat next to him, this night, tomorrow, everyday ahead without her. How was that possible?

As the taxi kept rolling westward, the shops along the side of the boulevard grew increasingly exclusive. On the sidewalk now were elegant shoppers carrying bags; robin-egg blue for Tiffany, Hermes orange, blood-red for Cartier, again blood-red for Wempe watches. The triumph of capitalism on display here in the windows, in the Porsches and Mercedes and BMWs gliding by, and in the eyes of the people walking. At the end of the twentieth century, this was the winner's circle.

The taxi turned onto Leibnizstrasse. On the right was a shop selling Russian icons. On the left, a Sushi restaurant, shoe store, bakery, copy shop and a dentist. At Mommsenstrasse another right and the taxi stopped. Cal paid and got out. As the car pulled away he stood with his backpack looking up at the elegant old yellow apartment building with its Art Nouveau flourishes and the date 1905 written proudly on its side. Survival here nothing to take for granted.

A row of names and brass buttons were next to the door.

Cal pushed the button beside the name Yermiloff. Waiting for the buzzer, he looked around. On the opposite corner was a bland apartment block from the fifties. One of so many that had sprung up after the war to fill the craterous gaps left by the bombs. No thoughts of beauty there. Just a practical way of putting roofs over peoples' heads and a toilet under their ass as fast as possible. On another corner was a gas station. Cal knew from his earlier visit here that they were open 24/7, and that as well as gas they also sold beer, wine and little bottles of Gorbachev vodka for two Deutsche Mark.

A familiar, friendly voice through the speaker.

"Yes? Hello?"

"Grisha, Cal."

"Hi Cal! Welcome to Berlin!"

A buzzing sound. Cal pushed the heavy door open and entered the dark marble corridor with the black and white tile floor and the little alabaster statues set up near the ornate ceiling. At the foot of the old stairs with the carved wood banister was a small elevator. Cal squeezed into it and, with his pack resting on his toes, rode to the top floor. Grisha was standing in the oversized doorway to the apartment waiting. A big warm smile and hand outstretched. Cal shook the hand, but then moved past it. He needed more, a real hug. Greetings are cultural moments, centuries in the making. Wherever he went Cal was a Californian, first name basis even with strangers, touching when possible. Grisha was more formal. Courtly, even.

"Look Cal, it's history of twentieth century. An American, a Russian, here in Berlin." Grisha laughed. "Come in."

Cal leaned his pack against a wall.

"Maybe you like something to drink, Cal? Some tea maybe?"

Grisha had a wonderful sense of humor.

"Umm..."

"Or, maybe something else? Maybe a little vodka after such long trip? Just to relax?"

"That sounds good, Grisha. Thank you."

One year together in New York, one month in Spain and a few weeks in Berlin the year before, and Grisha knew Cal as well as anyone.

He led Cal into the living room with its high ceiling and high bookshelves stuffed with books about art, history, literature, sex. Grisha's own paintings hung on the walls between the shelves. As a young man back in the U.S.S.R. he had risked much by belonging to non-conformist art circles. Then he had married a German woman, Elsa, and made it through here to the West. And the moment his brush was clear of the censors...

On one wall was a painting of a bust of a scowling Lenin rising out of the sea, a naked woman sunbathing on his rock-bald head.

"He had to be good for something," said Grisha as Cal paused to look at it.

On another wall, Stalin was strolling nonchalantly past the decaying carcass of his rotting philosophy. And there was an early oil-on-canvas of a fish and a loaf of bread. Like art, the church had offered the young Grisha welcome refuge from the dictatorship of the proletariat.

Finally there was a self-portrait, Grisha with maulstick standing in front of the church in Cadaqués. Cal pointed to the roof of the church and quickly told Grisha the story of how he had climbed onto it. Even the top of the Cypress tree was in the painting.

"You should have painted the tree a little bigger, Grisha. I wouldn't have had a problem then."

Grisha laughed. Cal had not laughed in days. He tried to do it now.

There was a big green sofa and a matching chair with low coffee table between them. Cal sat on the sofa. Grisha excused himself and went to the kitchen. A moment later he was back with some little things to eat, olives, cheese, smoked fish, and a frosty bottle of cold vodka from the freezer. Also one small crystal glass. He put the bottle and glass on the table in front of Cal.

Grisha himself was drinking tea. Cal knew his friend didn't drink during the day. Usually he didn't drink much at nights either, though on special occasions he could drink, and even get down on the sidewalk on hands and knees and bark like a dog as well as anyone. But that didn't happen often.

Grisha sat and looked at his friend, smiling.

"So Cal, tell me, how was your time now in Cadaqués?"

There was news about people they both knew, and about the book. Otherwise the talk turned quickly, the whole summer reduced to basically one word...Layla. And tears. Cal couldn't hold them back any longer.

"I'm sorry, Cal."

"I don't know, Grisha, why I keep fucking these things up. And she was so...perfect."

"It's okay, Cal. Really, it's okay."

Grisha waited for Cal to let it out. In his black slippers with the monogramed GY in gold thread, and that cup of tea beside him, there was something of David Suchet's Poirot here. Thoughtful, neat, wise. And so patient. This is what Cal had come for.

It was a great irony, this subversive painter living in the bourgeois heart of West Berlin. Comfort can disarm some artists, but it can also free others to focus on their work. After a childhood spent in the bleak middle of nowhere, where Grisha's parents had been forced into internal exile for "political crimes against the State," these days having icons, a nice bakery and a good dentist next door were welcome. Enough discomforts easily recalled to provide a lifetime of images. And for the student of history, Berlin supplied even more. The twentieth century would be gone soon, only three months left of it, and while many wounds had healed over, the scabs were everywhere still. An artist could pick at those whether the ceilings were high or not.

Grisha sat patiently listening to his friend, almost like Freud listening to a patient. Hunched forward on the couch, Cal went on about Layla. And as he sat nodding, Grisha thought it looked like the little glasses Cal kept shooting back were filled not with vodka but with tears. The stuff was leaking out of his eyes almost as fast as he could swallow it.

"It was *so* wonderful. *She* was so wonderful. I tried, Grisha. I really tried."

"It's very pity, Cal."

"I'm sorry. It's embarrassing. I feel like a baby."

"Well, okay then, Cal. Babies have long futures. And many possibilities."

Always so positive.

"It will be okay, Cal, you will see. Trust me. It will be okay."

The vodka was starting to work, fog softening the harder edges.

"And Elsa, where is she?"

"She is in Munich. She makes a story for her newspaper about Oktoberfest."

"I would like to go to Oktoberfest once."

Grisha smiled to picture it, Cal in the beer halls and tents.

After about an hour the well was running dry.

"So Cal, what do you think? You can stay here and sleep on

the couch like last year, only maybe not so comfortable. Or you can stay in my studio, where is more privacy. As you like."

"Maybe the studio, Grisha."

"Maybe you like to take shower after so long train?"

There was no bathroom in the studio which was in another building. While Cal showered, Grisha sat at the heavy wooden table by the window writing in his journal. In Cyrillic script, he wrote about how vodka looks like tears. And on the opposite page, he drew a picture of a man with his tongue stuck out catching his own tears as a child catches snowflakes.

Chapter LXIX

From the comfort of bourgeois West Berlin, to the withdrawn poverty of an artist's garret. Grisha's atelier was in the rough attic above an old beautiful white apartment building at number 60 Leibnizstrasse. This one had the date 1904 timestamped on its side. Another survivor.

Through the elegant foyer, up the elevator, then the creaking steps beyond that to the attic. Very La Boheme. Or, maybe Raskolnikov's garret in Crime and Punishment. Grisha unlocked the small unfinished door and, heads stooped through the low frame, it was into the hot broken expanse under the roof. Rough wooden beams transected the space, dusty boards haphazardly nailed together with gaps between them on the floors. There was a bucket of nails, and some metal strips and a roll of tar paper next to one of the beams. A dull light half-shone through one little window that slanted with the roof. Lying under the window on its side was a green ceramic two-liter jug. It had the name "Bulgaria" written on its side. A souvenir. There was no toilet in the attic, and later that night Cal would remember this little jug and use it.

Stepping carefully, Cal followed as Grisha led him to a second door, bigger than the first, also unpainted. There was a large padlock securing it. Grisha fished for the key among those in his hand, and unlocked it. A moment later they were inside Grisha's studio. Cal put his backpack down against the old gray sofa in one corner where he would sleep. The smell of dust here gave itself over to the smell of painting supplies. Turpentine, linseed oil, varnish drying, rags with paint on them. Two mansard windows spread pale gray light like in a Vermeer painting, and there were images everywhere hung or stacked against the cracked walls. On the floor, leaning against one wall, were three paintings of Cadaqués. No escaping it. The old stone watchtower Torre de les Creus, which had stood guard over the village in its earliest days, and where Cal and Layla had made love one afternoon when they spread out the green blanket and had their picnic and she told him about the little hiding place under the stairs where she would go as a girl. The second painting, of the Cova de l'Infern or Hell's Cave, where Cal and Layla had gone in the boat one day as they were poking around all those little coves. And finally the third painting, of the passeig with Boia and Imperial and Casino across the bridge. In it was the very spot where Cal had seen Layla that first day that now seemed years ago, but was really not very long ago. It just felt like forever.

"Cal, are you all right?"

"Yes, Grisha. I'm fine."

There were many more paintings, some finished, others in-progress. Men and women having sex, doing almost everything in almost every way; Grisha's illustrations to Krafft-Ebing's Psychopathia Sexualis. There were oil-on-canvas portraits of Stalin, Lenin, Hitler, and a large landscape of a destroyed city with dirty children struggling to play in the ruins. And there was a painting of an unmade bed. The bed had empty bottles of vodka, spent condoms, cigarette packs, and other detritus littered around it.

"I paint now the perversions, Cal. Shit sex, shit politics, shit art. Did you hear of lady called Tracy Emin?"

"No."

"Oh, Cal, she is..."

As Grisha explained the painting, Cal stood as if listening. But he was not listening. All he could think of were those fucking paintings of Cadaqués on the floor behind him, and the woman he loved, and how it was likely he would never see her again.

"...This lady Tracy Emin, everyone in London now they talk about her. They say she is artist because *she* says she is artist. She came from her bed one day, so dirty as possible like this one, and called it art."

"Interesting, Grisha."

"It's fantastic, Cal! Everyone can make art today, not just the artist. Even, the real artist cannot make art. Because better just the idea of art. It's perverted time, Cal. The idea of art, *this* is the new art. When Duchamp made it in 1917 with his *pissoir*, okay, it was interesting idea. What is the art? But now, this only repeats."

"Yes, Grisha."

"And her shit bed will not last. It will be dust in the museum where so many critic-ers, they write about it now. But the *painting* of the bed, Cal, the *painting* will survive."

"Yes, Grisha."

"The name of this painting Cal, *History of Art*. You see, dimensions of this panel, one meter by 1.62 meters. The famous Golden Ratio. Da Vinci, Dali, so many they used it. *Such* things will last, because if..."

Did she have any idea how much he loved her? How desperately sorry he was, and how he needed her? Tharrats knew where he was. She could find him that way. Would she ever even bother looking for him?

"...and I mix with the paint the real amber, that it survives. Rubens, van Dyke, all the great Flemish masters, they wanted what they made with their hearts, with their minds, and their talents, to survive. Today, it's only to make money with the fast idea."

Grisha grinned. "Avida Dollars," he said. Breton's cynical anagram for Salvador Dali.

"Yes, Grisha. You're right. You're very right."

Grisha continued, so excited to explain it all to his friend.

"Always, Cal, the artist must struggle against the Academy that tells him how to make, and what to make. Today's academy, they tell, instead of paint the animal or sculpt it, *just kill it*. It's enough. Put it in chemical, like the scientists they did always. Only now, just give it name and call it art. And the museums, they go crazy for it. It's incredible."

That wasn't love. What a bitch! Leave someone you care about when they're trying so hard to change, want to change, want to be with you always and forever.

Cal needed to sit. He crossed to the gray sofa as Grisha was pointing out how in the wrinkles of the bed he had built in secret images. Faces, words, the shadows aligning.

"You see Cal, even Picasso he is here."

Grisha pointed to one of the shadows. Cal saw it and nodded.

"And there are more things hidden, Cal. *Many* more. So you see, from Flemish masters to Picasso to surreal-like, to this shit art today, all history of art, it is here. Even, this is biological painting. The red, it has small moment of my blood in it. The brown, the yellow, even the white, all have small biological moments. So one day, Cal, because DNA, maybe even they can make the artist from the painting."

"Interesting, Grisha. Congratulations."

Not possible, life without her. No way.

All Cal really wanted to do now was to die. Even as Grisha kept talking, about art, about progress, about evolution not revolution, Cal began to imagine it...the quiet, the absence of pain that death might bring. He didn't believe in the fires later. The fires were now.

Chapter LXX

"Grisha, maybe we go someplace to eat? What do you think?"

Grisha understood. They went together to a restaurant close by, the old Mommsen-Eck, Haus der 100 Biere. House of a hundred beers. Cal knew it from his last visit and liked it. They sat outside under a green umbrella with the name of one beer written on it, Berliner. There was a linden tree close by, and a chestnut tree, and in the little square with the fountain there were plane trees like the ones in Ceret and Cadaqués.

The fountain was made of heavy stone and there were two boys climbing on it. There were yellow leaves scattered on the cobblestones. The trees knew already that summer was about to meld into fall. The sun had poked through the clouds and there were splots of warm light between the shadows already growing longer. The waitress came, an older woman with dark hair and serious face.

"Was wollen Sie trinken?"

Cal looked at the long list of beers on the menu. Grisha knew he would not work more that day and ordered a pilsner. It was light. Cal looked at the woman.

"What is the strongest beer you have?"

She didn't understand. Grisha translated.

"Mein Freund würde gerne wissen, was ist das stärkste Bier, das Sie haben?"

She reached over Cal's shoulder and pointed to several on the menu. Satan was eight percent alcohol. Delerium Tremens, also Belgian, nine percent. And De Verboden Vrucht...The Forbidden Fruit...8.8 percent alcohol.

"I'll have that one please, Forbidden Fruit."

"Ja, gut."

She left to go get them.

A leaf fell on the table. Grisha pulled the little camera he always carried from the breast pocket of his jacket and took a picture of the leaf. The waitress brought their beers and they ordered their food. As they waited for it, Grisha talked about art, Cal talked about Layla, and Grisha told him again that it would be all right.

"I think, Cal, maybe she just wants to know you take care of yourself. It would give her more feeling of safety. Every woman, she wants to feel safe enough."

"I don't even know how to fucking find her, Grisha."

"Okay. Well, maybe she finds you. Make that when she does, she will be happy to find you in strong condition. It's simple enough. Are you writing now, Cal?"

"Not really."

"Well then, my suggestion, start to write. Make that your mind has something to focus on. Something positive. Then more positive things, they can also happen."

The food came. Cal had already finished his first beer and ordered a second. Grisha was still sipping his.

"And Cal, maybe...how to say...maybe not to drink so much? For sure, Layla, she would be happy to see you healthy. Be careful Cal. Please."

The waitress brought the second beer. Grisha's words were a great comfort. Between them and the beer, Cal was feeling better.

Chapter LXXI

A knock. And another. Cal's eyes opened.

"Cal? Cal, are you there?"

It was Grisha's voice on the other side of the door. Cal looked around. The studio. Paintings. Light through the window. Berlin.

"Cal? Cal, excuse me, are you there?"

The door opened. Cal sat up, rubbed his face, cleared his throat.

"I was having a dream, Grisha. So incredible."

"Oh yes?"

"There were these horses in the water and Layla was lying under a tree and..."

As Cal told him all about his dream Grisha stood there looking down at his friend and at the empty little bottles of Gorbachev vodka on the floor next to the bed.

"...and the sea began to foam, and there was something red floating in it and then I woke up."

"Interesting, Cal. Very interesting."

Grisha moved toward some shelves.

"Cal, my gallerist in London, she has called me about this painting about the bed. She is so interested in it. I must wrap it, because later today the shippers they can come."

There was a plastic bag next to the bed. As Grisha turned his back to begin wrapping his painting, Cal reached into the bag, took out a bottle of Campari and drank from it.

Chapter LXXII

So many things to do in a city like Berlin. Cal wasn't interested in any of it. Two days and two nights he stayed in bed drinking himself to sleep, waking, glancing over at those paintings of Cadaqués and then just drinking again.

Elsa was back now. She and Grisha both tried to interest him in going out. To Rogacki, that great Berlin eatery where you eat standing up squeezed in with locals eating and drinking and laughing beside you.

"No, really, I'm fine."

There was an art opening in the east at a gallery on Auguststrasse.

"So many interesting people can be there, Cal. Come on, let's go. You will enjoy yourself so much."

"No thank you Grisha. I'll just stay here, maybe I write a little."

He did not write.

One night finally they did get him out, to the classic jazz and blues club Yorckschlösschen in Kreuzberg. Cal got so drunk he almost had a fight with a man who was arguing outside the club with his wife. Cal pushed the man hard, and then the wife stopped yelling at her husband and started yelling at Cal.

"I was only trying to help you," shouted Cal.

"I don't need your fucking help. Go away, leave us alone. Mind your own business."

Grisha and Elsa piled Cal into a taxi and took him home. On the whole ride back he kept mumbling, "I was only trying to help the bitch."

The following night Cal went with them to the Italian embassy, to a reception for an artist from Rome. Standing in the middle of the big room while chatting, Cal learned that the ambassador had once been a student of his father's at Yale.

"Your father was my favorite professor. I am not joking."

Cal was so thrilled he started slapping the ambassador on the shoulder. The ambassador was a small man, and while Cal held a glass of red wine in his left hand he kept slapping the ambassador's shoulder with his right.

"Are you joking? Hey, that's wonderful!" Slap on shoulder. And another. "Really, I can't tell you what a joy it is for me to hear that!" Like a drunk cowboy.

Grisha came over to him, leaned close, and spoke into Cal's ear.

"Umm, Cal, maybe to stop hitting the ambassador?"

"I'm sorry. I was just so...excited."

"It's not a problem," said the ambassador. "I understand." The ambassador then excused himself and walked away.

The next morning, such happy news. Cal went over to the apartment to grab a shower and found both Grisha and Elsa thrilled. Grisha was grinning.

"It's incredible! Really, Cal, so incredible! My gallerist in London, she sold that painting of that shit bed. For enough money."

"Really, it's fantastic," said Elsa, also grinning. "No, really, incredible. She sold it for *so* much."

"That's wonderful. I'm so happy for both of you. Congratulations."

"Cal, we make some celebration tonight at Paris Bar. Please to come, help us celebrate."

"Absolutely!"

Chapter LXXIII

After his shower, there was no going back to the studio. Cal had to move. A taxi through the Tiergarten, down Strasse des 17. Juni to Brandenburg Gate, and just walking now. Not even looking so much. People, places, floating by. This was not Walter Benjamin's *flaneur*. Not Baudelaire taking it all in. Cal was drifting through it all, his mind far off. Layla this, Layla that. A few images got through. A young couple laughing outside the Hotel Adlon. The Russian embassy. Aeroflot. A Bugatti showroom. A turn down Friedrichstrasse then, thinking about her still. That stupid turn on the road in France where he had almost hit that boy on the bike. Her outfit from Casablanca and the way people looked at her. Retracing every step he could.

A taxi horn blared suddenly. An old woman fell in the street and people rushed to help her. It jolted Cal back. He looked around. Crowds of tourists. Checkpoint Charlie. He couldn't remember getting here. Oh well, here now. Men on the sidewalk selling fake East German military medals, hats, uniforms. The little shack with the sandbags reconstructed for tourists to take photos. Nice. Souvenir shops. Little bags of concrete remnants of the Wall for five Deutsche Mark each. Magnets. So many magnets! *You are leaving the American sector...I am a Jelly doughnut* (Kennedy's "Ich bin ein Berliner" - he should have left out the "ein")...young Peter Fechter shot, crumpled, bleeding under the barbed wire...Brezhnev kissing Honecker on the lips...and there at the bottom of the carousel a real surprise. *It's never too late to be what you might have been* - George Eliot. George Eliot? How the fuck was that here? George fucking Eliot. He flew to the cash register to buy it. George Eliot! Unreal. And there she was back *again*, Layla, sitting at Imperial reading Middlemarch that first day. He couldn't even go to a fucking souvenir shop at fucking Checkpoint Charlie in fucking Berlin without being reminded that she had left him. Turned her back and walked away just like that, with her stupid little bag in her hand. Only one thing to do about that. Into a bar for a drink.

"A fucking vodka, please."

He even said it that way. Everyone around here spoke English. The young bartender smiled.

"You got it."

He got it all right. And the next one. And the next one. Out Russian the Russians! DE-LICIOUS, Robert would say. DE-LICIOUS, darling. Touché! Fuck you, George Eliot. Fuck you, Layla. Fuck you, fate, tricky devil of a jokester. The barbed fucking wire of life. George Eliot! Cal thought of having another, then looked at his watch, decided against it. Only a couple of hours now before he needed to be at Paris Bar for Grisha's and Elsa's big happy celebration.

Chapter LXXIV

The blue hour, day morphing into night. A taste of Paris in Berlin. When the Wall had stood, and travel not as easy as for those unencircled by barbed wire, isolated West Berliners could come to Paris Bar on the wide Kantstrasse to escape the everyday. The danger of those moments lent spice to everything here, the food, company, conversation. Oysters and spies and David Bowie, champagne and Helmut Newton and goose paté, Veruschka, Georg Baselitz, all eating, drinking, drinking more, smoking, laughing through it. The danger had gone now, but the rest of it here still. Everything packed in tight, as if the wire was still out there. Paintings, drawings and photos everywhere, on the walls, even on the ceilings. Human nature, too much of this to compensate for not enough of that. Actors and artists and politicians at the best tables, the black and white tiled floor, the waiters who didn't need you as much as you needed them. All here.

At the back hung a massive painting by Martin Kippenberger, showing the interior of Paris Bar itself. And at a long table in front of it, looking as much part of the painting behind them as of this place, Grisha and Elsa sat surrounded by close friends. Tables in the painting behind the real tables, chairs in the painting behind the real chairs, the painting of paintings on the wall... fiction and fact fused seamlessly. Grisha's mother was to his left, looking so proud. The Russian novelist Vladimir Sorokin and his wife Irina, Ukranian photographer Boris Mikhailov and his wife Vita, Cal, a few others, all there to celebrate their friend's success.

Food had already been ordered. There was a bottle of vodka in a silver ice bucket at the center of the table. Cal reached for it again. He was looking at the others, and listening to them.

A few tables over, Grisha spotted an old friend of his, Ottomar Rodolphe Vlad Dracula Prince Kretzulesco. Adopted son of the last known blood relative of the Prince from Transylvania. Cal had met him also the year before.

"Cal, look, it's our friend Dracula."

Cal turned to look.

This Dracula lived in a 46 room castle a few kilometers south of Berlin. The summer before, Cal and Grisha had gone to one of his parties. He hosted blood donation parties for the German Red Cross, and collected old Rolls Royces left covered with cobwebs for the tourists who paid to visit his castle. Now glasses hoisted high toward each other from across the room, happy greetings shouted over the heads of those sitting between them.

"Is it red wine?" Grisha called out, seeing the red liquid in his glass. Dracula just smiled, drank, and smiled again.

The starters came. Cal had ordered oysters to begin. They appeared in front of him now, splayed out on a bed of shaved ice. Grisha looked at them approvingly.

"Hmm, Cal, looks delicious."

"Do you want some, Grisha?"

Rhetorical question. Cal knew Grisha was allergic to oysters.

"Hmm, well..."

Elsa saw, heard.

"*No*! I say no, and no again!" She was smiling, but her voice was deadly serious. "You remember what happened last time."

"Yes Elsa, but that was San Francisco," said Grisha, grinning.

"Maybe these oysters are different."

Elsa looked at her husband, then at Cal.

"No! No, no, no!"

She and Grisha had visited Cal once in California. Grisha thought then that he would try "just one" oyster in San Francisco, at Alioto's on Fisherman's Warf. A cable car ride afterwards up Nob Hill, then walking, *Hmm, Elsa, Cal, I'm not feeling so good. Maybe...* Hours then invested in the men's room at the Fairmont hotel, while Cal and Elsa had sat listening to the piano player in the lobby.

Never again.

"No, and again no, Grisha!"

"Elsa, what's wrong? Maybe these oysters are different kind."

She just looked at him.

"Okay, Elsa. You win."

Cal took another shot from the bottle of vodka, then ate his oysters. Slurping the sweet juice from the shells, teeth taking that flesh of the sea, ripping at it, swallowing. Everyone was eating now, drinking, talking. Grisha stood up, his glass high in the air.

"A toast!" First in Russian, then repeated in English for Cal's benefit. "My friends. Really, today's night something so special. To be here with my dear mother, my dear wife, and my dear friends. For me, it's greatest honor to celebrate with you really such important moment. Thank you, dear friends."

At the same instant Sorokin and Cal both began to offer their own toasts. Sorokin stopped and gestured to Cal to go first.

"Please," he said, gesturing, "After you."

Cal stood up.

"I want to say...I just want to say that it's really such a wonderful painting our friend Grisha made of that stupid shit bed. What happens now with...with galleries, with art, with these stupid shit critics...it's only because of great artists like...like Grisha, that..."

Cal staggered backward. He fell. He tried to grab his chair but then that fell too. Some people sitting nearby jumped to help him. One gentleman in a tuxedo reached for his arm.

"Alles in Ordnung?"

Is everything in order? He was sitting on the fucking floor of this nice restaurant, so obviously not. Still, "I'm fine. I'm fine, thank you."

Grisha was trying to squeeze out from behind the big table.

"Cal, are you okay?"

"I'm sorry, Grisha. Really, I'm so sorry."

Cal tried to stand, one hand resting on the edge of his chair, but it slipped out from under him. He was on his knees now, vomiting. The man in the tuxedo stepped back quickly. Everyone was looking at him.

"Oh god."

It didn't stop. More vomit. Noises, colors, Elsa saying something, everyone saying something. Grisha again.

"Cal? Cal? Are you okay? Cal?..."

A waiter's black shoes, people moving. A woman leaned down to hand Cal a napkin. When he didn't take it, she dropped it gently onto the floor next to him. Grisha and Sorokin were trying to pull Cal to his feet.

"No. No, please. Can't move."

"It's okay," said Grisha. "Leave him to rest."

A waiter was saying something in German, probably that they couldn't just leave him there because people were trying to eat. Cal didn't care. He took the napkin off the floor and wiped his mouth.

Chapter LXXV

Two days later Cal was feeling better. He had slept most of the day before, had not drunk a thing, only water and a little of the soup that Elsa had brought up to him. She and Grisha had tried to get him to come stay in the apartment, but he had told them no, thank you, he wanted, needed even to be alone. Moving slowly he dressed now, then looked at himself in a small mirror leaning on one dusty shelf. Eyes still red. He needed to eat something. Down to the street, then along Mommsenstrasse to the Mommsen-Eck, Haus of 100 Biers. They also served breakfast. He sat outside and ordered. Boiled egg, some white cheese, bread, espresso. And maybe a beer. Nothing too strong. Just a pilsner. It came. He reached for it. Something stopped him.

No. Enough.

He started to cry.

Please god, enough.

He turned his head so that nobody could see him. Hand over his face, trembling even, he took a deep breath. He looked around. If anyone noticed they didn't show it. The waitress brought his food. He couldn't eat. He didn't want that beer either. Did and didn't.

"Just the bill, please. Die Rechnung."

She looked at him oddly, left, and came back with the bill. He paid. Not waiting for change he stood, then back up the street and over to Grisha's building.

The night before, one candle burning in the studio, he had written a song.

Nothing left to do but die it seems
The end of hope, the end of dreams
So close at hand
Would they, could they, understand?
Bottle of that Skull and Crossbones wine...

But he did not want to die. Not really. One died soon enough as it was.

The buzzer, then up the elevator, Grisha standing in the door.

"Cal, good morning. How are you feeling?"

Cal stepped into the apartment.

"Grisha, please, can I use your phone?"

"Yes of course."

"Do you have a phone book?"

Grisha disappeared into the kitchen and brought both back. He and Cal moved into the big room. They sat, Cal on the green sofa as before, and Grisha in his chair. Cal held the phone book in his lap.

"Is everything okay, Cal?"

"Not really, no."

"How do you feel?"

"Not so well. I'm sorry about the other night, Grisha."

"Oh, Cal, please, not to worry. Important thing is you feel better. Not so pleasant to be sick as that."

"No."

It was quiet in the room. Nothing moving.

"Grisha?"

"Yes, Cal?"

"I think...it looks like maybe I can't just drink normally. You know, I mean like most people."

"Yes, Cal."

"In fact, I think maybe..."

Grisha sat, waiting for it.

"...maybe I have a problem. I know I have a problem."

"Is it first time you think it, Cal?"

"No. No it's not. Just, maybe it's first time I say it."

Cal opened the phone book. Thumbing through the thin pages he found what he was looking for. Not just Alcoholics Anonymous, but a listing actually for *A.A. in English*. That was a surprise. He phoned the number. Grisha stood up and excused himself from the room as Cal began to speak with someone.

Epilogue

Five years later. Cal downshifted at the bend, then coming out of it he accelerated once again though not too fast. At the top of the mountain the sign ahead pointed to "Cadaqués."

So long since he had been here. He had come back just once, in the spring right after his little book was published. As promised, Tharrats had held an event in the bookshop. Grisha and Elsa had come for that, too. David had given a nice little speech, and other friends were there. Layla was not there. No one had seen her, or knew where she was.

Cal had hurried back to Berlin then. Bolted back. He felt safe there, focusing on getting well still. Something comfortable being in a place that had also reinvented itself, the new Germany, the new Berlin, so tolerant today. They had traveled light years in nanoseconds. He had stayed in Berlin a full year then, going to meetings almost every day. The program helped, the people helped, even the slogans helped. *Have a good day, unless of course you have made other plans...We're sick and tired of being sick and tired...A.A. spoils your drinking...Don't take yourself so damn seriously...There is no problem a drink will not make worse...You can do this...*

Finally then, at last feeling strong enough, he had gone back to California to his little mountain. There were meetings there, too. Different accents, but the stories more or less the same... wanting to get better and doing it. Drunks not drinking anymore, helping other drunks, all with their crazy stories. Best of both worlds, that sane glimpse of the madness.

Cal had brought with him to California a chip of painted wood from one of the fishing boats in Port Alguer. Cadaqués blue. He painted the Quonset hut white with that blue trim around the doors and windows so that it would look like Cadaqués. He had his dogs again, Dada, Suetonius and Moocow. They would lie in the shade of the big pine trees and watch him as he worked alone on the property. Every so often a truck would bring a big load of river rocks that he bought from a local quarry, and they would dump the rocks on the side of the long driveway. Then one by one he would carry them around the property, building stone terraces to make the land itself look as close to Cadaqués as he could. He planted fig trees and olive trees, and in winter when there was snow on the mountain and the wind was strong he had to cover the trees so they would not die. And then in the deep snow Cal would carry the wood in and sit by the fire and read, or else just look out the window. In the evenings he would soak in his outdoor tub and watch night settle in, with the snow falling around him and the steam from the hot water rising. And later, dead tired from the work and the cold clear air, he would fall asleep with the fire and the dogs close by.

It wasn't only the air that was clear. This was like a new high still, seeing things as they were really instead of through a prism clouded over. This was as new and exciting as the old highs had long ceased to be. Nice to have a new way of looking at the world. He felt young again for it. As if starting out all over.

The seasons ticked by. You could count on those like old friends. And the years ticked by. If you were lucky, you could count on that too.

Though he was being much more careful, still the money

from his father eventually ran its course. But then a stroke of luck. A film company in Barcelona had just bought the rights to his little book. Saved his ass. The reason he had flown to Barcelona three days earlier was to meet with them. They wanted to make a few changes before filming it. What the hell, he needed the money. They could set it in China if they wanted, and cast it with monkeys. It turned out they only wanted to give it a sadder ending than he had written. If Hollywood had bought it, it would have been just the opposite, everyone hysterically happy at the end, with the sun setting orange over the ocean. What the fuck, it was just a story. What mattered now was that he could pay his bills again, and that he had gone five years without a drink. Not even tempted any more. In the meetings they called that a miracle. And so he had begun to believe in miracles.

The road to the village began to slope downward now as Cal's mind kept turning like the car. It was not as if everything was okay. There was a hole there still, that was filling in only slowly. He missed Layla. He still had dreams about her. He would wake up sometimes, and a dream had been so vivid it was as if he had really seen her. He had tried every way he could to reach her. He wanted so much to tell her how well he was doing, and to know if she was okay. But he couldn't find her. As the Internet had grown he had tried again and again to find some trace of her. No luck. Once he even called Paul in Manchester. That was not very successful either. He listened to Paul's screaming for about a minute, and then as he was still screaming he just thanked him and hung up.

And now he was coming back here to Cadaqués. He had not planned this. The idea had been to sign the film deal, spend a couple of days in Barcelona visiting with Tharrats, and then fly back to San Francisco. But at the last minute he had decided instead to change his ticket, rent a car and come here. He could do it now, see his old friends. The twins, David, Wiggles and the others. It was all about facing things, wasn't it? He was ready. Also, maybe somebody would know where, or at least how, Layla was. He had to know.

The road twisted one last time, and then there it was, Cadaqués in the distance. His heart was racing. So strange to be back here!

He parked in the big lot near the entrance to the town. Then, as he had those years before, he walked down the Avenida Caritat Serinyana. As he came out into the main square, with Imperial and Casino to his right, he almost expected to see himself sitting at one of the tables with a glass in his hand. Like Scrooge sneaking a peak at Christmas past. Funny.

It all looked about the same, except everywhere the ground had been resurfaced. Where it had all been rough, now there were elegant black-slate paving stones stretching to and around the passeig, like the ones they use in upscale shopping centers in California. There was a white Rolls-Royce parked near the bridge in a no-parking zone. A policeman stood nearby ignoring it.

The little wine shop was to the left still. They had done something to it. It looked fancier, new windows or something. The two *chiringuito* bars, the Maritim and the Boia, were in front of the water just where he had left them. And between them, the statue of Dali stood holding court as ever. A young guy with a backpack stood next to it looking at a map in his hands.

Cal turned and looked up over his shoulder at Cassandra's. The shutters were closed. Probably off minding the shops. Just as well. Walking slowly, he moved toward the Imperial. Most of the tables were filled with strangers. At one table near the door to the bar there was a man reading a newspaper. As Cal got closer he could see it was Wiggles.

"Any good news in that thing?" asked Cal.

Wiggles put the paper down and glanced up.

"Well, if it isn't...Cal. Look at you! What a pleasant surprise." A nice warm grin. "Well now please, Cal, do have a seat."

He spoke as slowly as ever. Cal sat.

"How are you, Wiggles?"

"Well now, that's a complicated question, isn't it? I'd have to think about that. In the meantime, how are *you,* Cal? Haven't seen you for, well, for ages. We were all wondering what had happened to you."

Angela came to the table. Another sweet smile.

"Hola, Cal."

"Hola, guapa."

Cal stood and kissed her on both cheeks. A little small talk. Then, "¿Qué quieres tomar, Cal?"

At the next table there were some people laughing loudly, drinking. Cal looked over at them. One man had a cold beer in his hand. The woman next to him was drinking a glass of sangria. Cal could see the yellow and orange fruit floating in the red wine.

"¿Qué quieres tomar, Cal?"

Cal ordered a sparkling water. "Vichy Catalan."

Angela disappeared inside to get it.

"Well now, that's not like you, is it?" asked Wiggles.

Cal told him the short version of the story. Then he saw what Wiggles was drinking.

"And you? What's that, a cup of tea?"

"That's right. I do like a nice cup of tea these days. No, you see the thing is, I had to make a little change myself. That is, if I didn't want to have you come here for instance, as you are now, and have someone tell you, 'Oh well, old Wiggles, he overdid it, and he's off now with David and the others."

"What do you mean, David?"

"Oh, I'm sorry. Haven't you heard? He died."

"*What*?"

"Oh, we've had a rough few years here, Cal. Very rough."

Angela brought Cal's water.

"What happened?"

"Cancer of the jaw, I'm afraid."

"No."

"Well you remember David, always smoking. Sixty-odd cigarettes a day or something like that. One afternoon he went to the dentist. Perfectly routine. But then apparently the dentist found this odd green color in his gums. Well, he'd let it go so long by then, they had to take the whole jaw away."

Cal felt tears starting.

"Well now don't cry, Cal. It had to be expected really. The way he smoked."

"And that fucking cancer killed him?"

"Well not exactly. They had to give him anesthesia of course, before the operation. And the night before, it seems the doctors asked him if he'd been taking any other drugs. They have to know these things of course. And, well, apparently David told them no, he had not. But then you know David, he was taking pills left and right. To help him sleep, to calm his nerves, something else for depression I believe. And so, well, he just never woke up, that's all. Damned shame, really. We all miss him a great deal."

"And, you said something about 'others'?"

"I'm afraid it's a long list, really. Robin, you remember him. Always playing his guitar."

"No!"

"I'm afraid so. That was really a damned shame also. Not

his fault. Just standing next to the road up by the bus stop, and some young tourist, drunk as anything, ran off the road and straight into him. Died instantly."

"Oh god. Such a nice man."

"He was, yes. A very nice man."

Cal was looking out toward the water. It took him a minute.

"Any other good news?"

"Antonio. That fellow who cut off his finger. He's gone. Liver. And then there was this awful boating accident. Freddy had this boat, the African Queen. Do you remember that?"

Cal turned, looked at him.

"Yes, of course. I do remember it."

"Well, his boys took it out one day. A friend of theirs with them. They were all doing what boys do. And the friend drowned. Fell, hit his head on a rock, something like that. No, it's been a rough time here, Cal. Not easy. I'm very sorry to have to tell you these things."

"And the twins?"

"Ah, well, sadly there's another thing."

"Oh no! Please, don't tell me..."

"Robert."

"He's..."

"No, no. It's not that. He's in England. Not terribly well though. Again, something with the liver. Can't really travel. Richard's with him of course. I'm thinking of going up and paying a visit myself. No, it's been a rough time here, Cal. A very rough time. But so tell me, what brings you back here now? Plan to stay awhile, do you?"

"Not really. I hadn't even planned to come. I was in Barcelona, doing some business. I was about to head back to San Francisco and then at the last minute I just decided I was so close..."

"Well that's it, isn't it? Heading one place, suddenly find yourself in another. But anyway, it's very nice of you to visit us, Cal."

Cal was afraid to ask.

"And Layla? Have you seen her?"

"No, I'm afraid not. Not since long-ago days when you were here. But one does hear things, of course."

"What did you hear?"

"Well, I heard that she's living in Paris, that she's married, and that it seems she has a child. Now I did hear that some time ago, so please don't ask me who told me because I won't remember."

A man at the next table over was talking loudly into his mobile phone. Something about delivery of some furniture.

"Of course that's only what I heard, Cal. I don't know how much of that is true."

Like most gossip, what Wiggles had heard was only half the story. It was not Paris where Layla was living, but Lyon. Also, Wiggles did not know that the child was a boy, and that the boy was Cal's.

Cal was looking once again toward the water.

"Who would have thought it, eh Cal? You and me, sitting here now on this very nice day, you with your sparkling water there, me with my nice cup of tea. The last of the Mohicans, that's us, Cal. We're the survivors. But we had our go, didn't we? All in good fun."

Cal nodded.

"And how about you, Cal? Everything okay?"

"Yes. Yes, it's fine, thank you."

"Well that's good. I'm very happy to hear that."

They sat quiet for some moments.

"Look, Wiggles, I think I'm going to take a little walk around."

"You do that, Cal. Let it sink it. That was a lot of news just now."

"Will you be here?"

"Oh, I'll be here. I'm not going anywhere."

"Alright then. See you a little later, yes?"

"See you later, Cal."

Cal went inside to the bar. He paid for his and Wiggle's drinks. Then he came back out and began to walk. He stopped in front of the Boia for a moment, deciding if to turn left or right. He turned right and started to walk toward Port Alguer. Passing by the Casino he looked inside and saw no one he recognized. There was a crowd spilling out of the place, young people sitting on the window ledges in the front holding drinks in their hands, talking and laughing.

Cal took a few more steps, then stopped. He didn't have to see more. It was in his head, all of it. The bench where he and Layla had sat that night near where the road bends, the little beach at Port Alguer where he had written in the sand for her, the rocks where they had first made love. He did not have to look at any of that to see it, so instead he just turned now. There was a back way up through the village to the parking lot. He took it. He walked straight to his car, got into it and drove off.

As he was pulling out of the village, starting up the mountain he could see Cadaqués in the rear view mirror. It would always be back there, like childhood. Even as you left it you also brought it with you. Driving slowly he crossed over the Parafita pass, then down the other side of the mountain. There was the sweeping view of Roses in the distance ahead, with the sea and the fertile plain below.

In Barcelona there had been a young woman at the film company. Very pretty, smart, nice. She had smiled at him, and after they had finished their business she had asked Cal if he would like to meet some of her friends, writers, actors, artists. Maybe he would call her now when he got back to that city.

The road leveled out. With the window open, the warm air against his shoulder, Cal drove past the olive groves and the roundabouts and the long open stretches. Just beyond Figueres was the wide Autopista del Mediterraneo. One sign pointed toward France, another toward Barcelona. Cal pulled onto the big road and, heading south, leaned back in his seat, took a deep breath and stepped on the gas.

THE END

Aus dem Programm von PalmArtPress

Michael Lederer
Das Große Spiel, *Berlin-Warschau-Express und andere Geschichten*
The Great Game *Berlin-Warschau Express and Other Stories*
ISBN: 978-3-941524-13-2 Deutsch, 280 Seiten
ISBN: 978-3-941524-27-9 D (eBook)
ISBN: 978-3-941524-12-5 Englisch, 242 Seiten
Kurzgeschichten, Broschiert, 14,8 x 21 cm, 16,90 EUR

Michael Lederer
Nichts ist mehr für die Ewigkeit,
Nothing Lasts Forever Anymore
ISBN: 978-3-941524-32-3 Deutsch, 144 Seiten
ISBN: 978-3-941524-31-6 D (eBook)
ISBN: 978-3-941524-33-0 Englisch, 128 Seiten
Erzählung, 16 farbige Abb. Genia Chef, Broschiert
14,8 x 21 cm, 14,90 EUR

Wolfgang Nieblich
Wahr oder Nicht wahr - *Kurzgeschichten und Berichte*
ISBN: 978-3-941524-14-9
ISBN: 978-3-941524-28-6 (eBook)
Anthologie, 266 Seiten, Broschiert, 12 x 18 cm, 14,90 EUR

Anne Lorquet-Leithäuser
Kirschenzeiten
ISBN: 978-3-941524-17-0 Deutsch
ISBN: 978-3-941524-35-4 (eBook)
Roman, 299 Seiten, Broschiert, 14,8 x 21 cm, 18,90 EUR

Ingolf Brökel
minimals
ISBN: 978-3-941524-37-8
Lyrik, 60 Seiten, 30 Abb. W. Nieblich, Franz. Broschur
Sign. und num. limitierte Auflage
14,8 x 14,8 cm, 28 EUR

Reinhard Knodt
Schmerz - *Acht Miniaturen*
ISBN: 978-3-941524-39-2 Deutsch
ISBN: 978-3-941524-43-9 (eBook)
Kurzgeschichten, 80 Seiten, 8 Abbildungen, Broschiert
14,8 x 21 cm, 16,90 EUR

Maria Reinecke
La Rambla- *Barcelona Story*
ISBN: 978-3-941524-20-0 Englisch, 96 Seiten, 11,90 EUR
ISBN: 978-3-941524-24-5 E (eBook)
ISBN: 978-3-941524-02-6 Deutsch, 76 Seiten, 9,90 EUR
ISBN: 978-3-941524-26-2 D (eBook)
Erzählung, Broschiert 12 x 18 cm

Emily Pütter
Sandengel
ISBN: 978-3-941524-30-9 Deutsch, 60 Seiten / Abb.
Kunstbuch mit Audio CD: Michael Neil: **Ifitry Fragments**
Sign. und num. limitierte Auflage (100)
28 x 24 cm, 35,00 EUR

Michael Kromarek
KunstGeschichten *ernst und heiter*
ISBN: 978-3-941524-11-8 Deutsch
ISBN: 978-3-941524-19-4 (eBook)
Kurzgeschichten, 150 Seiten, Broschiert, 12 x 18 cm, 11,90 EUR

Wolfgang Nieblich
Das Ferne so nah oder **Die Currywurst**
ISBN: 978-3-941524-09-5
ISBN: 978-3-941524-29-3 (eBook)
Erzählung, 64 Seiten, 18 farbige Abbild. Lothar Hartmann, Gebunden
8 x 10 cm, 6,90 EUR

Bestellung: www.palmartpress.com
Versandkostenfrei innerhalb Deutschlands